BRENDA JOYCE

Deadly
KISSES

HQN™

Recycling programs
for this product may
not exist in your area.

ISBN-13: 978-0-373-77547-7

DEADLY KISSES

www.HQNBooks.com

Printed in U.S.A.

Praise for Brenda Joyce's Deadly series

"Joyce's latest 'deadly' romance is truly a pleasure to read, given its involving plot, intriguing characters and the magic that occurs as the reader becomes immersed in another time and place."
—*Booklist* on *Deadly Kisses*

"If this is your introduction to Francesca Cahill, you'll be just as hooked on the series as longtime fans. Joyce skillfully pulls you into her characters' tangled lives as they pursue a killer. The 'Deadlies' keep you coming back for more because you care about the people and you can sink your teeth into their complicated lives as they twist and turn with mystery."
—*RT Book Reviews* on *Deadly Kisses*

"As Francesca searches for clues and struggles with her complicated feelings for two different men, readers will follow her from turn-of-the-century New York's immigrant tenements to its wealthiest mansions. Fans of Joyce's Deadly romances will find the seventh in the series to be another entertaining blend of danger and desire."
—*Booklist* on *Deadly Illusions*

"Just when you think you have it all figured out, Joyce turns it all around, leaving you with a cliff-hanger, and eager for Francesca's next adventure."
—*RT Book Reviews* on *Deadly Illusions*

"Joyce excels at creating twists and turns in her characters' personal lives."
—*Publishers Weekly*

"An elegant blend of mystery and romance simmering with sexual tension."
—*Booklist* on *Deadly Promise*

"The steamy revelations…are genuinely intriguing, and just enough of them are left unresolved at the book's end to leave readers waiting eagerly for the series' next installment."
—*Publishers Weekly* on *Deadly Love*

This novel is dedicated to my sister, Jamie.
I miss you.

Jamie Lee Allen
1965–2005
Courageous in life.
Forever in Peace.

CHAPTER ONE

Monday, June 2, 1902,
New York City—Before Midnight

"FRANCESCA, I THINK IT'S wonderful that you have volunteered to chair the Ladies Citizen Union Funds Committee," Julia Van Wyck Cahill remarked, handing off her ruby-red velvet mantle to the doorman. Slim, beautiful and elegant, and wearing a very famous ruby pendant that had belonged to a Hapsburg princess, she stood with her daughter in the front hall of their Fifth Avenue home, beaming with pleasure.

Francesca, however, was preoccupied. She handed off her own light wrap, a turquoise satin to match her evening gown. "Mama, I did not quite volunteer. I do believe you and Mrs. Astor decided among yourselves to make me cochair."

Julia's blue eyes widened as she feigned innocent ignorance. "Darling! Whatever makes you say that? My dear, you are the youngest lady to ever chair the committee, and I know you will be superb, Francesca—you always are."

In truth, Francesca did not really mind being named the chair, as her current investigation was so routine. A neighbor had realized that certain items in her attics were missing, including several valuable family heirlooms, and having read all about Francesca's last case in the city's numerous newspapers, she had requested Francesca's sleuthing services. Francesca was almost certain that Mrs. Canning's son-in-law was the thief.

"It is a good cause and someone has to raise funds for the

party." Francesca sighed. "I simply wish you had asked me first if I had the time to give the position all of the effort and attention it deserves."

Julia took her arm. "I'm sorry, dear. Of course, I should have asked."

Francesca knew very well what her mother was about. Julia was a great society hostess, and she had been aghast by Frances-ca's new profession. Even with Francesca's success, she remained opposed to her daughter's involvement in any investigation, al-though she seemed relieved that Francesca finally had a case that was neither life threatening nor scandalous in nature. Francesca knew her mother wanted her so preoccupied with fundraising for the Citizens Union that she would have time for nothing else other than her fiancé.

At the thought of Calder Hart, her heart skipped uncontrollably. But then, Hart had that effect on her, from the time they had first met, when she had refused to admit her attraction to and fascina-tion with such a notorious man. He was one of the city's wealthi-est millionaires, yet he had come from humble beginnings, born out of wedlock on the city's poverty-stricken Lower East Side. Until recently, in spite of his reputation as a womanizer, he had been considered the greatest catch in town, with almost every socialite vying for his attention for their debutante daughters. Hart, however, preferred to attach himself to infamous courte-sans and divorcées, shying away from any serious involvement. Francesca still had to pinch herself from time to time, in order to realize that it was *real*—she, Francesca Cahill, who owned an equally notorious reputation as an eccentric, a bluestocking and a sleuth, had somehow snagged Calder Hart. These days, when she walked into a supper party or a ball, knives were sharpened and daggers were drawn behind her back. Once, the whispers and gossip had hurt her feelings; now she rather enjoyed the attention. But then, usually Hart was at her side, whispering in her ear, reminding her to revel in the limelight.

All was not perfect, however. Her father was dead set against Hart. An entire month had gone by since Andrew Cahill had broken off their engagement and he did not seem any closer to coming around, never mind that Francesca's mother was so angry she refused to speak to him unless it was absolutely necessary. In fact, Julia continued to gloat about the engagement to her society friends, as if it had not been terminated.

Francesca had come to realize she could not imagine a future without Hart in it, and she was determined to win Andrew over to their cause. Her father was one of the great progressive thinkers and leaders in the city. He was also a great humanitarian, and Francesca admired him immensely. She could not imagine eloping behind his back, although she and Hart had discussed it. This was the first time in her life that she had not been able to gain her way with her father.

Hart had suggested they not push Andrew Cahill just now. Calder was out of town right now, and Francesca missed him terribly.

As if reading her daughter's mind, Julia said softly, "When will Calder return to the city, Francesca?"

"In a day or two, Mama. He is in Boston, tending to his business affairs." Hart's fortune had been amassed through shipping, insurance and the railroads. He was also a world-renowned art collector, with one of the most extensive and valuable privately owned collections in America.

Several months ago, Hart had commissioned her portrait and Francesca had been hugely flattered. The portrait had been a nude, and she had been daring enough to pose for it. Last month, the painting had been completed—and it had also been stolen. With Francesca too upset to think clearly enough to investigate the theft, Hart had put private investigators on the case. But there had been no leads; it was as if the portrait had vanished into thin air. If it ever surfaced publicly, Francesca knew she was finished.

She had quite a few enemies, although many of them were now in prison.

Francesca did not want to worry about the missing portrait now. Instead, she thought about her reunion with Hart. She could barely wait to be in his arms, being soundly and thoroughly kissed. "Mama, I am going to bed. It was a pleasant evening," she said, kissing her cheek.

"Yes, it was, wasn't it?" Julia seemed pleased.

Andrew Cahill stepped into the spacious front hall, having been outside giving instructions to the coachman for the next morning. Francesca smiled at her father as he handed off his top hat, white gloves and scarf. Dressed in his tuxedo, he was a short man with a rotund build and excessive side whiskers. "Papa? Did you enjoy the affair tonight?" Her sister, every bit as successful a society hostess as Julia, had held a charity supper to raise funds for the vast new public library, soon to be erected on Fifth Avenue and Forty-Second street. There had been a hundred guests, with champagne, caviar, dinner, dessert and dancing, all in the ballroom of the Waldorf-Astoria Hotel.

"Of course I did," Andrew said, his expression somber. "It is a fine cause and I look forward to the day the library opens. Francesca, I should like to talk to you in the study before you retire for the night."

Francesca tensed. "Papa, can't it wait?" she began. She had the dreadful feeling he was going to talk to her about Hart, a subject they had carefully avoided for an entire month. Unless he had changed his mind about them, Francesca did not want to hear whatever her father had to say.

"I think we have gone on at great odds for long enough," he said firmly.

Francesca knew that tone. She waited while he kissed Julia's cheek, bidding her good-night. Then Francesca and Andrew started through the front hall, arm in arm. All of the servants had discreetly vanished, and their heels clicked on the black-and-white marble floors.

"I believe Hart is back in town."

Francesca was dismayed. "No, Papa, he is not due back for at least another day, and probably he will not be back until Wednesday."

"Ben Garret saw him this afternoon crossing the street," Andrew said curtly. And finally he softened. "Or he thought he did. We had lunch and he mentioned your engagement."

There was no mistaking her father's intended subject now. They paused on the threshold of his study, a large library with wood-paneled walls; high, pale green ceilings; hundreds of books, most political or philosophical in nature; electric lights; and the family's single telephone. Beneath the emerald-green marble mantle a small fire crackled in the fireplace.

"Papa, you broke off our engagement," Francesca said softly. But she twisted the huge diamond engagement ring which she still wore, refusing to take it off.

Andrew regarded her unhappily. "I intended to break it off, but your mother has openly defied me, gleefully telling everyone we meet about your engagement. In private, she won't even speak to me!" he exclaimed. "And do you think I am blind? I see the ring you continue to wear!"

Francesca flushed. "Calder gave me the ring, Papa, and it is a token of his admiration and respect. I simply cannot part with it."

He sighed heavily and walked over to the fireplace, staring down at the flames. "I could tell you stories until I was blue in the face about gullible young women falling for handsome rakes. But like each and every one of those young, naive women, you would not listen to me. You would think you are different, that you are the one to finally capture the cad's heart."

Francesca went and stood besides him nervously. "Unlike all those other cads, Hart has never suggested that I have captured his heart. But he has told me how much he admires and respects me, how dearly he needs my friendship, and how well he thinks we suit."

"So you are not marrying for love?" Andrew asked skeptically. "You are marrying for respect, for friendship?"

Francesca gave him a look. "I love Calder. I have never been so in love. He has a good side, Papa, one that quite contradicts his selfish reputation. And while he says he does not believe in love, he is very fond of me. I wish you could believe that! I think we suit."

"I never said he was not fond of you. I believe he cares for you. Why else would he want to marry you? He hardly needs your money—he is as rich as Hades! But I cannot approve when I know with all of my being that he will hurt you terribly one day. A man like that will eventually stray."

Francesca turned away, trembling. Hart had promised her undying loyalty and fidelity. He claimed he was tired of the life he had thus far led, and while Francesca believed him, she could not help but be afraid that the day might come when his head would be turned by a woman far more beautiful than she was. In fact, such a possibility was her single greatest fear.

"Papa, I hate being at odds with you. I know all of your arguments. We both know he has been a cad when it comes to women—just as you know I am the first woman he has ever asked to marry. Why can't you give him the benefit of the doubt? If I am making a mistake, isn't it mine to make?"

He faced her fully and clasped both of her hands. "I am so proud of you. You are so beautiful, so caring and so committed to humanity, Francesca. While I do wish your new profession was not so dangerous, you have saved many lives and brought justice to those who desperately needed it. You and Hart have nothing in common!" he exclaimed. "I understand that he has turned your head, but what about a dozen years from now? You have dedicated your life to easing the pain and the burdens of others less fortunate that yourself. Hart is the most selfish man I know. Passion will not ensure a successful marriage, Francesca, not for the long term."

She pulled away. "That is unfair! You are judging Hart based solely on his reputation. You do not even know him, Papa. He has been nothing but noble to me. If you cast stones at him, Papa, then you cast them at me, too. Please, please trust me now."

He appeared ready to weep. "Francesca, you have been too kind and trusting since you were a small child, bringing home stray dogs and cats. I keep thinking that Hart is another stray, a man with no real advocates. Are you certain that you really wish to rescue him this way?"

Francesca knew she was Hart's only genuine friend—he had admitted it. But surely, surely she wasn't rescuing him as she had all of those strays? If her feelings weren't love, then Francesca did not know what they could be. "If I am rescuing him, I cannot help myself. Papa, you know that I have never been accepted in society, not until this engagement. Mama's friends and their daughters always saw me as an eccentric, and they never even tried to make me a part of their circle. Has it ever occurred to you that Hart is rescuing me?"

Andrew looked at her with surprise.

She held up her hand and the huge diamond there caught the room's lights and flashed. "It feels so right, Papa, being with him. And not because of passion, but because he has become my dearest and best friend. I am begging you to give him another chance. Please. Because you love me, give Calder one more chance to prove himself to you."

He stared for a long moment. Francesca stood very still, praying he would agree.

"I have treated you as an equal your entire life," he said slowly. "And even though my heart is telling me not to do so, I surrender. You are a brilliant young woman, and I am hoping that you will come to your senses before it is too late. But until then, I will give Hart another chance—as long as you wait a year before you marry."

"A year!" Francesca gasped, her pleasure dissolving.

"A year," Andrew returned calmly. "I know that seems like a long time, Francesca, but it is nothing when you think of a commitment made for the rest of your life. If you still feel this way next June, I will give you my blessing."

Francesca forced her dismay aside and managed a smile. "Thank you, Papa. Thank you so much." She hugged him hard.

He tilted up her chin. "I have always been proud of your independent thinking," he said with a sigh. "I have been wrong to think I could dictate to you after allowing you a lifetime of independence."

She softened. "I am who I am because of you, Papa. I owe you everything." She kissed his cheek, suddenly lighthearted. If she could control her lustful nature—or convince Hart to take her to bed before they were married—maybe waiting to marry wasn't such a bad thing. The year would give Andrew enough time to really get to know and like Hart. "Good night, Papa." Francesca stepped into the hall.

"Miss?" Her personal maid, Betty, appeared at the far end of the corridor. In her hand was an envelope.

Francesca was surprised to see her. "Betty, why didn't you go to bed? I told you, I do not mind." She saw no reason for Betty to wait up for her. Other young ladies might be incapable of getting out of their gowns, but she could manage quite easily and hardly needed a servant to help.

Betty, who was Francesca's own age, smiled at her. "Oh, miss, it is so hard to get those buttons opened by yourself! And it's my work to take care of you. Besides, this come for you, and the cabbie who brought it said it was urgent, miss, terribly so."

As it was almost midnight, Francesca was intrigued. She took the small envelope, noting its premier quality. It was addressed to her at her Fifth Avenue home, but bore no sender's name. "A cabdriver brought this?"

"Yes, miss."

Francesca unsealed the envelope and pulled out a small parchment. The note was brief and handwritten.

Francesca, I am in desperate need. Please come to Daisy's.
Rose

FRANCESCA LEANED FORWARD eagerly in the hansom cab she had hired. Stealing out of the house at the midnight hour had been easily accomplished, with her father still in the library and her mother upstairs and presumably in bed. The doorman, Robert, had pretended not to see her escape—but then, she gave him a weekly gratuity to ensure that he look the other way at such times.

After leaving the house, she had walked to the prestigious Metropolitan Club, but a block south of the Cahill home. There, she had merely waited for a gentleman to arrive at the club. Traffic was light, as it was a Monday night, but this was New York City, and eventually a hansom had paused before the club's imposing entrance to discharge his fare. Not wanting to be recognized, Francesca had bowed her head as a gentleman walked past her, but she knew he stared, as genuine ladies did not travel about the city at such an hour alone.

Francesca clung to the safety strap, straining to glimpse Daisy Jones's residence as her cab rumbled toward it. She simply could not imagine what Rose could want.

Daisy Jones was Hart's ex-mistress, and one of the most beautiful women Francesca had ever seen. When they first met, she had also been one of the city's most expensive and sought-after prostitutes. Francesca had been on a case at the time, working closely with Calder's half brother, Rick Bragg, the city's police commissioner. In fact, at that time she barely knew Hart—and had thought she was in love with Rick.

Francesca had not been surprised when she had learned of the liaison between them. She understood why Hart would want to keep such a woman. In fact, she and Daisy had become rather friendly during that investigation—but any friendship had vanished when Hart had asked Francesca to marry him. Jilted, Daisy had not been pleased.

The large Georgian mansion appeared in her view. Daisy continued to reside in the house Hart had bought for her, as part of a six-month commitment he had promised her and was honoring. Francesca thought, but was not sure, that Rose was now living there, too. Rose was Daisy's dearest friend—and she had been her lover, before Daisy had left her for Hart.

The hansom had stopped. Francesca reached for her purse, noting that the entire house was dark, except for the outside light and two upstairs windows. Alarm bells went off in her mind. Even at such a late hour, a few lights should remain on inside on the ground floor.

Francesca paid the driver, thanking him, and stepped down to the curb. She paused to stare closely at the square brick house as he pulled away. There was no sign of movement, but then, at this hour that was not unusual. Uncertain of what to expect, she pushed open the iron gate and started up the brick path leading to the house. The gardens in front were lush and well tended and Francesca cautiously scanned them. Her nerves were on end, she realized, and she almost expected someone to jump out at her from behind a shrub or bush.

Just as she was about to silently reassure herself, she noticed that the front door was open.

Francesca halted, fully alert now. Suddenly, she thought about her mad dash from home. She had not bothered to go upstairs to retrieve her gun, a candle or any of the other useful items she habitually kept in her purse. She made a mental note to never leave home without her pistol again.

Francesca glanced inside the house. The front hall was cast in black shadow. She slowly pushed the front door open fully, the hairs on her nape prickling, and stepped in.

She had a very bad feeling, oh yes. Where was Daisy? Where was Rose? Where were the servants? Francesca moved quietly to the wall, groping for the side table she knew was there. Pressing against it, she strained to listen.

Had a mouse crept across the floor, she would have heard it, for the house was so achingly silent. She desperately wanted to turn on a gas lamp, but she restrained herself. Francesca waited another moment for her eyes to adjust to the darkness and then she crept forward.

A dining room was ahead and to her right. Francesca opened the doors, wincing as the hinges groaned, but the large room was dark and vacant. She did not bother to shut the doors but quickly crossed the hall, glancing nervously at the wide, sweeping stair-case as she passed it. The closest door was to the smaller of two adjoining salons. Francesca pushed it open. As she had thought, that room also appeared to be empty.

She paused, swept back to another time when she had stood in that room, her ear pressed to the door that adjoined the larger salon, spying upon Hart and Daisy. She had barely known Calder, but even then his appeal had been powerful and seductive; even then, she had been drawn to him as a moth to a flame. That day, she had been audacious enough to watch Hart make love to his mistress. Such an intrusion on their privacy was shameful, and Francesca knew it. Still, she had been incapable of stopping herself.

She shook the recollection off. That had been months ago, before she had ever been in Hart's arms, before Hart had cast Daisy aside—before she and Daisy had become enemies and rivals.

None of that mattered. If Daisy or Rose were in trouble, Francesca intended to help. She left the salon the way she had come in. The moment she stepped back into the hall, she heard a deep, choking sound.

She was not alone.

Francesca froze. She stared at the wide staircase facing her, straining to hear. The guttural noise came again, and this time, she felt certain it was a woman.

The noise had not come from upstairs, but beyond the staircase, somewhere in the back of the house. Francesca wished she had a weapon.

Throwing all caution to the wind, Francesca rushed past the staircase. "Daisy? Rose?"

And now she saw a flickering light, as if cast by a candle, coming from a small room just ahead. The door was widely open and she quickly discerned that it was a study, with a vacant desk, a sofa and chair. Francesca rushed to the threshold and cried out.

Rose was sitting on the floor, hunched over a woman whose platinum hair could only belong to Daisy. Rose was moaning, the sounds deep and low and filled with grief.

Surely Daisy was only hurt! Francesca ran forward and saw that Rose held her friend in her arms. Daisy was in a pale satin supper gown, covered with brilliantly, shockingly red blood. Francesca dropped to her knees and finally saw Daisy's beautiful face—and her wide, blue, sightless eyes.

Daisy was dead.

Rose moaned, rocking her again and again.

Francesca was in shock. From the look of her dress, Daisy had been murdered, perhaps with a knife. Horror began as she realized the extent of the wounds on Daisy's chest.

Who would want her dead, and why? Francesca recalled the last time she had seen Daisy. She and Rose had appeared at the funeral for Kate Sullivan, a murder victim from Francesca's most recent investigation. There had been no reason for her to attend, except one: to taunt Francesca. She had been hostile and bitter, and she had clearly wanted Hart back. She had done her best to cause tension between Hart and Francesca, and she had wittingly played upon all of Francesca's insecurities.

That day, outside of the church, she and Daisy had exchanged harsh words. Although Francesca could not remember the exact conversation, she knew she had been upset and dismayed, precisely as Daisy had planned.

But dear God, though Daisy had maliciously done her best to hurt both Francesca and Hart, she had not deserved this.

The questions returned. *Who would do this—and why?*

Francesca knelt. Rose had not stopped rocking her friend, weeping now in silent grief. Francesca reached out, grasping her arm. "Rose," she gasped. "I am so sorry!"

Rose froze, slowly looking up. Her green eyes were glazed with misery and tears. She shook her head, unable to speak.

Francesca quickly closed Daisy's eyes, shivering as she did so. Daisy was impossibly fair, blue-eyed, with platinum hair, her skin the color of alabaster. Delicate and petite, she had a sensuous grace that could only be inherent, never achieved. Now her small bosom was a mass of bloody, gaping flesh. Francesca would never become accustomed to death, and especially not violent death.

She stood, shaking, and decided against turning on more lights. The murder had been a brutal one. Rose did not need to be confronted with the extent of Daisy's wounds. Francesca took a soft cashmere throw from the sofa, feeling ill, very much so. She inhaled raggedly for control.

"I will find out who did this," she whispered, aching for Rose now.

Rose looked up accusingly. "Don't pretend that you care! We both know you hated her because Hart took care of her. I know you hated her for ever having been in Hart's bed!"

Francesca, still holding the throw, shook her head. She felt a tear tracking down her cheek. "You're wrong. I do care. I care very much. Daisy did not deserve this. No one deserves this!" She approached and laid a hand on the brunette's shoulder. "Please. Leave her now. Come, Rose, please."

Rose shook her head, choking, hugging Daisy more tightly. She was as dark, voluptuous and tall as Daisy was fair, slender and petite. Now she was covered with her friend's blood.

"I need to go to the police," Francesca said, thinking of Rick Bragg.

Francesca needed him now. They made an excellent team—they had solved a half a dozen dangerous and difficult cases together, and he remained her good friend. It was late, but he had to be summoned immediately. Together they would find Daisy's killer.

Hart's dark, smoldering image came to mind. He might not have ever loved Daisy, but how would he react to the news of her murder? Francesca realized she would be the one to tell him of the death of his former mistress, and unfortunately, she would have to do so the moment he returned home.

"The police?" Rose's voice was scathing and bitter. "*We* need to find Daisy's murderer! I am hiring you, to find the killer, Francesca. Forget those leatherheads! They won't give a damn about Daisy," she said, and she began to weep all over again.

Francesca nodded, but her instincts warned her not to take on Rose as a client. She took the opportunity to kneel and cover Daisy's brutally disfigured body with the throw, then somehow she pulled Rose to her feet, putting her arm around her. "Please, come sit down in the salon," she said, wanting very much to get Rose out of the room.

But Rose balked. "No. I am not leaving her alone like this!"

Francesca quickly knelt and pulled the throw over Daisy's face. "I do need to get the police. There has been a murder, and they must be notified. But I don't want to leave you here alone, Rose."

Rose sat abruptly on the sofa, her face collapsing into tears again. "Who would do this? And why? Oh, God why?"

Francesca sat besides her, her mind beginning to function fully again. She had received Rose's note a good half an hour ago, a few moments before midnight. Betty had said the note had been dropped off at the house just a few minutes before they arrived home. The trip uptown from Daisy's house was thirty minutes in light traffic, so Rose had sent the note around eleven-thirty. "Rose? Can you answer a few questions?"

Rose looked up. "Are you going to find her killer? The police won't care. I don't trust those flies."

Francesca hesitated, recalling Daisy's hostility the last time they had spoken, and Rose's own hatred of Hart for taking Daisy away from her. But how could she refuse Rose, who had loved Daisy so? "Yes. Yes, Rose, I will take the case."

"You will take the case, even though you hated her?"

"I didn't hate her, Rose. I was afraid of her."

Rose jerked, meeting Francesca's gaze. Slowly, she said, "All right. What do you want to know?"

"What happened here tonight? When did you find her?"

Rose swallowed. "I don't know. I was out for the evening. When I got here, the house was dark, I knew something was wrong! I called for her, but she didn't answer." Rose stopped, for out in the hall, a soft bump had sounded.

Stiffening, Francesca looked at the open door, as did Rose. The hall beyond was lost in shadow and she saw nothing. But she had heard a noise—someone was present.

Francesca stood. "Where are the servants?"

"The butler sleeps in his room behind the kitchens, as does the maid. The housekeeper goes home at five." Rose was ashen and wide-eyed now.

"Did you go below stairs when you came home?"

Rose shook her head. "No. I was about to go upstairs when I saw the light coming from this room." Her mouth trembled and she glanced at Daisy's covered body. She inhaled, clearly fighting more tears.

"Wait here," Francesca said. She glanced at the desk, saw a letter opener and took it. Then she changed her mind, putting it back and taking a crystal paperweight instead. After what had been done to Daisy, she did not think she could stab anyone. Clutching the paperweight, she left the study. The corridor outside remained dark and every blond hair on her nape prickled with dread and fear.

Someone was lurking in the corridor leading to the kitchen and servants' quarters. But it would make little sense for that someone to be the killer, who must have long since fled. It was probably just a servant.

On the other hand, murderers often defied every possible assumption one might make about them.

Francesca took a deep breath for courage, once more wishing she had her gun, and she started forward, trying to make as little noise as possible. She heard footsteps approaching—each footfall slow and cautious. She froze.

Her grip on the paperweight tightened. She debated turning to flee, but in a moment whoever was beyond her would appear and see her. Instead, she pressed against the wall, waiting. The shadowy form of a man appeared, carrying a candle. He saw her against the wall, halted in midstride and lifted the candle higher.

Francesca was illuminated—but so was he.

Standing there in the hall was her fiancé.

CHAPTER TWO

Tuesday, June 3, 1902—12:45 a.m.

FRANCESCA WAS DISBELIEVING. Hart was the very last person she had expected to see. What was he doing in the city?

And then she saw the dark stain on Hart's white shirt, where his suit jacket was unbuttoned. "Calder?"

He hurried toward her, his own surprise fading. "Francesca!" he exclaimed, and his expression changed, becoming displeased. "Why am I not surprised to find you here?"

"Are you hurt?" she demanded, but the beginnings of a terrible fear had crept into her mind. Somehow, she knew the blood was Daisy's. She stiffened, staring up at his dark, handsome face.

"I'm not hurt." He took her arm, as if to steady her. "Daisy is dead, Francesca."

She met his probing regard, her mind scrambling to sort through the confusion. "I know."

"The blood is hers, Francesca, not mine. I found her in the study. She had been stabbed."

Their eyes met. All of Francesca's shock suddenly vanished. He was supposed to be in Boston. When had he returned to town and why hadn't he called her? What was he doing here at Daisy's, in the kitchen and servants' quarters? Given the blood on the front of his shirt, he had held Daisy, too, the way Rose had. Something sharp and distasteful filled her: dread. "Calder, Rose said she found Daisy. In fact, she sent me a note asking me to come here."

"When I arrived, Rose wasn't here." His regard held hers. "I found Daisy on the floor of the study, very much alone." He looked away from her now. His composure was usually rock solid, but Francesca saw that he was struggling to maintain it. "She was already dead."

Francesca swallowed, feeling ill. "You checked for a pulse?"

He met her gaze. "Yes."

Francesca felt as if she were interrogating a suspect. Of course, that was not the case. "When did you arrive here, Calder?"

His look was sharp. "I left my home around eleven," he said. Then, softly, with warning, he added, "I do not want you involved, Francesca."

Francesca's tension rose. She was already involved, because Daisy had once been Hart's mistress, because she had once been Francesca's friend and because she had recently been her rival.

"Francesca," he said, his tone pointed, and he took her wrist.

She looked into his eyes. "Daisy is *dead,* Hart. She has been *murdered.* I think we are both involved."

He turned away, but not before Francesca saw the anguish in his eyes. She was shocked. Had she imagined it, or did Calder have some feelings for Daisy still, after all of this time?

He slowly faced her. "You are staring." His tone had softened and his hand slipped to her palm. "Francesca, I am also in shock. We had better summon the police."

Her heart raced with painful force. If she had seen anguish in his eyes, it was now gone. He seemed grim, but not grief-stricken. Of course he would be distraught that a woman he had once known intimately was dead. "Calder, what are you doing here?"

He hesitated, his expression hardening. "I finished my affairs in Boston earlier than expected. I arrived at Grand Central at a quarter to seven this evening." He met her gaze directly. "After I found Daisy, I decided to look for the killer. I was about to do so when Rose came into the house. She was not wearing any wrap—clearly she had just stepped out. I hid. She went directly to the study, Francesca, directly to Daisy. I followed her. She was not surprised to see Daisy murdered."

Francesca's mind raced. Calder had not answered her question. He had not told her why he was at Daisy's in the first place. Any affairs that remained between him and Daisy were of a financial nature. Such concerns could have waited. It was well after midnight now.

If he had left his uptown home at eleven, he would have arrived at Daisy's perhaps an hour ago. What had he been doing in the house for all of that time? Her pulse quickened with fear. She did not have to be thinking all that clearly now to know that Hart could be in trouble with the law. "And then what happened?"

"I left her and went to search the house." He released his hand from hers and tilted up her chin. "You're upset. I am, as well. We'll get through this, Francesca."

Francesca tried to smile at him and was fairly certain she had failed. "Of course we will. But Daisy is dead, Calder. As malicious as she was toward me, toward us—she did not deserve to die, and certainly not so violently."

His face tightened and something dark and deep flared in his eyes. "No. As much trouble as she caused us recently, she did not deserve to die."

Suddenly Francesca recalled that day last month outside of the church. After taunting her, Daisy had walked away. Hart had come outside, the memorial service over. He had been grim and resolute, and he had told her in no uncertain words not to worry.

I will take care of Daisy. Those had been his exact words. Now Francesca felt a surge of fear and she tried to think if anyone might have overheard his statement. Of course, Calder hadn't meant he would murder Daisy; he had meant he would make sure that she no longer bothered either one of them. But Daisy had been his mistress until a few months ago, and he continued to support her financially. Francesca had investigated enough crimes of passion to know that Hart should be kept out of this case. "Calder, you should leave right now. I will find a roundsman and alert Bragg. Did anyone else see you? Did Rose see you?"

He gave her an odd look. Softly, he said, "Are you trying to protect me, Francesca?"

She stiffened, but that single look caused her heart to skip. "Very well, I confess. Yes, I want to protect you. You should stay as far away from this house and the murder scene as possible." It crossed her still-dazed mind that she would have to lie to the police, if no one was to know that Calder had been at Daisy's that night. She didn't know how she would manage telling such a lie to Rick Bragg.

Hart's eyes smoldered. "I already spoke to Homer, the butler, and the housemaid. They are in their quarters, where I told them to remain. They both know I am here. I don't think Rose saw me. I found Daisy murdered, Francesca—I didn't murder her myself."

He was angry and she knew it. Quickly she took his hand but he shook her off. "Hart! I know you didn't kill her!" Of that, she had no doubt. "But you were here on the night of her death. You could be implicated." Francesca hoped that the coroner would discover that Daisy had been killed before a quarter to seven that evening.

"You don't need to protect me, Francesca," he said. "Besides, half the city knows I have been keeping her. I cannot deny our relationship. But remember, Rose was here before me."

"That is your word against hers." Francesca rubbed her temples, which throbbed. No good was going to come of this. A crystal ball could not have been clearer! If she did not find another suspect, and quickly, the police were going to consider Hart a prime suspect. She looked up and found him regarding her steadily, his gaze far too intent.

Suddenly he softened. He reached out and touched her cheek. "Why are we arguing? You don't need to protect me, Francesca, as I have done nothing wrong. And I have been fending for myself since I was a small boy, stealing scraps of food on the streets. And I have missed you," he added even more softly, and his tone was impossible to resist.

"I have missed you, too," she whispered shakily, moving into his arms as he reached out to her. She stood there, still grieving yet overcome with relief, pressed against his hard, powerful body. This was where she most wanted to be. Something terrible would come of this case, she just knew it. She was afraid for him, for her, for them both. But as afraid as she was, she had never loved him more.

Hart held her silently for a long moment, and she felt his strong heart begin to increase its beat. Her own pulse could not help but skip and dance when she was in his arms. Francesca lifted her face.

He touched her lips with his, once, twice, three times.

Beneath the gentle brushing, Francesca sensed his urgency and need. In response, as always, a fire roared to life in her veins. Their eyes met and held. Then Hart stepped back. "We should respect the dead," he said seriously.

"Yes, we should." Francesca folded her arms across her chest and gave herself a moment to refocus. "Rose is with…the body."

"Rose," he repeated. "Could she have murdered the woman she loved? Might she have already been here when I arrived? When did she send you this note, Francesca?"

Francesca could not imagine Rose killing her best friend, but she would consider it, of course. "The note arrived at my home before midnight. Let's estimate that it arrived by a quarter to the hour. Rose wrote and sent the note around eleven or shortly thereafter. She was undoubtedly sending me the note, which came by cab, when you walked in." It crossed her mind that most of the suspicion could be directed at Rose. "*She* found the body before you did. *She* was first on the scene."

He stared for a moment. "I have never trusted Rose. Why did she send for you, of all people? There was no love lost between any of us."

Francesca hesitated.

"Let me guess," he said sarcastically. "She wants you to find the killer?"

Francesca bit her lip. "Calder," she began, determined to head him off at the pass. Even though he was always supportive of her investigations and proud of her success in them, she knew why he did not want her on this particular case—and the reason was Daisy. "This is a crime of passion. I do not think it will be hard to find the killer. From what I saw," she added, an image of Daisy's mutilated chest coming to mind, "someone stabbed Daisy repeatedly in a fit of anger."

"You cannot predict the nature of this investigation!" Hart exclaimed. "Do not mistake me now, Francesca, this is one case where I do *not* want you involved." His look was uncompromising.

"But I *am* involved. She was your ex-mistress and I am your fiancée." Francesca tried to be firm and gentle at once.

He made an angry sound and took her arm. "I am asking you, this one single time, to leave the investigation of Daisy's murder alone."

That terrible feeling of dread rose swiftly up again. Francesca stole a look at Hart's angry expression, her heart sinking. Now was clearly not the time to tell him that nothing and no one—not even Hart—could stop her from finding Daisy's killer. But why did he want her off the case so badly? Surely he had nothing to hide, not from her.

"This is too personal for us both," Hart said in a calmer tone, as if that explained his reasoning, but it explained nothing at all.

"Yes, it is personal for us both," Francesca said non-committally. She was aware of the exasperated look he cast at her, but now she was wondering about Rose. She had yet to ask her exactly when she had found Daisy. Given the extent of her grief, it was possible she had sat with her dead friend for quite some time before writing Francesca the note. One fact was clear—Daisy had been murdered before eleven or half past eleven p.m., when Rose had sent Francesca the note.

Together, they moved toward the study, where the candle continued to flicker. As they approached, Francesca's steps slowed, as did Hart's. His grasp on her hand tightened, but with reassurance, not warning. Francesca glanced at him and he tried to smile at her, but the curve of his firm mouth could not extinguish the sadness in his dark navy blue eyes.

He was far more upset than he was letting on, she thought with dismay. God, what if he still had feelings for Daisy? Could she possibly manage that, when Daisy had always felt like a threat to her relationship?

Rose was now sitting on the sofa, curled up like a child, her knees to her chest, the dark green evening gown she wore stained with blood. Daisy remained on the floor, covered from head to toe with the throw. Hearing their footsteps, Rose looked up.

She shot to her feet, pointing, her hand shaking. "You! I should have known! You goddamned bastard! You killed her!"

Police Commissioner Accused of Dereliction of Duty
Commissioner Bragg Fails Reformers
Civic Leaders Outraged with Police Policy

IN DISGUST, RICK BRAGG swept all three newspapers from his desk, cradling his head in his hands. His head ached and he was impossibly tired. He had never felt more worn, and that had nothing to do with the fact that the grandfather clock in the hall had just chimed a single time, indicating it was one in the morning. Right now, he almost regretted accepting the mayor's appointment, an appointment that had initially been filled with excitement and hope. He was the first police commissioner since Teddy Roosevelt to attempt the monumental mission of reforming the city's notoriously corrupt police force. But the hottest issue of the day was his undoing, especially as the mayor had tied his hands behind his back, refusing to allow him to do his job as he wished to do it.

Bragg sighed and reached for his bourbon. Mayor Low was already afraid of the vast German vote and had decided to ask the police not to enforce the blue laws, which required the closing of saloons on the Sabbath. Yet every reform group in the city was in favor of such closings. But after a series of crackdowns, Tammany Hall had made it a point to stir up as much trouble for Bragg and his force as possible. The German workers of the city were in an uproar, demanding their rights in protests and petitions. Afraid of losing reelection, Low had told Bragg to back off.

Low was good for the city. He was a man dedicated to social and political reform and he was courageous enough to oppose Tammany Hall. He was also Bragg's boss. There was no way Rick could refuse his orders, even if it meant compromising his own oath to uphold and obey the law.

He could please no one now. The reformers, led by the clergy and the city's progressive-minded elites, wanted his head and his resignation. So did half of his own force, due to the internal shake up he had inflicted these past five months, reassigning officers left and right to break up the rings of graft and bribery that manacled the city in a web of corruption and lies. Low had made it clear that he wished for Rick to continue on; given the circumstances, he was pleased with the internal cleanup of the force. Rick hadn't really been considering resignation, but sometimes, on an endless day like this one, it crossed his mind.

He was never at home, and his family had never needed him more.

He drank, finishing the bourbon and pouring another one. *His family.* Images of his beautiful wife and the two little girls they had decided to adopt filled his mind. Who was he fooling? He had finished all the urgent paperwork an hour or two ago and had chosen to linger over the damn dailies, with their accusatory headlines, because he was afraid to go upstairs.

He was afraid to go to the bedroom he shared with his wife, afraid to go to their bed.

He leaned his face on his hands, closing his eyes, so tired he thought he could fall asleep at his desk. And it wasn't the job, it wasn't the corruption, it wasn't the politics—it was the impossible personal and private dilemma he found himself in. How much longer could he go on this way?

He had become a stranger to his family, a stranger to the little girls who needed him—a stranger to his wife.

And she wanted it that way.

He stood abruptly, terribly torn. A part of him was ruthlessly determined to go up those stairs, climb into her bed and simply hold her, even though he would find her stiff with tension, pretending to be asleep. When he reached for her, he knew she would turn away, refusing to allow him any opportunity for comfort or intimacy. And he could not blame her.

Leigh Anne had said she did not hold him responsible for the accident that had caused her to lose the use of her legs, but he blamed himself—and knew that, deep down, she blamed him, too.

Once, he had thought their marriage over. Years before the accident, soon after they were first married. She had left him to travel in Europe and he had hated her passionately. Now, too late, he had faced the extent of his passion. He still loved her and he always had. But it had become painfully obvious that she no longer cared in return. He knew what he should do. He should give her the freedom she clearly wanted, but how could he? Who would take care of her if he did so? And what about the girls? If he left Leigh Anne, it would mean the loss of his family.

His heart seemed to crack apart at the thought.

He stared at the dark, empty fireplace. The past flashed before his eyes—the moment he had first laid eyes on Leigh Anne, which was when he had fallen in love. Their wedding, and her happiness then. His sudden, unexpected decision to leave his profitable career to perform legal services for the poor and inopportune. Her unhappiness had followed, for he had turned his back on a sizable income and worked eighty-hour weeks instead. Finally, there was her betrayal. She had simply left him, walking out on their marriage. Too late, he wished he had never taken that damn employment, or that he had begged her to return.

But he hadn't. And four years of separation had limped by, until the night Francesca Cahill had come into his life.

He smiled, but his sadness increased. He wondered what would have happened if Leigh Anne had never returned to him. He still cared deeply for Francesca and he always would. Once, they had been on the verge of falling in love, but that seemed like a lifetime ago. Now he was committed to his wife and children—and Francesca was committed to his half brother. His smile vanished. Hart would break her heart. He knew it the way he knew that Leigh Anne wanted him to leave. He had not a single doubt, and the day Hart hurt her, he would break *him*.

A sharp knocking sounded on the front door.

Bragg was relieved, as he hated thinking about Francesca with Hart. It was terribly late, so the call could only be police business—an emergency. Bragg grabbed his suit jacket from the back of his chair and hurried down the narrow hall of the modest Victorian brownstone he leased.

A roundsman stood there with a lantern, his expression alert. Bragg was already shrugging on his jacket. "What is it?" He did not know the young officer who faced him.

"Sir, there has been a murder. Inspector Newman thinks you might want to meet him at HQ, immediately."

He was tense, and glad of the distraction. This could only be dire, indeed. "Who is the victim?" He stepped outside, closing the front door behind him. The early June night was cool, but not unpleasant.

"A woman. Her name is Miss Daisy Jones, sir."

An instant passed as he assimilated this stunning fact—Hart's mistress had been murdered. "Newman is at headquarters? He is not at the murder scene?"

"No, sir. There are some officers at the scene, but he has several witnesses to speak with, sir. He asked me to tell you that he is interviewing Calder Hart and Miss Cahill as we speak."

Bragg tripped. For one moment, he was in disbelief. *Hart was at HQ—with Francesca.* And he simply knew that no good could come of this case.

FRANCESCA SAT BESIDE HART at the long, scarred wood table in the conference room of police headquarters. The room was on the second floor, just a door down from Bragg's office. Inspector Newman, a rotund and pleasant man with graying hair with whom Francesca had worked many times, sat facing them, holding a notepad, and wearing his most professional demeanor. Francesca knew that was on her account, as he was very aware of her close relationship with Bragg.

Francesca had already heard Hart's story on the short ride from Daisy's to Mulberry Street, when they had had a chance to speak. Now she watched him closely, carefully listening to his every word. She could not help herself, for she had learned on her numerous past investigations to check and recheck every detail. Witnesses often confused facts and events; perpetrators often deliberately misled the police. Of course, she was not suspicious of Hart and she expected him to keep his facts straight, and although his expression was deadpan, his tone calm, she was certain now that he was very distressed by the evening's events.

"I left the train depot a few minutes before 7:00 p.m. As I was not expected, I took a cab home. Traffic was heavy and it was a good hour before I reached the house. An hour later I found a note from Daisy on my desk."

Which meant he had found her note at 9:00 p.m., approximately, Francesca thought.

"And what did her note say?" Newman asked.

"She wished to speak with me the moment I returned home and said it was very urgent." Hart's impassive expression never changed, but sitting beside him, Francesca could feel the tension coiled up in him. She could not help herself, and she reached out to cover his hand with her own. He glanced at her with a slight smile that failed to reach his gold-flecked eyes.

"And do you have any clue as to what could be so urgent?" Newman asked.

Hart did not hesitate. "I felt certain the matter was a financial one."

Newman glanced at Francesca, his cheeks becoming a bit pink.

Francesca was willing to let him off the hook. "I am well aware of the fact, Inspector, that Daisy was Calder's mistress."

He blushed. "I am sorry, Miss Cahill, to bring up such a delicate subject. You spoke as if the affair had ended?"

"It ended the day Francesca agreed to become my wife," Hart said flatly. "The morning of February 24."

Francesca looked at him in real surprise. He recalled the exact date she had accepted his proposal? He turned to smile at her, when Rick Bragg walked purposefully into the room.

Francesca leapt to her feet, very relieved to see him. Calder's half brother was a very handsome man, but the two men shared little resemblance. Bragg had tawny hair and a golden complexion, as did most of the Bragg men, while Hart was as dark as midnight. He glanced between Francesca and Hart as he approached them, his expression grim. Hart's face settled into an unreadable, emotionless mask.

Francesca was aware of the new currents of tension swirling in the room as she clasped both of Rick's hands. "I am so glad you are here! Calder was just giving his statement, Rick. Of course, you know that Daisy is dead."

"So I have been told," he said, kissing her cheek. "Are you all right?"

She nodded. "Yes, of course. But Rose is devastated." She hesitated, then dared to add, "Calder is upset, too."

Rick clearly did not believe that. "What are you doing here, Francesca? You are a witness to the murder?"

"Not really," Francesca said quickly. She realized Bragg had not released her hands and that Hart watched them like a hawk. She gently disengaged herself. "Rose found the body and sent a note, asking me for help. It appears that Rose discovered Daisy first, and that Calder found her while Rose was sending me the note. When I got to the house, Rose was with Daisy and Calder was looking for the killer. He had just spoken with some of the staff."

Bragg turned to Hart. "Don't let me interrupt your statement."

Hart shrugged as if he had not a care in the world.

Bragg leaned over Newman's shoulder and scanned his notes. As he did so, Newman said, "He received a note from Daisy requesting a meeting, sir. That would have been about nine o'clock."

Bragg nodded, straightening. His aloof gaze met Hart's. "So you rushed off to meet your mistress?"

Hart sent him a cold, unpleasant smile. "You know damn well I broke off the affair when I became engaged to Francesca."

Newman looked startled. He said, "Sir, she was living in Mr. Hart's house."

"I am aware of that. So, you rushed off to meet Daisy as she requested?" Bragg asked again.

Francesca walked over to stand beside Hart, dismayed that Bragg had instantly gone on an attack. Hart, who remained sitting rather indolently, did not give any sign of being shaken. "No, I did not rush off anywhere. It had been a long day and I had a drink, perhaps two. It was some time later when I decided to call on Daisy and conclude whatever affairs were bothering her."

Bragg made a mocking sound. "And those affairs were?"

"I assumed they were financial matters," Hart said, slowly rising to his feet, "as the only connection left between me and Daisy was financial. I continued to support her—we had a verbal contract, and it did not expire until mid-July. But you know all of that, don't you, Rick?"

Bragg stared and Hart stared back. Then Bragg glanced at Francesca. "I find it highly unlikely that you just returned to town and went to see Daisy to discuss a few bills."

"I don't care what you think," Hart said, finally appearing annoyed. "I never have and I never will."

Bragg looked ready to explode—or arrest him. Smiling tightly, he said, "Considering your mistress has been murdered, I think you had better start to care what I think."

Hart smiled as tightly, and for one moment, Francesca thought he was about to smash his fist in Bragg's face.

Francesca hated the hostility between the two brothers. She gripped Hart's arm. "A terrible murder has been committed," she said tersely. "There is no point in the both of you going at each other's throats. We need to find Daisy's killer. We owe her that."

Bragg gave her an undecipherable look and walked away, running his hand through his hair. Hart faced her, his rigid expression softening. "You don't need to be here right now," he said.

Francesca gaped. "Of course I do!" she cried. She could not

tell him, not in front of Newman and Bragg, how worried she was about his apparent involvement. "When we go home, we will go home together," she whispered.

Before Hart could object, Bragg returned to them, apparently having recovered his composure. "Let's leave the subject of why you went to see Daisy aside for the moment. Walk me through what happened when you arrived."

Some of Hart's tension eased. "I left the house around half past eleven, I think. When I arrived at her home, I saw that there were no lights on downstairs. No one answered the knocker, and that was odd. I did not have a good feeling at this point. So I tried the door, found it unlocked and walked in."

Francesca could not breathe and her heart raced. The mental note she had made earlier was glaring at her now. Hart had said he had left home at eleven, not half past. Was he deliberately misleading Bragg and the police, or had he, like most witnesses, made an innocent factual error? And she wondered again, if he had really left home at 11:00 p.m., what had he been doing for nearly an entire hour in that house? Was that why he was misleading the police?

Almost as if he were a mind reader, he turned to Francesca. "What time did you get there?"

She hesitated, her instincts rising up now. She did not want to lie, but she desperately wanted to protect Hart.

"Francesca?"

She wet her lips. "Before midnight," she lied. "I imagine it was just a few minutes after Hart." She could barely believe that she was lying to a man she had once loved and still cared so deeply for.

Bragg rubbed his jaw. "Calder?"

"I found Daisy shortly after I first walked in," he said, not looking at Francesca now. "It appeared as if she had been stabbed in the chest, many times. No one could survive such an attack, but I did check for her pulse." He spoke very calmly, as if they were discussing the next day's weather, but he was gripping the back of the chair he had been sitting in and his knuckles were white.

Francesca could not see his expression, because he had looked down, but she gave up all pretense now. Hart was distraught and anguished. He certainly still cared for Daisy, and Francesca was hurt and jealous, dear God.

But Francesca wanted to comfort him, too, and she moved closer to him. Instantly he glanced at her. She sensed he wanted to reassure her, and any grief he might be feeling was masked. Then he looked at Bragg. "I sat with her for a moment," he said calmly. "I was in shock. I was very much in shock."

Bragg nodded. "There's blood on your shirt," he said.

Hart had tossed his charcoal-gray jacket aside. His shirtsleeves were rolled up, his dark tie loose and askew. He rarely wore a vest, and dried blood stained the finely woven white cotton material of his shirt. Now he glanced down at his own chest.

"You held her?" Bragg asked.

Francesca tensed.

An interminable moment passed and Francesca thought Hart was recalling the moment he had first seen Daisy dead on the study floor. She touched his arm; he did not notice. "I saw her the moment I reached the study door. It was ajar. There was so much blood. I knew instantly that she had been murdered." Hart finally looked at his half brother. "But I checked to see if she was breathing. She wasn't. I was on my knees." He stopped. He had spoken as if reciting notes for a university class. Now he looked down. "Yes, I held her."

Francesca turned away. Her heart beat so hard it hurt her there, inside of her chest.

"Go on," Bragg said to Hart, as if he had not just revealed his feelings, when they all knew he had.

Hart shrugged. "I instantly wondered if the killer remained in the house. I was about to begin a search when I saw Rose coming inside, without any kind of wrap. Clearly she had only just stepped out. I was suspicious and I made certain she did not see me. She went directly to the study. She was not surprised to find Daisy dead there, but she was very distraught."

"She still did not see you?" Bragg asked.

Hart shook his head. "We all know that Rose was very fond of Daisy. Although her behavior seemed suspicious, I left to search the house, on the chance I might find either the killer or a clue. I had just finished speaking with the butler and a housemaid when I ran into Francesca."

"And that would have been at midnight," Bragg confirmed.

"I guess so," Hart said, suddenly sounding tired. "Are we through?"

Francesca would have been consumed with guilt for her deception, but there was too much worry and hurt. She could not get past the fact that Hart had admitted to holding Daisy in his arms, obviously grieving for her. She reminded herself that he had every right. After all, she still cared for Bragg. She would grieve until the day she died if anything ever happened to him. Why couldn't she accept that Hart had continued to care for Daisy, too?

Because she had always been jealous of the fact that Hart had once wanted Daisy enough to keep her as a mistress.

Francesca did not want to think about how insecure Daisy had always made her feel. She took a breath and plunged into the fray. "Rick, I arrived just a few moments before I bumped into Hart. When I arrived, the front door was ajar. I found Rose with Daisy, in grief. There was no sign of a murder weapon. I covered up the body and I also thought to look for the killer, as I heard a noise in the hall. That is when I ran into Calder on the stairs."

"And you went to Daisy, for what reason?"

Francesca reached into her beaded velvet evening bag and

handed him the note. He read it and gave it to Newman. "Tag it," he said. He faced Hart. "And the note Daisy sent you?"

Hart was rubbing his jaw. "It's probably on my desk, where I left it."

"I'm afraid I will need it, Calder."

"I'll send it to you," Hart said. He walked away from Bragg and Francesca, as if deep in thought. Francesca watched him, aware of Bragg watching her. This was one case that she was not going to be enthusiastic about working on. She turned to Bragg. "Rose has admitted to finding Daisy murdered, Rick. I think we need to pursue her as a suspect, as distasteful as that is."

Bragg spoke, not to Francesca but to Hart. "You have a houseful of witnesses, do you not, who will testify that you were at your home from the time you arrived there, at approximately 8:00 p.m., until you left for Daisy's at half past eleven?"

Hart faced them from a distance. "Alfred let me in when I returned from the depot. I am sure he saw me go out."

Bragg made a note. "And your driver can certainly testify to taking you to Daisy's at half past eleven, can he not?"

Hart's expression was impassive. "I took a cab."

Francesca almost groaned. "Rick! Hart was at home for at least three hours! I am sure quite a few staff can testify to that."

Bragg looked at her, not responding.

Francesca felt some panic bubble. Rick did not believe all that Hart had said.

"Rick, I want to speak to you alone," Hart suddenly said.

Francesca was instantly alarmed. "Calder!"

"No." His eyes had become shards of steel. "I wish to speak with my brother privately."

Francesca's worry knew no bounds. She hesitated and Rick said, "I want to speak to him alone, as well. Francesca, it is late. I will finish with Hart and he can take you home, as long as you promise me you will come in first thing in the morning to give an official statement." He smiled at her.

But she did not smile back. If they wished to speak alone, then they were going to discuss her—or discuss something they did not wish for her to hear. When both men united against her, it was a losing battle. She looked at Rick, who was smiling too benignly at her, then glanced at Hart, who was not smiling at all. He appeared ruthlessly determined, but to do what?

"I'll take you home in a few minutes," Hart said.

She knew she could not prevent this private discussion. She sighed and faced Rick. "Of course I'll come in tomorrow morning. What about Rose?"

"I'm going to interview her in a moment, if she is up to the task. If not, I will send her home with a police escort and speak with her in the morning, as well."

Francesca would be shocked if Rose were ever proven to be the killer. She felt very sorry for the woman. "Rick, she is in mourning."

"I know." He laid his hand on her back and guided her across the room to the door. "Newman? Why don't you see Miss Cahill downstairs and begin speaking with Rose."

"Aye, sir," Newman said.

HART WATCHED FRANCESCA LEAVE. He was very determined, but a part of him almost called her back. Before the door closed she sent him a reassuring look. He knew her so well now, better than he had ever known anyone. Therefore, he had not a single doubt that Francesca genuinely wanted to comfort him, just as he knew she wanted to protect him. It was amazing, and he knew that later he'd be grateful. Tonight, however, he had no use for any emotions whatsoever, not even those engendered by his fiancée. Tonight, he refused to feel anything at all.

Images of Daisy filled his mind, her anger, her tears, and later, her bloody corpse.

Hart turned to Rick and said, "I do not want Francesca involved in this investigation, not in any way. She thinks to protect me but it is hardly necessary."

Bragg's tawny brows lifted. "I could not agree more. How noble of you."

Inwardly he seethed. "We both know I am not noble, Rick, so don't even begin. But even I am not rotten enough to put Francesca in the awkward position of defending me in the murder of my ex-mistress." He did not want his past with Daisy—or any woman—thrown up in Francesca's face, time and again. In fact, he had regretted his hedonistic past ever since meeting Francesca, or shortly thereafter. Although he could not change the past, he hoped to keep Francesca as far removed from it as he could. Yet tonight, the past had somehow caught up with them both.

"I could almost believe you are putting Francesca first," Rick said, "except we both know you are not."

Hart despised his brother's self-righteous, judgmental nature. "Let's finish, Rick." His temper was explosive and *that* felt good.

But Rick was clearly not finished. "You don't want Francesca to know why you went to see your mistress tonight, do you?" Rick was furious. "We both know you did not ride downtown to go over her expenses and accounts."

Hart saw red. "Fuck you. I did not visit Daisy to sleep with her."

Rick stared. Finally said, "Then why? Because only some very urgent dispute or crisis would rouse you so late at night."

He tensed. Daisy's sobs filled his mind, and the image was hateful. "I told you, it was a matter of finances. I'm not even sure what, exactly, the matter involved. She probably wanted more funds. I had asked her to leave the house last month, earlier than we had agreed. She refused and I had decided to let it go. Maybe she was going to ask me for a payoff." He smiled coldly. "But we will never know now, will we?"

"How interesting this is, your word against the word of a dead woman. Why did you ask Daisy to leave the house earlier than the two of you had agreed she would go?"

Hart had to hand it to his half brother—Rick never missed a trick. Calder had learned long ago to stick as closely to the truth as possible. "She had become difficult, even malicious, toward me—and worse, toward Francesca. I was angry with her and I had had enough."

Bragg's brows rose. "Were you angry with her tonight?"

"No," Hart said, and that was the truth.

Rick saw it, too, because he nodded. "Is there anything else you wish to add?"

"No."

Rick nodded again. "Come in tomorrow afternoon. Your statement will be ready and you can sign it." He hesitated. "It wouldn't hurt, Calder, to bring your lawyer with you."

Hart stiffened. "I don't need a lawyer, because I did not murder anyone."

Rick shrugged and started for the door.

Hart seized him from behind. "I meant what I said. I do not want Francesca working this case with you. Turn her away, Rick, when you see her tomorrow. She doesn't need this."

"I can't dissuade her when she has set her mind to something."

"You can't, or you won't?"

Rick gave him an enigmatic look and he walked out.

Hart lost it. He kicked the door so hard that it hurt.

CHAPTER THREE

Tuesday, June 3, 1902—3:00 a.m.

FRANCESCA WAITED IN HART'S carriage, a large, elegant six-in-hand, while Hart and Bragg spoke. Although the station had been unusually quiet, she wanted to be alone with her thoughts.

The ward was almost deserted. Although numerous prostitutes worked the brownstones just across from headquarters, Francesca saw only one madam, outrageously dressed in a peignoir with a pink feather boa, smoking a cigar and sitting on the stoop of her building. A pair of officers was returning from a foot patrol in their blue serge uniforms and leather helmets, billy clubs in hand and wearing their new police-issue Colt revolvers. A horse and rider was approaching, and some raucous conversation was coming from a nearby flat. Otherwise, like the station house, the night was oddly quiet.

Why had Hart sent her out? What did he wish to discuss with Bragg alone? Francesca could not help but be worried. A part of it was simple—leaving both men alone together was like sending them an invitation to do battle.

Their rivalry was ancient, going back to when they were small boys. They shared the same mother, Lily, who had tragically died. Rick had been eleven years old at the time and he had been claimed by his father, Rathe Bragg. Hart had been unwanted, so Rathe had taken him in, too. Francesca knew Hart so well now and she understood. His mother had never had time for him, first fighting to provide for her children and later, fighting to stay alive, a battle she had lost. Somehow Hart had felt abandoned and unloved, first by Lily, and then, by his biological father. As foolish as it seemed, he had never been able to forgive Rick for being the wanted one, the favored one, the loved one.

And as children so often do, he had searched for Lily's and then Rathe's approval in a backward way, his behavior wild and out of bounds, testing first his mother and then his stepfather. But he hadn't really wanted to push everyone away—he had just wanted to be loved, in spite of who he was.

Francesca knew Hart had not been aware of what he was doing as a small boy or a rowdy adolescent. Yet she had come to realize that his behavior as a mature and powerful man was really no different than that little boy's. He claimed not to care what anyone thought of him, and he was well aware of his black reputation, but Francesca thought he *did* care—and that he refused to admit it, not even to himself. He refused to conform to the rules and mores of proper society; he had flaunted his lovers, many of whom were divorcées, and he displayed the most shocking and controversial art. Behind his back, society gossiped in absolute fascination. Hart laughed about it, but it was as if he had to see just how far he could go before being cast out. There had been difficult times when he had tried to push her away, as well. But Francesca understood that his actions were a test—a test of her loyalty, her friendship and her devotion. She was never going to fail.

There was another aspect to Hart's rivalry with his half brother. The two men were as different as night and day. Rick had given his life to social and political reform, even at the expense of his marriage. His reputation was as stellar as Hart's was not; he would never flaunt an indiscretion or compromise anyone's reputation. Hart was only accepted in good society because of his wealth and power. Rick was accepted not just because he was from that acclaimed family, but because he was a leader of the reform movement, universally respected and admired for all of his good works. No two men could be more different—on the surface, at least.

It also did not help that, when she had first met Hart, she and Rick had been romantically involved. Hart remained jealous of the fact that she had chosen Rick before him and that she maintained a genuine friendship with him. Rick clearly loved his wife, and Francesca often felt he would not mind her engagement—as long as it was to anyone other than Hart. She sighed. She could not undo the past. She could not stop caring about Rick Bragg and she could not stop loving Hart. Their rivalry had begun decades before either man had ever met her, but she was aware of being added fuel to the fire.

Francesca pushed open her window. The night was cool but pleasant; a few stars had come out to join the crescent moon. She felt a soft summer breeze and she let it caress her face. She was so worried about this case and where the investigation would take her.

Suddenly the other passenger door opened and Hart climbed into the backseat beside her, taking her hand. "Are you cold? Why are you waiting here, when you could be inside?"

Francesca met his dark gaze and tried to smile at him. "It can be so noisy in the lobby. I have a headache," she said truthfully.

His smile faded as the carriage rumbled away from the curb. He put his arm around her. "It has been a terrible evening," he said quietly. "I wish you hadn't been here tonight, Francesca."

She looked up at his face, at the strong and attractive features she had come to love, acutely aware of his powerful embrace. "I'm glad I was here," she said passionately. "You are not going through this alone!"

"Francesca, I know you mean well. You always mean well," he said roughly, and he smiled. "But this affair is already a sordid one. I have never asked you before to cease an investigation, but I am asking you now."

She pulled away from him, disbelieving. "Hart, don't ask me to drop this."

"You are upset with me," he remarked, his eyes moving over her face.

"I want to help," Francesca said firmly. "I can help. Daisy was murdered and we both know I can find her killer. Just as we both know that right now, the police think you might be involved."

His expression hardened and he glanced away.

She moved into his arms, turning his face toward her. Hart could be terribly insecure and vulnerable at times, as if still that small, unloved, unwanted boy. "I am not upset with you. You did not murder Daisy, Hart," Francesca said. "We simply need to bring her killer to justice."

He caught her hand, bringing it to his chest. Against her skin, Francesca felt the stiff material of his shirt, and she realized he had pressed her hand against Daisy's dried blood. "Why are you calling me Hart? You only call me Hart when distressed." His gaze was searching in the flickering lights of the carriage.

She wet her lips. "I am distressed. You are, as well. How can we not be distressed after what has happened?"

He studied her and said, "And that is why I don't want you on this case. It will only get worse."

She trembled. "And how will it get worse?"

He was incredulous. "I care enough about you not to want you reminded every hour of every day that I was in Daisy's bed a few months ago!"

Her mind became blurred. A little voice inside of her head said, *"Don't."* She ignored it. "Why did you call on Daisy tonight?"

His grip on her hand tightened as their gazes locked. "There was a matter she wished to discuss."

Francesca continued to tremble and she knew Hart could

feel it. She recalled Newman's expression of pity, and Bragg's. Both men thought Hart had gone to see Daisy to take her to bed. "What matter?"

He rubbed his face and Francesca realized how tired he was. "Can we let this go, at least for tonight?"

She knew he had not gone to Daisy for carnal reasons. While it was her worst fear that one day he would stray, they had only recently become engaged and the passion they shared remained vast. "What was so important and so urgent that you had to see Daisy tonight—the night of her murder?" She could not help herself. "Calder, we agreed to always be honest with each other. We both know that you didn't go to Daisy's to discuss financial matters."

"We had a private matter to discuss." He was terse and there was a warning in his tone.

Francesca became alarmed. "A matter you wish to keep private from me?"

"Yes." He turned away, resolute, his expression hard and tense. "Please. Just leave it for now."

She could not believe he would not tell her what he and Daisy had intended to discuss. But it was not his nature to ask for anything, and he was asking her now to let the subject alone. She didn't know if she could. Her mind was spinning. She simply could not imagine what had brought him to Daisy's in the middle of the night. "Your motive in calling on her is crucial to your defense."

He became rigid. "So now I am accused of her murder?"

"Hart, I am not accusing you of anything! I know you are innocent. But the police will want to know."

He was angry. "No, you want to know! You want to pry! Damn it! I just asked you to drop it! But when you get an idea, a clue, a lead, you might as well be a terrier with some damned bone. Usually your tenacity is endearing—it is not endearing now. Please, *leave it,* Francesca."

She recoiled. And against her will, an image arose of him with Daisy in an intimate embrace.

As always, he knew. He tilted up her chin, forcing her gaze back to his. His eyes were wide. "You cannot think I went there to sleep with her?"

Francesca felt her cheeks heating. She really did not doubt Hart, but she did doubt Daisy. Had the other woman somehow lured him to her home to seduce him, in the hopes of rekindling their affair?

And because she hesitated, he grew incredulous. "Don't tell me you have doubts about my loyalty," he began in warning.

She could not breathe. She shook her head. "I don't. Not really. It's just—" she managed to say.

"Not really!" he exclaimed, cutting her off. "It's just what?" he demanded.

Francesca saw from his shocked and angry expression that she had been wrong to even begin to doubt him. "You know I am insecure at times like these," she said. "I did not trust Daisy—and neither did you! If only I were half as beautiful as she was."

He leaned close, exploding. "I asked you to marry me because I had no wish to continue my philandering ways! I asked you to marry me because I was sick to death of all of those desperate women, and more important, of myself! I asked you to marry me because I wish to commit myself to *you,* Francesca. I *knew,* shortly after meeting you, that you were the one woman I wished to share the rest of my entire life with. I told you, in a true confession of my feelings, that I could no longer enjoy being with those faceless women, whose names I could never even recall! I asked you to marry me because you are the only genuine friend I have ever had, and because I have come to care deeply for you—because you have changed my life! Now, you believe I was sleeping with Daisy? I have never been faithful before, Francesca, but I have been faithful to you! And you are ten times more beautiful than Daisy!"

He was so angry. Francesca huddled against the velvet seat,
shocked by his passionate outburst—and thrilled, too. "Calder, I
was merely being honest. I don't really believe you went to Daisy
to sleep with her, of course I don't. But Daisy always worried
me. She was so beautiful. I am such a bluestocking, and I am
so different from women like her. I admit it—when it comes to
such women, I am a jealous, witless fool!"

He swept her into his arms. "Yes, you are jealous, witless
and foolish at times like these," he muttered, and he covered
her mouth with his. He moved so quickly that Francesca was
stunned, and then his tongue thrust hard and deep. Before she
could react, the kiss softened, becoming thorough, and more
thorough still. Francesca forgot the conversation, holding on to
his hard, powerful body, her blood surging with heat. When he
finally pulled away, she was dazed and throbbing with a terrible
need and urgency. His sexual tension emanated from him in
waves, but he gently brushed some strands of blond hair from
her cheek. "You are as different from Daisy and her kind as can
be—and I am so grateful for it! You tempt me, Francesca, as no
one else ever has," he whispered roughly.

It was always this way, she thought, recovering some of her
sensibilities. When she became terribly insecure, he would make
love to her and she would realize she had been a fool. When she
was in his arms, all doubt died. She smiled at him and clasped
his cheek briefly.

He smiled back and, his eyes closing, he kissed her hand.

The electricity that existed between them sparked. She covered his hand, pulling it against her face. Her heart pumped,
each beat solid and pregnant with desire, in the hollow of her
chest. She had missed him terribly while he was out of town and
it would be a few more minutes before they reached her home.

He sensed the direction of her thoughts and looked directly
at her. His gaze was brilliant as it met hers. Very softly, he said,

"This is a dangerous night. I don't feel in control, Francesca. I am not certain this is a good idea."

She slipped her hand under his shirt, against the warm skin of his hard chest, but his shirt remained stiff with dried blood. She looked at it; so did he.

Daisy was dead and Hart was in trouble, she somehow thought.

He kissed her cheek lightly and took her hand. Francesca fought the raging of her body until it softened. "I am sorry," she said when she could speak. "I am sorry for being so foolish and for having even the tiniest doubt. But I am afraid I will always be jealous when it comes to other women."

"You don't ever have to be jealous of another woman, Francesca," he said so seriously that her insides melted.

"I will try to prevent such a lapse in the future, I swear it, Calder." She actually managed to smile at him.

He glanced at her. "Maybe I should be more understanding," he said, surprising her. "Recently Daisy did her best to interfere in our relationship. Maybe your response to her was reasonable. But, Francesca, I have to remind you of one basic fact. Daisy had the airs of a well-bred lady, and I am rather certain she came from a genteel background, but she sold her body, Francesca. I *paid* for her attentions—they were never freely given." He held her gaze. "Darling, she was a whore."

"Calder!" She was shocked that he would speak so ill of the dead. But her mind quickly grasped the fact he had just tossed her way. Francesca sat up straighter. "Did she ever tell you anything of her background?" she asked. She had also realized upon first meeting Daisy that she was from society, although Daisy had never once referred to her background.

"It never came up. Frankly, I wasn't curious, not at all."

Francesca began to plan her next day. "This was a crime of passion, Calder, not some random killing. The killer knew Daisy and I think he knew her well. I must find out who she really was—where she came from, and why she left that life to become a prostitute."

He sighed. "I can see how determined you are. Well, if anyone can uncover the truth about her life, I am sure that person is you."

She barely heard him. She had so much work to do—and the sooner, the better, so she and Calder could get past this terrible tragedy and get on with their lives.

He tilted up her chin and their eyes met. "You lied for me tonight, Francesca," he said quietly. "I was at that house by half past eleven, an hour or so before you ever got there. You did not arrive until half past twelve."

She tensed. "I know what I did, Calder."

"You lied to Rick."

She bit her lip. "And I hated doing it. But you were at Daisy's for perhaps an hour after discovering her dead. And the police will think that terribly bizarre."

He took her hand again. "I told you—after Rose came in, I was looking for her killer."

"I know. And I believe you. I just want you off their list of suspects."

"You lied to Rick for me."

"I hated lying to him, but we are engaged," she said softly. "I will always be on your side, first and foremost."

His gaze moved slowly over her face. "I think I am finally beginning to understand that, Francesca," he said. He hesitated. "I am grateful."

She smiled warmly at him. "I don't want your gratitude."

He stared another moment, then faced his window, his face becoming a hard, tight mask of controlled emotion.

Her smile vanished. She knew his thoughts had veered away from her to the murder—and perhaps to the private matter he had wished to discuss with Daisy—and she could not help thinking that Hart was hiding something from her.

She was afraid.

FRANCESCA PASSED A MOSTLY sleepless night. At eight in the morning, dressed in her usual no-nonsense navy blue suit, she stared at her pale reflection in the mirror of her boudoir. She had thought about Daisy's gruesome murder all night, endlessly analyzing the little evidence she currently had. Maybe today Hart would tell her why he had called on Daisy. Maybe she would find a new lead, one that would point her in the direction of the real killer. As distasteful as it was, she had to acknowledge that Rose's behavior that evening had been odd and suspicious. Francesca could not come to terms with the concept of Rose murdering her best friend and lover, but she was clearly on the police's list of suspects and she would have to be considered a possible perpetrator. She could certainly deflect attention from Hart. Instead of worrying about what Hart might be hiding, she was going to focus all of her attention and efforts on finding the brutal killer. Sooner rather than later, she would interview Rose at length.

Francesca added some pins to her jaunty blue hat and left the dressing room, her long dark skirts swirling about her. She grabbed her reticule as she left the bedroom, having already placed her small derringer inside. A servant was coming up the corridor toward her. "Miss Cahill? You have a caller."

Francesca was taken aback. A call at eight in the morning was unheard of. This had to be urgent. "Is it Hart?"

The servant handed her a business card. "It is a Mr. Arthur Kurland, ma'am."

Francesca was filled with surprise and anger. Kurland was a newsman from the *Sun*. Usually he accosted her outside of her home or on the street. He had never dared to call in such a social way before.

"Should I send him away, ma'am?"

Francesca was certain he had learned of Daisy's murder. Half of the city's newsmen kept shop in a brownstone right across the street from headquarters, on the lookout for a hot scoop. As he seemed to have some kind of personal animosity toward Francesca, he had surely come to gloat over the fact that the murder victim was Hart's ex-mistress. Francesca had no doubt he had come to pry for information.

Oh, she would see him, all right. She would carefully feed him misinformation that pointed him in any direction but Hart's. "No. Where is my father?"

"He is in the breakfast room."

Francesca quickly led the way downstairs. She did not want Andrew learning of Daisy's murder, not until the police had an official suspect, other than Hart. Francesca had little doubt that if Andrew learned of the murder now, it would put the final nail in the coffin of his disapproval of her engagement. He would never give Hart another chance. "I'll entertain Mr. Kurland in the Blue Room, Mary. Bring two cups of coffee, please." As she entered the spacious front hall, she pinched her cheeks, regretting her earlier decision to forgo rouge.

She must not let Kurland suspect that *anything* was wrong. So she smiled, sailing forward to where he waited at the hall's other end, by the front door. His brows slowly rose as she paused before him and he carefully scrutinized her face.

Francesca hoped she did not look exhausted or distressed. "Good morning, Mr. Kurland. My, this is a surprise."

He was a slim man in his thirties with brownish hair and wearing an ill-fitting, equally brownish suit. He grinned. "I think the surprise is mine. You're not going to give me the boot?"

"If you are calling in such a pleasant manner, there must be an interesting matter to discuss." She gestured and he preceded her into a pale blue room with mint-green ceilings, gilded paneling and several lush seating arrangements. He paused before the large white-and-gold marble fireplace. Francesca closed the mahogany doors behind her.

"I don't know if murder should be described as interesting,

except that maybe it is interesting to you, because you are a sleuth." He smiled widely. "Come, do not play innocent with me!"

"Are we discussing the terrible, untimely demise of Miss Jones?" Francesca asked in a neutral tone.

"Yes, we are discussing the murder of your fiancé's mistress," Kurland said, regarding her closely.

Francesca's smile felt so brittle she did not know how long she could maintain it. "Mr. Kurland, everyone knows that Hart ended his affair three months ago, when we became engaged."

He rolled his eyes. "For such a smart investigator, you are awfully naive."

She tried to control her slowly rising temper. "I do believe I know Mr. Hart a bit better than you do. I would hardly agree to marry him if he were the cad society thinks him to be."

"Indeed, I'll bet a month's wages that you know him better than me!" He laughed, the implication clear.

Francesca fought to contain her temper. "If you wish to think Hart so immoral as to keep a mistress while engaged, so be it. But I find it hard to believe you have come all this way uptown to discuss Hart's private affairs."

"But that is exactly why I have come, Miss Cahill," Kurland exclaimed. He was eager now. "Good lord, the man's mistress— all right, his ex-mistress!—has been murdered. This smacks of being a true crime of passion. Hart wouldn't be the first man to rid himself of an unwanted mistress."

Francesca trembled, her fists clenched. "Did you come here to accuse my fiancé of murder?"

He sobered. "Nope. I came here to ask you how you feel about it—the murder, I mean, of such a rival."

She inhaled. "Daisy was my *friend,*" she lied. "We were friends before I ever became engaged to Hart, and I am going to find her killer." She still could not decide just how much

Kurland knew. "But I do agree with you on one point. I saw the body. It was a vicious and brutal crime of passion."

"You saw the body?" Kurland repeated eagerly.

Francesca was relieved. He obviously had no details of the murder. Of course, eventually he would uncover every detail, she had no doubt, but she would take all of the time that he could give her. "I found the body," she said, then she corrected herself. "Actually, we found the body."

Kurland whipped out a notepad and pencil. *"We?"* he echoed. "Surely you do not mean you and Hart?"

"I do," Francesca said smoothly, although her cheeks felt hot. "Hart and I had been out to supper. He had some papers to drop off at Daisy's. You surely know that she was living in a house he provided. In spite of the end of their affair, he had agreed she could stay on until July."

"So I've heard," Kurland said. "And at what time did you find Miss Jones?"

"It was about midnight." Francesca described how she had found Daisy, but did not mention Rose's presence. "We left the body and split up to look for the killer, but he or she was long since gone. When we returned, Rose was with Daisy."

Kurland stared. "This is very interesting, indeed! And where did you say you had dinner?"

Francesca smiled. "It was a private affair." She had no friends who lived downtown who would fabricate for her, but a maître d' could be paid off. "We took a private room at Louis'," she said, using the correct French pronunciation of the formal downtown restaurant.

Kurland suddenly smiled and shook his head. "So you are Hart's alibi, and he is yours."

"Excuse me?"

"Miss Cahill. Surely you must realize, with all of your vast experience, that you are as much a suspect as Hart?"

Francesca stared, her heart accelerating. "Just what are you trying to say?"

"I heard the rumor that Daisy's body was discovered independently by Hart and by Rose Cooper. I have heard no whispers that you were with Hart, although I had been told you were at HQ last night, looking into the case."

"I don't know who your sources are," Francesca said flatly, "but I would not rely too heavily on them. And no one has pointed a finger my way."

"Yeah, well, I can't imagine Bragg allowing that," Kurland said with heavy significance. "But I bet he wouldn't mind pointing the finger at your fiancé." He grinned.

Unfortunately, Kurland had caught her and Bragg in a somewhat compromising situation, well before Leigh Anne had returned from Europe to reconcile with him. "I am not involved," Francesca said. "You may think what you want, but in the end, the truth will out."

"Yes, in the end, I will learn the truth—every grisly aspect of it." Kurland slipped his notepad into his jacket. "I do appreciate your candor, Miss Cahill." He tipped his fedora at her.

Francesca turned to walk him to the door. In the hall, he paused, and Francesca tensed.

"Of course, I have only just begun to dig," he said. "And there is one more possible theory."

"I'm sure there are many theories," Francesca said.

"Perhaps you and Hart conspired to murder Miss Jones together?" he asked pleasantly.

"Hart has conspired to murder no one, Mr. Kurland, but if you wish to cast stones at me, so be it. I am not afraid of your slander," Francesca said. She did not wait for the doorman, but jerked the heavy front door open herself. "Good day."

"I hardly mean to upset you, Miss Cahill, but you and Hart had the most to gain from the death of his mistress."

"Good day, Mr. Kurland." She finally lost her composure

and slammed the door closed in his face. Then she stood there, staring at the beautiful grain of chestnut-hued wood, her heart hammering hard and fast. Kurland would probably learn the real facts of the case by the end of the day. He might be scum, but he was a tenacious and skilled reporter. That did not give her much time to unearth a valid suspect. Francesca had little doubt that if she did not find someone other than Hart with motive and means, tomorrow's headlines would be very distasteful, indeed.

"Francesca!"

Francesca stiffened in disbelief. Her mother could not be standing behind her now. Although Julia was an early riser, she never left her rooms before eleven, preferring to take care of all of her correspondence in the mornings.

"Francesca!" Julia clasped her shoulder from behind.

Francesca turned, aghast, to face her stricken mother. "What— what are you doing up and about at this hour?"

"I wanted to speak with your father before he left the house," Julia cried. "Hart's mistress is dead? Murdered?"

Francesca's mind raced. Her mother knew everything that happened in society. Of course, she would know about Hart's relationship with Daisy. Yet she had been Hart's biggest supporter and was so favorably disposed toward their marriage that Francesca had somehow assumed that she hadn't known about Daisy. She managed, "She was his ex-mistress, Mama. And yes, she was murdered last night."

Julia moaned. "And you and Hart are suspects?"

"Mama!" Francesca put her arm around her. "We are not suspects! Hart discovered the body, but Daisy's friend, Rose Cooper, actually found her first. Mama, I am investigating the case. So far, there are no suspects. We don't even have an autopsy report."

But Julia was shaking her head. "How could you allow that man into the house! His articles are scurrilous!"

"I know. I wanted to make certain he did not jump to the wrong conclusions."

Francesca knew what her mother was thinking—that Francesca wanted to make certain he did not suspect Hart. "Mama, please don't worry. I am going to find Daisy's killer."

"Don't worry. Of course I am worried. And not just because you are about to put yourself in all kinds of danger once again. Francesca, this scandal will be too much to bear!"

"Mama! Hart is innocent!"

Julia gave her an anguished look. "When the scandal breaks, it won't even matter."

FRANCESCA DECIDED TO TRY to catch Hart before he left for his offices, which were at the tip of Manhattan on Bridge Street. Hart had recently built a huge home for himself a dozen blocks farther uptown from the Cahill home. It had cost millions, and it rose up out of the wilderness of upper Manhattan like a royal palace. Sweeping lawns and lush gardens surrounded the house, and farther back on the property was a large pond, tennis courts and a redbrick stable. When Francesca had first met Hart, he had been living alone. She hadn't been able to understand how any human being could reside by oneself in such a huge home, with only staff for company, or why anyone would even want such a secluded and lonely existence. Had Hart not been so arrogant, she would have felt sorry for him.

He did not live alone now. His stepfather and stepmother, Rathe and Grace Bragg, had recently returned to the city, and were currently building a new and very modern home of their own. They had moved in with Hart some time ago. His nephew, Nicholas D'Archand, had also moved to the city and was attending Columbia University, and from time to time his various stepbrothers or his stepsister would also appear. Francesca was thrilled for Hart. He might deny it, but she felt strongly that being surrounded by family was the best thing possible for him.

Now, with the coach Hart had bought for her parked in front of the house, Francesca rapped on the front door. Hart worked long hours and slept little, but often he would work at his home in the early mornings. Still, it was a quarter to nine now and she was afraid he was already gone.

Alfred greeted her almost instantly. "Miss Cahill!" He beamed, clearly pleased to see his employer's fiancée and no longer trying to hide his feelings about their union. "Do come inside."

"Good morning, Alfred," Francesca said, dashing into the huge front hall where a great deal of Hart's art collection was displayed, including a shocking nude sculpture and a very sacrilegious Caravaggio. "Have I missed Calder?"

"I am afraid so. In fact, Mr. D'Archand has already left for the day and Mr. and Mrs. Bragg are in Newport for two weeks. However, Mr. Rourke is in residence. He arrived two days ago and he has yet to leave," the dapper, balding butler replied.

Francesca bit her lip, debating whether to send Hart a note. She had too much on her agenda for that day to travel all the way downtown to Lower Manhattan—even on an elevated railway, the trip would take a good forty-five minutes or so.

"Shall I summon Mr. Rourke? He is in the breakfast room."

"Alfred, that's quite all right." Francesca smiled. "I am on an investigation. I will show myself into the library and write Hart a note." Hart should be told of Kurland's visit. Thus far, Francesca had tried to avoid letting Hart know how bothersome and even malicious the newsman was. She had been afraid that Kurland would reveal the extent of her past relationship with Rick Bragg, but that did not matter now. Mama was right. If a scandal broke, it could destroy everyone. "But I do have a question or two I should like to ask you."

Alfred seemed surprised. "Of course, Miss Cahill."

"You were here, were you not, when Mr. Hart arrived home last night?"

"I most certainly was. I let him in."

That was a relief, Francesca thought. "Do you recall the hour?"

"It was a minute or two after the hour of eight o'clock—I happened to glance at the clock in his study, which is where he went directly upon arriving."

"And then what, Alfred? Did you bring him supper? Did you help him hail a cab when he left?"

"He told me he did not wish to be disturbed."

Francesca did not like the sound of that. "Do you know what time he left the house last night?"

Alfred shook his head. "I did not see Mr. Hart again until this morning, Miss Cahill. When he gives an order to be left alone, it is my responsibility to ensure that no one—not even family—intrudes upon his privacy."

Francesca almost moaned. Her heart raced. "You are telling me that no one in this house saw him after he arrived at eight?"

"I am the only one who saw him come in, Miss Cahill, and yes, he secluded himself in the library for the evening. Frankly, I had no idea that he even went out."

Francesca felt despair.

"Miss Cahill?" Alfred was clearly bewildered and worried now.

She stared at him, wondering if she dared ask him to lie for Hart. "Alfred, the police may wish to speak with you. They may ask you the same questions I have."

His gaze widened. It was a moment before he spoke. "I see. And what should I say to them?"

Was she really going to do this? She believed in the truth and the law! But Hart was innocent, and until the real killer was found, he was in jeopardy. "Perhaps you might suggest that you waited on Hart that evening," she heard herself say. "Once or twice. He did go out that evening—he went out at half past eleven."

"Very well," Alfred said with resolve.

"Thank you," Francesca whispered.

Almost unable to believe what she was doing to protect her fiancé, Francesca went down the hall. She had to find the real killer immediately, so these lies could stop. Hart's library was a huge, dark but pleasant room. Books lined three of the walls, but a number of windows and glass doors opened out onto the back gardens, showing a view of the tennis courts. His desk was at the far end. Francesca turned on a lamp and went to it.

The jacket he had worn the night before was on the back of his chair. Francesca hesitated, her gaze drawn to the stain on the right side of it. It was obviously dried blood.

Last night, he had gone into this room before going upstairs to bed. Francesca could imagine him removing his jacket, rolling up his sleeves and pouring himself a Scotch, the drink he preferred. Her eyes now found an empty crystal glass. Had he sat there, hunched over his drink, brooding about Daisy's death?

She shook her head. Of course he had. She wondered if he had thought about her, too. Had he regretted their argument? Had her doubt been on his mind? Or had he been too preoccupied with Daisy's murder?

Francesca told herself not to return to that place of doubt and insecurity. Instead, she briskly went behind the desk, reaching for a piece of paper. She scribbled a quick note, telling Hart that a reporter had been to see her that morning and that they should meet that evening to discuss the case. She added that she was on her way to interview Rose, and that the first thing she had to do was establish a timeline for the murder.

"Francesca?"

She started and looked up, only to meet Rourke Bragg's warm gaze and equally affectionate smile.

He seemed mildly bemused. "I didn't mean to frighten you,"

he said, coming into the room. He was Hart's stepbrother but Rick Bragg's half brother, and like his half brother and father, he had dark blond hair, amber eyes and a golden coloring. He was a medical student in Philadelphia and Francesca genuinely liked him.

Francesca straightened. "Rourke, I'm sorry! You didn't frighten me. I was so absorbed I did not realize you were there." She quickly came around the desk and he clasped her hands and kissed her cheek. "Are you on break from medical school?"

"The semester is over, actually, and I am waiting to see if my transfer to Bellevue Medical College has gone through," Rourke said easily. "And how is my favorite soon-to-be sister-in-law?" But his gaze was carefully searching.

Francesca hesitated. A tremor swept through her as she thought about the murder and Hart and she knew he felt it, because he became very alert. "You haven't heard."

Warily, he said, "I haven't heard what?"

"Daisy is dead. She was murdered last night."

He was clearly shocked.

"You haven't seen Hart?"

"I was out last night when he returned from his business trip. What is it that you are not telling me?"

She inhaled. "Hart found the body."

Rourke made a sound and looked away. Then, facing her, he said, "Don't tell me. He is the prime suspect?"

"I hope not! Rose also found Daisy, but independently, before Hart arrived at the scene. Or at least, that is how it appears. Rose is also a suspect."

Rourke shook his head grimly. "Is there any chance that you were with Hart last night at the time of the murder?"

"I wish I had been, but no. Rose actually sent for me. I found them both at the house with the body around midnight."

Rourke walked away, his expression hard. Then he hesitated,

glancing at Francesca. "At midnight? What the hell was Calder doing at Daisy's at that hour?"

Francesca flushed, wondering if he was thinking what Newman and Bragg had thought. She walked back to Hart's desk and sat down in his chair.

Rourke hurried to her. "Francesca, I did not mean that the way it sounded! We both know he had a good reason for being there. I just don't happen to know what that reason is."

"I should like to know, as well." Seeing Rourke's grim expression, she added, "Rourke! He was not there to rekindle their affair. Surely that is not what you think? Bragg and Newman think so, and the fact that he will not explain why he was there isn't helping his case."

Rourke paled. "No, I don't think he went to Daisy's for such a purpose." He sat down on the edge of Hart's desk. "Calder won't explain his actions? That hardly makes any sense."

Because Rourke had become such a good friend, she said, "I wish he would confide in me. For the life of me, I cannot imagine what could be so secretive. But in a way, he is right. He is entitled to his privacy. However, the police do want an explanation. And sooner or later, he shall certainly have to give them one."

Rourke smiled at her. "I am pleased to see that you remain as calm and sensible as ever."

She rolled her eyes. "It is a facade—I am worried. But not because I doubt Hart's innocence. Rourke, I wish Hart hadn't been at Daisy's last night—and I wish he would tell me why he went to see her in the first place."

He regarded her for a moment, as he absorbed what she had said. "Francesca, give him some time. I believe that Hart is in love with you. He has never been this involved before—or involved at all, really. He may not know how to confide in you. He may not understand that you need to know why he went to Daisy's last night."

Francesca was startled. Rourke's words made sense. Hart

had been reluctant from the first to share his real feelings with her. He kept a large part of himself closed off. He was adept at showing the world an arrogant facade, but Francesca knew it was only that, a front to hide the very complicated man behind it. Perhaps he didn't know how to be himself with her—and he certainly wasn't accustomed to having to account to anyone for anything.

"I know one thing," she said slowly. "Hart needs my trust. It is probably the greatest gift I can give him. So if I have to wait to discover his secret, I will do just that."

"I happen to agree. No one has ever believed in him before," Rourke said. He gave her a look. "Patience might be worthwhile in this instance, Francesca."

"Obviously, we both know that patience is not my strong suit." She sighed. "I am resolved to be patient now, but I am worried, Rourke. He lied to the police. I can't imagine why, but obviously he felt it was necessary. And I even lied to the police to cover for him." And now Alfred would lie, too.

Rourke took her arm in surprise. "You lied to the police—or to Rick?"

Francesca could not believe she had made such a blunder. "It was a very small deception, just until I can find the real killer!"

Rourke was disapproving. "They are both my brothers. You are on a tightrope, as long as you remain friends with Bragg while engaged to Hart."

She turned away. It was simply too much to ask her to end her friendship with Rick, but friends did not lie to each other. Then she faced Rourke. "Thank you, Rourke. Thank you for being so kind and so caring."

He grinned, revealing a rakish dimple. "We are almost family, and it's my duty to look out for you if my stepbrother is too negligent—and foolish—to do so."

Francesca thanked him again, this time hugging him. He was

blushing when she pulled away. She returned to the desk, taking up the note. "Are you going downtown, by any chance? I was hoping to send Hart this note."

"Actually, I had planned to cross town to the Dakotas. But I have a free day. I think I could manage it," Rourke said amiably.

Francesca's brows rose. Most of the city's residents referred to the distant and rather unpopulated West Side of the city as the Dakotas. She had no doubts as to why Rourke was making such a trip. Trying to be casual, she said, "Send Sarah my regards, will you?"

He glanced away. "I haven't seen her or Mrs. Channing in some time."

Francesca gave up and grinned, having wanted to play matchmaker for some time. Sarah Channing had become a dear friend, her best friend after her sister, Connie. Although most people saw Sarah as plain, mousy and reticent, Francesca had come to know her well. Sarah was as bohemian in spirit as Francesca, dancing to the tune of her own drummer and refusing to be cast in the mold of a proper, marriage-mad lady. She was, in fact, a brilliant artist. From their initial introduction, Rourke had been very attentive and kind to her. "We should plan to dine together, the four of us. How long will you be in town?"

Rourke eyed her. As if he had no real interest in such an evening, he shrugged. "I should not mind such a supper. Make the plans."

Francesca handed him the note, which she had folded in half. "Oh, I will. How about Saturday evening at seven, say at the Sherry Netherland?"

"You can be so transparent, Francesca!"

She batted wide, innocent eyes at him. "Transparent about what? I haven't seen you in weeks and we haven't had a social moment since well before my last case, in fact. And I haven't seen Sarah—I am killing two birds with one stone."

He smiled and shook his head.

Francesca was about to walk out with Rourke. Then she remembered to take Hart's stained jacket and she lifted it off the chair. On her way out, she would give it to Alfred for a cleaning.

A white stub fell from one of the pockets.

Francesca retrieved it, realizing it was the stub from a train ticket. She was about to put the stub on his desk when she saw the name of the city next to the punched hole: Philadelphia.

Her good humor vanished. She quickly told herself that the stub was an old one. Hart had not been to Philly since they had become engaged at the end of February. Becoming ill, she glanced at the date on the top of the stub.

June 1.

She inhaled, blinded by the date.

"Francesca?" Rourke asked in concern.

She hardly heard him. Hart had told her that he had gone to Boston. But yesterday he had returned from Philadelphia. She had the proof, right there in her hand.

Hart had lied to her.

CHAPTER FOUR

Tuesday, June 3, 1902—10:00 a.m.

LEIGH ANNE BRAGG WAS A petite woman with shockingly dark hair, green eyes and fair skin. She had been universally acclaimed as a great beauty her entire life. But now, applying rouge to her lips and cheeks, she saw a gaunt stranger in the mirror, a lackluster woman she did not recognize. Dark circles had been etched beneath her eyes, although she went to bed early, for she could not sleep. Worse, her eyes held a haunted look that matched the despair in her soul.

Leigh Anne sat in her wheeled chair, staring at her reflection, aware that the male nurse her husband had hired was in the hall outside of the bedroom, awaiting her every command. Her daughter, Katie, stood by her side, anxious for her to go downstairs.

Of course, Katie was not her biological daughter. When she and Rick had reconciled, he had been fostering Katie and her little sister Dot. Their mother had been murdered and Francesca Cahill had moved both girls into the house as a temporary measure. Yet months had passed and Leigh Anne had come to love both girls as if they were her own flesh and blood. Rick clearly felt the same way, and they had decided to try to formally adopt them. Leigh Anne couldn't imagine what the house would be like without the girls—or what her marriage would be like, either.

Once, long ago, she had been so terribly in love. It hadn't taken much to realize that, despite a four-year separation, she still loved Rick Bragg. How ironic it was to discover that her feelings had remained unchanged, in spite of so much discord, so much misunderstanding and betrayal. But it no longer mattered, because she was no longer suitable for him.

"Mama?" Katie smiled worriedly at her.

Leigh Anne hated the fact that the precious child was so astute. Katie watched her like a hawk, clearly aware of her depression and misery, rushing to fulfill her every whim, as if that might ease the pain. Leigh Anne knew the pain of loss and heartbreak would never go away. She smiled brightly at her child. "Can you call Mr. Mackenzie so we might go downstairs?"

Katie nodded eagerly and rushed out of the dressing room.

Leigh Anne watched the woman in the chair in the mirror, and saw her smile vanish the moment the child was gone. The woman she observed was attractive, though wan, and perfectly attired in lavender silk and amethysts. The woman sat in an odd chair with two huge wheels and handles that made it easier for an attendant to push. The woman was a cripple.

Leigh Anne looked away, but it didn't matter, because the image remained engraved in her brain. She knew that every time Rick looked at her, that was what he saw: a cripple.

She rubbed her thigh, reminding herself that his pity did not matter. Her right leg ached, but there was no feeling in her left leg and there never would be again. The doctors actually thought that, with time and intensive work, she might regain some use of her right leg, but there had been too much damage to her left leg. So why would she even try to regain some use of the one limb? She would never walk again, never dance, never make love....

Leigh Anne knew she was pathetic, to be feeling so sorry for herself. She reminded herself that she was alive and she had the girls. God, she didn't know what she would do without them! She wiped her eyes briefly. She only dared to allow herself such self-pity when she was alone. She reminded herself that she didn't need her legs, not when she had a chair with wheels and a nurse. She reminded herself that she was fortunate, so terribly fortunate, to have suddenly become a mother to two such wonderful girls. But no amount of rationalization would ease the melancholy that weighed her down. It was like being buried alive, she thought dismally, yet death was not an option.

The telephone, which had been recently installed in the house, rang in the bedroom just beyond her boudoir. Unthinkingly she reached for the wheels, trying to turn them, but she was so weak now. Tears of frustration came when she saw the nurse reach the phone. He was a tall, attractive young man and he said, "One moment, sir. I'll get her."

It was Rick, she thought, her heart accelerating, and the oddest combination of dread and anticipation filled her. She wondered if it would always be this way—if a part of her would always yearn for a word from him, a look, his presence.

Mackenzie came into the boudoir. "It's the commissioner," he said pleasantly, easily wheeling her into the bedroom. He positioned her near the phone and she reached for the receiver before he could hand it to her, as she was determined not to let anyone see how lost and incapable she had become. But the receiver was large and she was clumsy and it fell to the floor.

Leigh Anne blinked back more tears of frustration as Mackenzie quickly retrieved it, handing it to her.

Leigh Anne inhaled. She was doing her best not to let Rick know how miserable she was. "Rick?"

"Leigh Anne. How are you?" he asked, his tone carefully neutral.

But then, they had become strangers, which was what she wanted now. "I am fine," she said, aware of the enormity of the lie. "You went out last night," she said just as neutrally. He had not come to bed last night. Most nights he fell asleep on the sofa in his study, which she preferred—and which she knew he preferred. She had lain in bed, pretending to sleep, wondering if he would join her, afraid that he would, and worse, that he might think to hold her. But instead, someone had come to their front door and he had gone out for the rest of the evening. She was accustomed to police affairs requiring such strange calls.

"There was a matter that required my attention at headquarters," he said. "Did you sleep well?"

"Yes," she lied again, as she doubted she had actually slept more than an hour or two.

"What are you planning to do today?"

She had no plans. She was afraid to resume her old life, as she could not imagine the reaction of her friends if she called in her wheeled chair. She had accepted callers, however. Francesca Cahill called twice a week, and Leigh Anne genuinely liked her—she was very kind, pretending that nothing untoward had happened. Rick's parents also called frequently—Grace dropped by almost every day. But it had been simply awful when her old friend Countess Bartolla Benevente had called. Leigh Anne knew that the countess had been secretly delighted by her condition. How many other of her old friends would take pleasure in her downfall? "As Katie has finished school, I think we'll go to the park."

"It's a beautiful day. I'll try to come home earlier," he said, hesitation in his tone.

She swallowed, almost wanting him to return home at that moment. Images of their past raced through her mind, a jumbled collage of memories, all of them happy, playful or passionate. "If the matter is a serious one, do what you have to do, Rick. You know I don't mind."

He was silent, and she wondered if he was relieved or dismayed.

"Do you recall Daisy Jones?" he asked.

Her interest piqued. She understood the caution she heard in his tone, as the telephone operator was undoubtedly listening to their every word. It was the single drawback of the incredible convenience of a telephone—there was no privacy, ever.

Daisy was Calder Hart's mistress, or she had been, until recently. "Yes, of course."

Bragg said, "She was murdered last night."

Leigh Anne gasped. "That is terrible," she said, meaning it, even though she had never met the other woman.

"I may be late tonight after all," Rick said, sounding grim.

Leigh Anne had many questions now. As Hart was Rick's brother, even if they did not get along, she began to worry. "Of course."

"Thank you for understanding," he said. "I had better go."

"Yes," she said, still stunned by the news of Daisy's murder. She knew Hart somewhat, but not all that well, and wondered at his reaction to the news.

Leigh Anne replaced the receiver on the phone's hook. "Mr. Mackenzie? I'll go downstairs now," she said, thinking about Francesca now. How was she faring? she wondered. She almost smiled. Francesca was undoubtedly on the case, as no one was more intrepid than she.

As Mackenzie wheeled her out of the bedroom, Leigh Anne realized that Francesca would be working on the case with Rick. She refused to feel any jealousy, because she and Rick had a marriage of convenience and nothing more. But she knew that Rick had been fond of Francesca while they had remained separated, and no matter how she tried, a part of her hated them working together again.

"I'll have you downstairs in a moment," Mackenzie said with a smile. The nurse lifted her from the chair to carry her downstairs, Katie behind them. This was the moment Leigh Anne hated the most, when she had no choice but to be in the nurse's arms as he carried her down the narrow Victorian staircase.

Her cheeks grew hot. This was simply too intimate. Leigh Anne closed her eyes, forcing herself to endure the moment. And for an instant, she imagined herself in Rick's arms, the strongest, safest haven she had ever known.

But that was not to be. Not ever again.

"I'll get the chair," the nurse said, having carried her into the parlor. He placed her on the sofa and left.

Katie was watching her. Sensing her every emotion, she grasped Leigh Anne's hand. "Mama? Can we go to the park today? You, me and Dot and Papa?" Clearly she had overheard the telephone conversation.

Leigh Anne squeezed her hand. "I am afraid your father is involved in some urgent police affairs," she said. "But yes, we can go to the park and feed the birds."

"Papa never goes anywhere with us anymore!" Katie cried. "Mrs. Flowers can make us a picnic and we can fish, the way we did the last time he came with us."

Leigh Anne stiffened. The last time they had had a picnic, she had left, unable to bear such a family occasion, and Francesca Cahill had taken her place. Rick would probably still be in love with the other woman if they had not reconciled—a reconciliation Leigh Anne had forced him into.

If not for the girls, she would leave him and set him free.

Their single servant, Peter, a tall Swede, appeared on the parlor's threshold. "Mrs. Bragg? You have two callers."

Leigh Anne arranged her face into a smile. "Who is it, Peter?" she asked, filled with dread. If it was Bartolla Benevente, she would send her away.

"It's a man and a woman, Mrs. Bragg. He claims to be the girls' uncle."

Leigh Anne seized Katie's hand. "But that's impossible!" The girls had no family.

"He says he's Mike O'Donnell." Peter was grave. "I can send him and the woman away."

Leigh Anne began to shake. "No, no, send them in. We must find out what he wants."

A SHORT, POWERFULLY BUILT Spaniard, Raoul had been far more than Hart's driver and valet—he had been Hart's bodyguard.

Now he was Francesca's personal driver. Francesca had no delusions that, given the nature of her work, Hart wished to offer her protection at all times. Having been in dire jeopardy more than once, Francesca did not mind having such a driver. Now Raoul was driving Francesca downtown amid numerous drays, carts and wagons. The Lower East Side was as different from Fifth Avenue as night from day. Hers was the only elegant passenger vehicle on the cobbled street. Numerous vendors were hawking bolts of cloth, tallow for candles and lye soap, and other wares, and the pedestrians on the sidewalks were mostly women in aprons, carrying small children or groceries. Laundry lines were hanging from window to window. A gang of adolescent boys was playing a hard game of stickball. Even on Avenue A, the noise from the Third Avenue Elevated could be heard and its smoke and soot cast a gray pallor everywhere. Finally the coach halted.

Francesca had met Joel Kennedy, a young, street-smart kid, on her very first investigation. Joel was the oldest of four children, his mother a pretty, hardworking seamstress who was widowed. During the Burton abduction, Joel had helped her navigate her way through some of the city's seamiest sides. Francesca had needed his help, but she had also wanted to turn him away from his life of petty crime. After he had proved indispensable to her on several other investigations, she had hired him as her assistant. Now she picked up Joel Kennedy or had him meet her every day.

But young Joel was not on her mind, and neither was Rose nor the crucial questions she must ask her. Why was Hart lying to her, when they had come so far as a couple? Their relationship had been based on absolute honesty until now. How could he lie to her, and what did it mean for them and their future? *What was he hiding?*

Her first impulse had been to travel to Bridge Street and confront Hart in his offices, demanding to know why he had said he was in Boston when he had been in Philadelphia instead. But Francesca had instantly seen the folly of that action. Confronting Hart was never a good idea. He had a huge, quick temper, and she would only ignite it. The current investigation had already begun to place a strain on their relationship, and Francesca did not want to add to it. If she had judged him correctly last night, he had been grieving for Daisy. She could not attack the man she loved when he was mourning. But hadn't she seen and sensed something else in the nature of his tension? Last night, Hart had refused to discuss why he had called on Daisy. In doing so, he had pulled away from her, his usual response to a difficult situation— a response she dearly hated. Could his refusal to discuss his visit to Daisy have something to do with his trip to Philadelphia?

As rational as she was trying to be, it was hard not to be shaken.

The fact that he did not trust her hurt her terribly. She had been Hart's staunchest supporter and his biggest ally from the first moment they had met, when she had been investigating the Randle killing. Hart had been implicated, and even then, when she had not known him, when she had been infatuated with Bragg, she had known he was no killer. Even then, she had refused to judge him solely on his notorious reputation. From the first, she had seen past his reputation and his arrogant, at times callous behavior. Beneath the ego, the confidence, there was so much vulnerability. Hart was *good*. She still believed that with all of her heart and all of her being. But at times, his behavior made it so difficult to remain loyal!

She stubbornly refused to concede to his many critics now. There was an explanation. She knew it, the way she knew he was a good man. Surely he had a good reason for this last deception. She would bide her time, she would not push him, no matter how she wished to. She knew from experience that any impatience on her part would backfire. She would trust him as she worked on this case, because one day he would truly trust her in return and explain everything. No matter what, she was not giving up on Hart, and not this easily.

Joel appeared in front of the tenement building where he lived with his mother, his two brothers and little sister. He was a thin, short boy with a shock of dark hair and very fair skin. He grinned at her as he climbed up into the coach, allowing Raoul to open the carriage door for him. Joel had come a long way, Francesca thought, smiling with affection at him. Clearly, he enjoyed Raoul treating him as if he were a little prince, when just a few months ago he had been stealing purses.

"Thanks," he said to Raoul.

Raoul almost smiled and shut the door firmly before climbing onto the driver's seat.

Even though it was June, Joel wore a knit cap over his black hair, and Francesca tugged on it. "Good day, Miz Cahill," he said.

"We are on a new case," she told him as Raoul lifted the brake and clucked the two handsome bays on. "A murder investigation."

He grinned. "My favorite kind of case. Think it will be dangerous?"

"I hope not! And I also hope I am not jading you," Francesca said seriously. She sighed. "You know the victim, Joel, as do I."

He was all eyes. "Who got iced?"

She was not up to correcting his slang now. "Miss Jones."

He understood right away. "Mr. Hart's er…lady friend?"

"Hart's ex-mistress, yes."

His eyes bulged. "Ma'am! What happened?"

Francesca filled him in. "When we get to Daisy's, I will interview Rose. As usual, I need you to canvas the ward and find out if anyone saw anything suspicious between ten and midnight last night. To the best of my knowledge, we have lost the murder weapon, a knife. You can keep your eye out for that, too."

He nodded gravely. "Do we got any suspects?"

Francesca hesitated. "Not exactly. But I am afraid both Hart and Rose are at the top of the list right now."

Joel adored Hart. It was obvious that he clearly admired the man, as they had both come from the same desperately impoverished background. "Why would Mr. Hart off Miss Jones?"

"He wouldn't," Francesca said firmly. "But in a crime like this—I am sure the autopsy will reveal numerous stab wounds—the police always look at family and friends first. Whoever murdered Daisy, Joel, knew her and wanted her dead. We must find the real killer, and quickly."

"Before Mr. Hart gets in trouble," Joel said, nodding grimly.

Francesca tugged on his cap again. She had become as fond of the boy as if he was her little brother, but then, she was very fond of his mother. Maggie Kennedy had been acting somewhat oddly lately. Francesca had taken tea with her twice, and the Kennedy sparkle had been missing from her stunning blue eyes. "How is your mother, Joel?"

He grimaced. "I dunno. Something's bothering her. She's so sad all of the time. I mean, she pretends not to be, but I can tell."

Francesca hesitated. A month ago, she had witnessed her brother Evan saving Maggie from an insane killer, and there had been no mistaking his concern for her. As she had already suspected romantic sparks flying between the two, she had been delighted, never mind that an uptown gentleman should not dally with a downtown seamstress. Evan was currently living at the Fifth Avenue Hotel. He had been disowned by their father, much to Francesca's dismay, but the bright side was he seemed to have abandoned his notorious gambling ways. He was now making an honest living as a law clerk, and Francesca was very proud of him for standing up to their father.

While Evan was a ladies' man with a rather large reputation,

Francesca knew he would never compromise Maggie, and she
was certain he had strong and genuine feelings for her. Hart had
advised her to stay out of the affair, reminding her that Evan was
courting the Countess Benevente. Most of society thought he
might marry her, although Francesca wasn't so sure. She could
not imagine Bartolla Benevente marrying a law clerk. But then,
she was a wealthy widow, so Francesca could be wrong. "Joel?
Has my brother called at all?" She simply had to know.

Joel scowled. "I thought we were friends! He used to come by
all the time with all kinds of goodies an' gifts. I ain't seen him
since Father Culhane tried to kill my mother." He was angry now.
"I know what's up. He's too busy with that *countess* to bother
with me, Paddy or Matt."

Francesca reached for him but he pulled away. "He's having
a rough time these days," she said gently, and it was the truth.
"Imagine how you would feel if your father disowned you and
you had to move out of the house. Imagine what it would be like
if your father refused to call you his son."

"I don't have a father," Joel said sarcastically. "He's a grown
man, not a boy, so it don't matter, anyway."

Francesca sighed. Joel had come to care far too much for
her brother, and maybe Maggie had, too. She should not get
involved, but if ever there was a time to interfere, it was now.
If Evan was not going to pursue a relationship with Maggie, he
should have never treated her as he had when she had been in so
much danger. Francesca decided she would call on him later in
the day. And then Daisy's Georgian brick home came into view.
She tensed, instantly forgetting all about her brother. An image
of Rose, grief-stricken and holding Daisy's mangled body, came
to mind. Francesca was sobered by the recollection.

Joel had learned to wait for Francesca to alight from the
carriage first. When she had done so, he leapt to the street. "I'll
start talkin' about," he said.

"And don't forget Daisy's servants," Francesca reminded him

as he started off. She had discovered long ago that witnesses spoke differently to different interrogators. Often she could get more information than the police, and Joel would certainly be handier with the staff.

This time, the front door was firmly closed and her knock was promptly answered by Daisy's butler, Homer, a white-haired man of middle age. He ushered her inside, looking positively stricken. Francesca thanked him and handed him her card. "Good morning. I don't know if you remember me, but I was a friend of Miss Jones. I am a sleuth."

Homer read her card. It read:

Francesca Cahill
Crime-Solver Extraordinaire
No. 810 Fifth Avenue, New York City
All Cases Accepted, No Case Too Small

"I do recall, Miss Cahill. I am afraid that…" He stopped, unable to continue, clearly distressed.

"I was here last night," she said gently, laying her hand on his shoulder. "I am so sorry about Miss Jones." She would begin her investigation with Homer, she decided.

"Thank you," he whispered, ashen. "She was a good employer, ma'am. She was very kind to me and the staff."

"I know," Francesca said softly, although of course she had not known. "I came to see Miss Cooper, but I should like to speak with you first."

He nodded, not at all surprised. "Are you going to find her killer?"

"Yes, I hope so."

"Good! She did not deserve to die," he cried. "I know she sinned, but she wasn't a bad woman."

Francesca patted his shoulder. "Maybe you should sit, Homer. May I call you Homer?"

He nodded. "I am fine. It's just the shock…."

"I know. At what time did you finish your duties last night?"

"At half past five."

That was very early and Francesca was surprised. "But what about supper? Or did Miss Jones go out?"

He shook his head. "She was staying in with a guest. She dismissed me, Annie and Mrs. Greene," he said.

Francesca was surprised. It seemed that Daisy had been planning a private evening with someone. But she had to make certain she had not misunderstood. "When Daisy was entertaining, she dismissed the staff?"

He flushed. "Last night she wished for a private evening, Miss Cahill."

Francesca stared. What was he not telling her? "But this was her pattern of behavior?"

His color deepened. "When I first came to be employed here, she would dismiss us when Mr. Hart called."

Francesca's insides lurched and tightened. She should have been expecting that, she realized grimly. "And after Mr. Hart and I became engaged?"

"She entertained Miss Cooper a few times, but otherwise, she would go out, which was usual, or stay in alone."

Francesca blinked. "Miss Cooper does not live here now?"

Homer seemed surprised. "No, she does not. But she calls once or twice a week."

It did not sound as if Daisy and Rose had resumed their former relationship. Or, if they had, it sounded as if it had lost some of its fervor, Francesca thought. "Who did Miss Jones see last night?'

"I don't know," he said apologetically.

Francesca's mind raced. Before she and Calder had become engaged, he had called on Daisy and she had dismissed the staff. On a few occasions, she had dismissed the staff in order to see

Rose. Calder, of course, had arrived at Grand Central Station at seven o' clock—she had the ticket stub to prove it—so he could not have been her caller last night, for Daisy had dismissed everyone at half past five. Surely she had been expecting someone by six or seven o'clock. Had she been expecting Rose? "Perhaps she was going out?" Francesca had to rule this possibility out.

"Oh, no! She had me prepare a small supper, which she said she would take later. She also asked that I chill champagne and ice two glasses. It was odd, because the supper was for one."

Francesca tried to breathe. Daisy had intended to have drinks with her caller, but not dine with her or him. This was another fantastic lead! "You went to your rooms at half past five? And that is when Mrs. Greene went home and Annie went to her room?"

"Yes."

"And this morning? Was the champagne gone? Had both glasses been used? Had she eaten her supper?"

He met her gaze. "No one drank anything last night. I had opened the bottle for her, and two glasses had been poured, but neither had been drunk. Her supper was untouched."

Francesca tried to fight her excitement. If Homer had been instructed to open the bottle of champagne before retiring for the evening, then Daisy's caller had been expected shortly after five-thirty. Had Daisy greeted the killer with champagne? If so, she had seemed to intend an intimate rendezvous with her murderer. And if the drinks and her supper had not been touched, had she just narrowed down the time of her murder? "Did she say at what time she was expecting her caller? And did you see or hear anything last night?"

"She made no mention of when she was expecting her caller."

Francesca said, "And you did not see or hear anyone?"

"I went out for a while, Miss Cahill, to take a drink with some friends. When I returned, it was well past eight—it was close to nine-thirty or ten. The house was dark, which I found it a bit strange, but I saw some lights upstairs and I decided it wasn't my business. I was tired and I went to bed. Mr. Hart awoke me at midnight."

Francesca's mind raced. "So you did not hear anything when you came in at nine-thirty or ten?"

"No."

Francesca's thoughts veered. "Hart has admitted that he came to see Daisy last night."

"It was very odd, him calling like that," Homer said.

"Why? Why was it odd?" Francesca asked quickly.

"Well, he hasn't called in months." He blushed. "I am sorry, Miss Cahill, but this is so awkward, with this being his house and you being his fiancée."

"Please, Homer, do not fret on my account! When I accepted Hart's offer of marriage, I was well aware that he was keeping Daisy, and as we both know, he stopped seeing her at that time."

Homer glanced away.

Francesca did not like that. "That is what you said, isn't it?"

"Except for last week," he amended somewhat glumly.

Francesca tensed. "Last week? He came here last week?" And a treacherous image arose of Daisy smiling at Hart and handing him a glass of champagne.

Homer hesitated, wringing his hands. "I don't know what I should say or do," he said. "He is my employer."

She fought the dismay. "He called on Daisy last week."

Homer's brows shot up. "Not that way, Miss Cahill! He came in the afternoon, last Thursday, I think. The visit was a brief one, and there were no refreshments. Miss Jones made it clear she did not wish for them to be disturbed. I don't think he stayed for even a half an hour. I don't know what they discussed," he added hastily.

There was relief, but on its heels came fresh dismay. What affair had they been conducting? "You didn't hear anything?"

"She sent me away. No. I didn't hear anything."

Francesca inhaled. Hart's call had been the day before he had left on his business trip.

"Miss Cahill?" A woman whispered, her tone tentative.

Francesca saw a housemaid approaching, her dark eyes huge in her pale, freckled face. "Are you Annie?"

Annie nodded, appearing frightened and stricken. "I heard them," she said hoarsely. "I heard them shouting—arguing—and I heard Miss Jones crying."

Francesca froze. "What were they arguing about?"

"I don't know. But Mr. Hart was furious when he left. He was so angry that he broke the door—I saw him do it. And Miss Jones? She collapsed on the sofa, weeping."

CHAPTER FIVE

Tuesday, June 3, 1902—11:00 a.m.

MIKE O'DONNELL STOOD ON the threshold of the small parlor, a weather-beaten man with a suntanned face and hands and bleached-blond hair. He was not a gentleman, Leigh Anne saw instantly, as he wore a flannel shirt tucked into corduroy trousers, and the boots of a workman. An older woman accompanied him, plump and pleasant in expression, also dressed in the drab clothes of a working woman. Katie had not rushed over to him. Instead, she stood near Leigh Anne, wide-eyed and tense. She clearly recognized him.

"Why don't you sit down, Mr. O'Donnell?" Leigh Anne said graciously. She had been returned to her wheeled chair and Mr. Mackenzie stood behind her, ready to move her at her command.

"I should like to do that, ma'am," he said very deferentially. "An' thank you for lettin' me an' Beth in to see Katie an' Dot." He went to sit on the sofa, holding his knit cap between his hands.

The heavy older woman smiled at Francesca. "My nephew has no manners, Mrs. Bragg. I am Beth O'Brien, his aunt—Katie's great-aunt."

Leigh Anne was ill with fear and dread, but she smiled. "Do sit down, Mrs. O'Brien." She glanced at the door, where Peter stood. "Peter, please bring some refreshments for our guests, and ask Mrs. Flowers to bring Dot down."

The big man left.

But Beth O'Brien did not sit. She beamed at Katie. "You don't remember me, do you? But then, I haven't seen you since you were five years old, when I came to visit your mama for the Christmas holiday."

Katie just shook her head.

"I was living in New Rochelle until last month," Beth told Leigh Anne amiably. She had warm brown eyes with a kind sparkle to them. "But my mistress died and I came to the city to find a job. I decided to look Mike up—and Mary, my niece and the girl's mother. I was stunned to learn that she had died," Beth added, no longer smiling. "How tragic for the girls!"

"It was very tragic," Leigh Anne managed to say. What did these two want? Surely they only intended a brief visit! "But my husband and I have been caring for the girls for some time. They are well fed, Katie is in school, and they are very happy." She looked at Katie, desperately trying to keep her composure. "Isn't that right, darling?"

Katie nodded, reaching for Leigh Anne's hand. She clung to her.

"That is so generous of you and your husband," Beth said. "We are so grateful, aren't we, Mike?"

"Very grateful," Mike O'Donnell said. He suddenly stood and approached Leigh Anne and Katie. "Hello, Katie. Aren't you going to give me a hug? I know you remember me."

Katie's grip on Leigh Anne's hand tightened. She did not move—she did not seem to breathe—and Leigh Anne knew she was more than simply shy.

She was afraid of her uncle.

"So you are close to the girls?" Leigh Anne said quickly, wanting to avoid his pressuring Katie.

"I was very close to my sister, their mother," Mike said. "But before her death and the death of my wife, I did not appreciate the family God gave me." He shook his head, disparaging his own past.

"I am sorry, I did not realize you had lost your wife, too," Leigh Anne said, wishing Peter would hurry with the refreshments.

"Their deaths changed everything," Mike said softly. "I miss them both, very much. But God works in mysterious ways, and I have come to accept that."

Did he also miss his nieces? Leigh Anne wondered. "Yes, God seems to have answers only He knows."

"The Lord has changed me, ma'am," Mike O'Donnell said. "I've given up drink, given up cards and, if you beg my pardon, other forms of entertainment. I've been praying, ma'am. I pray every day, two or three times, for His help and His guidance."

"So you are a religious man," Leigh Anne managed.

O'Donnell only smiled, but Beth spoke for him. "My nephew was a bit of a rascal. But since Mary's death, he has found God."

Leigh Anne could only nod, sickened.

"I really needed to see my nieces," Mike said. He knelt, smiling directly into Katie's face. She did not smile back. "They are my family, my only family, and I miss them, I really do."

Leigh Anne put her arm around Katie, whose skinny body was frozen. "I am sure you do. Well, you may visit anytime," she said, lying through her teeth. She did not want Mike O'Donnell or Beth O'Brien in the girls' lives.

"That would be so fine," Mike said with a grin. "Wouldn't it, Katie?" He touched her cheek.

She flinched, tears coming to her eyes.

FRANCESCA GREW AWARE THAT someone was behind her, watching her. Filled with dread over Annie's revelation, she slowly turned. Rose stood on the stairs, a few steps from the ground floor, ashen in spite of her olive complexion. Her stare was hard and focused. She had pulled her dark hair tightly back, but tendrils were wildly escaping. That, coupled with her gaunt, haunted look, gave Francesca pause. The glint in Rose's eyes was almost frightening.

She turned back to the servants. Hart and Daisy had been arguing very emotionally just a few days ago, but Francesca could not dwell on that now. "Homer, thank you. And thank you, Annie."

They nodded and left.

Francesca turned back toward Rose, who was now approaching. "I am so sorry for your loss, Rose."

"I doubt it," Rose said coldly.

Francesca tensed. Rose had been very hostile toward Hart ever since Daisy had become his mistress, and some of that hostility had been directed toward Francesca, as well. But now she seemed to be seething. "I am sorry. Daisy did not deserve to die—"

"Daisy was murdered," Rose hissed, confronting Francesca. "And I am certain Hart did it."

Francesca was rigid. "I will find the real killer," she said carefully, "but you are jumping to conclusions. That will not help anyone—and it certainly will not help the cause of justice."

"Such fancy words," Rose cried. "You heard Annie! Hart was furious with Daisy last Thursday—just four days before she was murdered. And we both know that Daisy had been causing you some sleepless nights recently, now, don't we?"

Francesca was grim, her heart racing. "Rose, I am not going to try to hide the fact that Daisy seemed to want Calder back. She said some nasty things to me, more than once. You know as well as I do that Hart had no intention of returning to their affair. So if anyone has a motive, it is me."

"You would never kill anyone in cold blood, Miss Cahill, and the world knows it. And anyway, your dear friend the police commissioner would never charge you with such a crime. I know it was Hart. You heard the maid!"

"People argue all the time, and usually no one dies for it. Rose,

I understand that you are trying to make sense of this ghastly killing. But as angry as Calder was, he would never murder anyone."

"You don't understand—no one understands—and somehow, I don't think you know your fiancé all that well," Rose said harshly.

Francesca decided to retreat to a safer subject. "Have you given your statement to the police?"

"I gave it last night," Rose said.

That gave Francesca some pause. The police were a step ahead of her now. *Rick* would be a step ahead of her. But they were on the same side, weren't they? Not because they were friends, but because, in times like these, they were always partners. And no matter how Rick felt about Hart, they were half brothers. In the end, he would fight to prove Hart's innocence. Wouldn't he?

"I meant what I said," Francesca said briskly. "I am going to find Daisy's killer. If you wish to believe—conveniently, I might add—that the killer is Hart, so be it. But I am going to bring the real killer to justice. So I would like to ask you some questions."

Rose hesitated before nodding. "I need to sit down." She had become gravely ashen.

Francesca took her arm. "Did you sleep at all last night? Have you had anything to eat?"

Rose leaned on her. "How could I sleep? You know how much I loved Daisy! How can I survive without her now? How?" Rose clearly fought the rush of tears.

"It won't be easy, but you will survive. In time, you will be able to cope with your loss," Francesca said, leading her into the smaller of the two salons. Rose sat on the sofa and Francesca brought her a glass of water.

"I don't need your pity," Rose said with some heat.

"You don't have my pity, you have my sympathy and my condolences," Francesca said gently.

Rose looked away.

"Do you know why Hart and Daisy were arguing last Thursday afternoon?"

Rose shook her head. "That was the first I have heard of it." Rose's expression turned ugly. "Maybe they were arguing about their relationship—or about you."

"Why don't you tell me exactly what happened last night?" Francesca asked, ignoring that barb.

Rose paused. "All right. I was out with a gentleman—a client. I entertained him in his rooms at a hotel I prefer not to name. I left him at half past nine exactly—he was asleep and I looked at the clock."

"I have to ask, what was his name?"

Rose started. "I am afraid I cannot reveal his identity."

"Why not?"

"Francesca, he is a gentleman. Gentlemen do not wish to have their liaisons with women like myself made public."

"Didn't the police ask for his name?"

"I told them what I told you."

Francesca decided not to push. For the moment, Rose did not have a solid alibi, and that increased her significance as a suspect. Francesca knew she should not be relieved, but she was. "Go on," Francesca urged.

Rose shuddered now. "I took a cab back to the house. Daisy and I had agreed to meet later. There were no lights on and I was alarmed, Francesca. The moment I saw that, I knew something was wrong—I knew something had happened!"

"And you found Daisy?"

Rose nodded, covering her face with her hands. "I was in a panic. I ran inside and started calling her name. I ran from room to room and then I found her, on the floor, dead!"

Francesca went over to her, placing her hand comfortingly on her shoulder. Rose wept. "Why didn't you turn on the lights?"

Rose tried to speak. "I tried the first lamp, but it didn't work. I was so afraid—all I could think of was finding Daisy."

"Did you see Hart? Did you hear anything, or anyone?"

"No! I sat with her, my heart broken. I stayed until I realized we needed help, and that was when I wrote that note. The only time I left her was to go to the desk, write the note, and then I ran outside. I paid a cabbie to deliver it for me. Then I went back to her and waited for you to come. I didn't see Hart until he came into the study with you."

If Rose had left her john at half past nine, she had probably been at Daisy's by ten. Francesca had received her note two hours later, meaning Rose might have sat with Daisy for quite some time before recovering enough to write and send a note—if she was telling the truth. Rose's story confirmed that Hart had entered the house while Rose was looking for a cabdriver. "Why didn't you call the police?" Francesca asked.

Rose seemed taken aback by her question. "Those pigs don't care! They hate us—they *use* us. They would never try to find her murderer!"

"Rose, this is important. Do you know who Daisy was seeing last night?"

"She never told me who she was seeing, but I gathered it was some kind of old friend."

Francesca started. "Do you mean a friend from her previous life?"

Rose stiffened. "I don't know what you mean."

Francesca saw, in her dark eyes, that she understood quite well. "I mean, was it an old friend from the life she had before she became Daisy Jones?"

"I don't know!"

Francesca considered Rose's intense reaction. "Was Daisy still entertaining clients, Rose?"

"No. She left the business the day she moved in here."

That, of course, made sense. Why would Daisy continue to

solicit customers when she had no financial need? "Can you think of anyone she used to entertain who might have been so passionately involved with her that he wanted her dead?"

Rose was finally surprised. "You think a john murdered her?"

"It would hardly be the first time a prostitute was murdered by her client."

"I don't know. I need to think about it." Her face tightened. "Of course, there is one client we both know who had all the passion necessary to do the deed."

Francesca refused to do battle over Hart now. "What was Daisy's real name?"

Rose instantly turned away. "I don't know."

Francesca did not believe her. "You were best friends, and she never told you her real name?"

Rose stared into the distance. "No," she muttered.

Francesca decided to give that up, for the moment, anyway. "It was always obvious to me that Daisy came from a genteel background. She was well mannered, well spoken, clearly educated and as graceful as any lady from Fifth Avenue."

Rose did not respond.

"Why aren't you helping me?" Francesca cried. "Someone wanted Daisy dead—someone who knew her well. I have to uncover her real identity and her entire past."

"We both know who wanted Daisy dead," Rose said harshly.

"And what if you are wrong? What if Hart is not the killer?" Francesca demanded.

Francesca saw the conflict in Rose's eyes. She finally cried, "She never told me her real name, I swear! She was running from her old life, Francesca. She never spoke of it—ever."

That was very odd, Francesca thought. "How did you meet?"

Rose met her gaze, her own eyes turning moist. "Oh, God, that was so long ago!"

"How long?"

Rose smiled through her tears. "It was eight years ago. Daisy was such a beautiful young woman. She was fifteen, but she was really still a child. She was so innocent, so naive. I had been turning tricks for years—I was so much older than she was, although not in years. I was sixteen, Francesca, when we met and became friends."

"Where did you meet?"

Rose sniffed. "On the street." She looked at Francesca. "Can you believe it? Daisy was standing on the street corner, here in the city. She was so beautiful, Francesca, I can't even describe it." She bit her lip. "I had never been in love, not with anyone, but I was stunned by her beauty, even then. I could tell she was lost—she was bewildered—and she seemed so sad. I had been shopping with one of the other girls. I made an excuse— somehow I didn't want my friend to meet Daisy, to know about her. And then I went over to try to help." Rose hugged herself.

"What happened?"

"She was near tears. I saw that she was trying to sell her body to the gentlemen passing by, and that she had not a clue as to how to do it. She was so innocent. And obviously, she was desperate for funds. I couldn't understand—she was beautifully dressed."

"Had she run away?"

"Yes. She told me that much later. I couldn't stand to see her trying to sell herself like that, when she was so upset and inexperienced. I bought her a sandwich. We chatted a little and I could see she was frightened, and so relieved to be having a meal and not on the street, soliciting men. I told her she could come stay with me, and she did. I tried to hide her from the madam, Francesca. And I did, for about a week. I hid her in my room. When I had a john, she hid in the closet—or beneath the bed.

We became friends that week, until she was discovered. And then I couldn't protect her anymore."

Francesca was moved. How could she not be? "And the madam forced her into that life?"

Rose nodded. "But it didn't matter that much. We had each other now. I was already in love with her, Francesca. I fell in love with her right away."

Francesca paused to reflect on Rose's and Daisy's life. What could have caused a young lady to run from home and choose a life of prostitution over a genteel existence? She simply could not imagine. It was heartbreaking. "And she never told you where she had come from or why she was running away?"

"No! She refused to discuss her past, and do you know what? I was glad! Because I was terrified that one day she would come to her senses, go home and leave me."

"But she never did."

"No, she never did." Rose stared tearfully at her. "Daisy liked you," she said abruptly. "Before she got involved with Hart." And the tears began to fall.

Francesca tensed. She had come to believe that Daisy had developed actual feelings for Calder. Handing Rose her handkerchief, she said, "Daisy came to care for Hart, didn't she? That is why you hated him so much."

"I hate him because he took her away from me!" Rose cried.

Francesca studied Rose, who was wiping away more tears with her kerchief. Very quietly, she asked, "You were jealous, weren't you?"

Rose gave her a hard look. "What do you think? Daisy made you jealous, didn't she?"

Francesca intended to ignore that dig. "Did you fight about Hart?"

Rose became wary. "Daisy never stopped loving me," she said hoarsely. "But I admit that I was jealous—that I hated her being here, that I hated his keeping her. But you already know that. What are you getting at?"

"So you and Daisy fought when she was Hart's mistress."

Rose stared, breathing hard. "Yes. We fought."

Finally they were getting somewhere, Francesca thought. "Did you continue your relationship while she was with Hart?"

"What does it matter?" Rose asked hotly.

Francesca decided to press her. "Why don't you admit it? For a time, Daisy left you. She left you for Hart," Francesca said.

"She never left me!" Tears began to track down Rose's cheeks. "He refused to allow her to see me—he was that jealous, that controlling. How can you stand him?" she cried.

Francesca tried not to show her feelings. Hart could be very jealous, and she had not a doubt he could be controlling, but he had never tried to control her. "Rose, did you and Daisy reconcile?"

Rose turned away, crying. "She loved me," she wept. "And I loved her."

Francesca felt terrible, but she continued, "I know she loved you. I know you loved her. But your relationship changed, didn't it, the moment she became Hart's mistress? From that moment, it changed irrevocably, and it never returned to the way it was. According to Homer, your visits were once or twice a week. You didn't reconcile, did you?"

Rose covered her face with her hands.

Francesca clasped her shoulder, feeling very sorry for the other woman. But now she had to really consider the unthinkable. Until that moment, she had wanted Rose to be on the list of suspects simply to keep attention away from Hart. Now Francesca had to carefully think about the other woman's state of mind. Rose had been Daisy's lover, and she remained deeply in love with her. She was furiously angry with Hart, for supposedly stealing Daisy from her. And while she was blaming Hart for everything, she had been first at the scene of the crime—or so it appeared.

Rose was an angry, jealous and jilted lover. Could she have murdered Daisy? Had she done so? She would not be the first woman to resort to murder, either contemplated or not, in such an instance.

Rose turned her teary gaze on Francesca. "We did reconcile, Francesca. But it wasn't the same. As always, you are right," she cried bitterly.

Francesca dropped her hand, standing. She had to know the truth. "Was Daisy in love with Calder?"

Rose looked up. "Daisy wanted the life Hart could give her. She did not want to go back to being a whore, and she was determined to wait him out and get that life back."

Francesca was shaken. It was impossible not to feel some relief now that Daisy was out of their lives forever. She was instantly ashamed and guilty for feeling that way, even the slightest bit.

Rose's expression changed. "How can you be so calm about all of this? We are talking about the woman I love and the man you claim to love. Doesn't it hurt you that he once slept here? That he bought Daisy so he could use her as he willed?"

"Yes, it does hurt me, it actually hurts me very much," Francesca said sharply, finally admitting to her feelings. "But I wasn't with Calder when he and Daisy were having their affair, and I continue to remind myself of that. And no one forced Daisy to be Hart's mistress. She wanted to be here."

"Oh, that's right—at that time, you were in love with his brother, Rick Bragg!"

"That was a lifetime ago," Francesca said far more calmly than she felt. She understood Rose's pain, and that she was lashing out wherever and however she could. "Sometimes I wake up in the middle of the night, astonished with the twists and turns my life has taken, but there is no going back. I love Calder, Rose. And I know how much you loved Daisy. I know you are grieving, and that you are angry. But the more you tell me, the faster I can get to the bottom of this case."

"How can you be so blind?" Rose accused. "Daisy wasn't murdered because of her past. You heard the maid! Hart was furious with her, so furious he broke down a door! He was furious because she had been trying to get him back. He was furious with her for trying to hurt you, for trying to interfere in your engagement, for refusing to leave this house. No one wanted her out of the way more than he did."

Everything Rose had said was the truth, but it was also crystal clear that Rose was enraged with Hart. Francesca wondered how angry she had been with *Daisy.* "Is this what you told the police?"

Rose lifted her chin. "Of course. I told them *everything.*"

Francesca's heart lurched with dread. "What does that mean?"

Rose smiled and it was vicious. "I was at Kate Sullivan's funeral. I heard him, Francesca, as clear as day—I was standing behind you both."

"I don't know what you are talking about," Francesca lied.

Rose stood. "He told you he would take care of Daisy, and his meaning was clear. He would do anything, *anything,* to stop her. And last night, that is exactly what he did."

ROURKE LOITERED IN THE large front hall of the Channing home, the large trophy head of a white wolf snarling down at him. A servant had gone to inform both Sarah and her mother of his call and he was oddly anxious, as if he were a suitor. He reminded himself that he was merely a friend of Sarah's, although they had certainly been through quite a bit together. Francesca had provided the close connection. Once, Sarah had been engaged to Evan Cahill in a terrible mismatch that had made them both miserable. Rourke had never understood how either family had thought to match such a reckless rogue with someone as sincere and privately ambitious as Sarah Channing. The world thought her to be as eccentric as her father had been, and labeled her a recluse, but it was clear to Rourke that the world was wrong—she was a committed and brilliant artist. Her art was her passion and he understood completely, as he was privately driven, too. His intention was to heal the world's least fortunate, if he could.

They had both become involved in several of Francesca's cases, which was how their friendship had formed. Sarah had even been attacked in the course of one investigation, an incident Rourke did not like recalling, as he had been there and Sarah had been hurt. But that had been last February, and it had been well over two months since he had paid the Channings a visit. But his behavior was excusable enough—after all, he was attending medical school in Philadelphia, and like all med students, his schedule was hectic, allowing almost no personal time.

Still, given the time that had lapsed since he last called, he wasn't really sure of his reception. Rourke decided that was the cause of his anxiety. He paced, ignoring the other trophies alternately staring, grinning or growling down at him from the salon. Sarah's late father, Richard Wyeth Channing, had been an avid big-game hunter, and he had spent most of his life in the wilds across the world. Rourke wondered whether his widow would ever redecorate their huge West Side home. He tried not to be judgmental, but all of society seemed to delight in Mrs. Channing's extreme lack of good taste—behind her back, of course.

He heard a rustle of movement and felt his heart skip. Slowly, smiling pleasantly, he turned.

Sarah had just entered the hall from its far end, and her brown eyes were huge in her small oval face. She came forward, clad in a simple skirt and shirtwaist, her curly brown hair swept up very haphazardly. He noticed a smudge of paint on her white blouse and his smile became genuine. He crossed the hall to meet her.

"Good day, Sarah. I hope I am not interrupting, but I have the feeling that I am."

She did not smile back, her eyes searching his. "This is quite a surprise, Rourke," she said as if filled with tension.

His pleasure began to fade. "*Am* I interrupting?" he asked somberly.

She sighed. "I was in my studio, but I am afraid I have been blocked for some time. And how could you interrupt? You saved my life."

He hesitated, trying to read her, but all he could discern was that she seemed troubled—and that she did not seem eager to see him. Oddly, he was somewhat hurt. "That was a long time ago, and you hardly owe me."

She gave him a look, then smiled slightly. "I certainly owe you, Rourke. Come into the salon and sit down." She led the way. "I am afraid Mother is already out for the day. How have you been?"

He waited until they had entered the other room. "I have been very busy. I applied for a transfer to Bellevue Medical College, and I feel certain I will receive it. I expect to be moving any day now."

She turned away before he could see what she was thinking. "I had heard," she finally said, glancing up at him.

He heard himself say, "I had hoped to be the one to tell you."

She just stared, and he wondered if he saw hurt in her eyes. But that was impossible, wasn't it? "Sarah, I sense something is wrong. Have I offended you in any way?"

She seemed surprised. "Rourke, how could you have possibly offended me?"

Without thinking twice, he reached for her hand. She stiffened, but he clasped it, anyway. "I hope that is never the case!" he exclaimed. "I treasure our friendship, Sarah."

She blushed and tugged her hand away, avoiding his eyes. "When will you know if you have been accepted at Bellevue?"

"Any day now," he said, studying her profile. She was a petite woman, and while he clinically recognized the fact that she was somewhat plain in appearance, from the first time they had met he had been drawn to her in an unfathomable way. He had heard other young ladies calling her mousy behind her back, but she wasn't, really. She had a small, upturned nose, a sweet rosebud mouth, and those huge dark eyes, which could undo any man. And he had seen her hair down once. Sarah had the hair of a Greek goddess, waist-length, wild and curly.

She finally smiled fully at him. "And shall I be the first or last to know?"

He grinned back. "If I tell you first, will I be redeemed in your eyes?"

"Rourke, I meant what I said before. You saved my life—I will always owe you. There is no need for redemption."

He became aware of his heart pounding, slow and strong but almost aching, the hunger deep and quiet. "Do you want to tell me what is wrong? I should like to know. If I can, I should like to help."

She met his gaze, hers filled with worry. "No one has told you?"

"No one has told me what?"

She wet her lips. "You remember, don't you, that Hart commissioned a portrait of Francesca from me?"

He could not imagine where she was leading. "Of course I do. You were so wildly excited to do it."

Sarah bit her lip. "I finished it, Rourke, in April. Hart was pleased."

He did not understand. If Hart, a world-renowned art collector, had been pleased with the portrait, why was Sarah so upset? "I'm glad. Do I get to glimpse the work of art, as well?"

Sarah wrung her hands. "It's gone."

CHAPTER SIX

FRANCESCA RUBBED HER ACHING temples as her carriage moved up Mulberry Street, approaching the squat, square brownstone that housed police headquarters. She had not stopped thinking about her interview with Rose since leaving Daisy's and she was anxious to go over the case with Bragg. She was afraid Rose's statement had incriminated Hart even further in Daisy's murder. She continued to believe him innocent, but her protective instincts had never been as consuming. What was Bragg now planning? She felt as if a clock were ticking, right there in the carriage beside her. She had to find another suspect, one as apparently involved as Hart appeared to be—it had become her overriding priority. Of course, that suspect could be Rose.

Joel had stayed at Daisy's to continue to look for some kind of witness to the sordid and ugly affairs of last night. He despised the police, anyway, and Francesca had told him she would meet him on a designated street corner in a few hours.

Raoul braked the carriage. Through her window, Francesca glimpsed Bragg's handsome motorcar parked in front of the station between two police wagons. As usual, a pair of roundsmen was standing not far from it, keeping the passersby at bay.

Francesca was slammed into the past. Her heart ached now, the handsome black Daimler bringing back so many bittersweet memories. The inhabitants of Mulberry Bend had apparently become oblivious to the vehicle, although months ago, when

Bragg had first taken up his appointment, every crook and thug in the ward had gathered about it, wide-eyed with awe. Last January, before she had begun to fall for Hart, Bragg had been her best friend. It had been an exhilarating time when she had discovered her talent and passion for investigative work, and it had also been a time of awakening. Bragg was the first man she had ever kissed.

Since then, their lives had taken distinctly diverging paths. Still, a certain foundation remained—a foundation of respect, admiration and deep, abiding affection and trust. Up until last night, they had been so honest with each other. Francesca felt as if she were on the verge of lying to him once again. But wasn't she? After all, her motives in joining the investigation and finding Daisy's killer were clouded by her need to protect Calder Hart. Now Bragg was expecting her to give her statement to the police, but she was hoping to discern exactly what he was thinking and what the police intended to do next.

Her life felt as if it had become impossibly complicated. And if she dared to reflect on Calder's deception about his recent business trip, then she had to admit that it had.

Forcing her reservations aside, Francesca stepped down from the carriage and quickly went up the concrete front steps of the building. The lobby was crowded, with a number of civilians angrily and loudly lodging their disparate complaints at the front desk, where Sergeant Shea appeared irritated and harassed. An officer had a very scruffy sort in handcuffs, about to book him at another desk. In the far end of the room were the holding cells and they were full, half of the occupants sleeping off their drunks. One scantily clad prostitute was clinging to the bars, smacking kisses at the policemen who passed. Telephones were ringing, typewriters clicking, telegraphs pinging. Francesca looked across the crowded room to the elevator and stairs.

Her heart lurched, for Arthur Kurland was coming down the stairs, looking rather pleased with himself.

She was afraid he had just learned the actual facts of the case. And if that were so, he knew she had deliberately attempted to mislead him. Francesca hurried over to the front desk, rudely pushing to the front of the line, ignoring the protests and exclamations she was causing. There, she inserted herself between a pair of gentlemen, hunching over the counter and ducking her head. Hoping for invisibility, she waited breathlessly for Kurland to clasp her shoulder from behind and smugly claim victory over her, but a long moment passed in which no such event occurred. Francesca finally lifted her head and turned. Kurland was gone. She sighed in relief, and then apologized to the two annoyed men.

She gave Sergeant Shea a quick wave, but he was so busy he did not notice, and hurried to the elevator. She might have escaped a confrontation with Kurland, but he had probably learned the truth about last night. She could not imagine what tomorrow's headlines would be and she hoped they were not too malicious or defamatory.

She pushed open the door and entered the iron cage, closing the door again and pressing for the second floor. A moment later the engine whirred and the cage began its slow ascent. Francesca wrestled with the heavy door once more and then hurried down the hall to Bragg's office.

The door was open but he was not at his desk. It was a small room with a fireplace, above which he kept a dozen photographs of his family, his friends and a very interesting photo of himself with Theodore Roosevelt before he had become the president. His desk was in front of a window which looked down on Mulberry Street, a cane-backed chair behind it. Francesca walked in and paused by his desk. She stared briefly down at the stacks and piles of files and folders cluttered on his desk. Of course, she could not snoop, but she recognized one of the topmost folders—it was a coroner's report.

Her heart instantly accelerated and her fingers itched to lift it.

Fortunately, Bragg chose that precise moment to walk in. She straightened, smiling at him, feeling like a thief caught red-handed.

His gaze moved from her face to his desk, as if he knew exactly what she had been about to do. His smile was slight, as if reluctant. "Good morning, Francesca. I was beginning to think you had forgotten to come downtown."

She could not smile back, for she was too nervous now. "I think the morning has passed. Of course I did not forget that you need a statement from me." Their gazes held and she gave up her attempt at social niceties. "Rick! Is that Heinreich's report?"

"Yes." He nodded, studying her. "You look tired, Francesca. Didn't you sleep at all?"

She saw the concern in his eyes and she melted, remembering all of the good in their relationship instead of the distasteful positions they now found themselves in. Truthfully, she said, "How could I? I was Daisy's friend, at least until recently, and in spite of any awkwardness, I never wished her ill."

He did not speak for a moment. "Francesca, I know you as well as I know anyone, I think. You would never wish harm to a fly. Another woman might have despised Daisy, but you would never allow petty jealousy to rule you."

Francesca was grim. He still had so much faith in her. "But I *was* jealous of her, Rick."

"You weren't jealous of her. You were afraid of her—undoubtedly because you did not trust Hart where she was concerned."

She gasped and he gave her a dark look. "I know too much about your private life for you to attempt to mislead me, even in the slightest way."

Francesca inhaled. "I do trust Hart!" she exclaimed. "It was Daisy I did not trust!" And the moment the words were out of her mouth, she realized she had been manipulated. She stared at him, aghast.

He chose his words with care. "You have been in a difficult

position, Francesca. The outside world might see it very differently than I do. I know you were not involved in Daisy's death. But you cannot speak about your feelings so openly," he said seriously.

He was trying to protect her, she thought, melting all over again. She walked closer to him. "You don't have to protect me, Rick. Not in this case."

He smiled a little at her. "You are a dear friend. If I need to, I will protect you."

She was moved, and she turned quickly away so he would not see the sudden rise of tears.

He said softly, "Francesca, I know that you would never compromise your morals, not for anything or anyone, but I can also see that you are worried about Hart. And I know how big your heart is. No one is kinder or more caring than you. Don't be tempted into trying to protect *him*."

She wondered just how much he knew about Daisy's malicious behavior, and she faced him. "Rick, Calder did not kill Daisy and we both know it."

"I don't know who killed Daisy, and it would be unprofessional of me to release Hart from any suspicion, considering his relationship with Daisy."

Francesca was taken aback. She swallowed hard, folding her arms across her chest. "Then I should be a suspect, too."

"The coroner's report was clear. Daisy was murdered between 7:00 and 9:00 p.m. last night. You were out with your parents, and you did not arrive at Daisy's until midnight."

"So I am off the hook?" She was grim. "If we are being so terribly honest now, then you may as well admit that you would never indict me, even if my alibi proved to be a lie."

"But you have a solid alibi and it isn't a lie." He shook his head. "I told you before and I will tell you again—Hart is not good enough for you and you are only going to get hurt if you continue on with him, especially now."

She trembled. "I know you believe what you are saying. I really do. But I believe in him. We have become very close, Rick."

He started.

Francesca flushed, suddenly realizing he had misconstrued her words. "I know him well and he did not kill Daisy," she said firmly. "You almost sound as if you are hoping this case will break us apart."

Bragg walked away from the desk. It was a moment before he spoke, facing her. "I know you would be hurt at first, if the engagement ended. But you can do better."

She did not know why they always found themselves at this place, this point. "I don't want to do better," she said, and she had said those exact words to him before.

He made a harsh sound. "Daisy was killed in a fit of rage. She was stabbed six times with a medium-size bowie knife. While we have not recovered the weapon—and we may never recover it—the blade was probably five inches long and an inch to an inch and a half wide. The stab wounds were randomly placed, and some were so deep they were probably delivered in a two-handed manner. The conclusion is inescapable—the murderer was furious with Daisy."

Did this mean that Bragg also knew Hart had been furious with Daisy last week? She said slowly, with care, "I just interviewed Rose, and Daisy's staff."

"Good. Then you know that the maid stated that Hart fought with Daisy last Thursday afternoon, breaking a door and reducing Daisy to tears. I know that Daisy tried to hurt you recently, Francesca, in an attempt to get Hart back. Was that why Hart was so angry with her? Or was it because she refused to leave the house when he told her to get out last month?"

Francesca continued to hug herself. Bragg had definitely been doing his homework. She walked away from the window, away from him. "He was angry. So was I. Neither of us was furious,

Rick." She faced him. "Daisy was my friend—until recently. Recently, she became difficult. But Hart showed no inclination to bother with her. In fact, as you must know, except for last Thursday afternoon, he has not been at the house in months."

"But we really don't know that, do we?" He was hard. "Daisy always dismissed the staff when she was entertaining Hart. She would dismiss them two, three even four times a week. It was very rare for anyone to know who was calling on those evenings. I hate to be the one to point this out, but Hart could have been a frequent guest."

"Why are you doing this?" Francesca gasped, shaken and stunned. "Why are you suggesting that Hart was having an affair with Daisy behind my back? You are happy now, you have your marriage back, you are with your wife! Surely you do not want me! So why can't you leave Hart and me alone? I am happy, Rick!"

"Are you really? Do you really, in your heart, trust Calder? Is that why you lied to the police last night?" he demanded. "If you truly believed in his innocence, you wouldn't be lying to the police—to *me*—in order to protect him!"

She froze. "What do you mean?"

"I'm sorry Francesca, but I spoke with your father this morning. You got home at midnight last night. There is simply no way you were at Daisy's at midnight. The earliest you could have arrived there was half past."

Francesca closed her eyes in despair.

"How could you lie to me?" Bragg asked, agonized. "After all we have been through? Is it *me* that you don't trust?"

Francesca opened her eyes and their gazes met and held. "I hated lying to you. But I know how much you and Hart relish going at each other! You shouldn't be on this case if it is personal for you, if you cannot be objective, if you secretly think to crucify your brother!"

"I have no desire to crucify anyone." Bragg was shocked.

"And I hope for your sake—and my father's, and Grace's, and Rourke's sakes—that Hart is innocent. But damn it, Francesca! It doesn't look good! What in hell was he doing there in the first place, and what was he doing there for an entire hour?"

"The coroner said she was murdered between seven and nine," Francesca cried. "Not between eleven and midnight!"

"I can think of several good reasons for the killer to return to the scene," Bragg snapped.

"He is your half brother," Francesca cried desperately. "Rick, you are so generous with everyone else! If you can give a stranger the benefit of the doubt, why can't you give your own brother that same benefit? Can't you find it in your own heart to want to help him, and to want happiness for him?"

"Are we talking about the case, or your future and your marriage? Francesca, you chose to become involved with a dangerous, difficult man. I warned you. Your father is against Hart, too. But you can be impossibly headstrong, and you have made up your mind. I hope Hart is innocent, but I have no delusions about him—the way you seem to. Maybe *you* should walk away from this case, if it is so personal for you."

She was ready to cry. "I can't. And I know he is innocent. I *know* it."

"I think you protest overly. Rose said she overheard Hart threatening Daisy at Kate Sullivan's funeral."

She went rigid, shaking her head. "He did not mean it that way!"

"So he *did* say something to you about getting rid of Daisy?"

"No! He assured me that Daisy would not hurt us or our relationship, that is all," Francesca cried, painfully aware of what she was doing. Concealing Hart's exact words was no different from lying to Bragg again. But thankfully, Rose hadn't seemed to quote Hart precisely. "You are so busy preparing to indict Hart, have you even stopped to consider that Rose has just as much motive?"

"She is also on my list of suspects. Right now, Rose hasn't given herself an alibi. She refuses to identify the gentleman she was entertaining last night. I am sure her judgment is lacking because of her grief. I am inclined to think that shortly we will also have a rock-solid alibi for Rose."

Francesca spoke in anger now. "You want Rose to have a rock-solid alibi so you can continue to investigate Hart!"

Bragg seemed just as angry. He walked over to the fireplace and stared at some of the photographs above it.

"Rose hates Hart with a passion," Francesca cried, walking over to him. "She was insanely jealous of his relationship with Daisy. Because of Calder, she and Daisy broke up for several months. She was jilted by Daisy, Bragg, and we need to check this out."

"I intend to follow every single lead," he said slowly, with more calm. "But Hart is right on one point. He told me last night that he did not want you involved in this investigation."

Francesca dug in her heels. "Unless you think to charge me with obstruction of justice, I am on this case."

Bragg studied her for a long moment. "Maybe it is a good idea that you are on this case. Maybe you will finally realize just what you are in for, if you proceed to marry Hart."

"Maybe you will finally realize just how unfair you are to him," Francesca shot back. She grabbed his sleeve. "I understand why Hart hates you, Rick. He is jealous of you, because you have a real family by blood, because your father wanted you and his did not, because, to this day, he thinks your mother loved you more than she did him."

"Then he needs to get on with his life," Bragg flashed.

"He remains jealous that we ever were involved, too. But mostly, he is jealous that you have such a stellar reputation—one that is deserved."

Bragg stared. "What is your point?"

"I understand him, but I don't understand you. Why are *you* as jealous of *him?*"

Bragg searched her eyes; Francesca did not flinch. He finally said, "I'm not jealous. But because I continue to care so much for you, I hate the fact that he will ruin you, Francesca, in one way or another."

"You don't know that. And maybe it is not your place to sit in judgement on him as you do," Francesca cried.

"I am going to tell you something about your fiancé," he said very harshly. "I spent my childhood taking care of him, protecting him, rescuing him, until Rathe rescued us both. Our mother was too busy and then too ill to do any of those things. I remember helping him eat supper when he was in diapers—I couldn't have been much older than three! I remember going to the corner grocery, a few coins in my pocket, holding Hart by the hand. I was maybe six, maybe seven—he was four or five. I remember giving him a glass of milk for breakfast when Lily was too ill to do so. Damn it! He never tried to return a single favor, he never once showed any gratitude, he never even tried to be my brother. He has spent his life thinking only of himself, doing whatever he pleased, come hell or high water. It took me years to realize that the brother I yearned for and cared for didn't exist, and never would. Something is wrong with your fiancé. He has one goal in life—to serve his own selfish needs. I am judging Hart the way I would judge anyone."

"That's not true," Francesca whispered, stricken by Bragg's indictment. "And there are two sides to every story. Maybe he was too jealous of you to ever be the brother you hoped for and deserved. Somehow he was scarred terribly by his childhood, while you were not."

"We both grew up hungry, wearing hand-me-down, patched clothes. We both grew up watching our mother service men— until we had to watch her die. Don't tell me I am not scarred.

I knew I was never going to be like those johns—not *ever*—I knew I would never use anyone, and that instead, I would help everyone that I could."

"God knows why the very same past pushed you into a life of good works and Hart into a life of scandalous self-indulgence," Francesca said, saddened. "Isn't He the only one who should judge here? It isn't too late, Rick, not if you don't give up."

He stared, his expression twisted with his own anguish.

"It's not too late to forgive and forget. It's not too late for the two of you to find your way back to each other. You're *brothers*."

"Oh, it's way too late," Bragg said harshly. "Tell him to get a lawyer, because I am fairly certain he will need one."

She was alarmed. "Are you going to arrest him? How can you arrest him! You said yourself Daisy was killed before nine, and Hart didn't get there until close to midnight! What about Rose? She was there at the scene before Hart."

"I told you, I haven't ruled Rose out. But Hart could have gone to Daisy's directly from the Grand Central Depot, arriving at half past seven. What if they had another argument?"

"And he what?" Francesca said scathingly, furious now. "He stabbed her in a fit of anger and then ran away, but later returned to remove evidence of the crime? Hart is not a killer. And he has too much self-control to kill in such a manner."

"Oh, really? I seem to recall an explosive temper, Francesca."

"And have you questioned his staff? I am sure that any number of servants can testify to his presence at his house from eight o'clock on. That would not leave a very large window of opportunity for him to murder Daisy, now would it?"

"Newman is there as we speak." He didn't look at her now. Walking over to his desk, he sat down and began to read a file. Clearly he was upset and wished for their discussion to be over.

Francesca could not believe that Bragg seemed so ready to

believe the worst of Hart, and that he really thought him capable of murder. The tension between them had become huge, and it felt impossible to surmount.

Bragg looked up briefly, his expression closed. "We still need your statement. You can give it to Newman, or if he's not in, to a junior officer."

She nodded. Then she made a decision and she dared to walk over to him. "Rick."

He didn't glance up, so she covered his hand with her own and he was forced to meet her regard.

"I am going to prove him innocent."

His expression was rigid. "Believe it or not, I hope you succeed." He started to remove his hand from hers, but she grasped him more tightly, not letting him go. In surprise, he looked up at her again.

She held his gaze. "I don't want this case to come between us. We cannot argue this way. Your friendship is important to me, and it always will be important to me—even after I have married Hart."

He stared. "You lied to me, Francesca. Did you really think I would not find out?"

"Then be angry at me. But don't take it out on Hart," she cried, trying not think about the lie she had convinced Alfred to tell him.

He stared at her and she stared back. Then he sighed. "I despise arguing with you, but it's too late. Hart has come between us, hasn't he? You lied to me to protect him. And as long as you remain with him, he will always be between us."

His telephone began to ring and he promptly picked it up. Francesca turned away. It had been this way almost from the start, with her somehow caught between the two men, like some awful prize each intended to win.

Bragg's tone caught her attention. "Leigh Anne!" he sounded anxious and surprised. "What's happened? Are you all right?"

Francesca looked at him, instantly concerned, but he was so absorbed that he had clearly forgotten she was present. A ripple of sadness running through her, Francesca crossed the room and left.

LEIGH ANNE HAD *NEVER* called him at work, not even once, and he was seized with fear. "Is it the girls?"

"Rick," she gasped, and he realized she was highly distressed and close to tears. He did not know when he had last seen her cry, as she was so determined to pretend to be strong in front of him. "They are fine, but it *is* about the girls!" And he heard her choke on a sob.

He willed himself to be calm. "What happened?" he asked quietly.

He could hear her harsh intake of air. "We had a caller—callers. A man named Mike O'Donnell and his aunt, an older woman named Beth O'Brien."

He knew the name, but it took him a second to place the weathered blond longshoreman. "Mary O'Shaunessy's brother," he said grimly, and his heart quickened with dread.

"Yes, the girls' uncle—and Mrs. O'Brien is apparently their great-aunt. Rick! Why did he appear after all of this time? What does he want?"

He already suspected what O'Donnell wanted. The man was a ruffian in every way. He had been difficult during the course of the investigation involving the murders of his sister and wife, during which he had briefly been a suspect. Bragg and Francesca had learned that he had a quick temper, that he frequented bars and saloons, and that Mary had been afraid of him. O'Donnell was the kind of thug to take advantage of the new family connection. Leigh Anne had been through so much. She didn't need this now. "Tell me what happened," he said calmly. "Tell me everything."

"I don't want to lose the girls! Did our lawyer file those papers for their legal adoption yet?" Leigh Anne cried, desperation in her tone.

"We won't lose the girls," he said firmly, and that he did not doubt. "O'Donnell couldn't manage his own daughter—last I heard, she was in a foster home. There's no reason for you to worry."

"Katie and Dot have a cousin?" Leigh Anne gasped, and Rick instantly understood her concern.

He sighed. "I will check on her, but O'Donnell did not appear in order to take the girls away from us. Now, tell me what he said."

He felt her gathering her thoughts and composure. "He was very pleasant, actually, as was Mrs. O'Brien. He says that his sister's death changed him. He seems to be very devout, Rick."

Bragg doubted that. "Is that it?"

"He just wanted to visit the girls and make certain they were well. He asked if he could come again. What could I do? He was polite, I had to tell him yes."

Bragg thought about the visit he would make to Mike O'Donnell. The girls did not need such a thug in their lives. And he doubted that his sister's death had changed O'Donnell at all, much less that he was suddenly devout. "Did he tell you when he would come again? Did you learn where he lives?"

"I invited him back on Wednesday, so you could meet him."

"That was very clever, Leigh Anne," Rick said. He saw an officer passing in the hall and snapped his fingers at him. "Hold on," he told his wife. To the sergeant, he said, "Dig up the case file for the cross murders," he said. "And find me the last known address of Mike O'Donnell, husband of one of the victims and brother of the other."

"Yes, sir," the beefy sergeant said, exiting.

He returned to the conversation on the telephone. "Leigh Anne, I don't want you to worry. O'Donnell's visit doesn't change anything. I will call Mr. Feingold and see if the adoption papers were filed, and I will ask him to speed the process up. Meanwhile, I want you to think about something else. Are you still taking the girls to the park?"

There was a brief silence. "I hadn't thought that far ahead."

"I think you should keep to your original plans. It is a beautiful day."

She hesitated. "Rick, Katie was afraid of her uncle."

He could imagine why. From what he vaguely recalled, O'Donnell had bullied his wife and sister; he had probably bullied the girls, too. "Leave O'Donnell and the adoption to me," he said.

"Of course," Leigh Anne whispered.

"Leigh Anne," he said quickly, his grasp on the receiver tightening. "I will make it a point to come home at a reasonable hour, no later than six o'clock."

There was a moment of silence. She said, "I think that is a good idea, Rick. Thank you."

And oddly, his heart leapt with pleasure at her words.

FRANCESCA HAD RAOUL PARK her carriage around the block from Daisy's, out of view of anyone who might look out of the house's front windows. She did not wish to be discovered by Rose if she was still at the house. In order to make certain she could pass incognito, they had made a detour on their way to Daisy's, stopping at B. Altman's. Francesca had bought a ready-made skirt and blouse and had changed out of her own clothes in a dressing room in the store. She had also purchased a straw bonnet, which she now wore. At a quick glance, her disguise would do.

Joel would be waiting for her on the corner of Fifth Avenue, a half a block up the street from Daisy's. Francesca approached and saw him loitering beneath an elm tree. Sensing her presence, he turned, saw her and broke into a jog. "Miz Cahill!" He grinned at her, and she could tell that he was pleased with himself.

She tugged on his ear. "Spill the beans, my fine young man," she said, using slang she had learned from him.

"I got a neighbor who saw a lady calling on Miz Jones last night before dark, maybe at six or seven o'clock."

Francesca halted in her tracks, surprised. "Joel! Who is this neighbor and did she get a good look at Daisy's guest? Daisy was murdered between 7:00 and 9:00 p.m.—maybe she saw the killer!"

Joel continued to grin. "The woman wore a green dress and she had dark hair. She arrived by cab. The neighbor is right there," he said, pointing to the adjoining house. "Her name is Mrs. Firth."

Francesca could not move. She voiced her thoughts. "Rose was wearing a green dress last night—Rose has dark hair." And Rose certainly did not own a carriage. "How well did Mrs. Firth see the caller?"

"She said she only saw her briefly, as she was coming in, herself."

"Rose still has no alibi," Francesca said slowly. Her heart was thundering in her chest. "Perhaps this bit of news will provoke her into revealing the name of the gentleman she says she was with last night." Had Rose called on Daisy between 6:00 and 7:00 p.m.? If so, she had had a narrow window in which to have murdered her friend. Francesca knew she had to consider the possibility that Rose had called on Daisy at six, then gone on to meet her client, returning later, but that scenario felt awkward, oh yes. She made a mental note to question Rose again, as well as Mrs. Firth. Although it did not sound likely, it would be a great day indeed if Mrs. Firth could identify Rose as that caller. And she still wanted to search the house for clues. "Do you know if Rose is at Daisy's?"

"I saw her leave at least an hour ago," Joel said. "Don't you want to talk to her?"

"I do, but what I really want to do is search the house for any clues Daisy might have left behind as to her past, or other significant people in her life." Francesca tried not to think about the fact that searching the premises could be construed by the police as interference in their official investigation. She had briefly debated telling Bragg what she intended, but then she had decided against it. He had been very preoccupied when she had left. If she found something useful, she would certainly share it with him, she just wanted to analyze whatever she might find by herself first. Her every instinct told her to proceed alone now, just in case more incriminating evidence against Hart surfaced. As she and Joel started for the house, she said, "Does Mrs. Firth know how long the caller stayed?"

"I didn't think to ask," Joel said, clearly dismayed. "Darn!"

She patted his back. "You have done a wonderful bit of sleuthing today. Now, how can we sneak inside without alerting the staff?"

"They got a back entrance to the kitchens, but I wouldn't use that. There's a door on the terrace by the back gardens. It was open earlier, Miz Cahill."

Several moments later they had stolen past the delivery entrance without being remarked, had crossed the rioting gardens out back, and slipped into the house via the French doors on the terrace. There was no sign of staff. Francesca imagined they were worried about their future and that continuing their daily routine was the last thing on their minds.

At the bottom of the stairs, Francesca told Joel to hide behind an ornamental urn. "If you see anyone come in, make a ruckus so I can try to slip out without being detected. I am going upstairs to Daisy's private rooms."

Joel grinned and took a beautiful porcelain box off a nearby side table. He slipped it into his pocket and said, "Don't worry. I got my story all fabry-cated."

She patted his back and raced upstairs.

Once there, she quickly found Daisy's suite of rooms. Her sitting room was an elegant blend of cream, ivory and gold tones, just as Daisy had been. For one moment, as she paused on the threshold, she could see Hart standing by the white marble mantel, a Scotch in hand, with Daisy sensuously seated on the sofa in some kind of revealing peignoir. She shook her head to clear it of such provocative thoughts.

She had work to do. If something was here, some clue as to Daisy's past or the killer's identity, she intended to find it. She did not know how much time she had. A glance at the gilded clock on a side table told her it was a minute before 2:00 p.m.

Francesca crossed the room to where a secretaire stood. It was a delicate seventeenth-century piece of furniture, and she quickly checked the three drawers and the six cubbyholes. She did not think Daisy would stash any important information about herself in such an obvious place, and her search was a cursory one.

Most of the papers were bills, but one drawer was filled with bank statements. Francesca stared at the neatly wrapped stack, tied with a red ribbon, and a tingle swept over her. Hart had been keeping her; he must know all about her finances. Still, she could not help herself, even though she felt as if she were somehow violating his privacy. She took the bundle of bank statements.

Setting them aside, she began to search for a calendar. Everyone kept a calendar, but Francesca could not find one in the secretaire. Maybe Daisy had kept her agenda downstairs in the study, where she had died.

Francesca continued her search. She checked under the sitting room's furniture, beneath pillows and cushions, behind the pale cream-and-gold velvet draperies. Francesca swiftly moved into the bedroom, glancing at the gilded clock once more as she did so. It was eight minutes past two.

The bedroom gave her pause, her gaze instantly drawn to the canopied bed in its midst. It was covered in gold silk covers, with gold-and-burgundy velvet pillows and gold-velvet hangings. Hart had spent a number of nights in that bed.

She hated the very notion. She did not want to keep thinking about their affair. It had been over for months. Why had Bragg so cruelly suggested that it wasn't over? If only Hart would tell them why he had gone to see Daisy last night!

Trying not to think about it, Francesca glanced grimly around the rest of the spacious and elegant bedroom. She saw the armoire and the closet; if she were to hide something very important, it would be in one of those two places. She went purposefully to the armoire and rifled through a dozen silk underthings and several dozen peignoirs, trying to shut down her mind now. And beneath a neat pile of lacy white drawers and matching garters, her hand touched cardboard.

She jerked. This could be interesting, indeed.

Francesca shoved all of the underwear aside, revealing a cardboard box. It was about eight or nine inches wide by eleven or twelve inches long—the kind of box that could accommodate standard sheets of papers or standard business documents.

Her heart racing, she took the box, saw it was not sealed and removed the cover. A jumble of folded newspapers met her wide gaze.

Francesca went to the bed, removing the first piece of newspaper. It was a newspaper clipping, an entire page that had been carefully cut out of the *Albany Times*. It was dated February 3, 1902, and there were several articles on the page, all political in nature.

She reached for the next page. It was also from the *Albany Times,* but dated a year earlier. The name Judge Richard Gillespie leapt out at her. Hadn't she seen that name in the first clipping? She went to the first clipping, and saw a small paragraph about Gillespie's recent court decision.

The next clipping was from the *New York Times,* dated 1899, and it was a social page. One column was devoted to a charity event held by the Astors. Judge Richard Gillespie from Albany, New York, had been an honored guest.

Francesca did not want to interfere with the order that the clippings had been placed in the box, as it seemed to be chronological, so she carefully looked at three more pieces of newspapers. Most were from the *Albany Times,* but one was from the *Tribune.* Every page had an article about or mentioning Judge Gillespie.

She had hit the jackpot.

Francesca replaced the clippings in the order in which they had been removed, trembling with excitement. She had no idea why Gillespie was important to Daisy, but she would find out, oh yes, and soon! In fact, she would read every single article in the box, as quickly as possible. And if she had to, she would take the next train to Albany and speak with Gillespie directly.

But that plan, of course, was jumping the gun. Still, there was a connection. Now she merely had to reveal exactly what kind of connection it was. Replacing the cover on the box, Francesca heard a huge crash coming from the front hall downstairs.

Her heart skipped. Joel was making the ruckus she had requested, which meant that someone was downstairs. She hoped it was not a police officer.

The box in hand, she ran into the sitting room, seizing the bundle of bank statements. Then she rushed to the closest window and peered outside.

She was on the second floor, but the window of the sitting room opened onto the back gardens. Francesca quickly put the bank statements in the box, using the red ribbon to tie the box closed. Then she pushed the window open, and holding her breath, she let the box fall. She was relieved when she saw that it had landed in a shrub, the bush breaking its fall. The box had not opened, and it remained perched precariously there.

She slammed the window closed and fled across the room. She began to dash out the door, but as she did so, Rose came inside, causing both women to collide.

"What are you doing here?" Rose cried.

Francesca steadied herself, scrambling for an answer.

CHAPTER SEVEN

Tuesday, June 3, 1902—2:15 p.m.

FRANCESCA DECIDED THAT THE truth would have to do. "What do you think I am doing?" She tried to appear calm at being caught in Daisy's rooms. "I am looking for clues."

Rose appeared at once angry and disbelieving. "I asked you to find Daisy's killer, Francesca, but on second thought, I don't think you are the one who should be on this case."

Francesca smiled tightly and walked past Rose, wanting to leave the room. "And why is that? Because you have already tried and convicted Hart?"

Rose followed her into the hall. "Actually, that is exactly why! Do the police know you were here, searching the house? Is that legal? Or did Bragg send you here?"

Francesca faced her at the top of the stairs. "What I am wondering is if the police know that you were here last evening, between 6:00 and 7:00 p.m., before you met your client, the gentleman you have thus far refused to name?" She smiled sweetly.

Rose paled. "What are you talking about?"

"I have a witness, Rose, one who will testify that you were here last night at that hour." Rose's expression remained frozen in surprise. "Oh, haven't you heard? Daisy was murdered between seven and nine with a bowie knife. That places you here at the time of her murder. How odd."

Rose began to shake. "Just what are you saying, Francesca? Are you somehow accusing me? And if so, of what?"

"This was a terrible, brutal, vicious crime of passion," Francesca said harshly, leaning close to Rose. "The killer used a medium-size knife, one with a blade five inches long and almost two inches wide! Bowie knives are used for hunting animals, Rose. They are used for gutting carcasses." She stared, holding Rose's gaze. Francesca actually knew nothing about knives, much less bowie knives, and she was making up every word to provoke the other woman. "Daisy was stabbed six times, at random, some of the cuts so deep the killer had to have used both hands."

"Stop it!" Rose gasped.

Francesca seized her shoulder. "The two of you were together for eight years. Then Calder came along, took her to bed a few times, paid for her every expense, and she was in love. Isn't that what happened?"

"Stop it!" Rose screamed. She started to cry. "It wasn't love! She needed the safety he offered her!"

Francesca froze. What did that mean? She leaned even closer, for if Rose would break, the case would be over. "Daisy *chose* Calder's bed. She chose Calder."

Rose hugged herself, the tears streaming. "It was a temporary infatuation! He had wealth—she had never been cared for so well! He gave her freedom, Francesca, freedom! But that was all. She would have become tired of him, I know it. What we had, he could never replace!"

"Did you argue with her last night, about Calder? Or were you arguing about the fact that she would not let you move in with her here? Did you really have a client that night?"

Rose wiped her eyes with the back of her hand. "We were not arguing. But you are right, I was here. I stopped by on my way to visit my john. I begged her to reconsider what she was doing and move out immediately."

Francesca felt a surge of satisfaction. Rose had lied. Francesca had her suspect. "What time did you stop by?"

"Between six and seven. I didn't stay very long. I had my engagement—and she had one of her own, as you know."

Francesca studied Rose and could not decide if she was lying about her client or not. "What time did you meet this supposed gentleman of yours?"

"I told you, at seven. Or maybe a few minutes past." She flushed. "There is nothing *supposed* about him. But if Daisy was killed between seven and nine last night, I couldn't have done it."

Francesca wondered if the heightened color in Rose's cheeks was a sign of deception. "Rose, you need to tell me—or the police—the name of the gentleman you spent the evening with. Simply insisting that you were with someone else will not convince anyone of your innocence."

She shook her head. "I can't do that."

"You can't, or you won't?" Francesca pressed.

Rose glared at her. "You are not the nice person that you pretend to be!"

Francesca did feel like a heel, but she was not going to give up. She wanted a confession. "Until you give us that name, you are as much a suspect as Hart—if not more so."

Rose whirled, shaking her off. "I have to go. I have to get back to the house."

Francesca knew when to take a step back. She followed her down the stairs. "What did you mean, when you said Calder gave Daisy safety? Was she being threatened? Was someone frightening her in some way?"

"I never said that. I said Hart gave her freedom—because of him, she got out of prostitution, Francesca, a life she hated."

That gave Francesca pause. She knew Rose had said Hart gave Daisy safety. But safety from what—or whom? And what could have made her run away from home and take up a life she hated, as Rose said?

"Earlier you said an old family friend was going to call on her the night she was murdered. Was it Richard Gillespie?"

Rose looked bewildered. "I have no idea who it was. I knew better than to ask. If Daisy had wanted me to know, she would have told me. Who is Richard Gillespie?"

It was clear that Rose had no idea who Francesca was talking about. "A judge from Albany," Francesca said. "Have you considered what I asked you earlier? Have you thought of anyone who might feel so passionately about Daisy that he or she could want her dead?"

Rose sighed, appearing very worn and tired. "She had three clients, Francesca, that she was seeing for years. Their names are John Krause, George Holstein and David Masters. I happen to know that Krause is incapacitated—he had a stroke a few months ago. But these other two? They saw Daisy regularly before she moved in with Hart. Both men were very involved with her, despite their stellar reputations and their families."

"They saw her regularly for years?" Francesca asked with some excitement.

Rose nodded. "Masters has been around since the start, Francesca. As for Holstein, he appeared in her life a few years ago. I can get their addresses for you when I get back to the house."

"Please, maybe it will be helpful. Send a messenger to my home. Where is the house, Rose, that you are now living in?" Francesca was referring to the brothel.

"Off of Fifth Avenue, not far from here, on Thirteenth Street," Rose said. She folded her arms across her chest, sullen and perhaps worried. "Do the police really think I could have killed Daisy?"

"I won't lie to you," Francesca said. "You are a prime suspect." She watched her closely.

Rose flushed anew. "Of course I am—after all, I am a woman

and a whore! But Hart, who had every reason to want Daisy dead, is off the hook, because he is a man and because he is filthy rich."

Francesca said, "The truth is, Hart is hardly off the hook, either." She suddenly gripped Rose's arm. "*Rose*. Did you kill Daisy?"

Rose's gaze held Francesca's. "No," she said firmly, "I loved her."

And Francesca almost believed her. For one more moment, the two women stared at each other before Francesca released her. "I have to go. If you think of anything, you know where to reach me."

Rose hesitated. "Okay. Francesca? Thank you."

Francesca was surprised, but started down the stairs without responding. Rose watched her from the landing. "Francesca! What did you find in your search?"

Francesca waved up at her as she joined Joel. "Nothing at all."

ONCE SAFELY INSIDE THE carriage with Joel, Francesca asked Raoul to wait and she began to peruse the newspaper clippings. She quickly learned that Gillespie had been a New York State district judge for ten years. He had been born in Hartford, Connecticut, and seemed to come from a fine old family. Two years ago, the New York Grand Old Party had held a birthday celebration for him—he had been fifty years old. His wife, Martha, remained alive, and they had one unmarried daughter, Lydia.

"Miz Cahill?"

Francesca carefully closed the box. She would read every article that night and take notes. "I think we may be onto something. In any case, this is a lead that must be followed. We are going to Albany, Joel."

"Albany?" His eyes popped.

Francesca opened her door and poked her head out. "Raoul?

Headquarters, please." Then she closed the door as Raoul started to drive off. "Albany is many hundreds of miles northwest of the city, but we will take an express train. I imagine we can make the trip in four or five hours. Of course, you don't have to join me if you don't want to," she added teasingly.

His response was what she had expected. "I never been out of the city," Joel said, clearly excited at the prospect. "How long will we be gone?"

"I hope no more than a day, but it depends on the train schedule and Judge Gillespie." She sat back against the plush velvet seat, trembling with anticipation. Gillespie was obviously very significant to Daisy. Francesca hoped he was a relation, or even her father or uncle. Tomorrow, she would certainly find out.

A few minutes later she rushed into headquarters, Joel choosing to wait outside. Bragg was in his office, on the telephone, when she poked her head inside.

He seemed surprised to see her, but he waved her in and gestured for her to sit as he finished the call. Francesca pretended not to listen but quickly realized he was speaking with Low's chief of staff and that the conversation was about the recent newspaper headlines. To her chagrin, she had forgotten all about the mudslinging press and the pressure he was under. A moment later he hung up the receiver and faced her.

"Now, this is unexpected," he said with a slight smile, as if their earlier confrontation had never occurred. "You are glowing—I know the look. What have you found?"

She leapt to her feet, holding out the box.

"What is this?" he asked, standing and taking the box. He opened it and Francesca explained.

"I found this hidden in Daisy's bedroom. Every single newspaper clipping contains an article about Judge Richard Gillespie or a mention of him. Bragg! This has to be the lead to her past that we are looking for. I am going to Albany on the next express."

He looked up, his expression serious. "My men obviously missed this."

"Yes, they did. Before you chastise me, I know I should have asked for permission to search the house, but you were so occupied when I left here earlier. Is Leigh Anne all right?" she asked impulsively.

He hesitated. "Francesca, do you remember Mike O'Donnell?"

"Of course I do. He was Mary O'Shaunessy's brother and Kate O'Donnell's husband—a suspect in their murders. Why?"

"He called on Leigh Anne and the girls this morning."

Francesca felt a sudden dread. "What did he want?"

"According to Leigh Anne, he was very proper and very polite. However I expect extortion will be his game."

"He's an uneducated thug!" Francesca exclaimed, recalling nothing proper or even likable about the man.

"He claims that the death of his wife and sister changed him, that he has found God."

Francesca did not like the sound of that. "Do you believe it?"

"No. But I will have a better idea of what this is about after I speak with him."

She plucked his sleeve. "Do you want me to come with you?"

He met her gaze, his expression softening. "That is very kind of you, but I think you are right—you should go to Albany and check Gillespie out. Obviously, Daisy felt strongly about him. However, keep in mind that the connection may not have any relevance to our case."

She nodded, worried now about what O'Donnell wanted from the Braggs.

"Francesca, I am so sorry about what happened between us earlier today," he said suddenly. "It was wrong for me to speak as I did. It was out of place and entirely unacceptable."

She bit her lip. "Rick, I can't fight with you. I hate it. I still care too much," she whispered honestly. "And it hurts too much."

His expression tightened, as if he fought himself. "I am on your side," he finally said. "And I will always be on your side."

She nodded, tearing up. "I want to help you if I can. If O'Donnell is intent on some kind of extortion, you must tell me."

He walked out from behind his desk and reached out. She slipped her hand into his. "You don't have enough on your plate?" he asked softly.

She was aware of his body's heat, and she could not help recalling moments they had shared, before Leigh Anne had returned to their marriage, before she had fallen for Hart. She did not want to think of such intimacy and she moved away from him. Feeling herself flush, she said, "There is more. Rose was at the house between 6:00 and 7:00 p.m. She and Daisy argued over Daisy refusing to move out. And she still will not name her gentleman caller. I doubt she had a client that night, and that means she may have never left Daisy's."

Bragg nodded. "I think she would have revealed his name, if he did exist. Good work, Francesca."

She thrilled to his praise, but quickly sobered. "I asked her if she did the deed. She denied it. At the time, I believed her. But, Rick, I will say this again—Rose was angry with Daisy. She had motive, and she seems to have had means."

"I happen to agree with you," Bragg said. He hesitated, and his cheeks seemed to flush. "I really do hope that Hart is innocent. I know Hart and I are always at odds, and that your engagement has only fueled the rivalry we share, but in spite of what I said earlier, he is my half brother."

Relief made her knees buckle. She seized both of his hands. "I am so glad to hear you say that!"

He smiled a little at her. "I was angry when we spoke earlier."

"I know—and it is my fault for lying to you." She tried not to think about Alfred now. She wished she had not suggested that he alter his version of the previous evening's events.

He did not comment on that. "Try to convince Hart to come forward and admit his reasons for being at Daisy's last night."

"I will try, but I will wait until his mood improves," Francesca said. "He is very distressed about the murder." She paused. "Did Newman speak with Hart's staff?"

"Yes, he did." Bragg gave her a strange look. "Alfred claims Hart was at home, exactly as he said he was. I wonder."

She swallowed, her heart racing. "What do you mean?"

"I think Alfred is a very loyal servant. He has worked for Hart for years. No one else can corroborate his statement. I am not inclined to accept it just yet."

In a way, Francesca was glad. Still, she quickly moved to the next subject. "There is more." She told him about David Masters and George Holstein.

"I'll put Newman on it. Hopefully he can interview both men today—or at least before you return from Albany. I suppose you want to take the news articles with you?"

"I really need to read them carefully. I was going to do so tonight, but I can actually do it on the train."

"Check with the front desk when you leave. There might be a schedule lying about."

Francesca nodded. She had no excuse to linger now, but a part of her was reluctant to go. Somehow they had weathered the earlier crisis and she was so grateful. They were almost a team once again.

"I had better get going," she said. "Especially if I am off to Albany as soon as possible."

"By the way," Rick said when she was at the door, "your sister was here a few hours ago, looking for you. Apparently she heard about Daisy. She seemed very worried, Francesca. She asked me to tell you to stop by her home the moment you can."

Francesca was very close to her older sister. In that instant, calling on Connie and sharing all of her burdens and woes seemed the perfect way to end a long day of work. "I'll stop there on my way home," she said, wondering if Hart had ever received her note. They needed to meet that evening, especially as she now planned to leave town for a day or two.

Bragg nodded. When his telephone rang, he answered it, listened closely and said, "Send them to the conference room." He hung up abruptly. Francesca paused, glancing at him. He appeared grim.

Her heart skipped. "What has happened?"

"You should stay. Daisy's housemaid and housekeeper have just arrived, and apparently they have something they wish to say."

Francesca felt a new tension. "What else could they say? Annie already witnessed that argument between Daisy and Calder on Thursday." But she had a very bad feeling, oh yes.

Bragg stood, crossing the room. "I guess we are going to find out," he said, opening his door more widely for her.

Francesca felt ill. She somehow knew that whatever the two employees had come to elaborate upon, it was not going to be helpful to Hart's case. She could only hope that she was wrong.

An officer appeared at the corridor's far end, walking beside Annie, who was red-eyed from weeping. She was wringing her hands nervously together. Francesca had met the housekeeper, Mrs. Greene, on a prior occasion. Now, she was very pale and appeared tense. Both women were ushered into the conference room, where Bragg greeted them. "Thank you for coming to headquarters," he said. "Newman is in the field, but Miss Cahill and I will try to be of help."

Annie sat down at the long table, her mouth trembling. Mrs. Greene said, "We made a promise to Miss Jones, sir. All of us who worked for her, we made her the same promise, not to ever talk about the goings-on in that house." A tear slipped down her face.

"I understand," Rick said, glancing at Francesca.

She took her cue, stepping forward, trying to appear professional and not dismayed. "But Daisy is dead, and while we all should respect her wishes and her need for privacy, her killer must be brought to justice. If you need to break that promise in order to help us find her killer, that is what you must do." She smiled reassuringly at both women.

"We know that," Mrs. Greene said frankly. "I mean, we have spent most of the day thinking about how kind Miss Jones was, how fortunate we were to be in her employ, how she never treated us as anything less than thinking, feeling people. Never mind her unsavory reputation, she was a fine woman and a real lady."

Francesca found it interesting that her staff had thought so highly of her and that they now grieved so genuinely for her. "Do either of you know who called on her last night, other than Rose?"

Mrs. Greene and Annie shared a look. The housekeeper said, "We already told the police everything we know about last night, Miss Cahill. No, this is about the argument she had with Mr. Hart on Thursday."

Filled with dread and despair, Francesca knew she did not want to hear this.

As if reading her mind, Bragg laid his hand on her shoulder. "Go on."

Annie looked worriedly at Mrs. Greene, then turned imploringly toward Francesca and Bragg. "I wasn't honest when I said that I couldn't hear what they were saying. I could. They were shouting, carrying on so loudly, I heard every word," she blurted and tears welled in her eyes.

Francesca was so afraid now that she could not speak.

Bragg said, "It's all right. We understand that you had made a promise to Miss Jones. But your decision to come forward today and tell the complete truth is entirely appropriate, Annie. It is the right thing to do."

"I know," she whispered, looking with absolute worry at Francesca.

"I was there, too," Mrs. Greene suddenly said harshly. "Not the entire time. Annie was the one who eavesdropped from the first, but I was bringing refreshments and I heard them, just before Mr. Hart stormed out."

"Why were they arguing?" Bragg asked. "Why was Daisy in tears? And why was Hart so angry?"

Annie stood up, her hands moving nervously. Her whisper was so low that Francesca had to lean toward her to hear her words. She said, "Miss Jones was with child."

Francesca heard her own sharp intake of breath.

"Miss Jones was with child? Hart's child?" Bragg demanded, stunned.

Annie nodded, not looking at Francesca now. "Yes. She told him and he seemed not to believe it, not at first. But she would not back down. She told him to speak with her physician. And that was when he became silent and she began crying."

Francesca realized she was gripping the back of a chair. *Daisy had been carrying Hart's child.*

"Then what happened?" Bragg asked tersely.

Annie wiped her eyes. "She started saying she knew he would take care of her and the baby, no matter what, even if he married Miss Cahill. And he started shouting at her, telling her she had done this on purpose. I really can't remember everything, but it was awful, sir, just awful, the way she wept and the things he said to her."

Francesca sat down, her face in her hands, incapable of any rationalization now. There was only raw feeling, disbelief and shock and a deep, deep sickness.

"He was cruel," Mrs. Greene said abruptly. "I remember his exact words, as they were too horrible to ever forget."

Francesca closed her eyes tightly, reeling. Vaguely, she felt Bragg's clasp on her shoulder. "What did he say, exactly?" Bragg asked.

Mrs. Greene hesitated. "I don't want your goddamned child."

CHAPTER EIGHT

Tuesday, June 3, 1902—4:00 p.m.

HOW COULD THIS BE HAPPENING? Francesca wondered, vaguely aware of everyone leaving the room. She gripped the table, feeling dizzy and faint. Daisy had been pregnant with Hart's child and he hadn't told her. She reminded herself that he had only just found out, the day before he had left on his business trip—if he had actually gone on a business trip! Was that why he had gone to see Daisy last night? To discuss the child?

If Daisy had not been murdered, Hart would have had a child with another woman.

"Take this. It might help," Bragg said quietly, from beside her.

She realized he was holding a glass. She took it, her hand shaking. She had not heard him return to the room.

"It is bourbon. I plead guilty—I keep a bottle in my office for the nights I remain here working past any decent hour." He smiled at her but his gaze was terribly concerned.

She didn't even try to sip the bourbon. She didn't look at Bragg—she couldn't. Another woman had been carrying Calder's child, and the fact that she had conceived before Francesca had become involved with Hart didn't dull the sick sense of betrayal.

"Francesca, let me help," Bragg said softly.

How could he help? she wondered. If only she could think, then surely she would not feel so ill. Francesca tried to organize her thoughts. Daisy was dead, the illegitimate child she had shared with Hart was dead, and he had more motive than ever. *He was in trouble.* She looked at Rick Bragg. If she focused on the case, she could manage this crisis and recover her composure. "You know Hart would never murder a woman who was pregnant with his child."

He pulled out a chair and sat down beside her. Very carefully, he said, "I know you are upset. This is a terrible shock—a terrible situation. I don't want to talk about the case. I want to talk about how you are feeling."

She inhaled, forced a smile and said too brightly, "I am fine. I mean, this was an accident."

"Clearly," Bragg said with care, studying her.

Francesca realized she was hugging herself defensively. "Daisy conceived before I became engaged, Rick."

"Probably so. Francesca, do you really want to defend him now?"

"Yes, I do." Her eyes filled. "What am I going to do?" she heard herself whisper.

He put his arm around her. "Don't make any decisions just now, Francesca. Maybe you should attempt to discuss this with him."

"I know I should not feel betrayed, but I do."

He pulled her into his arms and held her there. Francesca finally allowed the tears to freely fall.

Stroking her hair, Bragg said, "Hart is not the first man to be confronted with an unwanted child."

She pulled away so their eyes could meet. "I know that. I can't seem to think clearly." She wiped her eyes. "He has always claimed his past was sordid and ugly, but I never cared. I genuinely didn't care about his previous lovers. Except for Daisy. She managed to bother me—I felt threatened! And now we find out that she was pregnant. Today, his past feels like the present. And I wish it weren't here!"

"He has a past, and the reputation to prove it," Rick said quietly. "You knew it from the start. But it's very different to be told about something than to have it strike you in the face. I am sorry, Francesca, truly sorry."

The implications of Daisy's pregnancy hit her then. If her parents ever found out, they would never support her marriage to Hart. This was another huge scandal in the making. Any other well-bred lady would disengage herself from her fiancé in such a situation. She was stunned, but she could never leave Hart—not even because of this. She could not imagine her life without him at its center.

Francesca stood, shaken. She must focus on the current investigation. There was no point in dwelling on her scrambled and uncomfortable feelings. "I am overreacting," she said flatly. "I am acting like a witless ninny—like a spoiled, selfish debutante. This happened in February, or even earlier than that. I hardly knew Hart last February!"

Bragg was silent.

She slowly looked at him. "Please don't look at me that way, as if you know what I should do—as if you believe I should leave him!"

"That is your decision to make."

"There is no decision to make."

Bragg looked away from her, clearly in disagreement.

And suddenly a bell went off in her mind. Francesca straightened, her thoughts racing. *Hart's child was dead.* And Francesca saw him as he had been last night, the shadow of grief in his eyes. In that lightning moment, she understood, and her own feelings did not matter. "Hart is mourning."

Bragg started and rose. "Francesca," he protested. "You had better look carefully before you leap. Hart didn't want the child and two witnesses heard him say so."

"No," she cried breathlessly. If there was one thing she did know, it was that he had not meant those terrible words of rejection. "He is grieving—I saw it last night, in his eyes, but I thought it was because he still cared about Daisy." She became grim. "Are you going to arrest him because Mrs. Greene and Annie both heard him say he did not want the child?"

"The evidence against him is mounting."

"It is circumstantial," she flashed, suddenly afraid for Hart in spite of her own confusion.

"Many murderers are convicted on circumstantial evidence," he pointed out.

She backed away. "Don't do this!"

He reached for her, but she dodged him. "Francesca! I am not going to arrest him without more proof."

She nodded. "Good. I have to go."

He grabbed her arm. "You are going to comfort him?" He was incredulous.

"Yes." More tears came, and she swatted at them. "I am going to get past this. He never meant to hurt me this way. Hart needs me now, more than ever."

Bragg was rigid. "Of course he didn't mean to hurt you—he will never *mean* to hurt you!"

Francesca saw his contempt and anger. She could not care, not now. She ran out.

ROURKE FOLLOWED A CLERK down the hall of Hart's office building, one of several from which Calder conducted his various business affairs. Hart's office door was open, revealing a large, spacious room with views of the New York Harbor and the Statue of Liberty. Hart was engrossed in the papers on his desk, but as Rourke and the clerk paused, he looked up.

"Mr. Bragg, sir," the young clerk said.

Hart smiled but it did not reach his eyes. Rourke hadn't expected to find him in the best of spirits, but instantly he saw the shadow of grief on his face. Uncertain now, he entered the room as Hart stood and walked out from behind his desk.

"Rourke! I am pleased you are back in the city," Hart said, clearly meaning that. He embraced him briefly, surprising Rourke, as Hart was not prone to displays of affection. A greeting from Hart was usually no more than a firm handshake. "Does this mean you have attained your transfer?"

"I'm not certain," Rourke said with a smile. "I'll know in a day or two."

"Are you certain you don't want me to pull a few strings?"

Rourke shook his head. Hart had offered to speak with one or two directors of the Bellevue Medical Hospital in order to make certain Rourke was transferred to the college. Rourke had refused, surprised to learn Hart would have leverage even at Bellevue. "Why don't we wait to learn my educational fate?"

"If you insist," Hart said, turning away, his smile vanishing. He seemed terribly preoccupied.

Rourke laid a hand on his shoulder. "I heard about Miss Jones."

Hart tensed and pulled away. He slowly turned. "And did you hear that I found her, Rourke? Stabbed viciously to death?"

Hart was distraught, Rourke saw—almost anguished. "I hadn't realized you still harbored feelings of affection for Miss Jones," he said cautiously, an image of Francesca coming to mind.

Hart gave him a hard look and wandered to the window. "I don't. But no one should have had to suffer such a brutal and untimely death."

Rourke didn't know what to believe. Hart was clearly in grief. "Are you somehow blaming yourself?"

Hart made a disparaging sound. "I am not so noble or so misguided."

"That is a relief," Rourke said before thinking about it. "Francesca asked me if I would mind coming downtown."

"So she is the one who told you about Daisy," he said, and it was not a question.

"She is very worried about you, Calder," Rourke said. He reached for Francesca's note. "She asked me to give you this."

Hart glanced at it and laid it on his desk. "She hardly need worry, because I did not kill anyone. The police will find the real killer, sooner or later." Rourke hesitated, and Hart narrowed his eyes at him. "What is it?"

Rourke knew he was intruding. "She loves you, Calder, very much, probably more than you deserve. But she is concerned, and after speaking with her, I cannot say I blame her."

Hart placed both hands on his hips, his stance braced for serious battle. "I see. She sent you here to plead her case. Or you have decided to become her defender?"

"She will be my sister-in-law," Rourke exclaimed. "I have become very fond of Francesca, not to mention that I truly admire her! Why won't you tell her why you were visiting Daisy last night, at such a socially unacceptable hour?"

"So you also think I have been unfaithful?" Hart was incredulous.

"No, actually, that is not what I think, not at all. I think you are head over heels for the first time in your life, and it frightens you so much you will not admit it, not even to yourself."

Hart softened briefly. "She is the blinding light of my dark and sordid life," he admitted.

Rourke went up to him. "She is doing what most women in her place would not do—she has chosen to trust you! But she needs an explanation, Hart. In fact, I need one, too."

"Like hell you do!" Hart exploded. He was furious. "It was a private matter, goddamn it, a very private matter!"

"What the hell does that mean?" Rourke demanded.

Hart shook his head, the anger gone, his expression ravaged. Clearly, he could not speak.

Rourke was concerned, vastly so. "Calder. I am your brother in every way but biologically. I want to help. I have never seen you like this. Are you sure you are not grief-stricken over Miss Jones's death?"

"No." He looked Rourke in the eyes.

"But you are grieving—I can see that—as if someone you cared for has died."

Hart stared. "My child died," he said. He suddenly seemed to choke up. He added harshly, "Daisy was carrying my child."

Rourke was shocked. It was a moment before he could speak. "Are you certain?"

Hart stood, tension rippling through his body. "I spoke with her physician just before I left on this trip. She appeared to be in her third or fourth month. Our affair was in February, before I was with Francesca. You can do the math. Even before she became my mistress, even when I saw her on a casual basis, Daisy always insisted I use protection—which is my habit, anyway. She was always so careful! *I* was always so careful! But one night in February, shortly after she moved in, the condom ruptured." Abruptly he sat down again, rubbing his temples.

"Could someone else be the father?" Rourke had to ask.

Hart looked up, briefly incredulous. "I never share. When Daisy became my mistress, our arrangement was exclusive. I have no reason to believe that she would deceive me in such a way. And what are the odds that she took another lover and that his means of protection also failed?"

"I am so sorry," Rourke finally said, meaning it.

"God, this was a terrible act of fate," Hart cried.

Hart's words were surprising because Rourke knew he did not believe in destiny. "It was an accident, Calder, an accident. It happens all the time."

Hart looked up. "I didn't want the child."

Rourke didn't know what to say. Hart needed comfort, yet he wasn't sure how to give it. "His or her death was not your fault."

"No! You don't understand. I genuinely did not want that child."

Rourke tried to remain calm. "Calder, you were shocked, and you were probably angry with Daisy—as anyone would be. But just because your initial reaction was to reject the child, that doesn't make you responsible for his or her death."

Hart shot to his feet. "Haven't you ever heard the expression *Be careful of what you wish for?*"

Rourke flinched.

"Well, I got what I wished for, didn't I," he said savagely. And he swept the files and papers from his desk.

FRANCESCA SAT ON THE pale green sofa in Hart's large, wood-paneled library, her hands folded in her lap, some of her composure recovered. Alfred had shown her in and had told her that Hart was not home yet. Francesca had told him that she would wait, and with a firm smile, she had refused any refreshments. She looked at the clock behind his desk. It was almost six. She had been waiting for more than an hour.

She would wait all night, if she had to.

Daisy's pregnancy still felt like a betrayal, but now she could think rationally and had shoved those feelings aside, to be dealt with at a later date. Her resolve had never been stronger.

Hart needed her now. He had never needed her more. No matter what the future might hold for them, she would see him safely through this terrible time.

She felt him behind her, before she even heard his footfall or the door open. Francesca tensed, forgetting to breathe. In spite of her resolve, a new nervous anxiety consumed her. She turned. The library door was open and Hart stood on the threshold, staring at her, looking as if he had spent the day in hell. Francesca slowly stood.

Hart came into the room. "This is a pleasant surprise," he

said, his tone carefully neutral. Francesca's tension increased. "Would you care for a Scotch?"

"No, thank you," Francesca said tersely. She went to the door and closed it.

He glanced briefly at her as he poured one Scotch. "Are you certain? This case just arrived and you have yet to try it."

She wet her lips. "Yes." She had no intention of pretending that nothing was amiss.

He smiled, his face terribly blank, as if they were strangers and nothing more. He obviously intended to play a game with her now. But then, Hart had never been an easy man to be with. In moments like these, he retreated with such icy calm behind such a wall of reserve that it was frightening to try to reach out to him. Francesca thought she understood. He was suffering and he did not want her to see. He must be suffering even more than she imagined.

I don't want your goddamned child.

Francesca did not want to think of that. He had spoken in shock and anger and she would never believe that he had meant his words. She started to approach. Not looking at her, he drained the glass and poured another one. Francesca refused to be intimidated, even though it was clear he was not pleased by her presence.

Holding the refreshed glass to his chest, he said casually, avoiding eye contact, "How was your day?"

She could not smile, but she did not want to play this game anyway. "Terrible."

His brows arched.

"But probably not as terrible as yours." She exhaled. "I know all about the child."

His eyes widened and their gazes clashed. Instantly, he turned away.

Francesca wanted to run to him and take him in her arms,

but she knew he would reject her. "Calder," she said quietly, in a plea. "Let me help you."

He did not move, not for a long instant. Then, not answering her and not looking at her, he asked as quietly, "How did you find out?"

"Annie and Mrs. Greene both heard your argument with Daisy on Thursday. They have amended their earlier police statements. The police know, Calder."

He turned. He was not smiling now. His face was strained, but his feelings remained so skillfully disguised that she could not read them. She was about to approach when he saluted her with his glass. "I should have known you would find out. It will be your epitaph, Francesca—No Clue Left Unturned." He was not mocking; he was resigned.

She was taken aback by that odd note of defeat. "I really did not make any discovery, as both women came forward."

He made a harsh sound and drained that drink, too. "I am sorry. You are the last person I should lash out at."

She started toward him.

He stiffened. "Don't."

She froze. "I am so sorry," she said, meaning it.

His eyes grew shadowed. "Only you, Francesca, would be sorry that my bastard is dead."

Tears threatened. "Just let me help you through this. You can feign apathy, but I know you cannot be indifferent, Calder. I know you are in mourning."

As if he had not heard her, he said, "Is my arrest imminent?"

"Why are you doing this? Why are you treating me as if we are polite acquaintances? We are lovers, we are friends," Francesca cried. "Another woman was carrying your child and she is now dead! Surely you wish to discuss this with me!"

"You must know—is my justice-driven brother preparing to arrest me?" he asked sharply.

"No!" She inhaled, shaking. "Hart—he did say you should get a lawyer."

Hart laughed. The sound was ugly, but Francesca recognized it—his pain was there, ready to erupt. Determined not to be pushed away, she walked over to him, her trepidation huge. He watched her very warily now.

"I know you did not kill Daisy."

"Do you?"

She paused before him, ignoring that provocation. "I am going to prove you innocent. If being nasty makes you feel better, then so be it. I will be your whipping boy."

He studied her, his face hard and set. "You heard them. I didn't want the bastard. I have motive, Francesca, lots of it, and I am sure the police will find opportunity, as well."

"Stop it!" She took his face in her hands, ignoring his tension. "I know you didn't mean it."

"I meant it," he roared at her.

Francesca cringed, releasing him.

He whirled away from her, pacing, then faced her again. He was shaking. "Why won't you stop being so goddamned loyal? When will you realize that your family and friends are right? You have made a mistake. I am no good. You have all the proof you need, do you not?"

She shook her head in protest. "You are a good man," she cried.

"I can think of nothing worse, *nothing,* than bringing an un-wanted bastard into this world. Do you understand me?"

She had never seen him with so much rage and anguish. "I understand," she managed to say, because it was hard to stand her ground, "that *you* were an unwanted bastard."

His look was murderous. "Please leave, Francesca. *Please leave.*"

Francesca was afraid. But she could not walk away when he was suffering so terribly. "Calder, stop," she whispered desperately. "I am here because I care. I know that from your perspective, learning Daisy was pregnant was the worst fate you could imagine. But you are not your father! Had your child survived, he or she would have been loved—by both parents! I am certain!"

He stared at her. "You have chosen to believe the best about me from the first. You have chosen to ignore my reputation and my past. When are you going to learn from your mistakes? The past is here, Francesca, in the present. My mistress and my child are dead, and I am the prime suspect."

"I am not making a mistake," she said, and she finally felt a tear falling, but the tear was for him. "I know you better than anyone. You are like a stray dog, Calder, all bark and no bite. One kind caress and the tail wags!"

"Am I supposed to be touched by your loyalty? Damn it, Francesca, I did not want you involved in this from the start!"

"I know what you are trying to do," she cried. "You are being cold and cruel, thinking to push me away. Undoubtedly you hope to protect me from the scandal! Well, this is not the first time you have tried to make me turn away from you. I won't do it. I am not a coward. I will see you through this crisis. I will prove you innocent."

He smiled at her now, chillingly, and stalked her. "And when I am a free man, when Daisy's killer is behind bars? Then what will you do, Francesca?" he purred.

She wet her lips. "I am here for you, Calder, no matter what happens. If you are waiting for me to tell you that, when this is over, I am leaving you, you are in for a disappointment. I won't pretend that I was not crushed by what has happened today. I know it is odd, but I felt betrayed. Maybe I was even jealous. I could not stand the idea of another woman carrying your child. But Daisy is the past. I am the present, your present, and I am not going anywhere."

He stared at her.

"And you can argue until your voice turns raw, but I know you would have loved this child," she added stubbornly.

He said, "You should run. Right now, as far as you can, as fast as possible. You should run from me." He turned toward the door, which she had closed. "Just go."

Something in her heart tightened. "No."

Speaking very calmly, he said, "You need not stay on the case. I am going to hire a lawyer and I already have a cadre of private detectives at my beck and call." He looked right at her.

She was shaking. "Even if I wanted to, I could not walk out that door, not now, not when you need me the most!"

"I am fine."

She choked on the stupendous falsehood of his words. "You are very close to being accused of murder! And you might fool the rest of town, but you can't fool me. You are suffering with guilt, and grief, and God only knows what else! I am staying on this case and I am staying with you."

He folded his arms across his broad chest and studied her. "And if I do not want your help? If I do not want you here? What if I tell you that *I* have changed my mind, that *I* no longer wish to be committed to you?"

His words stabbed through her heart like a knife. She wet her lips and dared to approach him.

She was aware of having become too physically close to him; as always, his body had a magnetic effect. "We need to talk about this, quietly and sincerely," she whispered.

He suddenly touched her cheek. Her pulse picked up a different beat, slow and deep, sending waves of heat through her body. "I have finally succeeded," he said slowly, "in pulling you down completely with me. And this is hardly the first time. Is this what you want, your reputation destroyed by your association with me?"

"I don't care about the scandal that is inevitable," she said, but her heart flipped, because she did care about how it would affect her family. And she saw the lost little boy in his dark eyes, waiting for another blow, waiting to be abandoned once more. She smiled just a little. "How many times do I have to tell you that I am not going anywhere?"

He took her hand. She stood still, her skirts brushing his thigh, and electricity seemed to leap between them as he answered. "Last night, I did not want you involved. Today, I am even more certain that you should be protected from all of this. I think, for once, I am capable of being selfless and putting you ahead of my own needs." He was grim as he raised her hand and pressed a lingering kiss there.

Francesca gasped, the mere kiss shafting through her. "Don't you dare tell me it is over," she gasped.

"Another woman was pregnant with my child. The police are preparing to charge me with her murder—and the murder of my own child. This is a very good time for us to part company."

"I know you didn't murder anyone. All I have to do is prove it," she declared.

He stood there staring at her, and when he finally spoke, his tone was raw. "Francesca, I didn't want to bring a bastard into this world. I can think of nothing more reprehensible, more irresponsible, but dear God, I never wanted this child dead."

"I know," she whispered. "I know all of that."

And his arms went around so suddenly she was surprised. Pressed against the solid and muscular wall of his body, she felt small and female and fragile, dwarfed by his power and his heat. He murmured thickly, "When will you stop believing in me? How could I possibly have found you?"

"I will always believe in you," she whispered against the fine wool of his suit. Not far from her lips, his heart pulsed, hard and strong. She had never needed to be in his arms more than she did at that moment, because there, the world was reduced to just the two of them, and nothing and no one else existed. "We may be engaged, and we may be lovers, but we are also friends. Friends fight for each other, Calder. People who care about each other do not jump ship at the first sign of a storm," she said, and she looked up.

His gaze was searching. "I have never known anyone as loyal or as brave as you, Francesca," he whispered roughly, touching her face and then stroking her lips with his thumb. "I must tell you, if you decide to leave me, I will understand."

Francesca shivered, her body already rigid with sexual tension. His thumb remained posed near her lower lip. "We are going to get through this, one way or another, together."

He choked, as if the distress he harbored was too much to bear, and he claimed her mouth. Francesca closed her eyes, accepting his hungry, urgent kisses with an answering passion, sucking back on his lips, his lapels in her fists. All worry, all fear and all thought vanished.

He held her head in his large hands and took her mouth, opening it, fusing with her. Francesca held on tight, straining against him, for him. Their mouths met and mated deeply and greedily, again and again, while her body raged for far more than a kiss. His hard hands moved up and down her back, shaking with his tension, and against her mouth, he said, "I have missed you."

She had missed him, too, but she could not speak. She cradled his face in her hands, kissing him, desperately and explosively.

He understood. Lifting her into his arms, he carried her to the sofa. As he laid her down, Francesca reached for his hand, guiding it down her body.

His smile was knowing, and his hand quickly slipped beneath her clothes. Francesca gasped wildly when he touched her wet and burning flesh.

Hart made a sound, hard and thick, his skilled fingers rubbing against her.

Francesca struggled with her skirts and petticoat, fighting a sob of extreme pleasure.

His eyes blazed. "I don't know if I can wait much longer, Francesca," he said harshly.

"Don't wait," she whispered. Their eyes met and she loved the blinding heat in his gaze. "Just hurry."

He gave her a look and bent between her legs, pressing one hand just above her sex and pushing his tongue against her.

And she surrendered to the exquisite pleasure building in tidal waves inside her. His clever tongue knew every fold, every peak, every valley of her sex, and in a moment, Francesca was sobbing her release and his name.

When she had floated back to earth and the sofa, she instantly recalled the past few hours. Refusing to dwell on reality, she opened her eyes. Hart knelt beside her, one hand remaining possessively between her legs. In the frenzy they had just shared, he had somehow jettisoned his jacket and his tie was askew. He was breathing hard and watching her intently.

Francesca's heart lurched with renewed need and great resolve. She reached out and seized his tie. "I seem to need you again," she whispered with a small, promising smile. She felt as seductive as the most infamous and desirable courtesan. "But I will be fair." She jerked on the tie.

He smiled slightly, allowing himself to be pulled down so she could kiss him, slowly and lazily, using her tongue with great skill against the mobile seam of his lips. As she teased, she held the tie like a leash so he could not move—at least, as long as he played along. With her left hand she reached for his belt.

Hart tensed, understanding.

Francesca nipped at him, jerking on his tie. "Stay still," she said, and unbuckled the belt.

He murmured one word, "Darling."

She stroked the bulge in his fly, just once, and looked up.

His smile was strained. "If you expect me to beg the way you do, it will never happen," he said. "I am a very patient man."

She loved the power unfolding in her now. She teased open a button, murmuring, "We shall see."

He sucked in his breath, giving her what was intended as a warning look.

Francesca freed him, releasing his tie. Hart leaned hard on the sofa now, his breathing loud rasps.

She bent and touched the fully distended tip with her tongue.

And Hart lost the battle. "Francesca," he cried, a plea.

CHAPTER NINE

BRAGG WAS AWARE OF the insistent pounding of his heart. He was preparing to do battle and he knew it. O'Donnell had not suddenly appeared in their lives to innocently visit the children. Tension filled him as he prepared to knock on the door of the rooms O'Donnell had let. A uniformed roundsman was with him. Bragg could handle any trouble by himself, but if there *was* trouble, he wanted a witness.

It had not been hard to locate O'Donnell, not once he had reacquainted himself with the man's file. An officer had learned of his present whereabouts from his parish priest.

He knocked. Bragg felt his tension rise as the door was opened. A plump woman with gray hair that was pulled back into a bun, an apron covering her blue dress, stood there. "Mrs. O'Brien?"

She seemed surprised, her glance moving to the policeman and then back to him. "Yes, I am Mrs. O'Brien. Can I help you?"

"I am looking for your nephew, Mike O'Donnell," he said. "I am Police Commissioner Bragg."

She opened the door more widely. "Mike? There is a policeman here to see you."

He thanked her and stepped inside, the officer following. Mrs. O'Brien closed the door and the suntanned, blond man sitting at the kitchen table, a book in front of him, slowly rose to his feet. "Sir," he said.

Bragg felt like rolling his eyes. O'Donnell's polite manner was absurd. He remembered the man too well: a thug who had left his wife and child, who had not cared for them in any way, and who had not been moved by either the murder of his wife or sister. "Please, don't stand on formalities with me. We are old friends, aren't we?" He had a sudden urge to smash the man's nose in. He was not going to let O'Donnell complicate their lives. Things were already difficult enough. Since the accident, Leigh Anne had become fragile, and she was so unhappy at times. The girls were her only source of joy.

O'Donnell was wide-eyed, as if in awe of Bragg. "Beth! Put up some hot water for tea. I'd offer you a whiskey, but I gave up drinking in March."

"How meritorious," Bragg said. He had already glanced around the small flat, commonly referred to as a railroad apartment because it was long and narrow, with a single window at the far end. He could see into the bedroom where a dress, a lady's coat and a scarf hung on the wall pegs, so he assumed Beth O'Brien was using the room. There was a quilt folded up on the sofa beside a pillow, so clearly, Mike O'Donnell slept there. The parlor and the kitchen were really one room, the sofa just a foot from the kitchen table. For dwellers in a tenement, O'Donnell and O'Brien were living like a king and his queen; usually several families shared such a flat. Although cramped, with the furnishings in dire need of new upholstery and the wood desperate for wax, the flat was as neat as possible, and it was clean.

Bragg gestured for O'Donnell to sit. "I see you are reading the Bible."

"Yes, I am," Mike said, taking his chair. "I find comfort in the words of the Lord now."

Bragg almost snorted. "I don't recall such devotion a few months ago, when Miss Cahill and I were trying to find the person who killed your sister and wife. I recall Miss Cahill being cursed at. And I recall your priest expressing that you had an unusually strong affection for your sister."

O'Donnell's eyes widened. "I am so sorry for that! But I have confessed to those sins—and other ones—many times over now, sir. I was terribly rude to Miss Cahill. I was mean to my own wife, God rest her soul. And yes, I had feelings I shouldn't have had for my poor, dear sister. I have confessed and I have been given absolution. I am not the same man now that I was then. After you found Kathleen and Mary's killer, it all hit me hard. I had lost the two people I loved most, after my precious daughter, and I could not go on. I was ready to kill myself."

"You didn't want anything to do with either your daughter or your wife."

"Sir, he is telling the truth." Beth stepped forward. She wore an earnest expression. "He sent this strange and incoherent letter to me, and I could tell he was about to go off the deep end. My mistress had just passed away—I worked in Hartford for many years—so I terminated my employment and came to the city, hoping to help him. Sir? I found Mike on his knees in prayer, a changed man."

Mike nodded. "God found me," he said with hushed reverence. "God saved me, and now I understand why He took my wife and my sister."

"Really? Care to explain it to me?"

"We must never question God's plans, but there is always a plan," O'Donnell exclaimed.

"Sir, if you have any doubts as to Mike's fine character, you need only speak with Father O'Connor. He gave up cards and liquor and he attends Mass twice a day. He is a good man now."

"Well, I am very relieved to hear this," Bragg said. "And where is your daughter, the child you abandoned when you left your wife? I mean, now that you are such a model Christian, shouldn't she be here with you and your aunt?"

O'Donnell was pale. "I tried to get her back, but it was too late! A couple from Brooklyn had already adopted her—they stole my child, they did." He covered his face with his hands, apparently about to weep.

Beth O'Brien went to stand behind him. "It isn't right," she said flatly. "To steal a man's only child that way!"

It was impossible to miss the implication—that he and Leigh Anne were stealing the girls. "It's too bad you didn't find God sooner," he said. He turned to Beth. "When did you arrive in the city to stay with your nephew?"

"A month ago," she said, "in early May."

He faced O'Donnell. "And why did you call on my wife and your nieces today?"

O'Donnell dropped his hands. "Sir, they are my flesh and blood. I have missed them terribly. I wanted to see if they were being properly cared for—and if they were happy."

Bragg laughed. "Your aunt may buy your theatrics, O'Donnell, but I don't. What is it that you really want?"

"I am a changed man," O'Donnell replied. "And God is giving me the chance to do things right this time."

A chill tickled the back of Bragg's nape. "I'd appreciate it if you spoke in plain English."

"My own child was taken away from me. That was God's hand, punishing me for my life of sin."

Bragg waited.

"But He is giving me another chance. I could see that the girls were fat and happy, but they belong with me."

Bragg stared. It was a moment before he spoke. "I'll see you in hell first."

O'Donnell flinched but did not reply.

The temptation to arrest O'Donnell on the spot was vast. It would be so easy to accuse him falsely and drag him downtown, throwing him in the tank. No one would care if he was being held there on trumped-up charges.

But the pursuit of justice and reform had ruled his entire life. It still did; Bragg simply turned and walked out.

FRANCESCA'S SISTER, CONNIE, lived just around the block from the Cahill home on Madison Avenue with her husband, the titled Englishman Lord Neil Montrose. She had supper guests, Francesca realized as she was let inside, as she could hear the sounds of quiet conversation and the tinkle of crystal. She had barely handed off her light wrap and gloves when another dinner guest arrived. Francesca was surprised, and then delighted, to realize it was her rakish brother.

"Evan? This is a surprise."

Evan was tall and slim, dark like their father, and very handsome, especially in his white dinner jacket. He quickly embraced her, his smile sporting a dimple. "Connie makes certain to invite me once a week to a society affair," he said, apparently in a good humor. "She is terribly afraid I will forget my roots."

Francesca laughed and it felt good. Enough time had passed that they could joke about his fall from Cahill grace. "Is Bartolla with you?"

His smile seemed to falter. "She was invited, of course, but she is resting this evening."

That was odd, as no one enjoyed society more than Bartolla Benevente. "And how is the beautiful countess?" She deliberately pried. Here was her chance to learn why Evan had not been to see Maggie for the past month.

He glanced away. "As beautiful and charming as ever," he said lightly.

She knew then that all was not well. She took his hand and pulled him away from the front door, where there was a bit of a chill. "Is everything all right?"

"Everything is fine," Evan said firmly, so firmly that Francesca knew it was not true.

It was wonderful to have someone else's problems to solve. "Do you want to talk about it—or her?" Francesca asked.

He gave her a look of some exasperation. "There is nothing to talk about! You must not be on a case, Fran, if you need to interview me."

She sobered. "Oh, I am on a case all right, and by tomorrow, you shall hear all about it. But I want to know why you are not happy."

"I am very happy," he snapped, his blue eyes flashing, but he started, as if caught in a trap.

"If you no longer love her, why not leave her?" Francesca asked quietly.

He gave her a dark look. "I hate it when you pry. Besides, I am committed."

"Committed?" Francesca was shocked. An image of Maggie in Evan's arms on the lawns outside of Hart's home came to mind, as he comforted her after a near brush with death. "What about Maggie?"

"I do not have a clue as to what you are talking about." He paused. "How is she?"

"She seems somewhat melancholy. I think her close call with the Slasher has had its toll," Francesca said, knowing she was being misleading. If her instincts were right, Maggie's spirits were low because of her feelings for her brother.

"Are you certain she is not ill?" Evan asked, with such concern that his own feelings were obvious.

"I don't know, Evan. Maybe you should call on her yourself and find out."

He looked away, his jaw hard. "That is not a good idea," he finally said.

She jerked on his sleeve. "Why not?" When he refused to answer, her annoyance escalated. "If you have no feelings for

Maggie Kennedy, then you should have behaved far differently with her. She is not like the countess, to be flirted with lightly and then dismissed!"

"I know very well that Maggie is not at all like Bartolla, Fran," he said quietly. "And if I have flirted with her, I am very sorry. That was never my intention."

"Then what was your intention?" she asked. "Because frankly, I thought you had genuine feelings for her."

He was taken aback. "Don't push me!" he exclaimed. "Has it ever occurred to you that in spite of the facade I keep, my life is far from jolly? I am trapped in a prison of my own making!"

She seized his hand. "What are you talking about?"

He shrugged free. "Everything. Do you think I like scrimping for pennies? Do you think I like making a commitment to a woman I do not care all that much for? Do you know that every single day I imagine returning to the tables, just for one roll of the die? One roll, Fran. I dream of it at night!" he cried. "And I still owe well over fifty thousand dollars to my creditors, not to mention another fifty thousand to Hart, who so generously helped me pay off LaFarge and saved my life in doing so."

"Hart doesn't care when he gets the money back, and once we are married, I am sure he will forgive the debt," Francesca whispered, aghast. "I thought you had gotten over the urge to gamble."

"I will never get over the urge," he said sharply. "Now, if you will excuse me, I really must greet Connie and Neil."

Francesca could not help herself. "Tell me one thing, Evan. If you do not care about Bartolla, why are you committed to her?"

He was angry. "I know you mean well, but you need to get the notion of a romance between me and Maggie out of your head! It is not happening, not now and not ever!"

She wet her lips. "I never suggested that you should have such a romance. But clearly, you have strong feelings for her."

He leaned close, his face grim. "You will find out eventually, anyway, so you may as well know. Then you can stop harassing me about Maggie!"

She recoiled, as he never spoke to her in such a harsh, rude and frightening way. It crossed her mind that her sunny-natured brother had changed, before everyone's eyes. "I will find out what?"

"The countess and I are eloping, sooner rather than later," he said, anger burning in his eyes, "because I have had the terribly good fortune of getting her with child."

WHEN BRAGG SLIPPED INTO the small, narrow foyer of his home, an hour later than expected, he was not sure of his reception. But just as Peter materialized, so did Leigh Anne. She was in her chair, of course, her nurse pushing her from the parlor, where, apparently, she had been waiting for him. Her green eyes were wide and worried.

"Sir?" Peter asked, as was his habit.

He had no coat to hand off, just a brown felt hat. "I will take supper later, in the study," he replied, his gaze on his wife.

Peter hesitated.

Leigh Anne's chair came forward. "I haven't dined yet," she said.

He was surprised. They hadn't shared a meal together in weeks. Even on Sundays, he had always found an excuse involving his work so that he might conveniently vanish.

She managed a slight smile. "But maybe we should have a sherry first."

He understood. "I'll take that," he told Mackenzie, moving behind the chair. Mackenzie and Peter left, and he pushed his wife's chair back into the parlor. The scene with O'Donnell tried to replay in his head, but he refused to allow it to do so. He had no intention of worrying his wife. Clearly, she was in a state of extreme anxiety already.

Leigh Anne never asked for anything, but the moment he had closed the doors, she said, her tone terse, "I will take a sherry, Rick, if you do not mind."

"Not at all," he said, pouring her a glass of wine. He handed it to her and their hands brushed, the brief intimacy making him ache for everything he did not have. Shaken by so much need, he walked away from her slowly.

"You aren't having a drink?" Her tone was sharp. "What has happened?"

He quickly turned. "Everything is fine, Leigh Anne," he lied.

She searched his eyes. "Did you see O'Donnell and his aunt?"

"Yes." He did not like lying to her, but he wanted to spare her the worry he was afflicted with. "He seems to be a changed man. Apparently he has given up alcohol and has become very devout. He seems to want to make amends, and visiting the girls is a part of that."

Her beautiful, perfect features filled with strain. "And that is all?"

He hesitated. "That seems to be all."

She seized the large, thin wheels and began to move them. He was shocked, as he had never seen her attempt to maneuver the chair before. Now she came right at him. "My instincts tell me this man is trouble, for us, for the girls!" she cried. "Rick, please don't coat this with sugar."

Her eyes filled with tears. He knelt before her and touched her face. Her skin was as smooth and soft as silk. She did not flinch. She looked at him as if begging for his help. A tear fell.

His heart tightened and he almost leaned forward to catch it with his lips. Instead, he said roughly, "I don't believe he has found God—or that God has found him. He's just a lowlife thug, Leigh Anne. He can't harm the girls and he certainly can't harm us."

She inhaled. "But what does he want? And did you speak with our lawyer? Can he hurt the adoption?"

He stopped the tear in its tracks with his thumb. "He probably hopes to extort a tidy sum from us."

"I knew it!" She seized his hand, gripping it tightly. "Just give him whatever he wants. I want both of them to go away."

He wanted to pull her close and comfort her, but he was afraid she would resist. He was acutely aware of her hand, clinging to his, and it was very hard not to raise it to his lips. "We decided to adopt the girls. I will make sure it happens. They need us—and we need them."

"I love them," she whispered, more tears falling. "Oh, Rick, I am so afraid. And Katie is afraid of that man—I saw it with my own eyes."

"He bullied her mother," Bragg said. "I don't want you to worry. I am going to take care of this. And I left a message for Feingold, so I will undoubtedly hear from him tomorrow, too."

Leigh Anne nodded, finally releasing his hand. She looked uncertain.

"Leigh Anne," he said softly. "I am the commissioner of police. O'Donnell is a lout, but he's not a complete fool. He knows better than to antagonize me."

"Have you told me everything?" she whispered.

He hesitated. "Yes," he lied.

She looked away, then back. "Rick? What if he is not lying? What if he has found God? What if…?" She stopped, unable to continue.

"What are you asking?" he said, his heart sinking. His wife was very clever, and clearly, she knew or at least suspected the truth.

"What if he wants the girls?" she cried. "He is their uncle. A judge would certainly decide that blood is thicker than water!"

He had to take away her fear and pain. He took her face in

his hands. "He hasn't found God and he does not want the girls: I want you to trust me," he said.

She closed her eyes, taking a deep breath. When she opened them, she said, "I do."

He still held her face in his hands, and now his heart changed its beat. She knew, because he felt her tense.

He almost kissed her, anyway. Instead, he let her go and stood. "Let's have that drink," he said.

"FRANCESCA!" CONNIE exclaimed, her face filled with worry as she rushed into the front hall.

Francesca had not moved after Evan crossed the hall and disappeared into the salon. She remained stunned, simply stunned, by his pronouncement. Now, of course, she understood. However, knowing Bartolla Benevente, she felt certain that nothing had been accidental.

She turned to her approaching sister. Connie was clad in a silk evening gown the color of moonlight with a triple-tiered diamond necklace around her slim throat and matching chandelier earrings. Connie was one of the most elegant women Francesca knew. She was also lovely. People often remarked that the sisters could have been twins, except for the fact that Connie was fairer in complexion and hair color than Francesca. If Connie favored ivory hues, Francesca chose golden ones. "Am I interrupting?" Francesca asked.

Connie grasped Francesca's hands. "We have several guests, but I don't care!" Her blue eyes were wide with concern. "Mama told me about Daisy Jones. Are you all right?"

Connie was Francesca's best friend, even though no two sisters could be more different. Connie had been a debutante while Francesca had been a student at Barnard College. Currently, she was a socialite, a society hostess, a mother and wife. Francesca was considered eccentric by most of society and she was now a renowned sleuth, which only heightened her reputation of strangeness. Yet somehow, they had always been confidantes. There had never been a time when Francesca had not been able to turn to her sister when in need, and that had always worked both ways. "I think I am beginning to recover from what has been a terrible day."

Holding her hand, Connie tugged and the two sisters ran down the hall, past the salon, where Francesca glimpsed a very important leader of the Progressive movement, and into the library. Connie closed the door and Francesca just stood there, preparing for a confession.

Connie took one look at her and pulled her into her arms. "You are putting up a brave front, Fran, but I can feel how worried you are."

Francesca hugged her back. "I am worried, but I am feeling much better than I was an hour or so ago."

Spending the past hour in Hart's arms had reminded her of how terribly in love she was and confirmed that her decision to stand by him, no matter what, was the right one. When they were alone together, she could feel the almost magnetic bond that coursed between them. In such moments, she had no doubts that he cared deeply for her.

Hart desperately needed her now. He had let his facade slip and she had seen how grief-stricken he was over the loss of his child. After their lovemaking, he had once again retreated into a somewhat cold and distant formality. Francesca could chalk some of his behavior up to grief, but she also knew he was at war with himself. His guilt over his behavior when first confronted by Daisy with the fact of the pregnancy—and his grief—were reflected in his eyes and there was no mistaking it. Francesca also suspected he continued to think that she would be better off without him now.

Connie led her to the gold velvet sofa, where they both sat down. A small fire leapt in the fireplace beneath an intricately carved wood mantel that had once graced the great hall of a sixteenth-century Austrian palace. Connie held both of Francesca's hands. "I am so sorry, Francesca. This is so terrible! But what, exactly, happened? Do you know who killed Daisy? Please, do not tell me that you and Hart are really suspects!"

"So Mama told you that Hart and I are suspects?" Francesca asked.

"Yes, and already word is out. I overheard two ladies at the luncheon counter at Lord & Taylor whispering about the murder and wondering if Hart had done it."

"He is innocent," Francesca said firmly, "but I am afraid he is a suspect. I, however, have a solid alibi."

"Thank God for that! Francesca, Hart would never murder anyone," Connie said, but her tone made it a nervous question.

"Connie, he is innocent and I am going to prove it. I am just hoping I can find the killer quickly, before this scandal becomes full-blown."

Connie stared at her for a moment. "What haven't you told me?"

Francesca had come to see Connie because she wanted to confide in her sister. "Even though I am certain that this will become news at some point, promise me that you will not say a word, not to anyone, not even to Neil—and certainly not to Mama."

"Very well, although I am quite nervous now. What bombshell is about to drop?"

"Daisy was pregnant with Hart's child when she was murdered," Francesca said.

Connie dropped Francesca's hands, turning starkly white. "Francesca!"

Francesca looked at her lap, surprised that she still ached in her heart over the unpleasant fact.

Connie inhaled. "Dear God! And the police think Hart killed the mother of his unborn child and that child?"

Francesca looked up very seriously. "He did not kill Daisy.

That is one fact I am sure of. They also suspect a woman, Rose Cooper."

It was a long moment before Connie spoke. "What are you going to do?" she asked.

Francesca knew exactly what she meant, but she said, "I am going to find the real killer. I have a lead, and I am going to Albany in the morning."

Connie seized her wrist. "That isn't what I meant and you know it."

Francesca met her gaze. "I was crushed at first. I was hurt and I felt betrayed. But Connie, Daisy became pregnant in February, before Hart and I became a couple—well before we became engaged!"

"Francesca, I do not care about the timing. No woman wants to learn that the man she loves has had a child with someone else."

"But the timing *does* matter. Connie, Hart has never lied to me about his past. When we became friends, I knew everything about him! He never tried to paint himself as a perfect gentleman. He even warned me that it was worse than I could imagine." Francesca gave a shaky laugh. "Of course, I never expected this."

Connie gave her a look. "That is hardly a relief, and this is no laughing matter."

Francesca barreled on. "And I knew all about Daisy when I accepted his proposal. The point is, he has never lied about his past and who he was. I agreed to marry him *knowing* that he'd had many affairs. Daisy's pregnancy was an accident. And, Connie, Hart needs me now. He is grieving over his lost child, even though he won't quite admit it. And he needs me to prove him innocent."

"Fran," Connie said, "have you even considered leaving him?"

"I love him," Francesca said, stiffening.

"Fran, he is accused of murdering both his mistress and his child! This is so serious. Even if he is proved innocent, how will polite society ever accept him again?"

Francesca was overcome with dismay. "Hart has never cared very much for polite society, and neither have I. Connie, he needs me—and I need you, now more than ever!"

Connie moved closer and put her arm around her. "I know you do," she said, and tears filled her eyes. "But this is unacceptable, Fran. Thus far, society has been able to ignore Hart's philandering. Now it will be the talk of the town." Connie looked closely at her. "Worse, people will debate whether he murdered his pregnant mistress or not!"

Francesca knew her sister was right. "Hart won't care."

"Really? And what about you? Won't you care what they are saying behind his back—and yours?"

Francesca inwardly cringed. "No, I won't care," she said, but the words felt hollow. She wanted to be strong enough not to care about any whispers, but the truth was, she did care.

Connie stood. "I don't believe you. It was only a few months ago that I would see you at a large charity event or a ball, standing by yourself, because other young ladies thought you odd and eccentric. Their gossip hurt you and you know it, Fran."

Francesca had to admit it. "Yes, their whispers did hurt, but I managed."

"So you are going to stand by Hart and marry him?" Connie was incredulous.

They shared a long, desperate look. Finally Francesca whispered, "But he didn't do it. I could never leave him now, when he is in such trouble. I will find the real killer, and eventually the scandal will be forgotten."

"Will it? Will it ever be forgotten? Hart has never tried to be a gentleman! You know as well as I do that he has always deliberately flaunted his inappropriate behavior to those who would object. He has delighted in doing so! This is their chance to get back at him. They are going to delight in his downfall," Connie cried. "I can feel all the knives coming out, and the points are being sharpened even as we speak!"

It was true. Until now, Hart did as he wanted and he had been accepted by society, anyway, because of his tremendous fortune. But he had spent most of his adult life mocking society openly. He had certainly flaunted his numerous affairs. His hosts and hostesses had turned a blind eye. But now his pregnant mistress was dead and he was a prime suspect. Francesca shuddered. No one would open their doors to Hart now. He would say he did not care, but the rejected child who still lived inside the man was going to be hurt very badly by this last rejection. "You have been in favor of this match. Have you changed your mind?" she asked slowly.

Connie did not hesitate. "Oh, Francesca! I will support whatever you decide to do. But society will have a field day with this! Hart is ruined. If you marry him, you will be tainted by association. I know that your life is sleuthing, but could you really live that way? And what about Mama and Papa?"

Francesca tried to imagine a future as Hart's wife, the two of them in his huge mansion, an island unto themselves. An image of Andrew came to mind, aggrieved and disappointed. His image was followed by Julia, who had been Hart's biggest supporter. Even her mother would be shocked by the scandal.

But they didn't need the rest of the world, as neither one of them cared about supper parties, balls and teas. He would continue his business affairs, she would continue to sleuth, and they would travel. And maybe, one day, they would have a family. She felt herself almost smile at the thought. Then she thought about that eventual time when the gossip reached their children's ears, and her smile froze.

"Mama and Papa will unite against your union, of that I have no doubt," Connie said. "Will you elope? I know you and Hart already discussed it."

"Eloping will be a last resort." Francesca knew that Connie was right. "And that is why I need you as an ally more than ever. I need you to help me win Mama and Papa back over."

Connie studied her with obvious resignation. "I have one more point to make. What if Daisy and the child had lived? Would you have been able to cope with Hart's having another family?"

Francesca winced. "What does it matter?" she asked, suddenly imagining Daisy, alive, with a small child in her arms.

"It matters. What if, one day, some other past lover appears—with his bastard in tow?"

Francesca's heart lurched. What would she do? Would there even be a choice? "I don't know," she said slowly. "Maybe we would have raised the child together, if Daisy would have allowed it."

Connie gave her a look. "Only you would come up with such a selfless solution."

"It doesn't matter. Daisy is dead. The child is dead. It's a terrible tragedy, but I am going to focus on the investigation at hand." Francesca stood.

Connie also rose to her feet. "You are so brave," she said. "How does Hart feel about your involvement?"

Francesca hesitated. She was afraid to tell her sister this last part.

"What aren't you telling me?" Connie asked slowly.

Francesca turned away, fighting the desire to confide the entire truth to her sister. But she had never needed a best friend more than she did now. She faced Connie again. "Hart's first reaction was to push me away. Hart doesn't want me involved, or hurt by association with him. He almost ended our engagement tonight, Con." She trembled at the recollection.

It was a moment before Connie spoke. Even then, she did so with care. "I would be very pleased if Hart forced you to withdraw from the investigation," Connie said. "And, at least temporarily, from his life."

Francesca worried now. "I should go," she finally said. "Tomorrow is going to be a long day."

Connie stopped her. "Fran? Please think very carefully about what you are doing. I know you love him, I really do. But you are about to become the victim of a monstrous scandal. Do you really need the heartache and the grief?" Connie bit her lip. "I hate to be the one to say it, but I love you, so I will. You should think about a future without Calder Hart in it."

CHAPTER TEN

Wednesday, June 4, 1902—5:45 a.m.

RAOUL DROPPED FRANCESCA AND Joel off at Grand Central Depot. As they hurried with the crowd toward the entrance of the huge limestone building, she heard a street vendor hawking newspapers. "Come an' read all about it! Murder's the name of the game! Come an' read all about it! Mistress slain!"

Francesca stumbled, praying she had misheard the young man. She turned, instantly locating a gangly adolescent boy in a felt cap, standing with a stack of newspapers, accepting a nickel from one gentleman. He started to shout at the rushing throngs again. "Come an' read all about it! Murder's the name of the game!"

"Miz Cahill? We got a train to catch," Joel said urgently.

Francesca heard him but did not reply, for she was already racing toward the newspaper boy. Before she reached him, she could see that he was selling the *Sun*—and she could see the prominent headline. Her heart lurched in dismay.

Ex-Mistress Slain; Calder Hart Suspect

Francesca seized the newspaper, instantly noting that Arthur Kurland had written the piece.

"Miss? That's five cents," the newsboy protested.

Francesca realized she would have to read the article on the train. She dug into her purse, the steel of her small gun hard against her gloved fingertips, and handed him the coin. Then she glanced toward the central tower of the depot where a huge clock faced the arriving world. It was ten minutes to six.

"Francesca," Hart said.

She gasped, whirling to face him. Hart was attired similarly to the other gentlemen on the street for a day of business, in a dark suit, white shirt and tie. He never wore a hat, and his black hair glinted in the early-morning sun. He did not smile at her. "What are you doing here?" she cried in alarm.

"I need to speak with you," he said, taking her arm.

"Hart!" She had a terrible inkling of what he wanted to say. "Not now! I need to make a six-fifteen train!"

"I know. You told me so last night." His eyes were dark and filled with unfathomable shadows.

"Don't do this!" she whispered.

"I care too much for you to hurt you this way," he said. "We can't go on, Francesca. I am a murder suspect. Today, the scandal erupts. And I won't have you a part of it."

"No," she protested frantically. "Damn it, Hart, I am not leaving you!"

His gaze became moist. "No, you're not. I am leaving you. Goodbye, Francesca," he said roughly. Before he turned to leave, he paused. "You are a miracle, Francesca."

She was in shock. She watched him pushing through the crowd, somehow comprehending that he had just ended their engagement—and their relationship. But he could not do this, because she would not, could not, let him. She ran after him, seizing his arm from behind. "I am not giving up on you!" she cried as he faced her grimly. "I am not abandoning you, not now and not ever!"

He disengaged himself, his face so taut it seemed in danger of cracking. He did not speak. He just looked at her, long and hard, and his eyes filled with tears. Then he turned away again. This time, his stride was brisk, carrying him swiftly away from her.

She was shaking like a leaf as she stared after him until the crowd swallowed him up. Tears were blurring her vision and she cursed, swiping at them. How could he do this? Why? But she knew why—he thought to protect her.

"Miz Cahill," Joel said tersely.

She recalled that Joel was present and that she had a case to solve—she had Hart's name to clear. She inhaled, wiping away the last of her tears, never having had more resolve. "Come on, we have a train to catch."

He was gazing at her with real worry and she tried to smile and pat him on the back.

"He didn't mean it," Joel said as they hurried inside. "He loves you, Miz Cahill. I mean, at least I think he does."

Francesca's heart cracked apart. Even though Hart was behaving in the most noble, selfless manner, what he had just done hurt beyond belief and comparison. "I think he does care for me, Joel. But you see, he has been accused of murder and he does not want me involved."

"I don't see," Joel said, as they hurried toward their gate, maneuvering though the crowds coming and going in the huge, marble-floored lobby of the train station. "You can find the real killer. He should want you involved!"

"People are going to say unkind and even cruel things about him," Francesca explained. "He doesn't want me there to hear those things."

Joel just shook his head. "But you can still get married. Because when you find the killer, no one will be mean to Mr. Hart anymore."

Francesca reached down to hug him. "Let's find the killer first."

IT WAS ONLY EIGHT, but Bragg had been at headquarters for more than an hour now. At the knock on his door, he slowly stood, his pulse accelerating. "Enter."

Sergeant Shea came in, gripping Mike O'Donnell's arm. The longshoreman was unshaven, bleary-eyed and in manacles. "Got your boy, C'mish," Shea said cheerfully. "An' he ain't very happy about it."

O'Donnell's expression was controlled, but Bragg could feel his anger. "Commissioner, sir," he said. "Am I being charged for a crime? 'Cause I just been dragged out of my bed!"

"You can take those off," Bragg said softly. He watched Shea unlock and remove the cuffs. "Thank you. Leave us."

Shea nodded and left, closing the door firmly behind him.

O'Donnell rubbed his wrists as if he'd been in shackles for hours. "I'm no criminal, sir," he said.

The man looked as if he had been drinking. Bragg circled him, but he could not detect the sour odor of last night's beer or alcohol. "I don't know. Should I charge you, Mike? Say, for extortion and blackmail?"

Bragg paused in front of him, their faces inches apart. The man's eyes were slightly bloodshot.

"Charge me? Charge me for extortion?" O'Donnell cried, his face the picture of aggrieved innocence. "Sir! This is unfair! I could never extort anyone, it is a sin!"

"Maybe you should have thought about the possibility that I could charge you with just about anything I choose—be it true or false—before you called on my wife and daughters."

O'Donnell was still, except for his chest, which heaved as he breathed. "Is that a threat?" he asked after a long pause. "I never asked for money. All I did was visit my girls. That's not a crime."

Bragg smiled tightly, not pleased that O'Donnell was sticking with his story. "We both know you have not found God and that you don't give a damn about the girls," he said flatly. *"How much do you want?"*

"They're my flesh an' blood," O'Donnell said, his expression relaxing, his tone earnest now. "And they belong with me. I feel certain it's what God wants. This isn't about money, sir."

Bragg had no patience left, not for this game. His wife was

upset and afraid. This ploy needed to end before it went any further. "God wants you to disappear," he snarled. "I want you to disappear. How much do you want?"

O'Donnell met his gaze, his expression deadpan. "Sir, I am not asking you for money. I have every right to see the girls. Beth an' me, we've been talking about it. How we can raise the girls. We can't give them all that you and your wife can, but we can get by. They're my nieces, sir, and they need to come home."

Bragg was in disbelief. O'Donnell was not going to crack!

O'Donnell smiled at him.

"Get out," Bragg said.

O'Donnell turned for the door when Brendan Farr, the chief of police, suddenly poked his head in. Bragg's tension skyrocketed. The chief had his own agenda, and Bragg did not trust him. "My door was closed," he said tersely.

"Sorry, boss," Farr said benignly. He was a very tall man with silver hair and pale blue eyes. "This a bad time?" He eyed O'Donnell as the blond man sauntered out. He turned back to Bragg. "I was hoping we could talk about Miss Jones's murder. The newsmen are having a field day, and we're looking bad—as usual."

Bragg sighed, rubbing his temples. "Come in, Chief."

Farr closed the door behind him. "Do I know that hoodlum who just left?"

"No." Bragg turned away. "I can't stop the reporters from writing their stories. But I will release a statement for the press before noon."

"And what will it say?"

He was not in the mood for games. "Whatever it is that you want to say, spit it out."

Farr's face hardened. "Yes, sir! Look, I know Hart's your half brother and I know he's engaged to Miz Cahill, but he's a real suspect here."

Bragg did not like Farr knowing that he and Francesca had

once had been romantically involved. "I am well aware of the facts of the case."

"We should bring him in for more questioning, but Newman's been treating him with kidskin gloves, just because he doesn't want to step on your toes."

Bragg realized with dismay that was probably the truth. Hart should be interviewed again, very thoroughly.

Farr saw the opening. "I can have my boys bring him in and I can do it."

"No." Bragg sat down behind his desk. "First of all, you have the entire department to oversee. You do not need to be personally involved in this case," Bragg said. He knew Farr had some kind of ax to grind, either against Francesca or himself. No good could come of his involvement in the case. Ironically, he now thought to protect Calder. "Newman can speak with Hart. But we'll do it uptown, at his home. He doesn't need to be dragged into HQ—the press will only write more misleading stories about that."

Farr nodded, his arms folded across his broad chest. If he was unhappy, he gave no sign. "I got one more thing to suggest, boss."

Bragg raised his brows, waiting.

"We need to search his house and his offices."

Farr was right. Inwardly, Bragg cursed. "Get a search warrant. Judge Hollister is usually accommodating."

Farr smiled. "Yes, sir. I'll put an officer on that right away." He started to leave.

"Farr!"

The chief of police halted and faced Bragg. "Yes, sir?"

"There'll be no search—none—until we have the warrant. When we do have it, I'm in charge."

Nothing flickered in Farr's eyes. "Yes, sir, I understand. Hollister may be in court. If so, we won't have a warrant until late tonight or first thing tomorrow."

Bragg nodded. "Just as long as we are clear."

"We are very clear," Farr said.

Bragg walked him watch out. Then he stood. O'Donnell was going to be a problem and he knew it. His worry had no bounds. He had to protect the girls and Leigh Anne, but he was going to have to wait for O'Donnell's next move. And then there was Hart. He could not help it—he was also worried about his brother.

CONNIE WAS VERY NERVOUS AS she was led down the corridor of Hart's huge home. She clutched her reticule tightly, reminding herself that she was fortunate to have found him at home. She had been prepared to travel to his offices on Bridge Street, however, for her sister's sake.

Connie followed Alfred, certain that her sister would not be very happy with her now. Had Fran known what Connie intended, she would have talked her out of it. Neil had advised that she not stick her nose into this affair, but she had tartly reminded him that Francesca was her beloved sister. She had to do what she thought was right. She had to convince Hart to break off his engagement to Fran.

Alfred knocked on the library door. Connie braced herself, because she was most definitely cornering the lion in his den. Hart was an enigma. He could be terribly charming and impossibly seductive, but he could also be blunt, rude and very difficult.

Hart appeared at the door, appearing uncharacteristically disheveled. He wore no jacket and no tie. His shirt was unbuttoned by two holes at the throat, revealing some dark hair there, and his sleeves were haphazardly rolled up to the elbows. "I said I did not wish to be disturbed," he said harshly. Then he saw Connie. There was no mistaking the fact that he flinched.

"I do beg your pardon, but Lady Montrose insisted she must see you, sir. As she is Miss Cahill's sister, I thought I must allow her in."

Hart looked past Alfred, as if he were no longer even there.

"This is not a good time," he said, and there was no mistaking his warning.

Connie's trepidation increased. "Good morning," she whispered hoarsely. Then she cleared her throat. "I know it is terribly early, Calder. I do apologize, and I could certainly come back later, if you insist. But I must speak to you, sooner or later, about Francesca."

An endless moment passed. Never taking his eyes from her, he said to Alfred, "That is all."

His words were very final and Alfred hurried away, not bothering to ask if they wanted tea or coffee.

Hart smiled at her, but it was a mere stretching of his lips. He gestured grandly—or mockingly—for her to come in. Connie knew that it was a mistake seeing him now, when he was so irritated and annoyed, but she hurried past him, breathing hard.

"Do I frighten you?" He laughed, walking past her toward his desk.

"Actually, this morning you do," she managed to say, her gaze riveted on him. She could understand Francesca's attraction, for once, briefly, she had felt it herself. Even now, there was something mesmerizing about his presence. Maybe it was the way he moved in such a predatory manner, as if he could barely control his own energy and strength. It was far more than his dark good looks, far more than his wealth and power. Perhaps it was his arrogance that was so fatally attractive to women.

"You are staring." He cut into her thoughts, lifting a glass from the desk.

Connie was shocked to realize he was drinking.

He smiled at her, but it was taunting. "I'd offer you a drink, but I feel certain you would decline."

And she knew then what made him irresistible. It was his anger, his wounded anger. It rippled through the man, making him unpredictable and dangerous. That was what the ladies found so fascinating, she decided. "Calder, are you all right?"

He saluted her and drank. Clearly he had no interest in providing her with an answer.

She bit her lip, wondering if she should have followed Neil's advice and stayed out of this affair. Then she took a step toward him. "Francesca told me everything last night," she said. "I am sorry for your loss."

He put his glass down and she saw that his hand was shaking. "Really? Forgive me, my lady, if I simply do not believe you."

She was thoroughly taken aback.

He smiled, but it came out a sneer. "Lady Montrose," he said, his tone as soft as silk, "we both know you are loyal to your sister. You must be thrilled that my mistress—excuse me, my ex-mistress—and my bastard are dead."

Connie hated being there. "Calder, I could not wish anyone dead, and especially not your child."

He shook his head. "As if you hoped my bastard would survive. And what then? Francesca and I should live happily ever after, with such a constant reminder of my black past?"

Why was he doing this? Connie wondered. She could see now that he was in pain. Fran had said he was grieving for his child, and she certainly understood that. "Francesca told me she would have raised the child with you," Connie said carefully. "You know how Fran is. She would have welcomed your child into her home."

He stared at her, his face stricken, and then he turned away from her, his body so rigid she thought it might snap. "Why the hell are you here?" he demanded, his back to her.

He needed comfort, she thought, and only Francesca could give it to him. Now was not the time to ask him to take a very high road, indeed. He was already down. How could she beg him to put Francesca first and break his engagement to her?

Because she loved her sister and she could not stand by and watch Francesca's life go up in flames.

Connie walked up to him, shaking with fear. She laid her

purse on a small table and put her gloved hand on his back. "I am sorry for your losses," she repeated, meaning it. "I am very sorry, Calder."

He whirled, clearly astonished by her gesture. Then his dark, gold-flecked eyes narrowed in suspicion. "What are you doing?"

She backed up. "I want to help."

"Are you thinking to seduce me?" he asked, angry and incredulous at once.

She was so shocked by his words that she gaped. She covered her mouth with her hand. Suddenly it was beyond amusing, and she was so nervous she laughed. "Calder! My sister loves you! I happen to love Neil! I was only offering you comfort!" She laughed again, helplessly, and then the laughter turned to tears.

He stared, noting the tears slipping down her cheeks. Finally, slowly, without anger, he said, "Women never offer me anything other than their bodies, Lady Montrose. Except for your sister, of course. So please forgive me for failing to appreciate your kindness."

She looked at him through her tears. He finally seemed sincere. He was odd, she decided, if he could not accept a simple gesture of sympathy from a woman without jumping to erroneous conclusions. Then she realized that *odd* was not the right word. He was jaded and terribly cynical—making him as different from her hopeful, optimistic sister as night and day. How did Francesca manage a relationship with such a dark man? "I understand," she said. "It doesn't matter. Calder, I know this is not the best of times, but I am terrified for my sister."

As if he hadn't heard her, he walked behind his desk. Connie watched him rummage through the jacket hanging on the back of the chair there. When he returned, he handed her a handkerchief, his initials embroidered on it.

She accepted it, wiping her eyes.

"Why are you here?" he asked harshly.

She finished drying her tears. "I know you are very fond of Francesca. I think you are even in love with her. I have been so happy for her—for you both." She prayed he would understand what she was about to say.

He waited.

She swallowed hard. "Calder, I can't stand by and watch my sister become a social pariah. If you really care for her, if you love her, you will surely break the engagement, so she does not go down in the flames of this scandal with you."

She thought she saw grief, anger and frustration all cross his face, shadowing his eyes. She knew she saw resolve. He finally said, "You are too late. I broke the engagement this morning. Your sister is finally free."

He strode past her to the door. There, he opened it widely, clearly wishing for her to leave.

Connie's heart beat madly. She understood his anguish now. Clutching her purse she went to the door. There, she dared to pause to face him, even though her instincts urged her to escape.

"Francesca has told me how good you really are. I can see that now. Thank you, Calder, thank you for protecting my sister."

His jaw ground down. "Get out."

Connie fled.

ALBANY WAS COLD. As Francesca and Joel traveled from the train station in an open horse-drawn buggy that was being passed off as a cab, she wished she had brought a coat with her. Although the sun was shining in a mostly cloudless sky, the pastures surrounding their route were muddy, and according to the loquacious cabdriver, last night it had snowed. "Might snow tonight, too," he cheerfully added. He turned to look at Francesca, several front teeth missing from his smile. "Ye need a coat."

"I have become rather aware of that," Francesca said. "How

far are we from the courts?" They continued to pass through a very rural area consisting mostly of dairy farms. Black-and-white cows grazed contentedly beside the road.

"Maybe five miles. The city's spread out, but all that's important is real close to itself."

Francesca quickly learned that the district court where Gillespie was seated was located in the city's civic center. A few moments later they reached the small two- or three-block area, where a handful of stately brick buildings had been built a century earlier. A quick inquiry to a passing gentleman yielded the information that the judge's offices were in the court building on the second floor. Several gentlemen, all carrying attaché folders, were coming and going as she and Joel climbed the wide front steps of the courthouse. Inside the spacious lobby, where several plaster columns formed a rotunda, Francesca saw a number of closed doors. Clearly, several court proceedings were in session. Above her, she saw gentlemen passing by on the mezzanine. To her right was a wide wooden staircase. She and Joel started up the stairs, Francesca hoping that Gillespie was not in session.

A moment later she found his office, his name engraved on the brass nameplate beside the door. Francesca told Joel that he could wait outside in the hall. A clerk with graying hair and spectacles opened the door to the office. "I am here to see Judge Gillespie," she said.

He seemed surprised. "I don't think the judge has any appointments scheduled for today, miss."

Francesca followed him into the antechamber where the clerk had a small desk. An equally small sofa was against one wall. The judge's dark wood office door was closed. The clerk went to the calendar on his desk. "No, he has no appointments today. I thought he might be in session until late."

Francesca glanced at the closed door. "But he is out of court?"

"Yes, but I am sorry. He won't see you without an appointment. However, I can make an appointment for you for next week."

Francesca smiled, handing him her calling card. "I am afraid that won't do, and I am sure the judge will see me. I am here to investigate a murder and I have traveled all the way from New York City today. More important, I am working with the police on this matter, as I frequently do. Commissioner Bragg encouraged me to meet with the judge. We both feel he could be helpful in solving this case."

The clerk was wide-eyed. "You're that female—I mean, that lady sleuth I read about!"

Francesca could not help being pleased. "Yes, I am. And this is terribly urgent. I'm afraid it cannot wait until next week."

"Let me ask the judge if he will see you," the clerk said to her. "I will do my best."

Francesca thanked him and paced nervously. Only an instant passed when Gillespie's door opened and he came out with his clerk.

The judge was of medium stature and build, with features that had remained distinguished and handsome in spite of his years. He had graying hair and blue eyes, and he greeted Francesca with some surprise and bemusement. "I am afraid I have not read about you as my clerk has," he said, shaking her hand and then glancing at her card. "But he tells me you are a very famous investigator and that you have solved some sensational cases."

"I am not certain I am all that famous," Francesca said with a smile. "But I have solved a number of cases. In each one, I worked very closely with the police, and I am assisting Commissioner Bragg now. Might I have a few moments of your time, Your Honor?"

"Of course," he said, seeming pleasant enough. He gestured, and she preceded him into his office. Unlike the Spartan antechamber, his office was wood-paneled and one wall contained a floor-to-ceiling bookcase filled with tomes. Behind his desk, a pair of windows looked out over the city square between the city government buildings. It was a lovely view of the small park, with some pedestrians passing through, and the horses and carriages queued up on the street.

Gillespie closed the door behind them, offering her a seat. Francesca took it and he sat down behind his desk. "How can I help you?"

Francesca spoke directly. "Do you know Miss Daisy Jones, Your Honor?"

He looked at her blankly. "I do not recall the name. It is unusual," he said, "almost comical, so I should think if I had heard it, or if I had met Miss Jones, I would at least vaguely recall it."

His blank look was at odds with his previous expressions—or so she thought. His denial almost seemed as if it was forced.

She had the strongest feeling that Judge Richard Gillespie knew Daisy Jones. "I have a sketch, made by a newspaper artist. Maybe you will recognize her."

He seemed indifferent. Francesca handed him that morning's *Tribune,* which she had snatched up just outside of her train's gate. A beautiful rendering of Daisy was on the front page, next to the headline, Prostitute Stabbed to Death. Anyone who knew Daisy would recognize her from the portrait.

Judge Gillespie took the page, glanced at it, and Francesca saw his hand begin to shake. He knew her—he was lying.

He quickly handed the front page back to her. He had become pale, but he smiled at her. "I am afraid I do not know Miss Jones," he said. His tone was strained.

Francesca slowly stood. "Your Honor, I am afraid I do not quite believe you," she said.

He gripped his desk, not rising.

Francesca thought he seemed distraught. "She knew you, and well, I think," Francesca said more softly. "I found an entire box of news clippings in her bedroom, and every single one of them contained a mention of you, Your Honor."

He continued to grip the edge of his desk, his knuckles white. "I did not know Miss Jones."

Francesca leaned over the desk toward him. "She was brutally murdered two nights ago, Judge Gillespie. Someone viciously stabbed her to death six times with a bowie knife. I am going to bring her killer to justice, but I need some help. If you knew her—and I am certain that you did—then help me find her killer. You are a judge. Your life is dedicated to the pursuit of justice!"

He did not look up at her. "I did not know her," he whispered harshly now.

Francesca felt her temper rising. "Well, she certainly knew you!" She took another card and laid it on his desk, not far from his hands. "I feel rather certain that the New York Police Department will want to speak with you. Whatever you know, we need to know it, too." She hesitated. "Daisy did not deserve to die. *Her child* did not deserve to die."

He flinched and looked up at Francesca. "She was with child?"

"Yes, she was."

And Gillespie moaned and covered his face with his hands. His shoulders began to shake. Stunned, Francesca realized he was weeping. She went behind him and laid her hand on his shoulder. "I'm sorry," she said. "I am so sorry for your loss. But please, help me now, so I can find her killer."

He pulled away. "You may be right. I think—" He choked, unable to continue.

Francesca was puzzled. "What do you think?"

"I think that she is my missing daughter."

tion; too much was at stake. "As you saw from the
owed you, Daisy—Honora—was a prostitute."
ute," he echoed, as if he had never before heard the
are you trying to say, Miss Cahill?"
a very expensive, very exclusive prostitute. Recently,
stress. Your Honor, why would she choose such a
e could have had a life of comfort and privilege in

e had become so oddly silent that Francesca could
breathing. "Dear God. I don't know."
could not decipher the look in his eyes. "There had
a reason that she left home," she began.
es that have to do with her brutal, vicious murder?"

now," Francesca returned softly. She would tell him
t another time, she decided. And she was not about
t her fiancé had been the man keeping Daisy.
ll destroy my wife," he said grimly. "Martha has
hor all of these years. She already suffered so vastly
disappeared from our lives. But now? I don't know
anage this. And my other daughter, Lydia, adored
er…she will be devastated. We have to bring Daisy
dded as he started to cry. His tears were very real.
d already known that Honora was turning tricks in
n he could be a suspect, too.
onor, I am sure you will be able to bring Daisy home.
ife will find out if you do not tell her. It is in all the
pers."
illespie held up his hand. "I will tell her—when the
."
s. Gillespie close to her oldest daughter?" Francesca

n to struggle for composure. "Of course they were
were very close. She adored Honora—as did I, and

CHAPTER ELEVEN

Wednesday, June 4, 1902—Noon

IN SPITE OF HER CONFUSION, elation swept through Francesca.
"You think she's your daughter?" Was this the connection to
Daisy's past that she had been hoping for?

Gillespie choked on a sob. "She looks exactly as Honora did,
but Honora, she…she left home…many years ago."

Francesca was almost certain that Gillespie had known that
his daughter was Daisy Jones from the start. From the moment
she had mentioned Daisy, his behavior had subtly changed. She
was operating on instinct now. If he had known that Honora was
Daisy, then he had probably known that his daughter had left
home to become a prostitute, Francesca thought. But she wasn't
sure he had known that she was dead. He appeared to have been
genuinely shocked by the news of her murder.

Francesca could comprehend why he had denied knowing
Daisy. He was a judge with a reputation to guard. He would not
want to admit that his daughter had become a woman of the
streets.

"Sir, if Daisy was your daughter, I am terribly sorry for your
loss," she said sincerely.

He inhaled. "Thank you."

Francesca hesitated. "You are very distraught. But before you
grieve, we should decide whether or not Daisy Jones really was
Honora."

He looked at her, ashen. "I know she's dead," he whispered. "I just do."

"Because you knew she had become Daisy?" she had to ask.

His jaw tightened. "I didn't know. She left us, without a word. There was not a single letter— God, it was as if she hated us!"

Francesca absorbed that. "May I sit? Can we try to discern whether or not Daisy and Honora was the same person?"

"Yes, of course, we must do just that." Suddenly his eyes filled with tears. "Martha—my wife—how will I tell her?"

Francesca waited for him to compose himself. He seemed truly shocked by Daisy's murder, but she knew very well that appearances could be deceiving. "I knew Daisy. We were friends."

"You knew her?" He seemed surprised.

"Yes, but not well," Francesca said. "I met her when I was on a case. Sir, it had always been obvious to me that Daisy came from a very genteel background. I learned from another friend of hers that she first came to the city eight years ago, having run away from home. You just said she left you?"

Gillespie replied. "Honora left home when she was fifteen years old. That was eight years ago—eight years and two months. She vanished in April."

This was the proof, Francesca thought. The dates could hardly be a coincidence. "Her friend told me that she was fifteen when she first arrived in the city. Given those facts and her resemblance to Honora, I think we can agree that Daisy was your daughter."

Gillespie just sat there. Francesca knew she was going to have to press him, but that could wait. His wife didn't even know about Daisy's—Honora's—death yet.

Gillespie finally said, "It's Honora. That sketch—it's identical to my daughter. I have a portrait of her at the house, painted on her fifteenth birthday, just two months before she went away. You'll see."

Francesca had to speak with
"I should love to see it, Your Hon

He suddenly looked her right i
did this to my daughter," he cried
to justice."

"The killer will be brought to ju
said. "Sir, I want to respect your g
tions I am going to have to ask if
was a crime of passion. Someone
her dead, and was very angry wh
afraid this investigation will be a

"I understand completely," he s
may have been killed by a woman

Francesca paused. She had to
Gillespie *hadn't* known Honora wa
known she was a prostitute until F
ing headline, and he didn't know t
lover, either. Even if he had known
she had been living, Francesca felt
doubt that he had loved his daugh
now.

"Miss Cahill." He was sharp. "
reluctant? What are you keeping fr

"Quite a bit," she said grimly. "
with your family before you learn
but it is very sensational, and the c
read any of the New York newspap
do, you are going to learn these fa
They will be difficult for you to un
go home, sir, and speak with your
conversation tomorrow."

He slowly rose to his feet. "I w
telling me. I want to know all of th

Francesca did not want to wait

her investig
headline I s

"A prosti
word. "Wha

"She was
she was a m
life, when s
society?"

The offi
hear her ow

Francesc
to have bee

"What d
he cried.

"I don't
about Rose
to reveal th

"This w
been my an
when Daisy
if she can
her older si
home," he
But if he h
the city, th

"Your H
And your
city newsp

"No!" C
time is rig

"Was M
asked.

He beg
close. The

as did her sister. Honora was beautiful and perfect in every way."
He paused.

"I want to see my daughter."

Francesca thought that was a very good idea. She wanted
Gillespie in New York City, where she and Bragg could interview
him at length. In fact, she wanted the entire family there.

"I think the police will want a statement from you, sir," she
said. "I happen to have a train schedule—"

He waved at her. "I am in the city frequently and know when
the trains run." He finally walked away from his desk to stare
out of the window at the city square. "I have to go home and tell
Martha that our daughter is dead," he said. "Dear God, how did
this happen? Why did she have to leave us in the first place?"

"You said she did not leave a note when she ran away?"

"No. She just left. At first, we worried that she had been
abducted from her own bed." He faltered. "She was so perfect,
Miss Cahill, and so beautiful. She was graceful, witty, charming
and kind. Everyone who knew her loved her. We had such plans
for her. She would have been a debutante the following year,
and one day, a great society hostess. There were no doubts that
Honora was special."

Francesca could imagine Daisy as a young lady and felt that
Gillespie had not exaggerated. "There must have been a reason
for her to leave like that. Perhaps your wife knows, or your other
daughter?"

"It has been years," he cried. "Why does it matter?"

"It might not matter—or it might be extremely relevant to
her death," Francesca said. "I am afraid that, at this point, I can
leave no stone unturned." She gave him a chance to assimilate
that. "I suppose the police ruled out an abduction?"

He turned away.

"Judge?"

"She went to bed that evening and was gone in the morning.
Lydia saw that she had taken a bag with clothes and jewelry.

So we immediately knew that it was not an abduction, Miss Cahill."

"You did not call the police?" This was very interesting indeed!

"It was bad enough that she was gone. I wanted to spare my wife and younger daughter any scandal."

Was that true? Or had he hoped to spare *himself* a scandal—protecting his own reputation at the expense of finding his daughter?

"We even considered that she might have run off with some young man—although Martha and I felt certain she hadn't been seeing anyone. Lydia assured us, as well, that there was no young man in Honora's life."

"I will have to speak with your wife and daughter at length, as soon as possible." She didn't add that she would also interview him again.

"They don't even know that she was in New York all of this time, selling herself to the highest bidder!"

"When will you be going to New York?"

"Tomorrow. I will be on the first train. I have to see her!"

"Maybe you can bring your wife and daughter with you."

His gaze widened. "I don't know. I can't seem to think clearly—yes, perhaps they should come."

"It would be very helpful to the investigation," Francesca told him, firmly but gently.

"I will take that into consideration," Gillespie said, very much speaking as if he were on the bench. "Miss Cahill, I need some time alone before I go home."

She understood completely. "Of course you do. Judge? I am very sorry. I liked Daisy very much. In spite of how she lived, she was a lady."

He brushed the rising tears. "Thank you."

Francesca nodded and started for the door.

"Miss Cahill? I will be staying at the Fifth Avenue Hotel. You may reach me there."

THE COUNTRYSIDE HAD CHANGED. Francesca stared out of the window of the speeding train, Joel napping beside her, his cheek on her arm. Farms and pastures were finally giving way to factories, busy cobbled and dirt streets, shops and tenement buildings. Working men and women with sacks of groceries were rushing on foot to their homes. They had reached the Bronx, but there would be no more stops until they arrived at the Grand Central Depot. She hugged herself, her heart aching terribly.

She had made copious notes about the case, until she could no longer avoid the huge hurt she had buried deep inside her chest. She would be home in an hour or so—and just ten blocks from Calder Hart's. Very, very shortly, she would be back in the city, and she could no longer avoid her feelings—or him.

She didn't see a single building, a single wagon, a single person or tree as the train raced on.

I am not leaving you.

No, you are not. I am leaving you, Francesca.

In the three months of their engagement, she had learned that his first response to a personal crisis was to withdraw from her and try to push her away. He did not like discussing his feelings, and certainly not his fears.

She had seen his guilt and grief and knew he was afraid of the future. These were matters she wished to discuss, and she was not giving up, even if this rejection had felt so final. Surely, when this case was closed and the real killer had been brought to justice, Hart would come back to her.

But Francesca could not deny her feelings. She was filled with doubts. She was very afraid. One of the problems with Hart was that he was so unpredictable. Only last month, he had confessed to her that he was falling in love with her. Francesca had been thrilled. Now she realized her elation should have waited. Leave it to Hart to refuse to admit to solid feelings of affection. If he had been falling in love with her, had he now simply changed his mind and resolutely brought that process to a halt? No one could be more stubborn and more effective than Hart. It was a reason she so admired him; now it was the reason she was so afraid.

This morning, he had meant what he had said, that their engagement was off. She had seen the anguish in his eyes, and knew it hadn't been easy for him.

She had told him she would never give up on him. In her mind, this was a temporary separation. Had he understood that? And if so, where, exactly, did that leave them?

She already missed him. Was she still allowed to call on him at whim? Why should she wait for their paths to cross when she desperately wanted to see him? When she desperately *needed* to see him? More importantly, once she saw him, she would have a better idea of the mood he was in. Maybe he was having regrets and a change of heart.

Her decision was made. She would make a quick stop at home to change her clothes—she wanted to look beautiful and attract all of his male interest and attention—and she would go directly to Hart's. Her train was arriving at half past six; she should be at Hart's shortly after eight o'clock.

FRANCESCA WAS SO INVOLVED in her decision to call on Hart that she had not thought about the morning's newspapers. But the moment she started through the spacious front hall of her home, her mother appeared, stepping out of the dining room. Julia was as pale as a ghost, her distress apparent. Instantly, Francesca remembered the terrible headlines and she halted, one foot on the bottom step, her hand on the brass railing.

"Francesca," Julia said, her voice hoarse. "Your father wishes to speak with you."

Francesca stepped away from the stairs. There was no doubt in her mind that both of her parents had seen the *Sun,* at least. The house was terribly quiet, which told her there were no supper guests. That was odd. Julia entertained every day of the week except for Sundays and Mondays, or she and Andrew went out.

Julia easily read her thoughts. "We canceled our plans to go out tonight, Francesca. Neither one of us was in a social mood."

Francesca approached her mother. "Mama, we discussed this earlier. Hart is innocent. Do not believe whatever you have read." But she kept her voice low, not wanting to alert Andrew to their conversation. Julia would surely move back to her side!

"Francesca, you know how fond of Hart I am. You know how thrilled I have been that you have managed to get engaged to him. I don't think he murdered anyone."

For some reason, Francesca was not relieved. "Thank you for your faith and loyalty."

Julia raised her hand. "Stop! It doesn't matter whether Hart is innocent or guilty. This scandal is simply unacceptable and you cannot be a part of it."

Francesca was in disbelief. Julia had been their biggest ally, their greatest supporter. "How can you say that his innocence doesn't matter? Of course it does! Mama, I love Hart. I am not going to back down now. He will be proved innocent and this terrible scandal will fade away and disappear. One day, it will be entirely forgotten."

"You may be right. On the other hand, this scandal may follow Hart for the rest of his life—unless he moves to Paris. But it might even follow him there!"

Francesca found it hard to breathe. "So what are you saying? You no longer approve of my marriage to Calder?"

Julia's face collapsed. "I have to protect you, Francesca. You are my child."

"I am a grown woman," Francesca cried in anger now. "Mama, I am begging you, do not oppose my marriage. I need you on my side." She felt frantic—a very rare moment for her.

Julia wiped the tears that had appeared. "Your father wishes to speak to you. He is in the dining room."

"I have to go out," Francesca said tersely.

Julia was incredulous. "Francesca! Andrew wishes to speak to you!"

Francesca steeled herself, hardly able to believe that she would be so disrespectful as to go out without giving her father a word. But she did not want that confrontation now.

It did not matter what she wanted, she realized, for Andrew had come into the hall, his face terribly sober, the light in his eyes as grim.

Francesca knew what he would say. She rushed to him. "Papa, you have always respected my judgment and my choices. You have been proud of me because I am an independent thinker. Do not do this!"

"Francesca." He actually hugged her. "You are right. I have allowed you the freedom of choice and action that no one I know allows their daughter. But like your mother, my duty is to protect you. I have been opposed to Hart from the start. Like your mother, I do not care whether he is innocent or not."

"That is not fair," she said bitterly.

"Life is not fair, and I know you know that." He hesitated. "I already ended the engagement, but neither you nor Hart seemed to listen or to care. I will not allow the marriage, Francesca, not now—and not ever."

In that moment, Francesca realized that her father, the most kind and rational of men, was going to close his mind forever to Calder Hart, and the choice she must make became crystal clear. It saddened her to no end.

"Did you hear me?" he asked quietly.

And because she had no intention of ending the future she had planned with Hart, she did not tell her father that Hart had ended their engagement that morning. "Yes, I did. I am very sad, Papa," she said as quietly.

"You will recover. I know you do not think so, but you are only twenty-one years old. Eventually, you will find someone else."

"There is no one else," she said calmly.

His eyes widened. It took Andrew a full moment to understand. "You are going to disobey me?"

"I am afraid so," she said evenly, but her heart raced with sickening speed.

He was shocked. "Francesca, I forbid the marriage! I forbid your seeing him, period!"

Behind them, Julia gasped.

Francesca wasn't certain she had ever been so hurt. A lifetime of memories flashed through her mind. She saw herself as a child eagerly and adoringly following her father about the house or his offices, soaking up his every word. There were other moments, too, sitting in his lap while he read to her, or his tending to her skinned knee. And later, as a young woman, there were the fierce debates they had shared, with one of them playing the devil's advocate, as they were always on any issue's same side.

"Papa," she whispered. "I wish you weren't making me choose, but you are. I am choosing the man I love, the man I trust, the man I believe in. I am choosing the future I am determined to have."

Andrew had turned white. "First Evan," he whispered in shock and disbelief. "But you, Francesca, you would oppose me this way?"

Nothing had ever been harder than turning away from the man she had loved, respected and admired for her entire life. She wiped away the moisture that was gathering in her eyes. "I can't stay here anymore." She closed her eyes, realizing that it was true. "I will move in with Connie."

Julia cried out. "Francesca! You can't mean it!"

Francesca smiled sadly at her. "I love you both. But Hart is in a difficult time. I am not abandoning him because of a temporary crisis. I wish you both could be supportive of me. But as you are not, yes, I do mean it. I am moving out."

Julia sat down on the stairs, tears running down her cheeks.

Andrew had not moved. "Francesca, I am your father. No one, *no one,* loves you more than I do!"

"And I love you, too," Francesca said. She hugged him briefly, kissing his cheek. "When Hart and I marry, you will always be welcome in our home." She realized she would not be changing her clothes. She had to leave, before she lost all control, breaking down in tears.

Francesca went back across the hall, aware of her parents standing at its opposite end by the sweeping staircase, in shock and disbelief. She vaguely smiled at the doorman, and as he blanched, she realized he had heard every word. "Have Raoul meet me at Hart's," she told him, her tone tremulous. She had no intention of waiting a half an hour for her carriage; she would take a cab.

"Francesca." Julia ran after her.

Francesca faced her mother and hugged her, hard. "Don't worry, Mama. It will all work out in the end. You shall see."

"Will it?" Julia cried, weeping.

"Yes, it will." She meant her every word.

CHAPTER TWELVE

Wednesday, June 4, 1902—9:00 p.m.

FRANCESCA STARED UP AT the elegant and imposing front entrance of Hart's home, past the pair of life-size limestone lions there, still stunned and shaken. The breakup with Hart had been hard enough to bear; now she knew she had hurt Andrew and Julia to no end. Yet there had been no other choice.

She slowly went up the front steps. A part of her was ready to rush into Hart's arms and tell him what had just happened, for she found so much comfort in his strong embrace, but she did not know what her reception would be. And even if he was pleased to see her, he had his own problems now. He did not need any additional burdens. Francesca realized that she was not going to tell Hart what had happened a few moments ago. Besides, facing him now was no simple or easy task. She needed all of her courage and all of her conviction.

Trepidation rising in her, Francesca waited for the door to be opened. Alfred did not seem surprised to see her, but then, Francesca didn't think Hart would tell his butler that he had ended his engagement. In fact, Hart might not have said a word to anyone. That would be a relief, indeed.

Alfred ushered her into the front hall. There, in the glow of the overhead chandelier, Francesca saw that he was worried. "I know it is late, but I need to speak with Calder. Alfred? Is something amiss?"

"I am afraid so," he said seriously. "It is Mr. Hart, Miss Cahill. I am afraid he is in one of his moods."

"What kind of mood?" Francesca asked warily. When she had first met Hart, Alfred had let her in on one of his employer's secrets. Hart would frequently dismiss the entire staff, so that he was alone in the huge house. Fearing for his employer, Alfred would retreat to the kitchens but not leave. Hart, unaware he was not as alone as he had intended, would then wander the halls, staring at his art while drinking heavily. Francesca still did not understand what dark despair drove him to such strange and solitary behavior.

Alfred, of course, had also witnessed his extreme temper, and his moments of cold, cruel reserve. Francesca did not think he could have dismissed the staff to indulge himself in an alcoholic binge, as his house contained too many guests. But with Hart, one simply never knew what was coming next.

"It is hard to say, Miss Cahill. He did not go to his offices this morning. He spent most of the day in the library, refusing all callers except one. I am afraid he was drinking. He seemed very distressed. Early this evening he went up to his rooms and I have not seen or heard from him since. I sent up a supper tray, but he would not answer the door and I did not dare take it inside."

Now Francesca was worried, very much so. "Was he inebriated when he went up to his rooms?"

"Mr. Hart can hold his liquor. So I would say, no, he was not."

"Who called?"

"Your sister."

Francesca was very surprised, and instantly, she was suspicious. If Connie had called on Hart to interfere in her relationship, she was in for a major set-down. Francesca was beginning to feel as if the entire city was aligned against their future together. "Is anyone home?"

"At this hour? No," Alfred said. "I do not expect Mr. Rourke back until much later. As for Mr. D'Archand, it is hard to say, but he also keeps late hours. Mr. and Mrs. Bragg will not be back until next week."

Francesca hesitated, trying to decide what to do. Alfred said, "Miss Cahill? I spoke to the police as we discussed. But I have seen the newspapers. We all have. How deeply in trouble is Mr. Hart?"

Instantly Francesca forgot her own worries and fears. "Alfred," she said reassuringly and firmly, "Hart is innocent. I am going to prove him innocent. But I am very moved that you care so much for him. And thank you for your loyalty," she added carefully.

He clearly understood. "We are all concerned," Alfred said. "He is a good employer, even with his moods."

Francesca was brought back to her own dilemma. "Alfred, can you tell Hart I am in the library and that it is urgent that I speak with him? I mean, I should understand if you are reluctant to go upstairs."

Alfred smiled grimly. "I have had to corner the lion in his den many times over the past six years," he said. "I will tell him you are here."

Francesca's heart began to beat far too swiftly for comfort. As Alfred went upstairs, she went to the library, her nervous anxiety escalating wildly. In just a few minutes, she was going to face Hart. She was afraid he had not changed his mind about her. She began to gather all of the arguments she would make. Then she reminded herself not argue about their relationship— she would discuss the case with him instead.

Francesca was standing in the center of the large room, trying to remain calm, when she felt him come to the threshold of the room. She slowly turned.

Hart leaned on the wall in the open doorway, appearing disheveled. There was a five-o'clock shadow on his jaw, and wisps of short, dark hair curled randomly against his temples and forehead. His white shirt was unbuttoned well past the throat. The shirt was in dire need of a pressing and his sleeves were rolled haphazardly up.

She forced a smile, her heart pounding. "I have just returned from Albany," she said brightly. "I found Judge Gillespie."

His expression remained impassive and impossible to read.

She faltered, wringing her hands. "He is Daisy's father, Calder. Her real name is Honora Gillespie."

"What are you doing here?"

She stiffened in dread. "Hart, don't you want to hear what I have found out?"

"Not really." He launched himself off the wall, his strides long and leisurely, at odds with the tension she sensed. He did not quite approach; he circled around her and walked toward the glass doors that opened onto the night. "I told you quite a few times that I do not want you on this case."

When he behaved like this, she was afraid. She was afraid it was too late, that he no longer cared and that she had already lost him. "I am not abandoning you in your time of need."

He faced her, his gaze raking over her features, shooting back to her eyes, where she was afraid all of her hurt and confusion showed. "But I don't need you, Francesca. Haven't I made myself clear?"

She was terribly taken aback. "We both know you do need me—or at least, you need my sleuthing services. Even if you do not want me involved in this case, it's too late. I *am* involved—not because I told Rose I would find the killer, but because I am not letting you down. Not now," she said, swallowing hard, thinking of a future apart from him, "and not ever."

"You are exasperating," he warned.

She shook her head. "No, Hart. You are the stupidly exasperating one!"

His brows rose in some surprise. "Now I am stupid?"

She was aware that she was losing all control of her emotions. "Do not even think to turn my words around. You are a difficult man. At times like these, you are beyond difficult, beyond unreasonable. And you are arrogant! We have been friends, partners and lovers for some time. But you decide without consulting me that it is over, just like that?"

"Welcome to the world of men," he said, but he never looked away, his gaze terribly intent.

She shivered. "What does that mean?"

"It means you are naive enough to have no clue that when a rogue is done, he is done, and it is never a two-way street."

She was going to break down, Francesca thought as his meaning became painfully clear. She fought to keep her composure about her, and her pride. "Fine. Jilt me, then. Papa feels certain I will find someone else, someone better, and maybe he is right."

His face darkened. "Oh ho! Do you think to madden me with jealousy? I set you free this morning, Francesca, and damn it, your father is right. One day there will be someone else. I will be first in line to send you a wedding gift," he snarled.

"Don't send me any presents!"

He gave her a long look and turned away.

She hesitated, then gave in to her impulses and ran after him. She seized his arm, forcing him to face her. "When you pursued me, when you seduced me, when you made me fall in love with you, then it became a two-way street, Calder. I am not like the other women you have chased."

Reluctantly, he said, "No, you are not like any other woman. I will concede that. Don't do this, Francesca."

She shook her head. "Don't do what? Don't make this hard for you? Don't make you hurt, the way I am hurting? How well do you know me, Calder?" she demanded. She was very angry now.

"Very well," he said more quietly, his gaze riveted on hers.

"If you know me so well, then you know I would never give up on you. If you really are tired of me, if you really wish to end our engagement, we both know, in the end, I will have to concede defeat. But I am your friend. I am your best *friend*, goddamn it. In times of danger, in times of need, friends stay the course! So end the affair, if you will. That only means you are a coward! But I am not leaving this case. I am going to find Daisy's killer. And when you are free of all suspicion, well, you can wander these halls all by yourself. No, better yet, you can find some whore to warm your bed and *I* will be the first to line up and congratulate you on a life well done!"

He smiled without any mirth whatsoever.

"Nothing I have said is amusing," she snapped. She had the feeling she had gone too far but she had meant her every word.

"I have done nothing to deserve a woman like you."

Relief overcame her and her knees buckled. Hart reached out to steady her. She clung to him in return. What did this mean? she wondered frantically. Was he finally going to give in and change his mind?

He did not try to release her. "I hate hurting you this way. I hate myself today."

She leaned closer, but he did not pull her into his embrace. "There is no need. I could never hate you. We are in this together, whether you want it or not."

He cupped her cheek. "Why can't you understand? I could never live with myself if I remained engaged, Francesca. I would hate myself even more than I now do. I am protecting your good name. I will continue to do so, no matter what you think, no matter what you say. Nothing is more important to me, not even proving my innocence."

"I don't want my good name protected!"

He shook his head. "Yes, you do. You merely do not realize it just yet."

He was resolute, she realized, disbelieving.

"But you are right. Friends do not jump ship at the first sign of inclement weather. We will always be friends, won't we?" he said, and she heard the uncertainty in his tone.

He wanted reassurance, she realized, dumbfounded. Her heart ached impossibly. "Hart," she said, only managing a whisper, "I will always be your friend."

He nodded and walked away from her. "I feel the same way."

Francesca dropped into the closest chair, incredulous. Why did he have to want to protect her reputation so badly, when he had never cared about his own?

He faced her from a careful distance. "I had my office release a statement to the press earlier today. It will be in all the morning papers."

She stiffened. "What kind of statement?"

"I announced that our engagement was over," he said. Softly, he added, "I am sorry, Francesca."

She just sat there staring at him, loving him so much that hope refused to expire. He wasn't going to change his mind—at least not now, not in the midst of this investigation, and maybe, not ever. It was hard to think, and even harder to know what to do. She tried to imagine a future in which they were merely good friends. It was impossible. "Do you still care about me?" she heard herself ask. "Or is this case a convenient means of ending an affair that no longer interests you?"

He wet his lips, never looking away from her. "I will never stop caring," he said.

She realized he was struggling to appear calm. Slowly, she stood. "Then don't do this."

"Don't," he warned.

She could not stop herself. She walked to him, determined, reaching for his shoulders.

"Don't," he said again, with some desperation flaring in his navy-and-gold eyes.

She ignored him, standing on tiptoe, pressing her mouth to his.

He did not move; his lips were firm and closed beneath hers. Francesca kissed him again, and then again, more insistently, and again, and even though he refused to respond, desire rose in a swift crescendo until he seized her in his arms, kissing her back.

Her mind rested, overcome by waves of dizzy relief. He kissed her urgently, mindlessly, hot and hard and openmouthed, as if this might be the last kiss they ever shared, and she knew his control had snapped. Francesca reached for his shirt, unbuttoning it and pulling it open, so she could run her hands up and down his broad, hard chest and solid, sculpted torso. His skin was smooth and warm. His chest hair was coarse, like the stubby hair on his jaw. He gasped, breaking the kiss and pushing her away from him.

Francesca was dazed from consuming desire. He made no move to close his shirt, which hung open, outside his pants, revealing a muscular body more fit for an athlete than an urban businessman.

"That doesn't help," he said hoarsely, his chest rising and falling.

"I had a point to prove," she managed to say as breathlessly.

"I told you—I will always care, and I will always want you." He finally reached for his shirt, buttoning it. "What difference does it make? You have brought out my noble side, Francesca, and I am not changing my mind. No matter what will remain between us, I am protecting you now."

"Fine," she said, trembling. But she was beginning to realize that, if he still cared and he still wanted her so passionately, there was hope. "The engagement is off, but we are friends and you shall continue to protect me from your big, bad self."

He gave her an undecipherable look.

"And Calder?" She smiled at him now, as sweetly as possible.

"You have the power to break up with me, but you do not have the power to stop me from investigating Daisy's murder."

"Oh, Francesca. Do not push me now, my darling."

"Why? Because you are angry with yourself for being an idiot where we are concerned?"

His smile was dangerous. "I am angry at life. As I said, do not push me now."

She decided to let go. "Do you want to hear about Gillespie?"

Walking over to the bar cart, he poured two very hefty Scotches. She was pleased to notice that his hands were shaking. Then he carried a drink to her. Francesca accepted it, noticing that he was careful not to touch her as he handed her the glass. "Yes."

She felt more satisfaction then. If he wanted to know the progress she was making, it would keep them involved. She sat down, taking a good long sip of the Scotch. She had never needed a drink more. The alcohol warmed her instantly, and she waited for it to have its intended effect. She wanted the tension in her to dim.

Hart clearly needed the drink as much as she did, for he did not press her to reveal that day's discoveries. He sipped his Scotch, staring at it very thoughtfully. No matter their current status, Francesca felt the same bond she always had with him. He slowly glanced up at her. His eyes told her he felt it, too.

Managing as his friend would be difficult, if not impossible, she thought with savage pleasure. It occurred to her that, instead of accepting his dictum, she could use every wile she had to attempt to seduce him. She knew that if she could get him to take her virginity, he would marry her, no matter his intentions today.

She began to like the idea, oh yes.

"I can feel you scheming," he remarked. "So, tell me about Gillespie."

Her thoughts veered to the case at hand. She leaned forward

eagerly, about to describe her meeting with Gillespie, when Alfred appeared on the room's threshold. Although they both looked up, he knocked lightly on the open door.

Hart was his usual abrupt self. "I asked that we not be disturbed."

Alfred shot Francesca a very worried glance. "Sir, it is the police. I think you had better come into the front hall. They have a warrant to search the house."

FRANCESCA HURRIED INTO THE front hall with Hart, Alfred behind them. Bragg was waiting there, his hands in the pockets of his dark brown jacket, Inspector Newman a portly figure at his side in an ill-fitting suit and a battered felt hat. Four officers in uniform stood behind them, staring at the life-size nude sculpture on the other end of the front hall. The moment she entered the marble-floored room, Bragg's gaze leapt to hers. In that single instant, she realized he knew about the failure of her engagement, for his expression changed, tightening. He glanced at Hart, looking disgusted and angry at once.

Hart's strides ate up the room. He halted before Bragg. "You have a warrant to search my house?"

Bragg glanced at Francesca again. "I'm afraid so. Given all of the evidence, there was no other choice."

Hart's smile was nasty. "There is always another choice."

Bragg handed him the document. "Why don't you read it?"

"No, thank you. You would never trump up such an important document, now would you?" He whirled, gesturing at the rest of his house. "Please, feel free. I have nothing to hide."

Francesca's heart was leaping wildly. She wished Rick had not done this. But of course, the police would not find anything, unless they found more evidence of his involvement with Daisy.

"Calder," Bragg said sharply. "I need that note Daisy sent you, asking you to meet her that night."

"I can't find it." Hart shrugged mockingly at him, as if to say, tough luck.

Bragg grimaced and turned to her, lowering his tone. "Are you all right?"

"I am fine," she lied, too brightly. She glanced nervously at Hart, but he was pretending to ignore them. "What do you expect to find here, Rick? Hart is not the murderer."

He sighed. "Francesca, Chief Farr approached me about the need to search the house. And he is right. It would be remiss of the department not to take a good look around Hart's home."

"Farr!" she exclaimed in disgust. "I still think he is up to no good."

He touched her arm. "Let's talk privately."

Unable to stop herself, she glanced at Hart. He had been very jealous of her friendship with Bragg until recently and she had no desire to provoke him now.

But he no longer pretended to ignore them. His smile flashed, as cold as ice. "By all means, have a little tête-à-tête. After all, you are a free, unattached woman now."

"We can speak here," Francesca told Bragg.

He took her arm. "I don't think so. He will have to get over it."

Francesca glanced once more at Hart as Bragg led her into an adjoining salon, often used by the family when they visited for smaller, more intimate gatherings. Hart simply stared at them before walking away, his gaze terribly intense. Rick closed the mahogany doors. "I heard, Francesca," he said quietly. "One of the newsmen told me of Hart's statement to the press. It will be in tomorrow's newspapers."

She searched his face for any sign of pleasure on his part, but she could find none. "Aren't you going to gloat? Or at least say I told you so?"

He started. "No, I am not." He touched her cheek briefly,

shocking her. Instantly he dropped his hand. "I know you have been smitten. And I can see that you are very hurt."

She turned away so he would not see the instant effect of his kind words. Moisture gathered in her eyes. "If I must admit it, then I will. My heart is broken, just as you have always claimed it would be." She dared to wipe a tear away and then smiled very brightly at Bragg. "But he is being very noble. He wants to protect me from his fall from grace."

Bragg studied her. "Francesca, I have always predicted this moment. Hart has a past filled with terribly reckless, self-indulgent behavior. It was simply impossible for the two of you to carry on and not have something or someone rise up from his past this way."

She hugged herself. "I thought you believed he would someday turn to another woman."

"There was always that possibility, too. I am not gleeful. I hate seeing you hurt this way. But I happen to agree with you. Calder is actually being noble, for once in his life. He is doing the right thing now. If he cares for you at all, he should be protecting you from shame and scandal."

She turned away restlessly. "He still cares for me, very much, and I am not giving up. I expect for us to be reunited, sooner or later."

He was silent for a moment. "I know you think that would make you happy, and I suppose it would, for a time. But what next? How much more of this could you take?"

"It won't be like that."

"What can I do to help you now?"

She smiled slightly. "Help me find Daisy's killer."

The light in his eyes flickered oddly. "That wasn't what I meant."

"That's all the help I need."

He regarded her, rubbing his jaw. Francesca realized he had not shaved that day, and that he had dark circles under his eyes.

She noted that he seemed tired, worn, strained. She touched his sleeve. "I have been so wrapped up in my own dilemma that I haven't asked you about yours!"

"Everything is fine," he said, pulling away. "What did you find out in Albany?"

Francesca knew everything was not fine, but she would not pursue that topic now. She told him every detail of her meeting with Gillespie, and that she expected him in the city the next day, hopefully with his wife and daughter Lydia.

Bragg was thoughtful. "So you do think he was genuinely surprised that she had been murdered?"

"Yes," Francesca said. "Frankly, he seemed stunned. But I am almost certain he knew that Honora had become Daisy Jones, and that implies he also knew that she had become a prostitute."

"So he becomes a suspect—if you are right," Bragg said.

"I can't imagine any man killing his own daughter."

Bragg remained calm. "It does happen."

"Yes, unfortunately, I suppose it does," Francesca acknowledged grimly. "Rick, we need to interview him very thoroughly. We need to confirm, once and for all, if he knew his daughter was Daisy, and if he also knew where she was and what she was doing. Did he have any contact with her? And what about Martha Gillespie and Lydia? Did they know, or was this the judge's secret?"

Bragg met her gaze. "Is there any chance he was *not* surprised by her murder?"

"I have already wondered if it was theatrics," she said slowly. "Right now, I cannot imagine him being the killer. He is so grief-stricken."

"We know one fact for certain," Bragg said after a thoughtful pause. "Daisy was a blot upon the Gillespie name."

"So you suspect Judge Gillespie? You think he murdered his own daughter in order to protect his reputation?" The concept was simply horrifying. But any alternative theory was far better than Hart remaining on the top of the police's list of suspects.

"I refuse to rule anyone out. And by the way, Newman brought Rose in today. She will not name the client she was with on the first. I am beginning to think she has no alibi for that evening, and that moves her right to the top of my list of suspects."

Francesca could not help but be relieved. She had to voice her thoughts. "That is odd. She has admitted to stopping by at six or seven—at a time when she could be accused of committing the murder. So why not make up an alibi for the entire evening?" She suddenly gasped. "Wait! Rick—if she murdered Daisy, she would know exactly when the murder happened. And that would explain Rose's odd alibi. For example, if Daisy was murdered at eight-fifteen, and Rose did do it, she would claim to be occupied at that precise time—which is what she has done. She would not know that we are looking at a larger window of opportunity, one in which she could still fit."

"That is excellent thinking," Bragg said with a smile, impressed. "Francesca, sometimes your mind is exceedingly clever."

"I am going to push Rose tomorrow," Francesca said firmly, elated with her latest theory. "I want a break in this case, Rick, a real break. What did she say about Daisy's pregnancy?"

"That subject was not raised," he said. "Unfortunately I was not present when Newman interviewed Rose and he did not think to ask her about it."

"Rose surely knew about the child," Francesca said with growing excitement. "That certainly adds to her motivation. She must have been furious that Daisy was having Hart's child! That would only solidify the bond between Daisy and Hart, while causing more conflict for her and Daisy." Francesca made a mental note to herself to discuss Daisy's pregnancy with Rose immediately. "Did you have any luck locating either George Holstein or David Masters?"

"Both men denied any involvement with Daisy—at first. I interviewed them myself. They were both very involved with her, but they both have solid alibis, Francesca. Masters was with his wife and two other couples at the opera. Holstein was at a restaurant with his wife, his brother and a dozen other guests for his wife's birthday celebration."

"So our list of suspects is a list of three," she said seriously. "I want Hart ruled out."

His gaze was direct, searching. "You are so loyal to him, still. If the two of you do not get back together, I wonder, will you continue to be so loyal and so supportive?"

Francesca was not going to think about a future without Hart. "He deserves my faith."

"Does he?"

She jerked. "That's not fair."

"I have always had a bad feeling about this case," he said quietly. "I really hope Hart is innocent, but I must consider that he has tremendous motive and all the means."

"So does Rose. And surely now you must agree she has even more motive and more means! She was there at Daisy's for most of the evening—for all we know, the entire evening. Hart was at home until well after the murder. He has an alibi," she said, flushing.

"So he *claims,*" Bragg said skeptically. "And so Alfred claims."

He seemed to know that Alfred was lying to protect Hart. Francesca was uneasy, and once again, she felt terribly guilty for her part in the deception.

He gave her a look. "Is there something you wish to tell me?"

"Only that Calder is not a killer."

"Again, I hope not," Bragg said. "In any case, we will be better able to proceed with Gillespie in town. I'll send word the moment we learn he has arrived."

"I am very eager to pursue this lead," Francesca admitted. She felt as if she had just barely escaped being caught in the terrible but necessary lie she had encouraged Alfred to tell. Sooner or later she was going to have to confess her deception to Bragg. Surely he would understand and forgive her?

Then she studied Bragg's handsome face. The lights were dim in the salon, but there was no mistaking the fatigue and strain she had glimpsed earlier. Her heart stirred. He was fighting to hold his marriage together and she knew it for a fact. "How is Leigh Anne, Rick?"

As if at a loss for words, he shook his head.

She took his hand. "What aren't you telling me?"

"I don't particularly wish to add to your burdens," he said.

"Do not be noble now! It's Mike O'Donnell, I can feel it," she exclaimed.

He sighed. "I expected O'Donnell to demand money—I even encouraged it. But he is too clever. He has not made any attempt at extortion, and he continues to insist that he has every right to the girls. I can't arrest him and end this if he does not do anything criminal."

Francesca was wide-eyed. It took her a moment to absorb what Bragg had said. "So he is playing you."

"Yes, he is. But sooner or later he will ask for the money."

"Rick—how is Leigh Anne managing?"

He became grim. "She is both distressed and afraid. I am worried about her. She has yet to come to grips with the fact that she can no longer walk. She doesn't need any more strain."

"No, she does not," Francesca agreed. She hesitated. "An arrest, a hearing and a court case will prolong this situation, Rick."

"What are you suggesting?" he asked sharply, their gazes meeting.

"You could pay him to leave town permanently—sparing Leigh Anne any further tension and worry."

He was silent for a moment. "I hate to admit it, but the thought has occurred to me. I want this over, Francesca, so Leigh Anne can genuinely recover from the accident. I want to see her happy again."

She knew he had no real means to pay off O'Donnell, if that was what he decided to do. As a city official, he had a very modest wage. Leigh Anne had no means, either. Of course, the Bragg family was very well off. So was Calder.

She wondered if this could bring the two brothers together. "I can help," she said slowly. "If you decide to proceed this way, I can help you get the funds."

"That's generous of you, Francesca. But if I do decide to pay O'Donnell off, I will go to the bank for a loan."

Francesca knew he was in a moral dilemma. Why not have Hart help his own brother—the brother he was so jealous of—for what might be the very first time in their lives? "Rick, I can help, and I would dearly like to."

He finally smiled at her. "There is nothing you would not do for a person in need, is there, Francesca?"

She smiled warmly back. "I don't even think about it."

A moment seemed to pass. Francesca was well aware that she shared a very deep bond with this man, and that she always would. Inspector Newman said, "Sir? You had better come into the hall."

Francesca had not heard him open the door and she turned. Newman stood on the threshold, appearing very grim. Hart stood behind him, staring at her and Bragg.

Bragg hurried out, Francesca following. She dared to look Hart's way, aware that her cheeks had warmed. He was eyeing her coolly and suspiciously. She knew she should be pleased he cared at all, but she genuinely despised his jealous moods and their ensuing tempers.

"What is it?" Bragg asked.

Newman nodded at a young officer. The man came forward,

holding up a knife with a large, crusty-brown blade. Francesca's heart turned over, hard. "Is that a bowie knife?" She was certain it was—just as she was certain the blade was covered with dried blood.

"Yes," Bragg said. "Bag it."

Hart strode forward. "Where the hell did you find that? That's not mine."

Bragg turned to the young officer, whose cheeks were scarlet. "Sir...sirs...ma'am," he said, almost stuttering. His eyes were huge Os. "I found the knife in that big coach in the stables, underneath the back seat."

An absolute silence fell.

This was not happening, Francesca thought, stunned.

"Sir?" Newman spoke.

Bragg flinched. Looking at Hart, he said, "I am afraid you will be spending the night downtown. Cuff him."

CHAPTER THIRTEEN

Thursday, June 5, 1902—10:00 a.m.

FRANCESCA SAT AT THE secretaire in the guest bedroom at her sister's house, hunched over Daisy's bank statements. It was almost impossible to concentrate. All she could think about was last night, when Hart had been taken away by the police in manacles to be detained for further questioning, while the knife was analyzed.

He had been furious, but he had not protested his innocence another time. Instead, when Francesca had run to him, about to tell him not to worry and that she was going downtown with him, he had turned to Bragg. "I don't want her coming downtown. I don't want her involved. I mean it, Rick," he had warned.

Aghast, Francesca watched as Hart was led away. After, Rick had reassured her that all would be well, while talking her out of accompanying him back to HQ. Bragg had been right—there was nothing she could do for Hart that night. Still hurt by another rejection, she had gone to her sister's. The household was asleep and a servant had let her in; Francesca had shown herself to a guest room. It was only while she lay in the peach-colored, canopied bed, trying in vain to fall asleep, that she had considered that Hart had been framed.

She had passed an entirely sleepless night. The investigation was spiraling out of control, with Hart more deeply implicated in Daisy's murder than ever. But he was innocent. Surely he would not be arrested. She was certain he had been framed—and very cleverly, oh yes. While Francesca remained convinced that the murder was committed in rage, the killer had carefully planned the crime well beforehand.

Rose seemed the most likely candidate. After all, she had been accusing Hart of Daisy's murder from that very night, and she hated him enough to want to frame him. She had motive, she had means and more than enough opportunity. After all, she did not have an alibi and they knew she had been at the crime scene just before the murder and just after it.

But Bragg was suspicious of Gillespie, too. Francesca would not rule out the judge, no matter how shocked he had seemed to learn of his daughter's death yesterday.

And where did his wife, Martha, and his younger daughter, Lydia, fit in? Why had Daisy left home, with such disastrous consequences, in the first place?

Unable to sleep, she kept imagining Hart in the holding cell just off of the lobby at police headquarters. The room was sparse, with several bunk beds and individual cells. He would, of course, be given a small cell entirely to himself. Francesca knew he could fend for himself and he could manage one uncomfortable night, but she ached for him. He had suffered enough in his life and he did not deserve to spend even a single night in jail.

Francesca believed in the American judicial system. She had no doubts that Hart would eventually be freed, but she was afraid now. She had never seen him so set against her. He did not seem to be having any second thoughts about them. She was afraid that if he continued to be so adamant, she would never be able to change his position, not even after he was cleared of Daisy's murder.

One thing at a time, she told herself, trembling from both fear and exhaustion. Today she had a case to solve. With any luck—and they certainly needed some good fortune—the Gillespies would arrive early enough to be interviewed. And then there was

Rose. If she had an alibi, Francesca thought fiercely, it was time to talk.

There was already some good news today. She had stolen downstairs at half past six to sneak a peak at the day's newspapers. Her sister received the *Tribune,* the *Times* and the *Sun.* Daisy's murder had only been on the *Sun*'s front page, and there had been no mention of the fact that she had been with child when she had died. In fact, that piece, authored by Kurland, had held no new information, not even the truth of Daisy's identity. On the flip side of that coin, however, Hart's announcement of their broken engagement had been on the social pages of all three newspapers. In each one, he had been labeled a suspect in the murder of his mistress.

The numbers and words on the bank-statement page before her blurred as she looked down. Francesca focused her eyesight. She had to concentrate. She glanced over the last statement. It was for May. This account had been opened in February—clearly it had been started by Hart when Daisy had become his mistress. Daisy had received two thousand dollars each and every month. The first deposit had been on February 10, the others on the first of the month. That amount would cover Daisy's entire household budget.

He had kept her well, she thought, a sick feeling in her heart.

And then another figure leapt off of the page at her.

Francesca saw that Daisy had deposited eight thousand dollars on May 8. As she read further, her tension and surprise increased. She had deposited twelve thousand dollars ten days later on May 18.

Francesca sat up, her mind racing. Daisy had deposited twenty thousand dollars into her account in May in a very short period of time. Had Calder given her the money? Daisy had been giving them so much trouble—maybe he had hoped to pay her off. There was another possibility, too, one Francesca prayed was wrong.

Maybe Daisy had been blackmailing Calder. That would take a lot of courage, indeed. But if that were the case, it only gave Hart even more motive.

Francesca stood. She had the perfect excuse to see Hart, never mind that he had been adamant she stay away. She had to know who had given Daisy those funds. She had to find out if they had come from Hart and if so, why.

"Fran?" Her sister's voice came from the other side of her closed door, as did her soft knock.

Francesca ran to the door and opened it. "You slept in," she cried, thrilled. She had never needed her sister more.

Connie was gazing at her with surprise. "I had a late night," she said, as she was usually up at eight with her two children. "Fran, what has happened? Mrs. Rogers told me you spent the night!"

Francesca took her hand. "Connie, I need to stay here for a while. Please tell me it is all right. I promise not to be a bother."

Connie seemed dismayed. "What is going on? I pray it is not what I think!"

"I'm afraid it is," Francesca said tersely. Connie was utterly different in nature from Francesca. She was never impetuous or rash—and never disobedient or disloyal. Francesca knew her sister would not approve of what she had done. "Papa forbade me from even seeing Calder, much less marrying him. I have moved out of the house."

Connie gasped and sank down on the sofa, stunned.

"It was awful," Francesca admitted. "And do not tell me I have broken their hearts, because I know that I have done just that. You know how much I adore Papa and how I love Mama. But Con, try to understand. I am a woman now. I am not a child, and I love Hart. I cannot be ordered about now as if I am still a little girl."

Connie shook her head. "But the two of you aren't even engaged anymore—he told me so himself."

Francesca was no longer angry at her sister for daring to approach Calder and interfere in their engagement. "Connie, I love him and he is in trouble. I shall stick like glue to his side. You would do the same for Neil. And I believe that, eventually, he will change his mind and we will renew our engagement. I have no intention of walking away from that man."

Connie hesitated. "I had to speak my mind, Fran. I had to try to do what is right for you."

"I know. And I was very angry at first. But too much has happened since then." She sat down beside her sister.

Connie took her hand. "I will tell you this, he is a very intimidating man. I don't know how you manage. But I like him even more now than I did before. He really does care about you. He was distraught. It was obvious that this breakup has hurt him terribly."

Francesca was pleased by Connie's words. She wondered if she dared tell her sister the latest news. It was going to be in the afternoon papers and certainly any evening editions. Sooner or later, all of society would know about Hart's arrest. She wished Bragg had waited.

"What is it?"

"Hart was picked up by the police last night."

Connie turned white.

"The police found what might be the murder weapon in his coach. Someone has very cleverly framed him for Daisy's murder!" She was grim. "Hart spent the night in *jail,* Connie."

Connie remained pale. "Fran! Can't you hear yourself! What if Hart hasn't been framed? Have you ever considered that the weapon was found in his coach because he left it there?"

Francesca stood. "Hart is innocent."

Connie also stood. "I hope you are right! Francesca, I don't really think Hart capable of murder, but it looks so terrible for him."

"Yes, it does," Francesca said seriously. She left her sister in the sitting area of her bedroom and picked up her purse. "I am going to visit him today." She opened it and removed the derringer, then emptied the gun of both bullets.

"What are you doing?" Connie cried, rushing to stand beside her. "I still refuse to believe you carry a gun!"

Francesca put the unloaded pistol and the bullets back in her purse. "I must carry a gun, as a sleuth. But I didn't want it loaded when I call on Rose today. First, though, I need to pay a brief visit to Bartolla."

"Bartolla! Fran, why are you going to see Bartolla Benevente? And what are you going to do when you call on Rose?" Connie asked with obvious concern.

Francesca smiled sweetly. "I have the oddest feeling Bartolla is playing games with our brother, Con, and I am going to put an end to them, once and for all." She paused. "Want to join me?"

"I am afraid I can't, not this morning." Connie worried her hands as they walked to the door. "You're going to threaten Rose, aren't you? You are going to threaten her with that empty gun!"

Francesca was resigned. "You know me better than anyone. Don't worry, the gun *is* unloaded, and I will only resort to threats if there is no other choice."

Connie did not look reassured.

FRANCESCA WAS SHOWN INTO the salon by a servant, who left to inform Bartolla of her arrival. The countess was a cousin of Sarah Channing's and was living with the Channings in their West Side home. Francesca had been to the Channings many times and no longer saw the exotic furnishings and trophy heads and hides as she paced. Once, she had genuinely liked the flamboyantly beautiful countess. Recently, she had realized she was not to be trusted and that she might not really be a friend.

Francesca turned when she heard rapid footsteps. As Bartolla would never hurry, she knew it was either Sarah or her mother approaching. Indeed, Sarah hurried into the salon. She was clearly on her way out of the house, as she was dressed in an unusually simple but attractive light blue suit. "Francesca!" Sarah beamed, obviously pleased to see her. She rushed forward and the two women embraced. "You are here to see Bartolla? I heard Harold upstairs, advising her that you have called."

"Yes, I have a matter I wish to discuss with her," Francesca said, truly surprised at how well Sarah was looking. Usually she wore overly bright and excessively adorned clothes that dwarfed her petite stature and washed out her complexion. But the light blue was lovely on her. Other than a flounce at the hem of the skirt and ruffled sleeves on the jacket, the suit was unadorned, in marked contrast to most of the clothes Sarah wore, and it displayed her slender figure to a great advantage. "How are you, Sarah? And I like your suit. Is it new?" Francesca guessed that Sarah had managed to go shopping without her mother. Mrs. Channing was renowned for her excessive and bad taste.

Sarah nodded. "Do you think it suits me? Bartolla took me shopping—we ordered three new evening gowns and as many ensembles for day. It is so plain! And I have never worn this color before. Bartolla insisted that I stay away from those dark reds and golds I used to wear. What do you think?" she asked anxiously.

Francesca knew that Sarah did not care one whit for fashion. But Rourke was in town. Two plus two equaled four. She grinned. "Light blue is a lovely color on you—it makes your eyes even darker, it puts a blush in your cheeks and your hair has such a rich hue now! Bartolla is right, the color and style suit you very much. So…where are you off to?"

Sarah glanced away, but her cheeks had become pink. "I am having lunch."

Francesca poked her. "With whom?"

"Just…a friend," Sarah said.

"Sarah!"

"Very well, I will tell you. But do not make anything of it!" Sarah cried, flushing.

"You are meeting Rourke for lunch," Francesca returned in absolute delight.

Sarah nodded. "But we are just friends, Francesca. I am not interested in romance—I am too busy with my art."

Francesca met her gaze, understanding perfectly. "It is not your fault that my portrait was stolen."

"I cannot believe that, with all those private investigators, Hart has not located it!" Sarah cried in distress.

"Perhaps it will simply remain missing," Francesca said, not believing it for a moment. Her portrait had no value. An art thief would steal a masterpiece. Someone had stolen her portrait for personal reasons, she was certain. She knew, with real dread, that one day that portrait was going to surface.

Sarah reached for her hand. "Oh, Francesca, here you are comforting me, when Hart is in so much trouble."

"You saw the papers?"

"Yes. But I know he is innocent, just as I know you will find Daisy's real killer," Sarah said earnestly. "Because you will never give up."

"No, I won't," Francesca said. "Sarah, I cannot tell you how much I appreciate your loyalty to Hart."

"You love him, you are my friend and he has been a great patron," Sarah said simply.

"This is so touching," Bartolla said, walking toward them. She was smiling, apparently having been eavesdropping for some time. Gorgeously dressed in a royal-blue ensemble that was low-cut for daytime and revealed a great deal of her stunning figure, she was dripping diamonds. "Francesca, darling!" She kissed Francesca on both cheeks. "How are you managing? What a terrible scandal! Hart accused of murdering his own mistress! You must be sick with worry!"

Francesca drew back, her heart pounding. "I am completely focused on the investigation. We have several very interesting leads. I expect to find the real killer any day. Hart is innocent, so I am not worried at all."

Bartolla smiled knowingly at her, clearly not believing a single word she had just said. "I agree with Sarah," she declared. "Hart would never murder his mistress. Besides, if he did, he is too clever to be accused of it."

It was hard to keep calm and even harder to smile back. "Daisy was his ex-mistress," she said, knowing full well that Bartolla already knew that, "and Hart *is* innocent."

"Of course he is," Bartolla soothed. "But it is awful, isn't it, that he was arrested last night?"

Francesca froze.

Bewildered, Sarah looked from her cousin to Francesca. "Hart was arrested?"

Francesca managed to breathe. "He was detained for further questioning. That is all."

"I must have misunderstood that article in the *World*. Hart is in jail, is he not?"

"Yes." Francesca turned away so Bartolla would not see how upset she was. Of course, last night's news would have broken later that day, but someone had worked very hard to get it in this morning's paper. Well, this time she could not blame that lowlife snoop, Arthur Kurland.

"Oh, Francesca," Sarah gasped, grasping her hand. "This is awful news! And you have been so brave and so confident! How can I help?"

Francesca faced her, unable to smile now. "Your loyalty and faith is all the help we need," she said softly.

"There must be something else I can do," Sarah whispered.

Bartolla patted Sarah on the back. "Come, dear, you heard

Francesca. Although we could have the cook bake a pie, and we could bring it to the jail where Hart is locked up." She seemed to think the idea very amusing.

Francesca itched to claw the other woman now. She said, dangerously, "That's a lovely idea, Bartolla. It is so thoughtful of you!"

Bartolla laughed. "Francesca, you are so nervous! I really am trying to help."

Francesca gave her a murderous look.

"Won't Hart get out on bail?" Sarah asked.

"He hasn't been arrested, Sarah," Francesca returned. She decided she despised the widowed countess.

"Thank God!" Bartolla cried. "You are very brave, Francesca, to stand by your man in such a time. Most women would turn tail and run the other way as fast as they could."

Before Francesca could answer, Harold announced the arrival of Rourke Bragg. He had not been home last night when Hart had been taken downtown, but of course, he would know about it now—the entire house would know. Francesca was relieved to see him stride into the room.

His amber gaze took in all three women. His expression grim, he paused by Sarah, kissing her cheek. He nodded politely at Bartolla and went right to Francesca, taking her arm and moving her aside. "Are you all right?" he asked quietly.

"Of course," she lied, meeting his intently searching gaze.

"How is Hart?"

Francesca pulled him across the room and out of earshot. "He refused to allow me to go downtown with him last night," she whispered. The anguish cracked open, and she looked at Rourke as if he might be the one to talk some sense into Hart.

He put his arm around her. "He wants to spare you exactly what you are going through."

"I need to see him," she said urgently. "Rourke, I will confess that I am afraid!"

"You don't think he did it?" Rourke was aghast.

"No. But he has decided we are through. I am afraid he will never change his mind. Maybe this is the excuse he needs!"

"If he doesn't, I will change it for him," Rourke said grimly. "Maybe this *is* an excuse—he has been a bachelor his entire life—but I don't think he has suddenly got cold feet. I think he cares very much for you and wants to spare you any more grief. How can I help, Francesca? Just say the word."

"He needs all of us now. He should not turn anyone away. But if he won't let me comfort him, then maybe you can do so."

"I am going to try to talk some sense into him," Rourke said grimly. "Of course I will visit him today. And by the way, Francesca, the family has already hired the best criminal attorney in the city, Charles Gray."

Francesca was relieved on that count. "Good. And I think you should visit—everyone should," Francesca said.

Rourke lightened. "Francesca, you do not know the Braggs if you think anything or anyone could keep them away."

She finally smiled. Then, slyly, "You are having lunch with Sarah?"

He flushed, glancing across the room at Sarah. "Yes, and do not play matchmaker," he growled.

"I would never sink so low," she said with a smile.

He rolled his eyes at her and they walked back across the room. Bartolla was wide-eyed, glancing back and forth between them both. She was obviously dying to learn what had just transpired.

"Rourke?" Sarah said. "Maybe we should invite Francesca to join us. I think she might like company today."

"No!" Francesca smiled. "Sarah, I have some key suspects I must interview. I wasn't exaggerating when I said I have some important leads to follow. Do not change your plans on my account. But I do need a word with the countess—alone."

"That will be our cue, then," Rourke said. "Francesca, where can I find you later in the day?"

She knew he intended to tell her about his visit to Hart and she loved him dearly for such loyalty and concern. "I am staying with my sister. But I have no real idea what time I will get home tonight."

Rourke looked at her in surprise. So did Sarah, who voiced what they were all thinking. "Francesca, you are living with Connie now?"

Francesca was all too aware of Bartolla's avid interest. "I had been thinking of moving out for some time now. It is hard to roam the city at all hours of the day and night while living under Julia's roof. She really does not care for my sleuthing. So I have moved in with Connie and Neil—but just until I can lease my own flat."

Sarah was stunned, and so was Rourke. Unmarried young ladies did not live by themselves. Trying to cover up his shock, he merely said, "Then I will try to reach you at Lord Montrose's tonight. Good luck, Francesca." He smiled at Sarah, who squeezed Francesca's hand, and they left.

Her heart began a more insistent beat. Francesca smiled at Bartolla. The countess smiled back. "What do you wish to discuss, Francesca?" She walked toward a chair, clearly about to sit.

Francesca said, "My brother."

Instead of sitting, Bartolla slowly turned.

"I saw him at Connie's last night."

"Really?" Bartolla's smile never wavered, but her gaze was searching.

"I have never seen him so moody," Francesca said, "I believe he is very unhappy."

Bartolla stiffened. "You are wrong. I know him better than anyone, Francesca. Of course, it has been difficult for him, being disowned by his own family. However, I have assured him that your father will eventually change his mind. If anything is bothering Evan, it is his relationship with Andrew Cahill."

Bartolla was smooth and clever. "And when do the two of you plan to elope?"

Bartolla looked as if she had been kicked. "He told you?"

"I am a sleuth, remember? I dearly love to unearth secrets—and lies."

"What does that mean?" Bartolla demanded with hard, cold eyes.

"It means that he also told me why the two of you are running off together in such a rush," Francesca said as coldly. She was furious.

Bartolla was rigid. "I do not know what you mean."

Francesca leaned toward her. "Evan told me that you are with child. Is the child even his?"

Bartolla slapped her across the face. "How *dare* you."

Francesca jerked, stunned, but even she had to admit that maybe she deserved that. She rubbed her throbbing cheek. "I am suspicious, Bartolla. I am not certain the child is Evan's. Worse, I am not even convinced you are with child." And she glanced at Bartolla's nearly flat abdomen.

"I am no trollop! I love your brother! There has been no one but Evan since I came to town," Bartolla exclaimed, her cheeks pink. "I thought we were friends!"

"So did I—until you betrayed me by sending Leigh Anne that letter," Francesca returned.

Her eyes widened. "Oh, come! You were about to have an affair with Rick Bragg, and she is his wife, even if they were separated. Considering you are now head over heels for Hart, you must not bear a grudge. I'd think you might consider some gratitude, really." Her eyes turned black. "Hart would never take Bragg's leftovers."

"My personal life is not at issue here. If you are with child, prove it. Because otherwise, I am going to recommend that my brother wait before he does something he may regret for the rest of his life."

"You plan to interfere in our relationship?" Bartolla asked, with obvious dismay.

"Evan doesn't want to marry you. I happen to believe he is in love with someone else," Francesca retorted. "I suggest you schedule an appointment with your doctor, Bartolla, for you and Evan. And do not think about bribing him to corroborate a lie, because I will find out."

Bartolla began to shake. It was a moment before she spoke. "I am carrying Evan's child, and it is his duty to marry me. This is not your affair!"

"Yes, it is," Francesca said.

Bartolla took one step closer, so they were nose to nose. "My dear, if you interfere, I will make certain that your relationship with Hart fails."

Francesca was taken aback. "What does that mean?"

"It means that I know Hart quite well. I know he is jealous—insanely so. I know that, for the first time in his life, he is in love. I know he is a man who will never forgive betrayal." She smiled coldly now.

"What are you saying? That you will somehow turn Hart against me?"

"Yes, that is exactly what I am saying." Bartolla laughed. "I will make certain he comes to despise you, Francesca. And don't think I can't do it. You are so naive! You cannot go up against me, my dear. I am a woman of the world. I know what makes a man like Hart breathe. I know what would make a man like Hart hate."

Francesca was actually shaken. Bartolla seemed inherently dangerous, far more vicious and malicious than she had ever dreamed. But she would not back down; she loved her brother too much to do so. She stared at the countess. It was a long moment before she spoke. "Sarah has no idea you are so ruthless, does she?"

"You started this war, my dear. You can end it easily enough by minding your own business."

Francesca knew when she should retreat. She simply turned and walked out. Bartolla could not turn Hart against her, could she? She had no clue as to how the other woman might accomplish such a feat.

One thing had become clear. They were not friends, oh no. They were bitterly opposed, they were enemies.

FRANCESCA ARRIVED AT POLICE headquarters on pins and needles at the prospect of seeing Hart. She was worried about what her reception might be, but hoped he would be pleased to see her, and not cold and distant in the hopes of continuing to push her away. Francesca hurried toward the front door of the station.

"Miss Cahill! Miss Cahill! Please, we'd like a comment from you!" several newsmen cried, leaping out from behind the two gaslights as she went up the building's front steps.

Francesca faltered. Three reporters had surrounded her and one of them was Arthur Kurland. She was very dismayed, but she managed a smile, facing them. "I will be happy to give you a comment," she said, drawing in an extra breath. She was going to profess Hart's innocence.

Kurland came closer. "How do you feel about the end of your engagement, Miss Cahill? And would you care to give me a quote for tomorrow's paper?"

Francesca froze, for she had not expected that question, although she should have anticipated it. Somehow she said, "I am afraid I cannot discuss any personal matters."

"Really?" Kurland laughed. "Can you make a comment about Hart's incarceration last night, then? Or is that personal, too?"

"Mr. Hart is innocent. He has been cleverly framed," Francesca said, flushing in anger.

Gasps greeted her declaration and lead pencils flew.

"Miss Cahill! Will you continue to investigate this case? Are you working for Hart, in spite of the end of your engagement?" This was from Walter Isaacson of the *Tribune,* a newsman Francesca thought fair and honest.

Francesca turned away from Kurland in relief. "I have been hired by Rose Cooper to find Miss Jones's killer," Francesca said. She held up her hand before anyone could speak. "There has been a major break in the case and I am pleased to share it with you." She paused for effect, having everyone's complete attention now. "Daisy Jones's real name was Honora Gillespie. She is the daughter of Judge Gillespie of Albany, New York."

"What are you saying?" Kurland cried. The other reporters were as surprised. Pencils raced, scratching over notepads.

"I think you heard me. Now, if you will excuse me?" She smiled pleasantly and left the stunned newsmen. No one made any effort to follow her, as they were so engrossed in making their notes. Inside, she sighed in relief. She had just deflected the entire story away from Hart. She had no doubt that tomorrow's headlines would be quite lurid. She was sorry for the Gillespies, but that news would have broken in another day or so, anyway. It was Hart she had to think of.

Francesca paused for a moment, seeking to recover her composure. The lobby was in chaos, with a number of gentlemen arguing at the front desk with a pair of bored officers. Telephones were ringing off the hook, telegraphs were busily pinging, and a drunk was singing. Francesca glanced across the crowded room toward the holding cells. They were all occupied—and Hart was not present. Had he been released? Her heart skipped at the thought.

"Miss Cahill!" An officer she did not know but recognized came up to her. "The c'mish wants you upstairs. He sent me to find you," he said breathlessly, and he glanced at his notes. "I called the Cahill house and then the Montrose residence and I was going to go uptown to the Dakotas, where they said you were. He's real eager to see you, miss."

"What has happened?" she asked quickly.

"He's got the Gillespie family upstairs—they just came in."

Francesca ran for the stairs, forgetting to thank him and hiking up her skirts as she went up. The Gillespies must have taken a sleeper train last night, she thought in real excitement.

The door to the conference room was open. Obviously Bragg wanted to appear casual and relaxed with the family. He and Newman sat facing the judge, who seemed to have aged a decade since the other day, and his wife, who was a small, pale, blond woman that reminded Francesca of a delicate bird. She clutched a linen handkerchief in her hand and frequently used it to dab at her eyes. Francesca saw that Daisy had resembled her somewhat, and she had certainly inherited her slender frame from her, but she doubted Martha Gillespie had ever been as beautiful as her oldest daughter.

She turned to Daisy's sister and studied her without anyone remarking her presence yet. Lydia, Francesca had learned, was two years younger than Daisy. She had hair that was neither brown nor blond, even, unremarkable features, and a much darker skin tone than her sister. In fact, other than her eyes, which even from this distance she could tell were a pale blue, Francesca saw no resemblance between the two sisters. She wondered at their friendship, then. She knew how difficult it could be growing up with a sibling who was remarkable in any particular way—in this case, being so beautiful. She wondered if Lydia had been jealous of her sister.

Lydia sat rigidly beside her mother, her hands clasped on the table in front of her. Like both of her parents, she seemed very upset.

Bragg noticed her and stood. "Francesca, come in. The judge and his family arrived very early this morning. They just came in to see me."

Francesca smiled at him and Newman, and then at the judge.

"Good morning, Judge. Thank you for coming—and thank you for bringing Mrs. Gillespie and your daughter."

He also stood. "Martha, this is the young lady I told you about, the very remarkable sleuth."

Martha nodded tearfully. "I still can't believe it. I can't believe Honora is dead."

Francesca glanced at Lydia, who did not move. She looked as if she wished to cry, but she did not. "I am very sorry," Francesca said. "Daisy was liked by everyone and she did not deserve her fate."

Martha Gillespie shook her head. "How is it possible? How is it possible that she gave up the life she had with us to become what she had? Please tell me, Miss Cahill, because I don't understand."

"I don't know, but I should like to find out," Francesca said softly.

The judge muttered, "I had to tell them. I told them on the train last night."

Francesca wished she had been the one to break the news, so she could have gauged both Martha's and Lydia's reactions. But Daisy's mother certainly seemed grief-stricken and shocked.

Bragg said, "The judge just gave his statement. It is brief and exactly as you described."

Francesca understood. He claimed to have no knowledge of Honora's whereabouts, until Francesca had appeared in Albany yesterday. She said, "Let's go back to Honora, the fifteen-year-old daughter. Mrs. Gillespie? Were you close to your daughter?"

Martha nodded. "Of course I was. I adored Honora. She was so beautiful and sweet."

Francesca was skeptical. If her home life had been so happy, why had Daisy left? "And there were family outings? Picnics, ice skating? Family vacations, family gatherings? Supper at home, at least on Sundays?"

Martha looked perplexed. "We went to church every Sunday.

We are Baptist. But my husband works very long, hard hours, and when he is not working, we have social obligations. And no one in my family cares for picnics," she added.

A picture was emerging, Francesca thought. "So you and the judge went out almost every night."

"If not, he would work in his study, dining there alone," Martha said.

"I take each and every case very seriously," Gillespie said harshly. "What is this about?"

Francesca just smiled reassuringly at him. "Did you take Honora shopping?"

Martha was taken aback. "We had a modiste come to the house to make both of the girls' wardrobes." She started to cry. "It feels like only yesterday. How could she be gone—and this way!"

Lydia said softly, "Honora liked horses."

Francesca turned her attention to Daisy's somber sister. "She did?"

"Yes. We would ride through the fields almost every day, in the afternoon." Lydia held her gaze. "And sometimes we took lunch. Sometimes we shared a picnic."

Francesca sat down besides her. Lydia's message was clear. Her sister had liked picnics, but their mother had not known. "Do you know why she ran away? Had she become unhappy before she left?" she asked softly, speaking only to Lydia now.

Lydia glanced at her parents. "I don't know why she left." A tear fell. "I don't know if she was unhappy."

"Were you close?" Francesca asked gently. If the two girls had spent so little time with their parents, if they had ridden together every day, she suspected they had been good friends.

Lydia nodded; and another tear fell.

"Perhaps there was a boy, a young man that she liked?"

"There were no boys," Lydia said hoarsely. "I wish she were here!"

Francesca glanced at Bragg. He said, "Did she tell you that she was going to run away, Lydia?"

"No!" Lydia was both adamant and aghast at the thought, and Francesca believed her.

Bragg turned to Martha. "Did you have any idea that your daughter was unhappy enough to leave home?"

Martha was pale. "No, of course not."

Gillespie said, his cheeks pink, "She was a very happy young lady, sir."

Francesca had the oddest sense that the Gillespies were not being entirely honest with her. "Happy young ladies do not run away from home, Your Honor."

Gillespie jumped to his feet. "How dare you! What does any of this have to do with my daughter's murder?"

Francesca turned to Lydia. "Did she write you, Lydia? Did she tell you where she was after she had left? Did you know that she was here in the city?"

Lydia hugged herself, her gaze downcast. "No."

Francesca knew a lie when she saw one. Lydia had either heard from her sister or had known where her sister was. "You have missed her, haven't you?"

Lydia nodded, closing her eyes briefly. "She was my sister. I loved her."

Francesca allowed that statement to resonate. She and Bragg shared a look and he spoke.

"Judge Gillespie. Did you know Honora had become Daisy Jones? Did you know she was in New York City before Miss Cahill spoke with you?"

The judge stood, his chair rocking back loudly. "Of course not! What are you insinuating? That I knew where my daughter was for all of this time? That I knew the life she had chosen, what she had become, and I did nothing to bring her home? Sir, I protest."

Francesca inhaled, and beside her, she felt Bragg's tension, too. After a moment, quietly, he said, "I apologize, but it was a question I had to ask. And it is a question I must ask your wife, as well."

Martha stared, horrified. "No," she whispered. "I did not know. Richard told me yesterday, when he told us Honora was dead."

Bragg nodded. "We may have more questions for you, but we are done for now. I would like to ask you to stay in the city for a few days, in case we have a new lead."

"Are you going to find Honora's killer?" the judge demanded.

"We will find him," Bragg said softly. "Have no fear of that."

"Is it true that you have detained a suspect? I glimpsed a headline on my way over here, but I have yet to read the paper," Gillespie said.

Francesca grew still.

"We have not made an arrest, and I am not convinced the suspect in custody is the guilty party," Bragg said.

Francesca faced him. What did he mean, the *suspect in custody?* Hart had been released, hadn't he?

"Who is he?" Gillespie demanded.

Bragg hesitated. "His name is Calder Hart. He had kept Daisy as his mistress for a brief time in February," he said carefully.

"I know that name," the judge cried. "He's a wealthy man, here in the city."

"He's my brother, sir," Bragg said, stunning Francesca.

The Gillespies cried out in shock.

"He is not the killer," Francesca said firmly. "And the police will do their job."

"This is rich! You have placed your own brother in custody for the murder of my daughter! What kind of investigation is this? Of course you claim he did not do it!" Gillespie stormed out. His wife and daughter followed.

But then, Lydia glanced back into the room—at Francesca.

Her expression was odd. It was almost desperate, like some kind of plea. And then they were gone.

Bragg rubbed his jaw.

"That was very brave of you," Francesca said. "What do you think?"

"It appears that the entire family is grieving and that no one has a clue as to why Daisy—I mean Honora—would leave home the way that she did," Bragg said.

Francesca was impatient. "Rick, I still think Gillespie knew all about Daisy and her life here in the city. I cannot shake the feeling."

"For once, I am not convinced that you are right."

Francesca sighed. "Martha Gillespie may have been left in the dark. However, I also think Lydia had been in touch with her sister. Either that, or she somehow knew where she was."

"On that point, you may be correct," Bragg said.

Francesca fell silent, mulling over the case. Finally, she said, "What did you think of that look Lydia just gave me before they left? It seemed so hopeless—it almost seemed like a cry for help. What did that mean?"

"Yes, it *was* very hopeless. But that might be due to her grief."

He could be right, Francesca thought. Her mind veered to Hart. "Rick, didn't you release Hart? He wasn't in the tank when I came in."

Bragg did not reply. Her heart sank. "Rick?"

"I cannot treat him any differently than I would anyone else! Good God, Francesca, I have the Progressives in this city breathing down my neck, led by the clergy, and your father's friends. And then there is the press."

"What are you saying?"

He turned away. "He has been arrested for Daisy's murder."

CHAPTER FOURTEEN

Thursday, June 5, 1902—2:00 p.m.

LEIGH ANNE STUDIED THE seamstress Rick had recommended, her gaze very intent. Apparently Maggie Kennedy had been friends with the girls' mother and was also a friend of Francesca Cahill's. She had also heard that Maggie had been attacked during Francesca's last case. The redhead seemed pleasant enough, Leigh Anne thought. She had a gentle way about her and surprisingly good manners, which Leigh Anne sensed she worked hard at. She was rather pretty, too, although sadness seemed to shadow her remarkable blue eyes and her smiles seemed forced. Leigh Anne intended for her to make a wardrobe for the girls. It was greatly needed.

At first she had been dismayed by Rick's recommendation. She hadn't wanted someone else from the girls' past entering their lives, not when they still did not know what their uncle really wanted. But Rick had mentioned that Maggie, a widow, had lost her factory job, yet had to support four children. That had finally settled it—Leigh Anne had decided to use Mrs. Kennedy. Having met her, she was glad. The woman was pleasant to be around. Just then, Maggie was leaning over Dot, who was pretending to read the story in a wonderfully illustrated children's book. Maggie exclaimed over the drawing of King Arthur and Guinevere. Dot laughed, but clearly did not remember her.

Children were blessed with very short memories, Leigh Anne thought with a small pang. She wished her own memory of the past would vanish, too. She was beginning to realize that she must forget the woman she had once been, if she was to be a good mother to the girls. Recalling the fairy-tale balls, where she had danced the night away in gorgeous evening gowns, saddened her. Somehow, she must think of the future now. She smiled a little, imagining herself as a plump matron with some gray hair, the children a few years older. In the scenario, she remained in a wheelchair, but she was content and the girls were beautiful and happy.

In the fanciful daydream, Rick was there, strong and handsome, an integral part of their lives.

"Read! Read!" Dot cried, smiling devilishly.

Leigh Anne jerked back to the present. Katie, as serious as usual, took her little sister's hand. "Mrs. Kennedy is here to make us clothes, real fancy clothes, the kind Mama wears," she admonished. She smiled just a little, at Leigh Anne.

Leigh Anne's heart turned over. She knew the children had been raised in a fatherless, working-class home with few amenities. In spite of how serious Katie was trying to be, she saw that her eyes sparkled with excitement. Leigh Anne had sent the nurse away. Now, she turned the wheels of her chair, moving it closer to the sofa where Dot sat, and Maggie and Katie stood. A sense of triumph filled her as she approached. It was so strong she did not care that her hands were blistered from turning the wheels.

She could actually move about. It felt like a miracle. Maybe she could actually become that plump, happy woman....

"Can I help you?" Maggie asked, moving nervously to stand beside Leigh Anne.

Although she was breathless from the exertion, Leigh Anne was also aware that the smile she gave Maggie was genuine—a reflection of her real pleasure. "I am fine, Mrs. Kennedy, but thank you."

"Shall I bring my samples in? Some clients wish to detail the order first, while others prefer to look at the fabrics. They often

change their mind when they find a color or a material they like."
Maggie smiled, but her blue eyes remained lackluster.

Leigh Anne recognized the sadness in the other woman, as
much as if they were kindred spirits. Maggie Kennedy was in
some kind of distress. "I should love to see some swatches," she
said. "But I do wish to see Katie in a bright, daffodil-yellow.
Katie? Would you like a yellow dress? I think the color would
suit your complexion and your hair."

Katie nodded, her eyes huge, clearly too excited to speak.

"Daff! Daff! Dot want daff!" Dot shrieked.

Leigh Anne reached for her chubby hand. "You, my dear, I
should love to see in pastels—a pastel green, a sweet baby blue.
Wouldn't that be lovely?"

Dot held her arms wide. "Mama! Mama, Mama!"

Leigh Anne's pleasure vanished. She knew Dot wanted to
be picked up and placed in her arms. But of course, she could
not manage that feat, and she would never manage it again. The
sadness returned, tenfold.

"Here you go," Maggie said, moving before Leigh Anne could
react. She lifted Dot and handed her to Leigh Anne.

Leigh Anne held her tight, just for moment. The girls were the
real miracle, she thought. Then she smiled at the other woman,
who regarded her kindly but without pity. Leigh Anne knew, in
that moment, that she liked her very much. "Thank you. Do you
approve of my color choices?"

"It is not my place to approve," Maggie said quietly.

"But I should like your honest opinion."

Maggie smiled. "I think bold colors will suit Katie, and you
are right, soft pastels for the baby."

Something clicked in Leigh Anne's mind then, something
about Maggie Kennedy that she should know. An image of the
countess Benevente assailed her, and Leigh Anne recalled the
gossip she had heard and shared with the widow. She made the
connection, at last. "I beg your pardon," she said, "but are you

the woman with whom Evan Cahill was dining, along with some young children, at one of the hotels, perhaps a month ago?"

Maggie Kennedy turned crimson. She glanced away. "He is very good to my children," she murmured. "I have four." She smiled too brightly now. "My oldest, Joel, is Miss Cahill's assistant. Evan—I mean, Mr. Cahill—often visits the children, bringing them cookies and gifts." Her tone dropped. "We haven't seen him in some time." Then she smiled at Leigh Anne again. "I'll go get those samples. I left my case in the front hall."

Leigh Anne watched her go out, bemused. She hoped the pretty seamstress wasn't in love with a man she could never have, not in any proper way. Worse, Cahill was a rake and everyone knew it. Bartolla suited him; they were a good match.

Peter came to the parlor door. "Mrs. Bragg? O'Donnell is at the front door."

She froze. "Send him away!" she cried. And panic consumed her.

Rick had said he was taking care of O'Donnell—but the man had come back! Why was he there? Rick had told her that Feingold had already filed the adoption papers, but he said the process usually took several months. In that moment, Leigh Anne knew that they could not wait. Rick had implied that O'Donnell was going to leave town—immediately. Had she misunderstood?

Peter was striding down the short hallway to the front door. Suddenly fury added to her panic, fueling her as nothing else could. She seized the wheels of the chair, turning them fast and hard, racing down the hall after Peter. She heard Katie calling her, but she did not stop. There in the front hall, not far from Maggie, was Mike O'Donnell. He dared to grin at her. Leigh Anne feared him, but in that moment, she hated him, too. He was not going to be a part of the girls' lives—and he was not going to take them away.

Huffing and puffing, Leigh Anne rolled the chair so fast that he had to jump out of the way or be hit by it. Peter caught the handles, braking her before she crashed into the wall. "Turn me around," she told him.

Instantly he turned the chair to face O'Donnell.

"Good day, Mrs. Bragg," he began. "It's lovely day and I was thinking—"

She rudely cut him off. "Don't tell me it is a lovely day! What do you want? Why are you here?"

Peter, who rarely spoke and never volunteered advice, leaned low. "Mrs. Bragg, I'll get rid of him."

She reached behind her, stopping him. "No." She stared coldly at O'Donnell.

"Like I said, it's lovely day, and I was thinking to take my nieces for a little stroll in the square."

"Never," Leigh Anne cried.

His smile flashed. It felt ugly and dangerous. "I got every right to take my own flesh and blood out for a walk," he said, pleasantly enough.

All she could think was that he intended to abduct the girls and she would never see them again. "No. You don't have every right. They live here with us now. You may be their uncle, but you are a stranger. I cannot allow you to take them for a stroll."

His smile faded and his gaze held hers. "I got every right. I know my rights, 'cause I just got a lawyer."

Her heart seemed to stop. "You have retained a lawyer? Why would you want a lawyer?" she managed, hoping her horror didn't show.

"Well, the girls are my nieces. I know you got a fancy house here an' lots of money, but I've been thinking about it. They belong with me and Aunt Beth."

Hadn't she sensed all along that he wanted to take the girls away? It was her worst fear come true. It was worse than losing the use of her legs. It was worse than anything she could imagine.

Maggie had stepped close. She said, lowering her tone, "Call your husband, ma'am."

Leigh Anne heard her. She wet her lips as her mind raced furiously. "You can't give them the life that we can. And…and we love them. *I* love them."

"Now, isn't that nice! I'm glad you're so fond of them, and I know you're right. You can give them pretty French dresses and brand-new toys, and I'm just a hardworking, God-fearing plain and simple man. But I can give them a roof over their heads, a bed, home-cooked food and schooling."

She realized she was shaking. "We plan to adopt them, Mr. O'Donnell."

"Really?" His eyes widened. "Don't I get some say in that?" He began to think, rather theatrically, his gaze on the ceiling. "Maybe that's not such a bad idea." His dark eyes narrowed. "Send the big servant and the lady away," he ordered.

Her every instinct told her that it was not a good idea to send Peter away. He had often served her husband as a bodyguard, and she knew he carried a concealed weapon. "Peter," she began.

He faced her, his expression one of protest.

"Could you step outside the front door," she asked softly, holding his gaze and hoping he understood. She would somehow settle this.

He did. His expression changed and he nodded. If O'Donnell thought to grab the girls and make a run for it, his way would be blocked. He walked out. She turned to Maggie, but the redhead said, "I'll go into the parlor and show the girls some fabrics." Maggie looked alert and wary now and her tone was strained.

When she had left, Leigh Anne found herself very much alone with the weathered longshoreman. Instantly she was afraid of him. "What is it that you wish to say to me?"

"I guess you and your hubby aren't all that close, now, are you?" He leered softly, leaning down so that their faces were inches apart.

Leigh Anne flinched. She didn't want him so close to her. It felt as if he were invading her body somehow, but she was helpless now, because she could not move her chair backward. "What does that mean?"

"It means we had a little chat," he said softly, smiling at her now. His lips were very close to hers. He murmured, "I told him how much I miss the girls."

Leigh Anne thought her heart might pound its way right out of her breast.

"I really do miss them," he added.

Leigh Anne swallowed hard. "How much?" she whispered. Her lips felt heavy, paralyzed. "How much do you want? What will it take for you to leave us alone?"

He grinned. "Are you offering me a *bribe,* Mrs. Bragg?"

Somehow Leigh Anne said, "I am offering you a helping hand. I know times are difficult for you now. And you are the girls' uncle. I should love to assist you and your aunt."

"That is mighty generous of you."

O'Donnell was looking at her mouth. Leigh Anne stopped breathing. The look was very male—as if he was about to kiss her. She seized her wheels so tightly her hands hurt and tears of helpless rage filled her eyes.

He raised his gaze and their eyes met. He saw her fear and smiled. "You're a real pretty woman, for a cripple," he said softly. "You got two legs beneath that nice silk dress?"

She was shaking with fright and she did not want him to see, but she could not control it. She wanted to tell him to get out of her house, but she opened her mouth and no words came out.

He placed both hands on the arms of her chair, thoroughly trapping her there. "I might not care about the legs," he said, low, "'cause the rest of you sure is fine."

Leigh Anne felt as if she were being strangled. "How much?"

He touched the bare skin above the neckline of her pale silvery-gray dress. She shivered reflexively and he laughed. He suddenly straightened. "Times are tough. And you're right. We're relations now, and I could use some help. But you know what? I don't want to piss off the police commissioner," he said with wide-eyed innocence.

She understood. "I'll get whatever you need for you—and I won't tell anyone, not even my husband."

He smiled. "Such a pretty and smart lady!" The smile vanished. His gaze was cold. "Tomorrow. You got until tomorrow night—fifteen thousand dollars will do." He gave her a hard look and hurried out of the house.

Leigh Anne sat in the chair, shaking like a leaf, so ill she thought she might vomit. Peter rushed inside, took one look at her and said, "I'd like to call the boss."

"No!" she cried. Peter stared at her, clearly disbelieving. She somehow smiled. "I am fine, now that that odious man is gone. There is no need to worry Rick."

"Mrs. Bragg," Peter began.

Miraculously, she spoke even more firmly. All the while, her mind was planning. "I am *fine,*" she stressed. "You are not to call the commissioner," she said, and it was an order.

Peter slowly nodded. "Yes, ma'am."

Leigh Anne felt utterly violated, as if she had been brutalized. But she had been abused, hadn't she?

You're a real pretty woman, for a cripple.

I don't want to piss off the police commissioner...

Fifteen thousand dollars will do.

Fifteen thousand dollars was an astronomical sum. And she had only been given twenty-four hours in which to somehow attain the funds. She could not ask Rick for help. Her every instinct begged her to rush to him, because she wasn't sure she could manage this crisis or that horrid man, but she didn't dare.

Somehow she would borrow the money. Somehow, by tomorrow evening, she would meet O'Donnell and get him out of their lives.

She was so afraid.

"Peter, ready the carriage," she said. "I am going out."

THE CITY PRISON WAS A LARGE, almost square, concrete building a few blocks farther downtown. It was dark and gloomy inside. The long, grim corridors matched her mood. She understood the very difficult position Bragg had been placed in. Apparently, Hart's case was so sensational that even the mayor had pressured Bragg to arrest him. She was never going to forgive Rick for caving in to that pressure and arresting Hart so suddenly. Nor would she forgive him for sending Hart to the city's notorious prison.

Images of Hart in shackles filled her mind as she followed a security guard to the visitors' room. She was ill. She reminded herself that Hart would get out on bail shortly—wouldn't he? She wasn't certain she would be eager to release a suspect like Hart on bail, if she were a judge. She had to speak with his lawyer. And even more important, she had to find Daisy's real killer, so Hart wouldn't have to suffer any more such indignities.

The visitors' room was a small and square, with a single pine table in the middle. The exterior wall was a large window, so prison officials could observe the prisoners and their guests. As she stepped inside, she was relieved to find the room brightly lit. It was whitewashed, although the walls were more gray than white. Francesca looked toward the forbidding iron door on the other side of the room. She was eager to see Hart but she was also anxious and afraid. It opened almost immediately and Hart came in.

Instantly she saw that he was not happy to see her. She had hoped that his attitude would have changed by now, given the enormity of the crisis they faced. He was still dressed in his dark trousers and white shirt from the night before—there was no prison uniform. He had no shackles on his ankles, but his wrists were manacled in front of him. In spite of their surroundings, his presence remained magnetic and invulnerable. In spite of everything, he appeared tired but unchanged. Relieved that he did not seem to suffer from any anxiety, Francesca started towards him. The guard restrained her.

"The prisoner could be dangerous, ma'am."

She whirled, angered. "He's my fiancé!"

Hart stepped away from his guard. "We are no longer engaged, Francesca."

She quickly faced him, sensing a much larger problem. "Prison visits are restricted to five minutes, Calder. Please, let's not argue!"

"I wasn't expecting you," he said tightly. He turned. "Take me back to my cell," he told his guard, clearly giving an order.

"Yes, sir," the guard said.

"No!" Francesca cried in disbelief.

He stopped, his shoulders rigid. Slowly he faced her. "I asked you not to come," he said very quietly now. "What is it that you want from me?"

His words stabbed her. "I don't want anything from you, Calder. I only want things *for* you. I want you to have peace of mind and happiness. I came here to discuss the case, and to make certain you were being treated fairly."

Something unsettled and dark was mirrored in his eyes. "I am a rich man, Francesca. I have paid off everyone in this prison. I am being treated like a king. In fact, I had a sirloin steak for breakfast. Do you feel better now?" There was a sarcastic edge to his words.

She hugged herself. "I do not feel better. I will not feel better until you are released from this awful place. In fact, I am furious with Rick." But she absorbed what he had said. "So you are being given special treatment?"

"Yes, I am." He eyed her. "He was only doing what he had to do. I don't think he dared show me any favoritism."

"Now you defend him?" She was incredulous.

"Yes, now I am defending him, believe it or not." His expression hardened. "I am sorry you made the trip downtown. But seeing you now like this is the last thing I intend to do."

Her anger exploded. "You will not treat me this way! If you think that extenuating circumstances can allow you to behave like such a boor, and that down the road we will be all chummy again, then you had better think again!"

He started, his gaze wide. "You are threatening me?"

Suddenly, she realized her power. He had been counting on her friendship for many months now. He claimed he could not live without it. "Ask the guards to leave us. Tell them we want fifteen minutes, not five."

He smiled tightly, without mirth. "Someone has taught you well, Francesca."

"It was you," she said with heat.

He glanced at the tall guard who stood just behind him. "I believe you heard the lady."

"Yes, sir, Mr. Hart," he said. "Johnny." He walked to the other side of the room and the two guards left together.

Whatever Hart was feeling, it was impossible to read. But he said, very softly, "I never expected you to be so ruthless, Francesca."

"I am not being ruthless and I did not threaten you," she said, but she had discovered his Achilles' heel. "I merely spoke the truth. You can't expect my friendship when it suits you, yet reject it now in an act of pure madness."

He hesitated and she saw the conflict in his eyes. She wanted to take him in her arms and reassure him, for she sensed that he was not quite as confident as he appeared. Instead, she walked around the table so she stood in front of him. He said warily, "What do you wish to ask me?"

He was steering her away from anything personal, she thought. But clearly they needed such a diversion. "Your family hired the best criminal attorney in the city," Francesca said.

"I know. Charles Gray was here."

"When will there be a bail hearing?"

"Francesca, I do not want you there."

She ignored his warning. "When does Gray think you will be released on bail?"

"What do I have to do to get you to promise me that you will not come to the bail hearing? If you still care about me the way that you claim, then you have to try to understand me now. The press will be present. You should not be there—they will descend upon you like vultures."

She hadn't thought about the press being at the hearing, but he was right. She did not want to add to his worries. Most important, his passionate insistence meant that he still cared for her. "I promise I will stay away from the bail hearing."

Relief covered his features. "Thank you," he said. And finally, his tone very low, added, "The hearing is in two hours. You don't have to worry. Everything has been taken care of. I will be released there."

She began to understand. The judge presiding over the bail hearing had been paid off. The hearing was only a formality. And while she hated the corruption in the city's judicial system, she could not think about her hypocrisy now. She desperately wanted Hart to be released. He was going to be freed in a few hours, she had never been more thankful. But as she met his gaze she saw that his was searching. He knew very well that her choice would have been a fair and honest hearing. He was wondering just how upset she was at the corruption he had encouraged.

"The evidence is stacked against me. You cannot have it both ways," he said, clearly understanding her exactly. "No honest judge in his right mind would release me now."

She impulsively touched his arm. His sleeves were rolled

down but the cuffs were open. "That's not necessarily true, but I am not going to argue with you. I want you out of here. I can accept this, Calder."

He looked away, and as he did, she glimpsed something in his eyes that might have been fear. She had never seen Hart afraid. Surely she was imagining it.

"I never thought to see the day when you would compromise your morals for me."

She became alarmed. Hart might use this as more evidence that he would drag her down with him. She thought of the lie she had encouraged Alfred to tell. "You have been framed for a murder you did not commit. You have been falsely imprisoned!"

He just gave a doubtful look, and no words could have been as clear. He felt that she had compromised her values for him.

"The Gillespies are in town, Calder," she said, changing the subject. "I have just interviewed them and I am now on my way to see Rose. I am suspicious of the judge. I think that he is lying about not knowing that his daughter was in this city, using another name. And Daisy's sister knows something, or wants something from me, I am certain of it."

"Are you thinking that the judge killed his own daughter?" Hart asked sharply.

"No, I am not, although Bragg does not rule out the possibility that public knowledge of his relationship to Daisy represented a huge embarrassment to him."

"She would have been a lit fuse, Francesca, considering his profession and reputation," Hart said. "But I cannot imagine any father murdering his own child."

She stood close behind him, aware that he was thinking of his own murdered child. "It is permissible to grieve, Calder."

He shook his head. "You are usually the one to jump to those kinds of conclusions," he said, ignoring her last remark.

"I know. But I am very suspicious of Rose. Especially as someone framed *you*," she said.

"My affair with Daisy was hardly a secret. Anyone who murdered her and wanted to cast suspicion elsewhere would easily conclude that he might get away with pointing the finger at me."

"Someone planted a knife in your coach," Francesca exclaimed.

"Have the police determined if it is the murder weapon?"

"Not yet. I don't think they can conclude that, but I do think they might be able to determine if the knife is *not* the murder weapon."

He smiled, just a little, at her.

Her heart leapt with hope. It was his smile of old, heart-achingly familiar. "What is it?"

He rearranged his expression into unreadable lines. "No one is more intent than you when you are on an investigation, Francesca."

"I can't help it. My mind spins with thought after thought. Hart, I have to ask you about Daisy's finances."

He nodded. "What about them?"

"In May, she deposited eight thousand dollars in her account, and ten days later, another twelve thousand. Did you give her the funds?" She feared what his answer might be.

But he was clearly surprised. "No, I did not. Why would I?"

"Thank God!" she exclaimed. "I was afraid you had tried to pay her off."

"For what? For sniping at us? For refusing to leave the house? I am a patient man, Francesca. Besides, if I really wanted to do battle with her, I would simply refuse to pay her household expenses. I had decided not to further antagonize her. She would have moved out in another month," he added.

"And then she told you she was pregnant," Francesca said, watching him closely.

Grief flickered in his eyes. He walked away from her, pacing.

Why wouldn't he share his feelings? She followed him and took his arm, stalling him. "Hart, I am here for you, always."

He suddenly faced her. "Do you have any idea who was paying Daisy off?"

"Is that what you think the money was? A payoff?" she asked, eyes wide.

"That is too much money to have come from her gentlemen customers. Of course, if your theory is right and Gillespie knew his daughter was here, maybe he was giving her the funds. He wouldn't be the first father to support his daughter in such a way."

She was intrigued with the idea. "But the funds were deposited in May, and only then. If they came from Gillespie, that might mean he didn't know where she was before that."

He smiled. "I would think so."

She seized his hand. "Hart! I am sure you are well connected with the Bank of New York. How do I find out where that money came from?" She was very excited now. This was a huge lead, indeed.

"Darling, I own half of the bank. Speak with Robert Miller, the bank's president. He will tell you what you need to know—if the money is traceable, of course."

She blinked. "I doubt Daisy marched into the bank with a valise filled with bills!"

He shrugged. "One never knows."

Her own excitement faded. He glanced sidelong at her and their eyes met. The bond between them was tangible, unmistakable, and she knew he felt it, too. "How are you?" she whispered. "How are you, really?"

He regarded her very seriously now. "I am fine. I would be better if you hadn't come here, Francesca."

He was admitting to his genuine feelings. This was the

opening she had wished for. "Asking me to somehow ignore the fact of your arrest and imprisonment is like asking me not to breathe. I am not turning my back on you. I can't."

"Why," he finally said, "are you so impossibly determined—so impossibly loyal?"

"Do you want a glib answer?" she asked.

"Not really."

"I believe I already told you that I am in love with you, daring, foolish woman that I am."

"Even now."

He hadn't said the words as if they were a question, but Francesca saw the uncertainty in his eyes. She saw the little boy, forever causing trouble, forever attracting attention and criticism, feeling abandoned and unwanted. "Even now."

"I truly did not want you to ever see me like this."

"Like what?" she asked, pretending she did not understand. But she did. Power had become his refuge; in prison, he could so easily be reduced to helplessness. "You were served a steak for breakfast and the guards call you 'Mr. Hart' and 'sir.' I know you are wearing handcuffs. I know you cannot walk out of here right now. That doesn't change all you have done with your life. It doesn't change the fact that in this prison you have circumvented the rules, it doesn't change the road you have traveled, and it certainly doesn't negate all of your accomplishments."

He almost smiled. "Do you really want the truth?"

She was afraid, and she hesitated. "Yes."

"You are my only accomplishment."

"Calder, that is hardly true. You left home at sixteen with nothing—and look at the fortune you have made for yourself! Look at the collection of art you have amassed. Look at the companies you manage and own. Your accomplishments are vast."

"Persuading you to agree to marry me is my only genuine accomplishment."

Did he have any idea, she wondered, that his words were terribly romantic? "I recall very little persuasion," she said tartly, but she did recall his heated kisses and she felt herself blush.

He knew, because he gave her a look. "The attraction between us did make persuasion rather easy," he said.

"It wasn't that," she said, very serious now. "You showed me that beneath that dark reputation you seem to cherish and even flaunt, you are a very good, noble man."

"When will you doubt me?" he exclaimed.

"Never," she said firmly. "Nothing has changed, Calder. You are the most powerful man I know. Even now, in handcuffs, in a prison cell, you are a dominating force, someone to be reckoned with."

He raised his dark gaze to hers. "Everything has changed, has it not?" He said slowly. "Daisy is dead. My child is dead. I am charged with murder. And we are no longer engaged."

After a hurtful, sinking moment, she said, "That was your choice, not mine. It will never be mine. My feelings haven't changed—and I know yours haven't, either."

He did not look away. "My feelings will never change," he said very quietly. "I don't want you here with me, like this. But you remain the sunshine in my life, Francesca. Even now, you brighten up this miserable place and my entire existence."

His words thrilled her, but she remained uncertain. She felt as if they were at a dangerous crossroads, and that he might choose to stay on his lonely, isolated path, without her, even after she had solved this case. "I want to be the sunshine in your life," she whispered unsteadily. "You never have to be alone again. But if you shut the windows, if you close the drapes, how will I ever get back in?"

His expression twisted with grief, misery, and perhaps confusion and doubt. She did not look away, even though she felt foolish tears rising. She tried to smile at him, hoping he would not see.

But he did. He wiped a drop of moisture from her cheek, having to raise both cuffed wrists to do so. Instantly her body tightened and her eyes drifted closed.

"I don't know," he whispered, and he leaned close.

She felt his hands on her face. Her heart filled with hope. He tensed and his mouth took hers, brushing, until his lips firmed in the most urgent, uncompromising manner. Francesca reached for his shoulders and held on, wishing she might never let go. The kiss raged, openmouthed and deep. Finally he pulled away.

She looked into his eyes and smiled at him. "It will never be over, will it? No matter what."

"No, it will never be over," he said. He stepped away from her. "You should go."

He was right. She started to leave, when she realized she hadn't asked him about the money Bragg needed to pay off Mike O'Donnell. She hesitated.

"What is it?"

She faced him. "Rick is also in trouble, Calder."

Surprise flickered in his eyes. "If you mean his head is about to roll over this investigation, I have no intention of blaming myself. His job has been on the line for some time."

"No, it's not about his job. It's about his family," she said.

CHAPTER FIFTEEN

Thursday, June 5, 1902—3:00 p.m.

HART SEEMED TAKEN ABACK. "What are you trying to say?"

"A man named Mike O'Donnell has come forward," Francesca said. "He is the girls' uncle, and a lowlife thug with questionable morals, although he claims to have had a religious awakening. I don't know if you are aware of it, but Rick and Leigh Anne are trying to adopt the girls. He has *suggested* that he could raise the girls himself."

"Why doesn't Rick arrest him for extortion?"

"He never actually asked for money directly. Rick is afraid for Leigh Anne, Calder. She is very fragile now and he doesn't know if she can withstand a prolonged crisis. I suggested that he pay O'Donnell to leave the city."

A moment passed as he considered her words. "I know what you are after, Francesca. But he would never take any money from me."

She was grim. Was Hart refusing to help his own brother? "How do you know that, if you do not ask him if you can help? Would you help, if he let you?"

His eyes flashed. "Of course I would help! I would gladly give him the funds. But I am telling you, he would die before ever being beholden to me."

She was relieved Hart would come to his brother's aid in an emergency. "Rathe and Grace went to Newport for the week.

Who else can he ask? Can I tell him that you have offered him the funds?"

He gave her a look. "He's going to be angry with you for interfering, Francesca. He will be angry with you for approaching me behind his back."

"What do you want to do, then? Wait for him to ask you himself?"

Hart was thoughtful. "He will never come to me in a million years. Go ahead. Offer him the money. But be prepared—he isn't going to be grateful."

"I don't care. I think this is the best solution, considering all that Leigh Anne has been through. We need to pay off O'Donnell and get rid of him," she declared. "It's best for O'Donnell and it is best for the girls."

Hart made a sound, shaking his head as he did so. "You are loyal to the very end."

"I will always be there for your brother, just as I will always be there for you."

"Then we are both fortunate, are we not? That you care so much for us *both*." He was mocking.

She closed her eyes in dismay. Hart was never going to forget her brief romantic interlude with Bragg. "Do we have to argue over my friendship with Rick now? When we are arguing about everything else?"

He studied her, his gaze ominously dark. "Our fifteen minutes are up, Francesca."

Her heart tightened. "Calder…"

"You should go."

MAGGIE BENT OVER THE only table in the one-bedroom flat she leased, sewing industriously by the light from a kerosene lamp. She had lost her job at the Moe Levy factory, due to the excessive number of days she had missed, the manager had said. No amount of explanation had convinced the manager to change his mind. She had four children to support, but before she had been able to spend one single day looking for new employment, Lady Montrose had appeared at her door with Francesca, ordering six new gowns and as many underclothes. Francesca had ordered an evening dress, as well, although Maggie knew she did not need another one, as she had recently finished a large order for her. Then Joel, who was Francesca's assistant, had received a raise in his wages. And just when she had finished the Montrose order, Mrs. Bragg had ordered an entire new wardrobe for Mary's children, Katie and Dot.

Maggie paused in her sewing. Mary O'Shaunessy had been her friend and her death continued to sadden her, but it was a blessing in disguise. Katie and Dot had been taken in by the Braggs, and clearly, they were thriving in such a wonderful family. It was obvious that Leigh Anne thought of herself as their mother. Maggie shuddered, recalling how brave she had been confronting that awful Mike O'Donnell. While she had never met Mary's brother, Maggie knew Mary had been afraid of him, especially when he was drunk.

She smoothed down the bright yellow fabric she was working on. Maybe losing her job at the factory was a blessing in disguise, as well. At first, she had thought that Francesca had maneuvered her sister into ordering so many dresses as an act of kindness and charity. But in the several fittings she had had with Lady Montrose, they had become rather friendly. Francesca's sister was terribly elegant, but she was as kind, as warm and as considerate as her sister. Maggie had come to realize that Lady Montrose had genuinely wanted several new dresses, and that she had admired the two evening gowns Maggie had made for her sister.

Now, with the order Leigh Anne Bragg had just placed, Maggie was beginning to think that maybe, just maybe, she could make ends meet as a seamstress. Maybe she would not need another factory job. Before her husband had died, many years ago, she'd had a foolish but wonderful dream. She had dreamed of one day having her own dress shop. It would be in some fabulous location—perhaps Union Square or the Ladies' Mile. All of the most fashionable uptown ladies would frequent her shop, begging for her services. She would have to turn away customers, for she would be one of the city's most sought-after dressmakers. Her husband had shared her dream. He had sworn that one day she would have her own shop.

It was impossible, though, and she'd never shared her thoughts with anyone else, knowing that it was just a foolish hope. It would be enough to sew for the uptown ladies out of her home, in the darkest hours of the night, barely making ends meet, while she worked by day as a housemaid or candle maker. Still, the possibility now loomed that she might not need the daytime job. She would be happy if she had enough food on the table for her children, four little beds and a roof over their heads. What else did she need?

An image came to mind of a dark and handsome man, a thought she did not want to entertain. Maggie quickly picked up her needle and thread, blinking back unwanted tears—tears she refused to identify. She began to sew, her fingers swift.

A knock sounded on the door.

Paddy and Matt walked together the few blocks to and from the public school they attended, but they never knocked; they shouted and screamed. Her toddler, Lizzie, was on the floor, examining her most precious possessions—two stuffed animals—a spotted horse and a shaggy dog, both gifts from Evan Cahill. But then, the gifts he had given her children were all over the flat. "I'm coming," she said softly, unable to ignore the ache in her heart as she went to get the door.

I told you all along, Maggie girl, he's not for you.

Although her husband had died three years ago, when she was pregnant with Lizzie, he was with her still. Months might go by without a word, and then suddenly he was there in her mind, offering her all kinds of advice and his particular brand of wisdom.

Ye got to move on, me girl. There's someone else out there for you, someone as kind, just not as rich or handsome, someone who will do right by ye and the girl and boys.

Maggie had not a doubt that he was right. She had never expected anything from Evan Cahill. She had never understood his interest in her children, his warmth, his smiles or his visits. But those visits were over anyway. He was marrying the countess.

Maggie opened the door and went into shock. For standing there was none other than the stunning countess herself.

The auburn-haired woman smiled. "Hello. You are Mrs. Kennedy, are you not? The seamstress?"

Maggie realized then that the woman had come to place an order. Somehow she nodded and smiled, but her gaze veered to the woman's waist.

Evan had told her the countess was carrying his child. He had seemed so terribly unhappy when he had spoken, yet she had known that one day, he would be thrilled. One day, the child Bartolla Benevente carried would be the greatest joy in his life. She had told him just that, but he clearly hadn't been able to believe her.

The countess wore a resplendent royal-blue gown that hugged her lush figure and was cut low enough that the dress should only be worn in the evening. It was an expensive, stiff satin, trimmed with equally expensive lace. She wore matching sapphires. Maggie saw that her belly was slightly curved, but still in perfect proportion to the rest of her figure. Maggie did not know how far along she was, but she wasn't showing yet.

Realizing she had been staring in the most inappropriate manner, she jerked her gaze upward. "Do come in, Countess," she stammered in haste, and with the same confusion, she curtsied.

The countess was a head taller than Maggie and she looked down at her with a mixture of amusement and condescension. "Thank you." She swept into the two-room flat, glancing curiously around. "I don't believe we have ever met, although I have heard *all* about you."

Her tone dripped with smug superiority. Maggie was taken aback, but then, perhaps she had become too accustomed to being treated as an equal by the Cahills and Lady Montrose.

Yer a hardworkin', God-fearin' Irish woman, me girl. Ye can be proud of who you are, but you ain't one of them an' you never will be—no matter that he kissed you.

"I have also heard about you," Maggie said, blushing now. She had done her best to forget that Evan Cahill had kissed her, just once. It had been an impulse on his part, obviously, but she had secretly dreamed of his kisses for months afterward. "I am very pleased to meet you, Countess."

"Really?" She glanced at the table where Maggie was working on Katie's canary-yellow dress. "And how would you know about me?" She faced her, a beaded blue purse in her hands.

Maggie was disconcerted. The other woman did not seem pleasantly disposed toward her. "I…I…I am a friend of Francesca Cahill's," she managed to say. "And a friend of the family's." Her cheeks were even hotter now and Evan's image loomed in her mind when she did not want him there, not ever, and especially not now. "Have you come to order a gown?" she asked in some desperation.

The countess raised her eyebrows. "My modiste is in Paris, my dear," she said coolly. "I would hardly order a dress from you."

Maggie was shocked by her rudeness.

Bartolla spoke again. "And I do think you meant that you are a friend of Evan Cahill's?"

Maggie felt cornered, trapped. She did not want to entertain the other woman now. Worse, she had an idea of why Bartolla Benevente had come.

"What is wrong? Do I frighten you?" Bartolla mocked.

In that instant, Maggie realized that this woman hated her. The countess wasn't the lady she had thought her to be. She was too terribly nasty. Had Evan told her about the kiss? There could be no other explanation! "I don't know why you are here," Maggie whispered. "Would you like some tea?"

"I am not sitting down at *your* table with *you* to sip tea," Bartolla said, her tone vicious. "I am a countess! My home in Italy is a palace! I live uptown in a mansion! I did not come here to be a friend to you, Mrs. Kennedy!"

Maggie backed up. The apartment was small and she hit the edge of the kitchen table, where she had been working. "He told you," she whispered, her heart racing with alarm and fear. "It was a mistake—it is my entire fault—I am sorry!"

Bartolla's eyes widened. There was outrage in them. "He told me what?" she demanded. "You little whore, what have you done? Do I even have to guess? You jumped into his bed, didn't you?"

Maggie gasped in shock at being called such a name and at the suggestion that she had behaved so shamefully. "No! I would never do such a thing. It was only a kiss! Just one single kiss! And I know you are marrying him. I am happy for you both. It will never happen again, Countess!"

Bartolla was still, and she lifted both dark, plucked brows. "A kiss," she repeated. "One single kiss?"

Maggie nodded, biting her lip. "It should have never happened."

Bartolla took two steps and loomed over her. "You are damn right it should have never happened. He is not for the likes of you, Mrs. Kennedy, but you already know that, don't you? Gentlemen only use trollops like you as a diversion, as entertainment, on a cold, lonely night. They *marry* women like me."

Maggie stiffened. "I am not a trollop. I work very hard to feed my—"

"Yes, you work," Bartolla said low. "You are a *seamstress*. He is a *Cahill*. I am a *countess*. I am sure that even your befuddled brain can do the arithmetic."

Maggie somehow drew herself up. "You do not need to be so insulting."

"How dare you tell me anything!" Bartolla exclaimed. "He is *not* for you. So turn those blue eyes elsewhere—or you will be very sorry, indeed."

Maggie held her head high. No one had ever spoken to her in such a manner before. "I know we come from different worlds. You do not need to threaten me. The kiss was a mistake. It will never happen again."

"I will do more than threaten you, Mrs. Kennedy. Do you not have four children?"

Maggie felt the world stop turning. The flat had become still.

"You have four small children," the countess said again with a smirk. "It would be a shame if anything were to happen to any one of them—like that sweet little girl on the floor?"

Maggie ran to Lizzie and picked her up so abruptly that the toddler wailed in protest. Holding her tightly to her breast, she faced the countess, shaking with fear and outrage. "You would threaten my children?"

"Stay away from Mr. Cahill. He is not for your kind," she said, marching to the door. She paused, glancing back at Maggie with visible anger. "I strongly suggest you send him away if he ever calls here again. Good day, Mrs. Kennedy." She left, closing the door behind her.

Maggie moved. She put Lizzie down and ran to the door, throwing the bolt home. Then she stood there, aware that she was panting. She could not seem to get enough air.

It had only been a kiss.

And then she could no longer deny the truth. She was desperately in love with Evan Cahill, a man who was so far above her he might as well have been the king of Great Britain. Somehow, the countess had guessed.

Maggie wiped her eyes; only then realizing she was crying. She had thought the countess a great lady, like Francesca or her sister. But she wasn't a lady, never mind her wealth or her breeding. She was horrid and nasty, she was evil. Maggie had genuinely wanted Evan to have a life of happiness and love. Now she was appalled. But the countess was pregnant. It was his duty to marry her, no matter her real nature. Maggie hurt for Evan now, but there was no helping it—there was no helping him.

Bartolla Benevente had no right to threaten the children. But Maggie had the terrible feeling that the countess had meant her every word. She tried to tell herself that she need not worry. After all, she did not expect to see Evan Cahill ever again.

HART STEPPED OUTSIDE OF THE court building with his lawyer. He rubbed his wrists, feeling the cold steel of the manacles he no longer wore against his skin. He wasn't sure he would ever stop feeling it. It was a gray day that looked as if it might rain, but he did not notice the cloudy sky or the buildings lining the street. He kept seeing the dark gray walls of his cell, the single narrow mattress, the dirty sink, the iron bars and the hostile but avid stares of the other prisoners. He kept seeing Francesca, whom he had ruthlessly hurt—and who would never give up on him, or so she claimed.

There had never been any doubt that he would be released immediately on bail, but beneath the clothing he wore, his skin was damp and clammy.

"Calder, don't you dare throw that rock."

The boy ignored his brother, grinned, and threw the rock— hard. They had just arrived at his brother's father's house. His brother had a father—a real father—and a pretty, kind stepmother and a bunch of other brothers and even a little sister, too. The boy saw that he had missed the window by an inch. He laughed at his older brother, running away, outside.

But Rick followed, seizing him and dragging him back. You need to apologize! Why did you have to do that? Did you want to break the window? Do you want them to send us away? Do you want them to send you away?

The little boy had apologized, carefully watching the pretty red-haired lady, wary and waiting to see what she would do. But she hadn't beaten him or yelled at him. She hadn't said a word about the rock. She had asked him to sit down at the kitchen table, where she had given him a cookie and a glass of milk.

"Calder stole my notebook!"

The entire family turned to stare at the little boy.

"Calder, did you take Rourke's notebook?"

Of course he had, because the boy was a spoiled prince and he loved his stupid notebook, which was filled with really stupid notes so he could achieve stupid high grades, making his parents love him even more than they already did.

"It's only a stupid notebook," he protested stubbornly. He already knew that they whispered about his incorrigible behavior at night when they thought they were alone—and now he could see their disappointment. He was glad—he didn't care—he didn't need this big, fake family that wasn't even his.

His brother's father trapped him in the bedroom he shared with his brother and one of the man's other sons. "You can't do whatever you feel like doing! You know better—I know you know better. You have to apologize to Rourke.

The little boy watched the man closely, waiting for the real punishment. But he sighed and came closer, clasping his shoulder. I know this is hard for you. I know you miss your mother. Losing someone is hard, and it's hard fitting into a new family. Just try, please? I know you know the difference between right and wrong."

Hart shut off his thoughts abruptly. He hated thinking about that pathetic child. He had desperately wanted to belong—no matter how badly he might behave. He had desperately wanted any kind of attention, and he had been as desperate to push and test the Braggs, to see if they might love him no matter how he behaved. But it had been a losing battle. That child had not belonged, certainly not in the Bragg family. He hadn't even belonged in his own mother's family. Remembering that hurt.

His mother, Lily, had given her love to her firstborn, Rick. Not that he could blame Lily. She had been too tired and then too ill to deal with his wild antics. It had been easier for her to let her older son manage the young, recalcitrant one. And that had only led to more mischief and disobedience. It was almost as if Lily had stopped caring, as if he could do anything and she would merely smile at him and collapse in her bed. And then, of course, she had died.

The Braggs had been stronger. By the time he'd moved into their home, doing whatever he wanted had become a part of his nature. He had even known that he was testing them, waiting for them to grow tired of it all and just send him far away. But they had not ignored his behavior. Not a single incident had ever passed that he was not reprimanded or punished. They refused to give up on him, but by then it didn't matter. He was not a Bragg. They had five other children that they obviously and openly loved. He was the outsider. They could be kind, they could feed him, put a roof over his head and chastise him for being rude and mean, but it didn't change anything.

Hart felt sorry for that child who had never been able to fit in, who had never been wanted, who had only been tolerated, first in Lily's sordid home, and then in the Bragg mansion.

That child was a painful and constant reminder of far too much. And now, with Daisy and his child murdered, with his relationship with Francesca formally over, Calder felt alone. He reminded himself that the boy he was had died a long time ago— Hart had buried him with no small amount of satisfaction. But the reminder did not work. This time, there was a strong chance that he was really going to be sent away—to prison.

"Things went well, as expected," he said quietly to Gray, as if his fears were not lurking.

"Things went very well, and you should not worry about anything. The police will find the real killer and this case will be closed," Gray said firmly. He was a tall, thin man with a deep, resonant voice that would serve any Shakespearean actor well. It had served him well in court, time and again. "I know you have ended your engagement to Miss Cahill, Hart, but her reputation as a sleuth precedes her. I should be very pleased if she were to stay on this case."

He did not want to think about Francesca. She had been the light in his life. Now his world had turned gray, like the skies overhead. "I'm not worried," Hart said flatly. It was a lie, of course, but Gray could not know it. "And frankly, Miss Cahill is an independent woman. I could never dissuade her from pursuing an investigation." His mouth softened as he spoke. Maybe that was why Francesca was so hauntingly beautiful to him, more beautiful than any other woman he had ever known. If he dared feel, it hurt so much to be without her now. But he'd had no choice. Besides, eventually she would have seen the light and left him.

Before Gray could respond, the reporters who had been present during the hearing raced out of the court building, calling his name. A dozen questions were shouted at him, all at once.

"Mr. Hart! Can you comment on what it was like to spend the night in jail?"

"Mr. Hart! Do you have any regrets regarding the death of your mistress?"

"Mr. Hart! Is it true that Miss Jones is really the daughter of Judge Gillespie? Did you know, sir?"

"Mr. Hart! Are you worried about being charged with the murder?"

Gray faced the reporters, whispering to Hart, "I suggest you leave, sir. I will take care of the newsmen."

"Thank you," Hart said, very surprised that the press had already learned about Daisy's real identity. That would work to his advantage, and he had the inkling then that Francesca might have leaked the news. As he turned to go down the courthouse steps, he glimpsed his brother coming out of the building behind him. Rick had been present during the bail hearing, although he had not been called to the stand.

Hart had nothing to say to him and he started down the wide limestone steps. His six-in-hand was waiting at the curb.

"Calder." Bragg caught up to him.

Hart did not pause. "I didn't expect to see you here."

Bragg took his arm, forcing him to pause. "Why not? In spite of our differences, we are brothers. I came to show my support."

Hart saw with surprise that his half brother was being sincere. But then, it would be easy for Rick to be supportive now, as he had gotten what he really wanted. Francesca was now free. "Really? And what is it that you want now? My thanks? My undying gratitude?" It had been a hellish twenty-four hours and he lost his temper then. "Oh, wait! You need funds, and you need them from me." He smiled coldly.

Bragg turned white.

But Hart could not stop himself, and he felt savagely satisfied that in spite of being a murder suspect, in spite of losing Francesca, in this brief moment he had all the power. "You are welcome to the money—I already told Francesca that. Just tell me how much. But I want something in return. I want Daisy's killer found. I have no intention of going back to jail."

Bragg was turning red. "She asked you for the funds?" He was incredulous now. "I don't want a damn thing from you—and I haven't, not in years!"

"I was under the impression you were desperate," Hart said, aware that he was lashing out at his brother, when his brother had nothing to do with the deaths of Daisy and his child, or the loss of Francesca. He was the one who had wished his own child into nonexistence; he was the one who had terminated the engagement with Francesca.

"If I decide to pay that thug off, I will go to the banks," Bragg said curtly. "But thank you for so kindly offering me the money!" He turned to go.

Hart seized his arm. "Wait. Stop."

Bragg turned in disbelief.

Hart took a moment to gather his composure. He was angry and frustrated, but Rick was in trouble. "I am more than happy to give you the funds, Rick." He spoke seriously now. "It has been a rough night. I am sorry for behaving like a boor. Francesca told me all about O'Donnell. You need to think of the girls and not our rivalry."

"You are hardly a rival," Bragg said tersely. "And do not dare tell me how to prioritize! I have always put family first." His meaning was clear—that Hart would only put himself first.

"Of course you have, because virtue and family devotion go hand in hand. Tell me something I don't already know, Rick, such as what you will do, now that Francesca and I are no longer engaged?"

Bragg shook his head. "You know, Calder, you haven't changed. You love to provoke! I will always care about Francesca, and I am very happy that you two are apart. She is too good for you. She deserves more than you can ever give her."

"I happen to agree," he said tightly. "But oddly, she accepted my proposal. I never really thought she would."

"How could she refuse, when you could not restrain yourself from seducing her?" Bragg asked with scathing bitterness.

"I haven't seduced her." His anger instantly imploded. "I would never sink so low, not with Francesca." He saw that Rick was startled. "But as we are being so honest with each other, what about your wife? Will you really remain wed to her now that she is paralyzed? Wait, I asked the wrong question! Now that Francesca is free, will you finally do what you really want to do, will you pursue her?"

Bragg's expression quickly became one of disgust. "I should have known that you could not understand duty, devotion and love. I am not going to deny that I care deeply about Francesca, and I always will. But I would never turn my back on Leigh Anne now, when she needs me the most."

Hart laughed. "You and Francesca are exactly alike. What a shame the timing has always been off for you both!"

"Why are you doing this now?" Bragg was incredulous.

Hart wondered the same thing. It made him ill to think of Francesca returning to his brother, but he could not ignore the dreadful certainty consuming him. Now that he had walked away, sooner or later, Bragg and Francesca would find their way back to each other. He was certain.

Bragg said quietly, "You did the right thing, Calder. Francesca has a good name. She doesn't need to be a part of this scandal. I have come to realize that you really care for her. I know this wasn't easy for you. You put her first. It was a noble act."

He stared at his brother. "I cannot believe you are flattering me."

Bragg shrugged. "You have protected her from an ugly scandal. No one could deny your actions were heroic."

Such praise and candor from his brother left him speechless. It was a moment before he spoke. "For once, we are agreed—Francesca doesn't need to be associated with me now." Then he met his brother's gaze. "Actually, when it comes to Francesca, we usually agree."

"I hate to admit it," Bragg said, "but you are right."

"Then admit I am right once more," Hart said.

"I don't understand."

"I want you to have the funds you need. I want the girls to be safe with you and Leigh Anne," Hart said, meaning it. "You don't have to pay me back. Consider the money a gift—an overdue Christmas present, if you wish."

"I can't accept."

"You would put your pride first?" Hart was incredulous. "For God's sake, the money isn't dirty!"

"I will get the money, if I have to, but I am not taking it from you," Bragg said harshly.

The brief amicability they had shared had vanished into thin air. "I knew you would die before taking one red cent from me." He reached for the door to his carriage.

Bragg seized his arm. "Have you really ended it with Francesca? She thinks so, but I know you. Is this a ploy on your part?"

Hart smiled at him strangely. Then he climbed into the carriage, signaling his driver to leave.

AFTER PICKING UP JOEL, Francesca had Raoul drive them to the brothel where Rose lived and worked. But Rose was not in. Instead, Francesca had interviewed the madam, Mrs. Delaney, and two of her girls. Everyone agreed that Rose had become increasingly angry in the course of the past few months—and not just with Hart, but with Daisy. Rose had changed, becoming sullen, hostile and withdrawn. According to Mrs. Delaney, there had not been any reconciliation with Daisy. However, no one believed her capable of murdering the woman she so loved.

Mrs. Delaney told her that Rose had said this morning that she was going to Daisy's. Now, as Raoul parked the carriage across the street from Daisy's brick home, Francesca wondered if Rose could really be the murderer. If she was, wouldn't she avoid the scene of her gruesome crime? But if she were innocent, being at Daisy's might provide some comfort in her time of grief.

As Joel and Francesca began to step down from the carriage, Francesca saw the front door of Daisy's house open. Instantly she recognized the large, gray-haired man leaving. She seized Joel's arm, pulling him back inside the coach, in shock. Brendan Farr, New York City's chief of police, hurried to a small carriage that was waiting. He climbed in and the carriage drove off.

What was Farr doing at Daisy's? He might have been there on police business, but he was not an inspector—he had an entire police force to run. Not only that, he had not been with any other police officer, and policemen rarely conducted their affairs alone. Her instincts screamed at her. Something was amiss.

"Miz Cahill?" Joel was wide-eyed. "Wasn't that the chief?"

She reached for his shoulder, her mind spinning. "Yes, it was." How calm she sounded. Had Farr been at Daisy's to look for evidence? If so, the fact that he was alone spoke volumes. If he was on this case, he was clearly acting on his own. She knew he despised her. She knew he was not loyal to Bragg. She thought he was only loyal to himself, and possibly to his own select group of men. Did he wish to crack the case himself? Did he want the glory, the fame? Or did he hope to circumvent her? Hart was both Rick's brother and her former fiancé. He would be pleased, she thought, if Hart took the fall for Daisy's murder.

But would he tamper with evidence? Hart had been framed. Francesca was uneasy. She had suspected Farr of criminal activities in prior investigations. She did not trust him and she knew he was ruthless. In this case, however, he had no motive for murdering Daisy.

She turned her gaze to Joel. "I am very suspicious," she said.

He nodded. "Want me to tail him?"

It was a brilliant idea, but if Joel was caught, she would be afraid for his safety. "No. He's a dangerous man, Joel. I'd worry what he might do if he ever found out that you were following him."

"But he wouldn't find out," Joel said, his eyes dark with excitement.

"I can't put you in that kind of danger," Francesca said firmly. As they stepped onto the sidewalk, she tried to think of some other reason for his presence at Daisy's. The more she debated the subject, the more she became convinced that he was up to no good—and that he was a threat to Hart.

Homer answered the door. "Good afternoon, Miss Cahill." He seemed to have come to grips with his mistress's murder and he let her in with a slight smile. "How may I help you?"

"Is Rose Cooper here, by any chance?" Francesca asked.

Homer nodded. "She is in the salon."

Before he could lead her the short distance to the salon, Francesca restrained him. "Homer, what did Chief Farr want?"

"I don't know, Miss Cahill, but he and Miss Cooper spoke for a few moments."

Francesca rubbed her jaw. So he was investigating the case on his own! "Did he snoop about the house?"

"No." Homer seemed surprised. "I believe he came here looking for Miss Cooper."

Did he also suspect Rose? she wondered. "How long did they speak? Were you present?"

"He was only here for a few moments, perhaps five minutes, maybe ten. And I am sorry. They spoke behind closed doors. I didn't hear anything."

Francesca hesitated. "Homer, if he comes back, would you please tell me? And if he does, could you possibly, discreetly, eavesdrop?" She smiled sweetly at him.

Homer's eyes were wide. "He is the chief of police," he said in surprise.

"Yes, he is. But the department is terribly corrupt. I do not know why he is here. He is not an inspector. If Newman had come today, I would not be so dismayed."

Homer nodded, appearing uneasy.

Francesca smiled reassuringly at him and he showed her to the salon doors. Although Rose was not the mistress of the house, Francesca waited while he knocked. Rose answered the door immediately.

Instantly, Francesca saw the dark circles under her eyes and the downward turn of her mouth. Although she was beautifully dressed in a dark blue velvet suit, it was obvious that she had just been crying. "Hello, Rose," Francesca said softly, and she could not help but feel sorry once again for the other woman. The truth was, she hoped Rose was not the killer. "Are you feeling any better?"

Tears filled Rose's eyes. "I will never feel better," she said.

Then, her gaze flashed. "No, I will feel better when Hart is in prison for his crimes."

Francesca decided not to argue about Hart's guilt or innocence. "I am glad I found you. I have some new leads and I need to ask you some questions."

"This is not a good time," Rose said.

"Has something happened? Did Chief Farr upset you?"

Rose spoke in anguish. "Did you know? Did you know that Daisy was pregnant with Hart's child?"

It took Francesca a moment to realize that Rose had not known about the pregnancy. And in the next instant, she realized that the discord between Daisy and Rose must have been even greater than she had thought, for Daisy not to have said a word. "I found out yesterday," she said. "Farr told you?"

"Yes." Rose wiped at the tears that were falling. "I am unbearably hurt." She turned abruptly and walked back into the salon.

Francesca followed her inside. "Did you and Daisy reconcile at all?" She wanted Rose to admit that they had not, as Mrs. Delaney and her girls had said.

Rose whirled, weeping. "I had thought so. I had thought there was hope. I mean, we did spend some time together. She said I was her dear friend. I thought that when she got over Hart, things would return to the way they were. But she was planning on having his baby and she did not tell me!"

Francesca put her arm around her. It did not seem as if Daisy had remained in love with Rose. "You don't know that things wouldn't have returned back to normal, in time," she said, trying to comfort her.

Rose gave her an angry glance and pulled away. "Daisy misled me, and not for the first time!"

Francesca saw her sudden, open anger. "How else did she mislead you?"

"Does it matter?"

"I want to help," Francesca said, but in truth, she wanted to know if Rose had been angry enough to murder Daisy even though she hadn't known about the child.

Rose sank down on the sofa. "We spent a few nights together and that was why I had hope. She would act as if nothing had happened between us, and then it was all about her scheming to get Hart back. There were times when I felt used, Francesca. I didn't want to admit it, not even to myself. Do you think she was using me?"

Francesca was beginning to wonder that herself. "I think she cared about you."

"When she told me she was going to accept Hart's offer and become his mistress, I begged her to reconsider. I knew no good could come of it! She laughed. She loved me then—she told me not to worry. But within weeks, I was worried. Within weeks, Hart refused to allow me in this house, and she was happy! Do you know what it is like to have your heart broken, not once, but many times, by the same person?"

"No, I don't. Did you share your feelings? Did you confront her?"

"Do I seem like the kind of woman who would keep my feelings to myself? Of course I told her how I felt, and we argued madly! We have been arguing for months."

Francesca looked at the floor, her heart pounding.

Rose seized her arm, standing. "You are looking for evidence against me!"

"Rose, I don't blame you for how you feel," Francesca began, in the hopes of placating her.

"Get out!"

Francesca wished she had had more tact. "Rose, if you did not kill her, then the killer is out there. I found Daisy's real family and I need to ask you some questions."

"You found her family?" Rose seemed astonished.

Francesca told her about Judge Gillespie and his wife and daughter.

Rose sat down, staring at her lap. "She came from such a good family," she whispered.

"And she left them to become a prostitute," Francesca said. "Rose, I have to ask again. Please, are you certain she never alluded to her reasons for running away?"

"Never," she said firmly. "The one time I tried to ask her, she made it very clear that if I ever raised the subject again, our friendship was over." Rose finally glanced up, meeting Francesca's eyes.

Francesca absorbed that. "Do you know anything about the twenty thousand dollars Daisy deposited in her bank account in May?"

Rose's eyes widened. "She deposited twenty thousand dollars in her account?"

"Yes, she did. Do you have any idea how she got a hold of such a large sum?"

"No. I don't. This is the first I have heard of it." Rose became bitter. "So she was keeping another secret from me!"

Francesca noted how hostile toward Daisy Rose seemed. "Well, I certainly don't think she was paid such a sum for her services," Francesca said. "Someone was paying her off. The question is, why?"

"Paying her off?" It took her a moment to understand. "Well, we both know who had a motive."

"The money did not come from Hart." Francesca decided to change the topic. "I have one more question. What did Chief Farr want?"

"He wanted to ask me some questions," she said, looking away. "I think he thinks I am involved—just as you do."

Francesca felt certain that Rose was lying about Farr. "What kind of questions did he ask?"

Rose shrugged. "He wanted to know where I was that night. I told him what I told you—what I already told the police."

"Is this the first time he questioned you?"

She hesitated. "Yes."

She was lying again. "Why won't you tell me the truth? I want to find Daisy's killer, Rose, and you are making it very difficult for me!"

"I am telling you the truth. I never met Chief Farr before today," Rose cried, standing. "And I didn't like his questions, just like I don't like him!"

Francesca sighed. "Very well. If you recall anything Daisy said, anything you did not understand, or anything that might relate to the investigation, please contact me."

Rose nodded, clearly relieved that Francesca was leaving. Francesca entered the front hall, Rose remaining behind. Homer materialized and opened the door for her.

Francesca felt as if she were very close to solving the case, as if the answers she was seeking were right there in front of her.

She faced Homer with a smile, handing him one of her cards. "Please, do not hesitate to call me if you think of something that seems relevant to the case."

"Miss Cahill? I couldn't help overhearing. I think there is something you should know," he said, surprising her.

"What is that?"

"You mentioned a Judge Gillespie."

"Yes, I did. Why do you ask?"

He was eager. "Because Judge Gillespie was here, twice."

"You mean today?"

He shook his head. "No. Last month. In May. He came to see Miss Jones."

CHAPTER SIXTEEN

Thursday, June 5, 1902—4:00 p.m.

LEIGH ANNE HADN'T MADE a single social call since the carriage accident had destroyed her ability to walk. That had now changed. The episode with that hideous O'Donnell replayed time and again in her mind. But she was determined: O'Donnell was not going to destroy her family. So she was calling on the only person who might actually lend her fifteen thousand dollars—and do so discreetly. She intended to convince Bartolla Benevente, the wealthy Italian countess, to lend her the vast sum, and if persuasion was not enough, she was prepared to go even further.

Her stomach was in knots. Trembling, she remained seated in her wheeled chair in the foyer of the Channing home, Peter hovering by her. Bartolla was wealthy, although no one knew exactly how great the fortune was that her dead husband had left her. She certainly had fifteen thousand dollars, Leigh Anne thought. However, Leigh Anne knew Bartolla well enough to know that she was selfish and even malicious.

Leigh Anne wished she could share this terrible burden with Rick. She had actually considered doing so, but she had realized almost instantly that she could not tell him what had happened. He would arrest O'Donnell, she was certain of it. What if the courts failed to convict him? Or what if he was released on bail before any trial? She was terrified of him. He would come back, she knew it, only this time it would be worse. Perhaps he would go so far as to abduct the girls. He was clearly evil and vengeful.

Or he might harass her again. She knew he would not be adverse to using his male power over her and that thought sickened her impossibly.

She was shaking with her fear and her determination. Rick's income was modest and they had little savings, so she could not go to the banks, as they would never extend such credit to her. Nor could she go to his wealthy family without Rick knowing. Her sole recourse was the countess.

The last time she had seen Bartolla was when the countess had called on her at home, at least a month ago. Bartolla had seemed to delight in Leigh Anne's new circumstances. Leigh Anne had understood. Bartolla enjoyed being the most beautiful woman in any room, and she had always looked at Leigh Anne as if they were rivals, when that was not the case. While they were not exactly friends, Leigh Anne had never considered her a threat, and they were certainly more than acquaintances. They had spent some time together in Europe, and not just on social occasions. It had been completely natural for two American women in a foreign country to seek each other out for shopping and luncheons and chitchat.

God, it seemed like a different lifetime, Leigh Anne thought, perspiring.

Bartolla sailed into the entry hall, a bright smile on her face. As always, she was beautifully attired in silk and diamonds. "Leigh Anne! I am thrilled that you have decided to get out and about, at last! I wondered if you would ever return my call. You must be feeling so much better," she gushed, bending down toward Leigh Anne so she could peck her cheek. She made an effort to do so, just so Leigh Anne might notice how inconvenient it was to now greet her in her chair. "Or have you become used to that chair?"

Leigh Anne felt herself smile. The act was a monumental feat. She did not miss the verbal barb, but she would take any knives that Bartolla wished to throw her way. "My dear, please forgive me for my rudeness in taking so long to return your call. But you are the very first call I am making since my accident." Leigh Anne's mouth was dry. This was the first time she had ever referred to the accident with anyone other than Rick.

Bartolla must have somehow known. Her eyes widened a fraction with some surprise. "I am so flattered." She turned toward Peter. "Please, push Mrs. Bragg into the salon so we may sit and chat more comfortably."

Peter obeyed. The big Swede had been in a state of distress ever since O'Donnell had left and Leigh Anne had refused to let him summon Rick. She knew how loyal and devoted he was to them both, and he had witnessed firsthand her depression, her sorrow and her inability to get out of the house these past few months. Understandably, he was suspicious of her outing now.

When he had wheeled her into the salon, Bartolla following, Leigh Anne smiled firmly at him in dismissal. He left the room, leaving both women alone in its vast, exotic interior.

"How is the police commissioner? He must be frantically trying to solve Daisy Jones's murder."

"He is deeply involved in the investigation. Of course, he does not apprise me of police affairs," Leigh Anne said, although that was not quite the truth.

Bartolla gave her a skeptical look. "Is he hoping Hart really is guilty of the dastardly deed?" She laughed.

Leigh Anne controlled a flash of anger. Hart was Rick's half brother and despite their enmity, that made him family. "Hart is not a murderer. Surely you remain friends with him, and with Francesca?"

Bartolla merely smiled benignly. "Hart despises me—and I despise him. But of course, I adore Francesca. She is so good and she can do no wrong, ever!"

Leigh Anne did not like the sound of that, but she could not be diverted now. "Bartolla, how is Evan?"

"Wonderful, wonderful, and thank you for asking. We are

more in love than ever." She lowered her voice. "We shall soon tie the knot, I think, my dear, and I have never been happier."

"I am so happy for you." Her heart continued to race madly in her chest. "Our lives have certainly changed, haven't they, since we were both in Europe?"

"Yes, our lives have changed. I hadn't really thought about it."

Sweat ran down Leigh Anne's body in streams. "Dear, I was actually hoping to ask a rather important favor of you. I am in a bit of a difficult situation," she managed to say.

Leigh Anne could feel Bartolla's avid curiosity—or was it delight? "You wish to ask *me* a favor? How odd! What trouble could you possibly be in? Other than the fact that you have suffered a terrible, tragic accident, of course."

Leigh Anne smiled stiffly. Bartolla was never going to let her forget that she was crippled for life. "I really cannot say. I do know this request is somewhat unusual, but…could you lend me some funds? It is *extremely* important," she added nervously.

Bartolla was clearly stunned by the request. "You wish to borrow money from me? But of course, Rick works and makes a modest living. Are you thinking of buying some expensive jewelry? Why wouldn't you approach his father? Rathe Bragg is a millionaire."

"I can't. This favor must remain a private matter, strictly between you and me."

Bartolla understood. "You don't want Rick to know."

It was so hard to do this, Leigh Anne thought. But then an image of the girls swept through her mind, Dot so blond and angelic, Katie so worried and needy. "No, he can never know."

Bartolla took a closer seat. She leaned forward. "This is intriguing!"

"It really isn't," Leigh Anne somehow said.

"Well, what do you want the money for? I must know!"

Leigh Anne had no intention of telling her. "Bartolla, I am

afraid that is also a very private matter. But I am quite desperate. I am asking you for help. I will be indebted to you forever."

Bartolla blinked, sitting upright now. After a thoughtful pause, she said, "Well. How much do you need?"

Leigh Anne felt her lips stretch into a frozen smile. "Fifteen thousand dollars."

Bartolla cried out. "That is a small fortune!"

"Yes, and your husband left you a fortune. Please." Leigh Anne felt as if she could no longer breathe. *"Please."*

Bartolla stood up and she looked down at Leigh Anne. "Darling, I cannot help you. I am sorry. I simply cannot lend you such a sum, as we both know you would never be able to pay it back."

Leigh Anne instinctively seized the arms of her chair, her body urging her to leap to her feet. "Of course I will pay it back."

"How?" Bartolla was disbelieving.

"In a few months, I will borrow the money from Rathe. He will not hesitate to loan it to me and I know you are aware of that."

Bartolla seemed perplexed. "Then borrow the money now."

"I can't."

Bartolla was clearly trying to ascertain what Leigh Anne was up to. "Darling, I do apologize. I simply cannot help you. You will have to go to your father-in-law."

Leigh Anne was ready to weep. Instead, she said tersely, "Will you change your mind if I invite Evan for supper, and regale him with tales of our adventures on the Continent?"

Bartolla blanched and Leigh Anne knew she understood.

Bartolla had married an Italian count at the age of sixteen. He had been sixty. Within a month of that highly publicized marriage, she had begun a series of sensational, very public affairs. Those affairs had continued for three years, until his dying day. The count had not seemed to know—either that, or he had not cared.

Leigh Anne hated descending to blackmail. She had no choice.

"I will deny everything," Bartolla finally said.

Leigh Anne shrugged. "I intend to tell him the truth, Bartolla. I hate doing this, I do. But I desperately need fifteen thousand dollars—and I need it by tomorrow night."

Bartolla was tight-lipped with anger now. "Evan will not believe you."

Leigh Anne said nothing.

"Why do you wish to hurt my chances for marriage with him?" she cried.

"I don't. I just need the money. Please."

Bartolla remained as white as a sheet. "I am with child, Leigh Anne. Now I am asking you for a favor—do not say anything to Evan."

"If you do not loan me the funds, I am going to tell Evan about all of your affairs, every single one, and I will give him *names*," Leigh Anne said. "Pierre Maurier is in the city, by the way."

Although it was almost impossible, Bartolla blanched further. "I can't give you the funds."

"Then I am afraid Evan will learn of your prior infidelities," Leigh Anne said.

Bartolla seemed close to tears. "Do you think I am living here in the middle of nowhere by choice?" she cried. "I have no wealth! I am impoverished, completely so. My life here as the wealthy widow is a sham! My husband left me a pittance, a pittance, Leigh Anne. He left everything to his children, damn them all!"

FRANCESCA AND HOMER WERE still standing in the open doorway when Francesca realized someone was slowly walking up the brick path to the house. She turned and saw a woman with vaguely dark hair. Her eyes widened as she recognized Daisy's sister, Lydia.

Lydia's brownish hair was pulled into a severe chignon and she was beautifully dressed in a black mourning dress. Her face, despite its olive complexion, was pale, and she seemed tense and strained as she hesitantly approached. Francesca quickly went to greet her. "Miss Gillespie! This is a surprise. Can I be of any help?" she asked. This was an opportunity and she knew it.

Lydia was staring into the house, her eyes wide. She finally looked at Francesca. "So this is where Honora lived."

Francesca nodded. She glanced toward the street, where a hansom was pulling away from the curb. "You are alone?"

Lydia nodded. "I need to see where my sister lived."

"Come in, then," Francesca said gently. She stole another glance at Lydia's profile; she remained distressed and grief-stricken. "How are your parents?"

Lydia paused in the front hall, looking at the Venetian mirror, the fine side table, the potted palm in its Oriental vase. "They are in mourning. Honora did very well for herself, living as she did."

"Yes," Francesca said carefully.

Lydia turned to her. "You said you were friends."

"Somewhat. The moment I met D—Honora—I liked her."

"Why? She was hardly a lady."

"I do not judge books by their covers, Miss Gillespie," Francesca said. "And Daisy—I beg your pardon!—your sister was intriguing. She was a study in contradictions. She was clearly well-bred, and gracious and graceful. And she was helpful to me in an earlier investigation."

"I don't see how you liked her. How could you like her when she was the mistress of your fiancé?"

Francesca winced. "I take it you have been reading the newspapers?"

"He kept her here. Your fiancé."

"Hart broke up with your sister in February, when I accepted his proposal."

"But she continued to live here, in his house. It's so odd." Lydia looked away. "She was always that way, even at fifteen."

"What do you mean?"

Lydia shrugged. "She was so beautiful. Everyone would stare at her—women as well as men. Everyone fell in love with her." Lydia met Francesca's gaze. "Did Mr. Hart fall in love with her?"

Francesca tensed. "You will have to ask him." Lydia seemed to be asking a lot of questions.

"Did you and your fiancé end your engagement because of her?"

Now warning bells went off, but Francesca smiled. "Hart wants to protect me from scandal. We broke up because Daisy was murdered. It had nothing to do with their past affair." She stressed the word *past* slightly.

"I don't mean to be rude, but what if you didn't like my sister very much? What if Mr. Hart was still seeing her?" Lydia's eyes were huge.

Francesca realized her instincts had been right. Lydia was interrogating *her*. "I have an alibi, Miss Gillespie. I was out with my parents at the time of the murder."

Lydia flushed. "That was rude of me, when you are trying to find my sister's killer." Tears came to her eyes. "I miss her still!"

"Do you want to sit down?"

Lydia shook her head. "I wish she had never run away."

"Lydia, why did she leave home? I know the two of you were close. You must have an idea."

Lydia's expression closed and she glanced away. "I don't know."

Francesca was certain that Lydia knew exactly why Daisy

had left. "She had to have been very unhappy to run away from home and never come back."

Lydia shrugged, moving away from Francesca now. Francesca followed her. "If you want to find her killer, you need to tell me everything that you can."

Lydia faced her abruptly. "The police have arrested Calder Hart. They seem to think your fiancé murdered her."

"And I know he did no such thing." Francesca stared back. "Did you ever hear from her?"

"No." And tears began to fall. "You are right, we were very close! Sometimes we stayed up late at night, gossiping about this and that, discussing clothes, just chatting. We rode our horses together every day. She helped me with my schoolwork, and I helped her. We ate our meals together, because Mother and Father were always out, or Father was always working late. Then she disappeared. And I never heard from her again. How could she do that to me? How?"

Francesca put her arm around her. "Something terrible must have happened to cause her to leave home like that, without a word, at least to you."

Lydia reached for a locket she wore on a gold chain about her neck. She took it off and showed it to Francesca. Inside was a portrait of the two sisters as small girls. "Since the day she vanished, I have never taken it off." She hesitated, closing her eyes in a sudden flood of anguish.

"Lydia, please, what aren't you telling me?"

Lydia looked sadly at her. "She did leave me a note, Miss Cahill."

Francesca was seized with excitement. "She did? What did it say?"

"She told me she was never coming back. She told me she would soon have a better life." Lydia wiped at her tears. "She said she loved me and she always would. She told me not to worry, and that was all."

"And she did not say why she left?"

"No." Lydia sniffed. "I never showed anyone the note, not even when she first disappeared, when Mother and Father were afraid she had been abducted."

Francesca thought that odd. In a way, Lydia had been a co-conspirator in Daisy's disappearance. Francesca sensed that Lydia still wasn't telling her everything she knew. "Do you know how I found your family?"

"No."

"I found a box of newspaper clippings in your sister's bedroom. Each and every article was about or referred to your father."

Lydia blinked. The rest of her face remained a neutral mask.

Francesca wondered at her reaction. "Your sister had been following his life, so to speak, for years. Clearly, although she left, her home and her father remained hugely important to her."

Lydia shrugged. "Well, I suppose I would have done the same thing if I were her."

"You would have done what?" Francesca asked softly, certain she was onto something.

Lydia turned away. "I should go. I shouldn't be here. Mother needs me." She started toward the front door.

Francesca followed. "Lydia, wait! What would you have done?" She grasped her arm, detaining her.

"I don't know why she cut out newspaper articles about our father." And suddenly Lydia seemed angry. "Why don't you admit it, Miss Cahill? You are not the right person to be investigating this case. All the evidence points to your fiancé. You are hardly objective."

"I know Hart," Francesca said tersely, frustrated that she must defend him to Lydia. "And he is innocent. Don't you want to find your sister's killer?"

Lydia jerked free. "I really have to go. I left Mother alone at the hotel, and that is not a good idea."

"Where is your father now?"

"He is having lunch with some associates at the Waldorf-Astoria."

Francesca decided to ask Lydia what she wished to ask the judge. "Did you know that your father visited Daisy here in May? Not once, but two times? Did you know that he had found her and was in contact with her?"

Lydia paled, which was answer enough. She had known, all right. The mire of family secrets had just gotten deeper.

SUPPER WAS ALWAYS A very chaotic time of day—sometimes, Maggie felt as if the small kitchen table was a moving railroad car. She was serving a soup made of mutton bones, onions and potatoes with a loaf of hot bread. Matt, who was seven years old, was helping Lizzie with her spoon. Lizzie, apparently, did not want to eat and she was being vocal about it. Paddy, who was five, was acting three, making waves in his soup and giggling about it. His soup was getting all over the table. Joel, who was supposed to be present at supper, had yet to arrive.

Maggie looked at her three beautiful children and recalled the countess's unbelievable threats. Inside, dread curdled. She went to Paddy to take his spoon from him. "I am very proud of this soup," she admonished. "The bones have plenty of meat. If you do not eat it tonight, you may eat it for breakfast." She meant her every word. With the new order from Mrs. Bragg, she had been able to provide her children once again with healthy meals. She had even snuck a can of green beans into the soup. Canned goods were expensive and, until recently, not in her budget.

Paddy regarded her solemnly. He had the same red hair and blue eyes that she did, and he seemed to have inherited her somewhat shy nature, too.

"You know I mean it," she said, but she clasped his little shoulder.

Paddy sighed and picked up his spoon, dutifully beginning to eat.

"Lizzie's not hungry, Mama," Matt announced. Like Joel, he had dark hair inherited from their father and their father's very fair skin. "Where's Joel?"

"He is with Miss Cahill, of course." Maggie spoke with some pride. Once, her son had been a cutpurse on the run from the police. His reformation in these past few months continued to amaze her, and it was a source of pride as well as relief. "But unless they are in some circumstance, I am sure he will be here at any moment." The words were hardly out of her mouth when there was a knock on the door.

Joel had a key. Maggie's heart flipped unpleasantly. She was afraid to open the door and find that cruel, cold countess standing there, with a nasty smile on her beautiful face. Wiping her hands on the apron she wore, Maggie went to the door. She almost fell over when she opened it. Evan Cahill was standing there.

He held a brown shopping bag, and a small bouquet of lovely hothouse flowers.

She could not breathe. She looked from the items in his hands to his dark, handsome face, uncertain as to why, after all of this time, he had come, and suddenly recalling the single kiss they had shared. Then she recalled the countess.

"I know I am intruding," he said softly, his Cahill blue eyes on hers. They were searching. She knew him so well that she saw they were haunted by his sadness now. "Hello, Maggie."

He had never brought her flowers before. She could not accept them—he could not be there! She had missed him terribly—just as a friend—and the children had missed him, too. But he was marrying the countess, who was carrying his child.

"I see I have shocked you," he said.

She nodded and found her voice. "Yes, you have." How could she throw him out, when she did not have a rude bone in her entire body? "Evan, you should not be here."

"I just thought to say hello. It's been so long… I have missed the children and I brought them presents."

Maggie bit her lip. She knew she had to close the door on him and send him away. The countess had threatened her children, and she had meant her every word.

"Maggie?" He seemed puzzled by her lack of graciousness.

How could she chase him away? she wondered desperately. She slowly lifted her eyes to his.

"What is it?" he asked sharply. "Is something wrong?"

"No, of course not," she replied. She opened the door more widely. "I suppose you can come in—for a moment—to see the children."

He gave her an odd look. She had never managed his visits before, or been so clear about their nature.

The children now saw him. "Mr. Cahill!" Matt shouted, leaping to his feet.

Paddy also cried out. Getting up, he knocked over his chair. Both boys barreled over to him and he laughed, kneeling to hug them at once. Lizzie howled in protest, banging her spoon on the table, wanting to get out of her chair.

Maggie rushed to her, so she would not try to get down by herself and hurt herself in the process. She glanced at the trio. Both boys were talking at once, Matt telling Evan about school, Paddy trying to tell him about the neighbor's new cat. Evan was laughing and trying to listen to both boys at once.

She was filled with so much love. It was hopeless, she thought, to feel this way about such a man. He was a gentleman, never mind his being disinherited and disowned, and she was a poor Irish woman who worked for a living with her rough, red hands. But it was so good to see him. His presence filled up her small flat, warming it the way the sun did the city after a good rain.

"I am very proud of you," Evan told Matt, his hand on his back. To Paddy, he said, "One day you can show me the cat. But

I have an even better idea. Maybe this weekend we can go to the zoo."

"The zoo!" Paddy nodded eagerly, beaming.

"I want to go zoo," Lizzie cried, clinging to Maggie.

Evan slowly looked at her. "With your mother's permission, of course."

She could not allow it now, could she? She must send Evan away forever, or live in fear of the countess. "That is a wonderful idea," she said, unsmiling, "but it will have to be another time."

He stared more closely at her, clearly surprised.

Maggie let Lizzie go. The little girl ran to him, stumbling as she did so.

"Lizzie, my girl," Evan said, lifting her into his arms. He glanced at Maggie, who now refused to meet his gaze, and said to the boys, "There are some items in the bag that might be of interest to you and your sister."

He spoiled them terribly, but it was a wonderful gesture on his part, because they had lived with so little for their entire lives. Maggie watched the boys exclaim over a set of toy soldiers, replete with a cannon and horses, and Lizzie was given another stuffed toy animal, this one a furry black-and-white pony. Lizzie shrieked in happiness, hugging the toy to her chest. Then she began to gallop around the room with the pony.

With the children now busy with their gifts, Evan shoved his hands into the pockets of his jacket, his expression uncertain. He looked from Maggie to the dinner table. "I am sorry I interrupted your supper," he said quietly.

"We can finish it later," Maggie replied, fingering the back of Lizzie's chair.

He took in the chair and basket set aside from the table, where the yellow dress that Maggie was working on lay. "I hear you have been given quite a bit of business these past few weeks."

"Yes, your sister ordered quite a wardrobe, and so did Mrs. Bragg."

"I am glad." He hesitated, as if confused by her answer.

Maggie knew her cheeks were hot. It was so awkward now.

Evan picked up the bouquet of flowers, which he had set down on the sofa. "These are for you."

She wanted to take the flowers, but she could not. What did the flowers mean? An image of the countess filled her mind instead.

"Maggie, what is it?"

She looked up, trying to control her raw emotions. "I cannot accept those. You know that."

His jaw tightened. "It is only a token of friendship, nothing more."

She braced herself. "I think you should leave."

His eyes went wide. "You do not want me here?"

There was no point in reminding him that he was marrying the countess, and they would have a child soon. She did want him there with her and the children. Maggie was unable to find any words now.

He was pale. "Very well. I thought we were friends," he added with some anger.

Maggie closed her eyes, tightly. The sooner he left, the better.

But he just stood there, and she had to open her eyes. "I just had to see you," he said.

She flinched. She longed to tell him that she had desperately needed to see him, too, but she knew better, and she kept her mouth closed, afraid the words might come out, anyway.

He turned to go. But suddenly he about-faced and came back to her. "I am sorry about everything, Maggie. But please don't do this. You and the children have become so important to me."

Maggie felt tears building and she gave up. "You have become important to us, too."

Relief filled his face. "We can be friends." He lowered his voice. "I am sorry about the kiss."

She shook her head as a tear fell. "I'm not." She wished she hadn't been so honest and she glanced aside.

He seized her hand. "I wish things were different, Maggie," he whispered. "I wish—" He stopped.

She met his intense blue eyes. "What do you wish?"

His expression hardened as he fought himself. "I want to make certain that you and the children are cared for," he said. "I know you are independent and you think to go it alone, but I want to help. Please, let me help."

"No!" She was aghast, and it had nothing to do with her pride and everything to do with the countess. "Why can't you understand that we cannot continue to be friends?"

"Why not?" he demanded.

She pulled away from him and went to stand at the sink, her back to him, shaking.

He came up behind her, so close that her body tightened, warming inside and out.

"Why not? We have been friends for all of this time. Bartolla will understand. I promise to keep my distance—"

She whirled, and she was almost in his arms. "She will not understand!" she cried. Then, realizing she had said too much, she clasped her mouth with her hand.

His gaze narrowed. "What is going on here? Why are you speaking like this? What aren't you telling me?" He took her hand and removed it from her mouth but did not release it.

She felt desperate and tried to pull free. He refused to let her go. His touch made her yearn for so much more. "She just seems to be a very possessive and jealous woman," Maggie managed to say. Her heart continued to thunder in her chest. Fear, love, desire and grief all managed to mingle and blur together there.

"You don't even know her," Evan remarked. His gaze was piercing. "But I do. In fact, I know her too well. What has happened, Maggie?"

Maggie jerked her hand from his and covered her face.

"Maggie?" Concern sharpened his tone. And suddenly he was holding her and she could feel his lean, hard body, her cheek against his chest. He said, "You have met her, haven't you? Did she come here?"

Maggie was mesmerized. She nodded, unable now to speak, aware of every inch of him.

His hands tightened on her waist. "She came here?" He was incredulous.

"She was very angry," Maggie whispered.

"She was angry with you?"

"She threatened us," she breathed.

He released her. "She came here and threatened you?" Anger began, tightening his face, darkening his eyes.

She knew she should not tell him, but she was afraid, and Evan was strong, secure and capable. He had been looking out for her and the children for months now. "She threatened the children."

He grasped her shoulders, his eyes wide.

"Evan, now you must understand why we cannot be friends."

And his expression turned hard and dangerous. "She has gone too far!" He released her.

"Evan," she cried, following him as he strode to the door. "Evan! What are you going to do?"

He spun. "I will never forgive her for this," he said harshly. Then he cupped her chin. "She is not going to interfere in our relationship, Maggie."

"Don't say anything!" Maggie begged, terrified for the children. "Please don't!"

"You let me handle the countess."

BRAGG HURRIED INTO THE narrow front hall of his home. He had had a telephone installed in the house last month, due to the demands of his job, and Peter had reached him a half an hour ago. Although Peter had reassured him that Leigh Anne was all right, he was torn between fury and concern that O'Donnell had dared to call on her. He hurried down the corridor. The parlor door was open, but a quick glance inside showed him that she was not there.

He hurried out and bumped into Peter by the stairs. "Where is my wife?"

Peter was very grim. "She has been resting upstairs, sir."

"And the girls?" Bragg demanded, aware of his heart pounding with unusual strength. Every beat was filled with worry, with fear.

"Mrs. Flowers has taken them to the park. They should return shortly."

Bragg nodded. "What did he say? What did he want?" he demanded. "And Peter, why the hell did you wait so long to call me?"

"Mrs. Bragg wished for me to undertake an errand, sir." Peter's round face was flushed. "She insisted."

"She insisted on an errand? Next time, you call me first!"

"Sir," Peter appeared agonized. "Mrs. Bragg asked me to take her out."

He was confused. His wife no longer went out. "Take her where?"

"She asked me not to say. This is very hard for me, sir. I do not wish to betray Mrs. Bragg."

He was very alarmed. "O'Donnell was here—and then Leigh Anne went out?"

"Yes, sir." Peter clearly did not wish to say any more. "She was very upset when O'Donnell left. I heard him say that he wanted to take the girls for a walk in the park. Mrs. Bragg refused."

"Is that all?"

"No. He said he had a lawyer, sir. And then he told your wife to send me and Mrs. Kennedy out."

Bragg tensed. "You left her alone with that thug?"

"I didn't want to, sir, but she gave me an order." He hesitated. "I wanted to call you, as well. I am sorry."

Bragg could not imagine what Leigh Anne thought she was doing, but he had a very bad feeling. "You should have called me then and there," Bragg said harshly. He turned and ran up the stairs, taking them two at a time, grateful the girls were out.

The door to their bedroom was open. He saw Leigh Anne instantly. She sat before the hearth in her wheeled chair, staring at its empty darkness. A cashmere shawl was around her shoulders, a dark green that was several shades darker than her remarkable eyes. Instantly he saw how worried and upset she remained. "Leigh Anne."

She said nothing but her eyes turned moist.

He rushed to her and knelt before her. "Are you all right?"

"No," she said hoarsely, her gaze intent on his. "He was here. I am very frightened, Rick."

His heart lurched. "I told you, I will take care of him."

"He is going to fight us for the girls, I just know it!" she cried.

He tried to cup her cheek but she jerked away. "The lawyer is a bluff, Leigh Anne. No judge is going to choose him over us and he knows it. He is going to blackmail us, I am certain, and when he does, I will arrest him."

"You should just pay him to go away," she said tersely, her gaze wide on his.

Maybe she was right. Everyone seemed to think that paying O'Donnell off was the best solution. "I spoke with Mr. Feingold today. He said our chances of adopting the girls are excellent. O'Donnell's shady history makes it unlikely that any court would give him custody of the girls," he added, hoping to reassure her and chase the terror in her eyes away.

But a tear fell. "I am sick with fear, Rick. You have to get rid of him before he destroys us!"

She was keeping something from him. He knelt before her, taking her stiff, frozen hands in his. "What happened, Leigh Anne? If I am going to take care of O'Donnell, I need to know everything."

She was as pale as a ghost. She shook her head, incapable of speech. She was clutching a handkerchief and she dabbed her eyes. He suddenly saw that her hands were bandaged with gauze. He took her wrist. "What the hell happened?"

"I hurt myself rolling the chair without help. But it's only a few scrapes."

"Why did you do that?" he asked, still holding her arm.

"I was so angry and so afraid," she whispered.

Acting on sheer impulse, he placed her bandaged hand on his chest and held it gently but securely there. "You don't have to be afraid," he said thickly. "I am going to take care of O'Donnell. But you have to trust me."

His every instinct told him that his wife was in trouble now. "What happened, Leigh Anne? What happened here today? What aren't you telling me? Please, let me help you."

She met his searching gaze. "He doesn't want you to know."

He was sick. "He doesn't want me to know what?"

She trembled. "I promised to get him fifteen thousand dollars by tomorrow night."

His blood surged red-hot now and his fury threatened to erupt. "He blackmailed you." He was amazed at how calm and quiet his tone sounded.

She shook her head. "No. He never asked for money. He is family now, isn't he?" More tears fell. "I would merely be helping the girls' uncle a bit."

His wife had been thoroughly manipulated. "Thank you for telling me," he said quietly. "I will take care of this." But in his mind, he saw himself strangling O'Donnell, squeezing the life out of him.

"I tried to borrow the money from Bartolla," Leigh Anne whispered, more tears tracking down her face. "But she is not wealthy at all. As it turns out, her husband left her nothing."

He was beyond anguish for what she had been through, and what she had tried to do alone. "Why didn't you come to me?" he asked, cupping her cheek. "You used to trust me." He rubbed at some tears with his thumb.

She tried to nod and glanced up, holding his gaze through her tears. "I was a fool. There is no one that I trust more."

His heart stilled. He wondered if she knew how much that meant to him, and how much he still loved her. He could not help himself—he leaned closer to her. She had become very still, but she did not press back in her chair. "I will get the money by tomorrow night," he whispered, his mouth close to hers. "Tomorrow this will all be over."

He saw the relief in her eyes, and something else, something he had not seen in months. He saw desire and need.

All thought vanished, because he needed her, too, terribly. He touched her mouth with his. The soft, full feel of her lips sent blood pulsing to his loins, hot and hard. The bare kiss wasn't deliberately planned, and he certainly did not mean to escalate it, no matter how much he wanted to, if Leigh Anne did not want him to. But she did not move and she allowed her lips to ever-so-slightly part. He felt her hesitation.

"Leigh Anne," he whispered, suddenly desperate to make love to her. He kissed her again, and her lips parted even more beneath his.

He began to kiss her more urgently, his need rising so hard and so fast that he was stunned by it.

"Rick," she managed to say, a whisper of protest.

"You are still the most beautiful woman in the world," he

cried against her wet, full mouth. And he kissed her throat, a man telling a woman he wanted her and that she must submit.

"I'm not beautiful anymore," she gasped, but she was trembling.

He stood, lifting her into his arms as he did so. She wrapped her arms around his neck and opened her eyes, and their gazes met. He carried her to the bed, whispering, "I have to make love to you. Please, don't ask me to stop."

He laid her down. She pushed once at his chest, and her bandaged hand slid to his neck. "This isn't a good idea."

"I think it is a very good idea," he said, already poised over her. He kissed her again, and this time, as he slid his tongue deep, she opened widely and a shudder racked her body. He could not wait. He slid his hands over the bodice of her dress and Leigh Anne arched wildly in an invitation she apparently could not control. It had been so long.

Somehow his hands were under her dress and petticoat. Leigh Anne's eyes flew wide the moment he touched her. She was wet, but she was also afraid.

He understood. "Give in," he pleaded. "Darling, give in to me."

She cried out, her eyes closing. "Then hurry," she whispered. "Oh, Rick, hurry!"

It was an invitation he had dreamed of hearing again. Pushing her skirts up, he kissed her deeply and darkly, no longer able to think. She writhed against him and he thrust hard, again and again, while she sobbed her release and he sobbed his.

When his breathing slowed, he was shocked to realize that he had just made love to his wife. He moved onto his side, overcome with the ballooning feelings in his heart. Taking her into his arms, he glimpsed her long, naked legs. The left one was twisted now. His heart lurched and he smoothed her clothes down. Now all he wanted to do was hold her for a very long time.

So much joy expanded in his chest. He studied her as he held her, amazed by how beautiful she was. Her eyes remained closed, but he knew she wasn't sleeping; she was merely relishing the aftermath, as she was wont to do. His heart tightened and he kissed her cheek.

Her lashes fluttered and she looked up at him. He smiled, but she did not.

Some dread began. "Are you all right?" he asked, praying she would not pull away from him now.

She smiled briefly, but it was forced. "You didn't hurt me, Rick."

He did not want to go back to that dark place in hell where they had so recently lived. "You're so beautiful," he whispered. "Leigh Anne, I need you."

She stared, the tip of her nose turning red. "I don't understand."

"You don't understand that your husband loves you and wants you?" he asked, but he tried to keep his tone light.

"How can you want me? I am a…cripple!"

He was shocked. He sat. "How could you call yourself such a name?"

"But it's true, isn't it?" Then she glanced away. "He called me that."

He felt his world still and reality intruded, ugly and dark. "Who?" But he already knew.

"O'Donnell. It doesn't matter," she said. "Rick, we shouldn't have done that."

"No, making love to you is right."

Leigh Anne tried to sit. Instantly he helped her to do so. "Everything has changed. If we didn't have the girls, I would set you free, Rick, so you could be with a real woman—not a crippled one." But her gaze was searching.

He understood what he was fighting for and he chose his words with care. "You are a real woman. And we have the girls. But even if we didn't, I would not let you go."

She studied him and he smiled, just a little at her. "I want to take care of you no matter what—and I would like it very much if you also took care of me."

Her eyes were wide. "How?"

"I think you know how." He touched her face. "Please don't turn away from me now. *Please*."

She simply stared, appearing torn.

Although he very much wanted to make love to his wife again, he got up. His shirt was open and he began to button it. Hart's image came to mind. He saw himself groveling before him, and how Hart would gloat. Then he saw O'Donnell in some dark, dank cell, waiting for his turn in the electric chair.

"Where are you going?" she asked.

"I am going to borrow fifteen thousand dollars," he said.

THE MAIN BRANCH OF the Bank of New York was downtown and not far from Hart's Bridge Street offices. It was a large, handsome building built well over a century ago. Inside, the oak floors gleamed with wax beneath several large Oriental rugs, a huge chandelier dominating the wood-paneled room. Francesca had inquired after Robert Miller and had been asked to wait in a small reception area, set somewhat apart from the tellers and the vaults. She had made it clear to the bank officer that she was there as an emissary of Mr. Hart.

She gave herself a moment of pure release and sank deeply into the plush blue velvet sofa. She was so tired. The truth was, the strain of this separation from Hart was frankly unbearable. Thus far, she had been focusing on the case and avoiding any thought of the future. But now she could not help think about it. She had not been able to identify herself as Hart's fiancée to Robert Miller. Fear twisted inside her, edged with panic. What if she had really lost Hart? What if he never came back to her?

There had to be a way, when this was all over, to convince him that letting her go served no one, that it was *not* in her best interest. But she knew him so well now. Once Daisy's murder was solved, there was still the issue of her missing portrait. Francesca knew he had been blaming himself for ever commissioning that portrait. And even though she had agreed to pose nude, he insisted that it was his fault. She knew he was not going to change his mind and share the blame.

He could be such an impossible man. She missed him. She had never missed anyone more.

"Miss Cahill?" A short, slim man with a goatee approached, smiling. He was immaculately dressed and had an unmistakable air of authority. "I am Robert Miller," he said, extending his hand. "I am very pleased to meet you."

She realized he knew who she was. "Thank you. Calder directed me to you, Mr. Miller, in regards to the current case I am on."

He nodded. "Come onto my office," he said, and they traversed the spacious hall where a few customers were at the long, gleaming counter, conducting their banking affairs. "May I be so bold as to ask how Mr. Hart is?"

"He is doing as well as can be expected, considering the nature of all that has happened," Francesca said as he closed the door behind him. His office was a smaller version of the public room outside. "And he is innocent, of course."

Miller smiled. "I had no doubt. How can I help you?" he asked as they took seats.

"Miss Jones made two unusually large deposits into her account in May, for eight and then twelve thousand dollars. We need to know where that money came from," Francesca said.

Miller stood. "As a favor to Mr. Hart, I will see what I can find out. Why don't you make yourself at home? I will be right back."

Five minutes later he came back with a file in his hands. "I think I may have some useful information for you, Miss Cahill."

"Do you know where the money came from?"

"Yes, I do. Miss Jones deposited two bank checks from First Federal of Albany."

Francesca felt her world still. *The money had come from Albany.* "Is there any way to find out who drew those bank checks in the first place?"

"Yes, but it will take some time. And you would have to approach First Federal directly. I think they might need the police to request the action, Miss Cahill."

"Consider that done." Her excitement grew. "How much time?"

"Days, I should think. You would need to send someone to Albany to go over the bank records there."

"Can we send a telegram and wire instructions to the bank there?"

"I suppose so." He hesitated. "Miss Cahill, what is this about?"

Her day had become exceedingly bright. "This is about uncovering the identity of a murderer, Mr. Miller." And as she left his office, she was almost ready to skip her way out of the bank. Clearly, Judge Gillespie had sent Daisy the money. Now the only question was why.

She paused outside of the bank, unable to stop smiling. Daisy had never let go of her father and the clippings were proof of that. As far as was known, Gillespie had been to see her twice in May—but not at any other time. Only in May had she received money from him. Francesca was ready to conclude that Gillespie hadn't known his daughter's whereabouts until then. Had he merely been giving his long-lost daughter funds to supplement any allowance she was already receiving? After all, that was what fathers did for their children.

On the other hand, Daisy had been a huge embarrassment to him, and his lying about knowing her when she had first confronted him in Albany was proof of that. Had she been enough of an embarrassment for him to murder her?

It was a leap, but Francesca was close to the truth now and she could feel it. She *had* to discover the real reason Daisy had left home in the first place. It was the missing puzzle piece.

She needed to see Bragg. Maybe they could decide on a plan in which to pressure the judge. And of course, the police had to contact the Albany bank. She had yet to learn about the knife discovered at Hart's last night. By now, that report should be in. She started toward the curb, raising her arm to signal Raoul to bring her coach from farther down the block, where he had found a place to park.

The person passing by her turned around. From the corner of her eye, still focused on her driver and coach, Francesca saw a gloved hand being raised, a dark object there, but it was too late. Pain lanced the back of her head and, with it, the realization that she had been attacked. Then there was only darkness.

CHAPTER SEVENTEEN

Thursday, June 5, 1902—6:00 p.m.

FRANCESCA LAY ON THE sofa in her sister's home while Rourke took her pulse for the third time. An ice pack was beneath her head, which ached and throbbed. The moment she had been struck from behind, Raoul had rushed to her aid, apparently having seen the tail end of the attack. But instead of pursuing the assailant, he had helped her into the coach. Unfortunately, the blow had been damaging enough that she had lost her wits for a moment and had not been able to identify her attacker. However, within moments, she had recovered enough to instruct Raoul to tell her everything that he had seen and to search the area, where she had found a small sterling shaving cup. It was dented, and clearly, it had been the weapon with which she had been hit.

"How is your headache?" Rourke asked with a kind smile, while Connie fussed over her sister.

"It isn't as bad as earlier," she admitted. "I am fine, Con. It was just a tap on the head with a little cup. Could you call Bragg? I have to speak to him."

"You are not fine!" Connie cried, as pale as an alabaster statue. "Rourke, should she be investigating this case now?"

"Absolutely not," Rourke said firmly. He closed his black satchel, but before he stood, Francesca seized his hand.

"I need to talk to Rick. It is urgent—it cannot wait."

"Francesca." He said patiently, sitting back down by her side on an ottoman. "If you are right and you were hit with that shaving cup, it is quite serious, indeed. You have some swelling on the back of your head. You may have a slight concussion. You can consider yourself fortunate that the cup did not cause a gash, which might have required stitches. You need to rest, but you must stay awake for the next twelve hours." He glanced at Connie. "Someone needs to stay with her through the night. I do not want her falling asleep. She can have plenty of liquids, but only something very light to eat—maybe some jam and toast."

Connie nodded, her expression fearful. "Neil and I will take turns," she said.

Francesca was not about to give up. "Raoul managed a glimpse of my attacker. He needs to tell Bragg what he saw. He thinks the attacker was a very slim man, or it might even have been a woman. In any case, he or she was wearing a large overcoat and a fedora, a man's fedora—and this in June!" She could not help but wonder if Gillespie had been her attacker. He was only of medium height and build. After all, she had been investigating his transfer of funds to his daughter.

"I will be back in the morning," Rourke said in a friendly manner. He patted Francesca's shoulder. "Francesca, it is six at night. You are not going to solve the mystery of your assailant this evening. Whatever you need to do, it can be done in the morning—after I check on you."

She was annoyed. "Then come early, if you please." In a way, Rourke was right. No one would be at the First Federal Bank of Albany at this hour to receive a telegram. Of course, Gillespie could be interviewed. Francesca was very impatient to hear just what he had to say about his visits to his daughter in May, and about the money he had obviously sent her. And where had he been an hour ago, when she had been struck on the back of the head? She shivered. She was lucky to not have been seriously hurt. "Rourke? Are you on your way back to Hart's?"

"Yes."

She hesitated. By now, he should have been released on bail.

Wouldn't he come running to her side if he heard about this mishap?

"I am not sure what you are thinking, Francesca, but I have every intention of telling Calder what has happened. He would want to know. Besides, I don't want to risk my neck by withholding this kind of information. Now, try to rest—but do not fall asleep."

Connie walked with Rourke to the salon door, and Francesca heard them exchanging a few words she could not distinguish in a low tone. When Connie returned to her side, as worried as ever, Francesca met her gaze. "I saw Calder today. Nothing has changed, Connie. He remains as recalcitrant as ever."

Connie understood. "Fran, if that man doesn't come running to see you after what has happened, I will be amazed." She sat down on the ottoman Rourke had vacated. "You could have been badly hurt—what if you had been killed?"

"But I wasn't, was I? You do know what this means, don't you?" Francesca gazed at her sister. "I am very close to solving this case, Con. And Daisy's murderer knows it."

"Fran! I hope you are wrong, because if you are not, that means that the murderer wishes to stop you!"

Francesca sobered. Her sister was right and she had to proceed with caution. From that point forward, she would be armed, wary and very defensive. "The sooner I close this case, the better." She thought about Hart and her heart tightened. "Hart can be so stubborn! Connie, he doesn't see himself the way that I do. He has always claimed he is not good enough for me and that I deserve someone far nobler. Now Daisy's murder has become some kind of excuse for him to break off the engagement. I am afraid that even when this is over, he will not come back to me."

Connie was thoughtful and sad. "Then he doesn't love you enough, Fran. Either that, or he loves you too much."

Francesca started.

"You know I supported this match. But I must tell you, to be with someone who has such a reputation and such a past seems a bit daunting. And he is so difficult! I don't know how you manage sometimes. I found him very intimidating when I spoke to him yesterday."

"He can be difficult," Francesca admitted. "But when he becomes cold and even cruel, that is his way of lashing out, because he is really scared."

Connie's pale brows lifted. "I cannot imagine Hart frightened of anything."

"Beneath the arrogance, behind the wealth, and power, he can be very vulnerable," Francesca said.

Connie gave her a look, one that said she clearly did not believe that. The salon doors were open and they both heard the knocker on the front door of the house. Connie grimaced. "I do hope you won't be too angry with me."

"Why would I be angry with you?" Francesca asked warily.

Connie hesitated, and their mother's voice could be heard in the hall outside. "Where is Francesca?" Julia was demanding, her heels clicking on the marble floors as she approached.

Francesca groaned. "Why did you call her? She worries excessively."

"Because you were hurt and she is our mother!" Connie said, standing as Julia rushed into the room.

Julia took one look at both her daughters and hurried to Francesca's side. "What happened?" she cried, clasping Francesca's hand.

"I am fine, Mama. It was just a little tap on the head."

Julia's blue eyes were wide with worry. "Have you seen a doctor? Connie, is she telling me the truth?"

Connie stood beside their mother. "It was more than a light tap on the head, Mama. But Rourke was here and she seems to be fine, nevertheless."

Julia sat down, still holding Francesca's hand tightly.

"You know how afraid I am for you when you are on these investigations. Why does every case have to become violent?"

"Mama, I am fine," Francesca stressed. "You do not need to worry."

"How can I not worry? You are my precious daughter, my youngest child. I worry day and night! It is my duty to keep you safe—it is my duty to worry about you! When will you come home, Francesca? Your father and I are brokenhearted. We both miss you so much." Tears had gathered in Julia's blue eyes.

"I can't move back," Francesca said. "I am so sorry, but nothing has changed. I love Calder and I intend to marry him. If Papa cannot support my decision, I have no other choice. Mama, it hurt me terribly to move out."

Briefly Julia closed her eyes. "Do you now how much he adores you? Do you know that you are his pride and joy? Do you know how proud of you he is, how he boasts about you at every party?"

"I love him, too," Francesca said quietly. "And I already feel guilty, so you do not need to make me feel more so."

Julia smoothed her hair. "That is not what I am trying to do. But it hurts me to see Andrew in such a state, just as it hurts me to have somehow lost you."

"Mama, you haven't lost me! I have merely moved out. And while I may marry against your wishes, that doesn't mean we are not family." Francesca's secret fear leapt out at her now. "Please, do not let Papa disown me the way he did Evan."

"Darling, he would never do such a thing!" Julia cried.

Francesca somehow nodded. "I love you both so much," she said shakily.

"Then come home," Julia whispered, her tone pleading. "Please."

It was so tempting, especially now, with her head throbbing and her heart hurting over the breakup with Hart. "I can't."

Julia was grim. "I really don't understand why you are doing this. I saw the announcement in the paper. We both did. Your engagement is off. So why not come home?"

"It is temporary," Francesca whispered. "I am going to get him back."

Julia regarded her daughter and a long moment passed. Julia said very quietly, "If you are so determined, if you trust Hart so much, if you love him this much, then I will support your marriage, Francesca."

Francesca sat straight up. "Mama! Thank you!" She flung her arms around her mother, holding her hard.

Julia's gaze was moist. "I have always adored that man, anyway."

Francesca smiled brightly, relieved. "I know. And he is innocent."

"I never thought him guilty!" Julia exclaimed. "That wasn't the point. The point is that this scandal will follow him forever. And if you are with him, it will hurt you, too. Are you really prepared to be ostracized from polite society?"

Francesca could not tell her that Hart's breaking off the engagement hurt far more than any nasty gossip. "We will still have your invitations, Mama," Francesca said. "I do care what people say behind our backs, but I care even more for Calder. I know we may never be invited out again. If that is the case, we will manage."

Julia regarded her sadly. "You are very brave. I just want you to be certain that this is the life you want."

"I am certain."

"Then I will do everything I can to help."

"Will you help me persuade Papa?"

"Yes, I will make certain your father changes his mind. And if I have to spend my entire life campaigning among society to see you included again, then that is what I will do." Francesca saw that her mother had a new cause. She was one of society's reigning matrons, and in the past, no one had ever been able stand in Julia Van Wyck Cahill's way.

"Thank you," Francesca whispered. She had never loved her mother more.

"SIR, COMMISSIONER BRAGG is here to see you."

Hart did not look up. He sat on the sofa that was in front of the fireplace, staring at the dancing flames, a letter in his hand. He hadn't intended to go through his mail tonight. He had only done so to try to get his mind off the dismal grayness that threatened to overtake his life. The letter had just arrived—and it was from the dead.

Dear Calder,

You have made yourself very clear, and I will never make the mistake of approaching you personally again. You do not want this child—our child—just as you no longer want me. Your life is with Francesca now. Everything is always about Francesca and you could not care less about me. I never expected you to give her up or change your plans for a future with her. But I did expect you to be more generous toward me, in light of the fact that I now bear your bastard. I wonder what Francesca would think—I wonder what she would do—if she knew I was carrying your child?

Of course, she will never find out, will she? My lips are sealed. Because I expect you to provide very generously for me in return for my silence. I will even relocate to a new city, as long as the house you provide for me and my child is in my name. I will also need a vastly increased allowance. And finally, I should prefer a gift of shares in your insurance and railroad companies as well as Treasury bonds.

I would also like the Titian painting you once
showed me.

As soon as my needs have been met, I will gladly
remove myself to my new home in the city of your
choice and you will never have to lay eyes on me
again—or on your son or daughter. And of course,
Francesca will never have to suffer the humiliation
of chancing upon me and our bastard on a public
street.

Daisy

THE LETTER WAS DATED May 30. Daisy had written him after
he had stormed out of her house, furious by the news that she
was pregnant.

There was so much anguish that he simply could not stand
it. Faced with Daisy's death he could not care less that she had
dared to blackmail him, much less demand one of his favorite
oil paintings.

"Sir? Commissioner Bragg is here and he wishes to see you.
Should I tell him you are unavailable?" Alfred asked, his tone
edged with worry.

Hart closed his eyes, fighting for composure, but the grief
that had been welling up in him, the grief he had so resolutely
shoved aside, felt like hot lava in a volcano, about to erupt.

Hart won the battle. As he stood, he wondered how many
more battles he could actually win with himself. Placing the
letter in the interior breast pocket of his jacket, he faced his
butler. "Send him in," he said. Maybe Bragg had good news—he
could certainly use a single lucky break.

Bragg appeared on the library's threshold a moment later.
Hart took one look at his tight expression and ravaged eyes and
knew there was no good news. Trying not to succumb to dread,
he nodded in greeting. "Scotch?"

"Thank you," his half brother said.

Hart walked across the room to the gilded bar cart, where he poured two doubles. Then he handed his brother a glass with what he hoped was at least the shadow of a smile. The police would have a field day with that letter, he thought grimly. It was as if fate were determined to punish him for the sins of his entire life with a crime he hadn't committed.

Bragg drank. "Are you all right?" he asked cautiously.

Hart managed a smile this time. "I have never been better." The smile died. "I was actually hoping you had brought me some good news."

"I have," Bragg said. "The knife we found in your coach is not the murder weapon."

Satisfaction slowly began. "You would think that whoever was framing me would have the good sense to do so with the murder weapon."

"Yes, you would." Bragg finished the drink. "Do you mind?"

"Help yourself," Hart said. He watched as his brother replenished his drink and it occurred to him that the usual animosity they shared seemed strangely absent in that moment.

"The knife is too small to have been the murder weapon," Bragg said. "Not only that, Heinreich feels certain the blood isn't even human."

"It's animal blood?"

"He thinks so. I can't see the difference on the slides, but apparently he can."

"What are you thinking?" Hart asked, settling down in a chair.

Bragg also sat. "You were deliberately framed, Calder. That much is clear. Perhaps the murderer got rid of the weapon and only decided to frame you well after the murder, when he or she learned you had been present at Daisy's that night."

"That is a theory I could agree with," Hart said thoughtfully. "But that means that framing me was incidental to the murder."

"Yes, it does. There is another possibility."

"Which is?"

"Maybe the murderer didn't frame you, and someone else did."

Hart absorbed that. "I like your first theory better. But I have plenty of enemies and any one of them could have taken that opportunity once the news of the murder broke the following morning."

"I also prefer my initial theory," Bragg said. "In any case, you have been moved down the list of suspects."

Hart drank and then eyed him. "Is it not a very short list?"

"It is," Bragg admitted. "I cannot rule out Rose. And while I do not agree with Francesca, I do admire her instincts, and she is convinced that Judge Gillespie lied about knowing that Honora was Daisy—although we have no proof."

Hart grimaced. "You do not seem to be making any headway, as far as I can see."

"It has only been a few days." Bragg stood and he hesitated.

Hart slowly rose, aware that Bragg had something else to say. "What is it?"

"It's not about the case," Bragg said, and he flushed.

Instantly, Hart knew. Bragg had come to ask him for money. The devil in him told him to wait and enjoy this single moment when his brother was reduced to asking him for help. But some other more sensible and reasonable part of him stepped forward. "I already told you that I would give you the funds you need. I am happy to do so."

Bragg's jaw was set. "I need fifteen thousand dollars."

Hart didn't blink. He walked across the room and paused before a large landscape painting. "Help me with this," he said.

Bragg joined him. "I will repay every penny."

"So you will not arrest O'Donnell?"

"Leigh Anne is in terror. She is nervous to the point of exhaustion. I have decided to get this thug out of our lives once and for all."

"It will be quicker," Hart agreed, surprised that his brother would succumb to buying off a thug, but he understood. If such a blot were on his and Francesca's life, he, too, would remove it in the timeliest manner possible. "You do not have to repay me," Hart said as the two men removed the large painting from the wall. "I don't need the money and I don't want it back."

Hart opened the safe that was now revealed and removed several stacks of bills. "I *am* repaying you," Bragg said.

Hart shrugged and they replaced the painting. "I have an extra case that you can use to carry the funds."

"Thank you," Bragg said tersely.

Hart saw that he was perspiring, his jaw remaining tight. "Why is this so hard for you? I seem to recall a childhood in which you were always watching out for me. Why can't I repay you this one time?"

Bragg started. "It is a matter of pride," he said after a pause. "And I am your older brother. It was always my place to take care of you."

"Actually, Lily was supposed to do that," Hart said, an ancient ache piercing through him.

"She worked long hours and then she was ill," Bragg flashed. "She did the best that she could."

The money in hand, Hart moved to the desk. His brain told him that Rick was right, but he still couldn't accept it or understand it.

"What are you two doing?" Rourke asked.

He was in the doorway. Now he strode in, his gaze going back and forth between the two brothers and to the money on the desk.

Hart did not flinch, laying the six stacks on the desk. "You need to rediscover the socially acceptable behavior of knocking," Hart said.

Rourke was mildly taken aback. "The door was ajar. That's a lot of cash."

Hart ignored the comment, retrieving an attaché case and laying it flat on the desk. He opened it and placed the money inside.

"This is not your concern and I expect your discretion," Bragg said.

Rourke faced his brother, appearing uncertain. "This feels like foul play."

"This is not your concern," Hart repeated Rick's words firmly, buckling the case closed.

"Fine!" Rourke threw up his hands in annoyance. "I need to speak with you, Calder."

"Can it wait?" Hart asked mildly, and then he did a double take. Rourke's expression was grim. He recognized that the little brother was gone, replaced by the doctor. His heart leapt in alarm. "Is this about Francesca?"

Rourke nodded. "She is resting now, but you both should know that she was attacked this afternoon."

CONNIE HAD INSISTED THAT they play cards. Francesca had never liked card games and thus far, her sister had won every hand while she brooded about the nature of her attack and the identity of her attacker, the money from Albany, and Gillespie's lie that he did not know about Daisy. She had removed her shoes and stockings and she remained seated on the sofa, her legs folded up beneath her skirts. Her head barely throbbed now. One conclusion was inescapable. The money was tied to Daisy's murder. Otherwise, why would anyone try to stop her from uncovering the source of the funds? And had the assault been a warning—or an attack with lethal intent?

Connie sighed as someone pounded on the front door. "Gin. That must be Hart." She laid her hand down on the ottoman that was between them.

Francesca thought so, too. Then she heard voices in the hall. Bragg was asking for her and she was disappointed. Still, they had to discuss the case, and the sooner the better.

Connie gave her a look. "It's the police commissioner," she said softly. She stood and went to the doorway. Bragg and Hart appeared there. She greeted them and slipped out.

Hart's gaze instantly connected with Francesca. He was clearly distressed. Before he could say a word, she smiled at him. "I am fine."

He strode past Bragg. "You are not fine!" he exclaimed. "Rourke told me you have been hit on the head. He thinks it possible that you have a concussion! What happened?" He sat in the chair her sister had vacated, taking her hand, his gaze on her face.

She felt certain he did not know that he had reached for her hand. "I was leaving the bank where Daisy had her account," she said. "Someone hit me on the back of the head with a sterling cup. I was hailing Raoul. Apparently, he saw the entire incident and he carried me to the coach."

"I may dismiss him for this," Hart said with tightly controlled fury. "He is supposed to protect you!"

"How could he stop the assault?" Francesca cried. "He was waiting in the street and I was on the sidewalk. This isn't his fault."

"Did you see the assailant?" Bragg asked quietly.

She met his gaze. "No. I saw his or her gloved hand—and we found a man's dented shaving cup on the street. Raoul glimpsed the attacker from a distance and thinks it might have been a woman, or a slender, short man. Rick, Gillespie is on the short side and he is of medium build. The assailant wore an overcoat and fedora."

"You think the attacker was Judge Gillespie?" Hart asked sharply.

"Someone doesn't want me investigating the deposits Daisy made in May. So I am sure they are tied into Daisy's murder," Francesca said eagerly.

Bragg and Hart exchanged a glance.

"I have saved the real news!" Looking back and forth between both men, she smiled. "The money was a bank check—from First Federal of *Albany*."

Bragg's brows arched upward. "That could mean Gillespie was giving his daughter some additional funds. Now we have proof that he did know all about Honora's new life. You were right—he lied to you and to the police."

"Oh, it gets even better! Homer has told me that Gillespie came to see Daisy at her house *twice* in May." She grinned, waiting for both men to react. When neither spoke, she said, "Has Gillespie climbed to the top of your list of suspects?"

"Obviously," Bragg said somberly. "Francesca, he may have lied about knowing Daisy merely to protect his reputation."

"He may have killed to protect his reputation," Francesca said to him, desperately wanting Hart off that list.

Hart understood. He stood, releasing her hand. "Francesca, I also have news. The knife the police found in my coach was not the murder weapon."

Francesca was thrilled.

"But I happen to agree with Rick," Hart said grimly. "Gillespie would not be the first father to benevolently send his daughter funds. It is a rather common gesture. I was hoping the deposits would lead us to someone Daisy was blackmailing—someone who had motive, someone who wanted Daisy dead. I cannot imagine Gillespie murdering his own child."

Francesca wanted to take his hand, but he had paced away, his expression strained. She studied him for a moment before looking at Bragg. "Rick, Daisy has had no clients since February, when she became Calder's mistress. It is unlikely an old client decided to suddenly murder her, and, anyway, we have ruled out the clients who were consistently involved with her. Very little has happened in her life since February. Then, in May, for the first time in eight years—or at least, that is how it appears—her father visits her twice. He gives her a large sum of money, twice. A few weeks later, she is dead."

He understood. "Do you think she was blackmailing her own father?"

Francesca hesitated. "I can't help it!" she exclaimed. "She hated home enough to run away and become a prostitute. That is beyond extreme! She wasn't mildly unhappy—she had to have been miserable. And what mementos did she keep for eight years? Clippings of her father! I think she may have been obsessed with him. I think she may have hated him! What other conclusion is there?"

"We simply don't know that she hated him, and certainly not enough to blackmail him," Bragg said.

"We need to speak to Gillespie and trap him in his lies," Francesca said.

"Daisy may have loved her father," Hart said bluntly, facing them. "She may have missed him and her family and that is why she kept the clippings."

"Then why run away in the first place?" Francesca asked. "Something is very wrong in that family. By the way, Lydia also admitted that Daisy left her a letter, telling her she was never returning home. Oddly, she never showed that letter to her parents or the police. I think she knows even more than she has told me."

Hart resumed his seat beside her, taking her hand again. "You need to rest," he said quietly. "These are good clues, but I mean it. You must rest, Francesca."

"I *am* resting," she said, feeling hopeful. He had come running to her side, just as she had wanted. "Calder, you *were* framed. That is very good news, is it not?"

"Yes, it is."

She longed to move into his arms, overcome with her feelings for him. She glanced at Bragg. "Well, if that isn't proof of his innocence, what is?"

Bragg eyed her and then turned away, pacing to the marble fireplace.

Francesca pressed further. "It is highly unlikely that he murdered Daisy and some extraneous person decided to frame him, as well!"

"It is highly unlikely," he agreed, glancing once at his brother. "But stranger events have happened."

"Rick," Francesca said. "Do you want to meet me tomorrow at the Gillespies'?"

"Why don't you come to headquarters at noon? I'll have Newman bring him in for questioning then."

She nodded. "Meanwhile, tomorrow you need to send a telegram to First Federal in Albany. Direct them to reveal who ordered those two bank checks. We can lock that lead up."

He walked to her. "I'll have it done by the time the banks open," he said. He leaned down, squeezing her hand. "Try to follow Rourke's advice, Francesca. A concussion is no laughing matter. Get some rest and we'll work on Gillespie tomorrow."

She would always be pleased by his concern, she thought. "I have every intention of obeying the doctor's orders," she said with a smile. "And Rick? I'd like to see that report on the knife tomorrow."

"Of course." He glanced at Hart. "I'll be in touch," he said, his demeanor strained.

Hart shrugged. "Don't worry about it."

Bragg hesitated. "I am very grateful," he said. And then he left.

Francesca studied Hart, who turned his dark blue eyes back on her. "What was that about?"

He touched her cheek briefly. "That," he said, "was about a private matter between Rick and myself."

"You lent him the money!"

He sat back in his chair, just eyeing her. Finally he said, "Can the matter remain a private one, between me and my brother?"

She nodded, thrilled. "You did the right thing, Calder."

His face changed. Abruptly, a haunted look appeared in his eyes. "Do not award me another prize for nobility," he said, and suddenly he rubbed his face with his hands.

When he had first come into the room, he had been distressed because of her condition. But Francesca knew him very well now. She saw that he remained upset, but the matter was a different one entirely. "Has something happened that I should know about?" she asked very quietly, reaching for his hand.

He leapt to his feet and away from her. "Nothing has happened. I have to go. It is late." He forced a smile. It did not reach his eyes. "You need to rest, and I am keeping you."

She did not want him to leave and not like this. "I am supposed to rest but I am not allowed to fall asleep," she said softly. "Can't you keep me company for a while? Although, Connie and Neil are going to take shifts to make certain I don't sleep at all tonight."

His eyes widened. "Rourke is that worried?" Instantly he sat back down. "Of course I'll stay. Damn it, Francesca," he began.

She knew he was going to complain about the attack and the nature of her work. She touched his lips with her finger. "It was a tap. Rourke is being overly protective. I am *fine*."

Agony shimmered in his eyes. "I cannot lose you, too. Maybe I have been wrong, to be so supportive of your independence and sleuthing."

She was startled. "You are not going to lose me." And she thought then about the child he had just lost.

But he was staring at his knees, rubbing his jaw. "I am sorry. I have to go." And he stood, unexpectedly starting across the room, his strides long and hard.

Francesca leapt up, racing after him in her bare feet. "Calder, wait!"

He turned as she rushed into his arms. "You need to be resting!" he cried. "You were hurt today, damn it. Why can't you ever listen to anyone?"

She flinched, but his face had cracked into a dozen lines. She could feel how distressed he was. "What is it? This isn't about me."

"Of course it is," he said harshly, looking away and releasing her.

She clasped his cheek. "When are you going to grieve?"

His gaze shot to hers. "Don't," he warned.

Tears filled her eyes. "Don't grieve for your child? I'm sorry, Calder, but even with the trouble she caused, I wish Daisy were alive and I wish we had that little boy or girl to raise!"

Abruptly, his eyes swam with tears. He turned, reaching for the door.

She clasped his shoulder and felt him trembling. "Please don't go."

He shook his head, and when he spoke, his words were hoarse. "You don't want to see me this way."

"What way?" She tugged on him but he refused to budge. "Your child deserves your tears."

He leaned his head against the door.

Francesca suddenly realized he was crying. She did not know what to do. She hesitated, but no rational thought came. There was only her own answering grief and all the compassion she felt for him. So she put her arms around him.

A long moment passed, shudders racking his body. And then the silent sobs were gone. "I am fine."

She decided not to refute him. "Just come here," she whispered to his back.

He turned and Francesca took his face in her hands. "It's all right, Calder, to mourn the death of your child."

He fought the grief and she saw it. "I lied. I would have taken care of that child. I would have never let him or her grow up abandoned, unloved and alone."

"I know."

"Would you have really helped me? You wouldn't have left me?"

"Of course I would have helped you," she said, smiling just a little. "I don't care who the mother was, I would love any child of yours," she said truthfully.

"What have I done to deserve you?" He tilted up her chin. "Francesca, last Thursday I did shout at Daisy. I was furious. I really don't remember what I said, but when she first told me the truth, I did not want the child. And now I am paying for it."

"You are not paying for anything." She hesitated, then decided to be honest. "I told you once that when I give my heart away it is forever."

He started, his eyes widening. "You said that when you were in love with Rick!"

"But I wasn't in love with him. I think I had confused my admiration and my respect for love. And I will always care about him. But you are the one I have given my heart to. And with my heart comes faith and trust. Forever."

He stared. Then he reached into the interior pocket of his suit jacket and withdrew a folded piece of paper. "I have just read this," he said seriously.

Francesca had a bad feeling then. "What is it?"

"A letter from Daisy. I only received it today. She wrote it Thursday after our argument. It must have arrived at the house when I was away. It is fortunate Rick has proved I have been framed, but this letter is damning."

Francesca trembled. "May I?" she asked, holding out her hand.

"Please." He handed it to her.

Francesca quickly read the letter, an image of Daisy sitting at the small desk in the study where she had been murdered filling her mind. Every word Daisy had written added to Hart's motive for murder. She finished reading and slowly met his gaze. "The police do not need to see this."

"You are going to withhold evidence?"

Francesca realized that was exactly what she was doing. "We both know you are innocent. And you are no longer at the top of the suspect list. I'll hold on to this." While she knew she should destroy the letter, she could not go that far.

Hart was grim. "You don't need to protect me this way, by compromising your honesty and morals yet again."

"I am not compromising anything," she retorted. "I am fighting for the man I love!"

A heartbeat passed, and Hart pulled her close. In spite of the slight throbbing in her head, her body responded as he plied her mouth very thoroughly with his. Then he pulled away, keeping one large hand behind her nape. The matter of the letter must have been settled, because he said, "I need you to understand why I have left you, Francesca." He was dead serious now.

She tensed. "I do understand."

"Do you?" His smile seemed fragile and it was brief. "You have become everything to me. No one and nothing is more important. Can you understand that?"

A thrill began coursing through her. "Really?"

"Why else would I have asked you to marry me?" he asked.

"You told me then that you were tired of your philandering ways and that we suited nicely. You were very casual about it."

His eyes warmed. "You are so naive! I wasn't about to reveal my hand, Francesca." He became intent. "But I must reveal it now."

She nodded, not daring to swallow or breathe.

"I can't hurt you. I won't. And if we went on, you would be hurt by your association with me. Can't you see that?"

She had thought his confession would lead to reconciliation, not a deeper and more entrenched split. "What are you saying?"

"I could not live with myself if we remained together. I am ruined, Francesca. It will be a long, long time before society forgets that I was a suspect in the murder of my ex-mistress and child. I can survive—I have survived all the whispers behind my back thus far. I am, frankly, used to it. Truthfully, I have been indifferent to what others thought since I was a small child. But you are thin-skinned, and do not tell me otherwise! I know you would pretend to manage, that you would pretend indifference, and I also know you would cry in your bed every night, behind my back. I am not going to be the cause of such misery and distress."

"This isn't fair," she somehow said, backing away from him. "You love me and I love you! It is my choice to make, not yours!"

"I will always be here to protect you, Francesca—always. And you will always be the most important thing in my life. I am never going to let anyone harm you. I will always help you if you ask for my help. But I will not be the cause of your ruin and disgrace and, worse, real heartbreak."

She could not speak. If she could, she would tell him that he was the entire cause of her broken heart, and the pain was far greater than any hurt society might ever inflict.

"Darling, tell me you understand. I could not look at myself in the mirror if I did not protect you now. If I went merrily along with our engagement, I would be the selfish cad society accuses me of being."

Francesca stared at him, her vision blurring. "I do understand," she managed to say. "You really think that what you are doing is best for me."

He nodded, and he pulled her stiff body close. "I know that what I am doing is right. I have respected all of your choices. Can you not respect mine?"

He *had* respected her from the first moment they had met. What he was now asking was very reasonable, in fact. But how could she agree? "I want you. Apparently I am the selfish one in this relationship."

He smiled. "But you have me. You always will."

His words, uttered in prison, echoed. *It will never be over.* And Francesca suddenly realized that their engagement might be off, but their relationship hadn't ended, not at all. Hart had made his feelings for her terribly clear. Their relationship hadn't ended—it would never end. It had *changed.* In fact, if anything, their love suddenly seemed stronger than ever, although the circumstances were far more complex. "I don't want to agree to your choice," she finally said, stunned by her own revelations.

His smile faded. "I am asking you to respect my decision, not to agree with it. I have to do this, Francesca."

"I do respect your decision, Calder. But where does that leave us, precisely?"

"It leaves us in a very strange place," he admitted softly. "I will not return to our engagement, but I am selfish enough to need you in my life." He spoke slowly now. "I suppose that leaves us as friends, as genuine friends." There was a question in his eyes.

Francesca knew she was never going to stop loving Hart. And while he could not say the words, it had never been more evident that he felt the same way. He was not going to revive their engagement but he wasn't really walking away from her, either. Still, could they go back to being friends, when they had been lovers in almost every way?

If the alternative was losing him, she knew that her answer was yes.

Besides, she intended to persuade him to change his mind, even if it took years. "So we will be loyal friends—and nothing more," she said softly. "Will there be other women now?" And she felt a terrible pang of jealousy.

"I don't want anyone else!" he exclaimed.

"So you will become a monk?" If marriage was not a possibility, why couldn't they become lovers? She had never been like the other young ladies in town. She hardly needed a traditional relationship.

His jaw tightened. "It appears that way. I know what you are thinking, Francesca, but having a love affair with a supposed murderer would be far more scandalous than marrying one." He flushed. "Remember, I wish to protect your reputation, not ruin it even further."

"But you just kissed me," she pointed out.

His color deepened. "As you know by now, I am hardly perfect. But I intend to control my passion for you, if that is what I must do."

"You are so stubborn," she whispered. But she cupped his cheek, and unthinkingly, he turned his lips to the inside of her hand.

"I have never cared about you more than I do now."

Her heart lurched with such intensity it was frightening. She would never stop loving or wanting this man. The territory that lay ahead now was scarily unknown, but when had Hart ever been predictable? When had the map of their future ever been clearly charted? "You do realize that, right now, I desperately want to be in your arms," she said.

"Yes, I do realize that, but I am trying to keep myself in check."

Something hot, white and electric leapt between them—

Francesca actually thought she saw the sparks. This would be a huge challenge, she thought.

At that moment, to her relief, Joel burst into the room. "Miz Cahill!"

Francesca faced Joel, and saw that he was hopping from foot to foot in his excitement. "Joel! What is it?" She hurried toward him.

"I beg yer pardon," he cried. "I didn't mean to barge in."

"It's all right," she said, studying him. "What do you wish to tell me?"

He grinned. "I tailed Chief Farr! An' I found him, all right, just like I found you an' Mr. Hart!"

"Joel! I told you not to follow the chief. Did he catch you?" she cried.

"No, ma'am. He never saw me, not once."

Francesca was relieved. "What did you discover?"

The color in Joel's cheeks increased. He shot a glance at Hart. "He was with Rose, Miz Cahill, just like you and Mr. Hart."

It took Francesca a moment. "Farr and Rose are lovers?"

Joel nodded.

CHAPTER EIGHTEEN

Friday, June 6, 1902—10:00 a.m.

THE BANGING ON HIS door awoke him. Evan groaned, his head pounding with the force of an anvil, wishing that whoever it was would go away. Then he recalled the prior evening and instantly he was ill.

"Evan! The maid said you haven't left yet. Please, open the door and let me in," Bartolla Benevente said, sounding quite annoyed.

He did not really listen. He lay very still, recalling every bet he had placed, the roll of every pair of die, the spin of the roulette wheel, and finally, the far too serious game of poker.

How much had he lost last night? He seemed to recall the sum of eighteen thousand dollars, all of it credit, and he already owed Hart fifty thousand, not to mention that he owed more than that to another creditor. He had been so upset last night that after three drinks he had wandered to a club, never mind that he had told himself he would not go inside. But he had. Then he had told himself he would only drink and watch, and he had—for a few hours. And then he had told himself he'd only place one bet—one single bet—and he'd leave. But he had known he was lying to himself. One bet had brought back that familiar rush and he had forgotten everything—Bartolla, the child she claimed was his, Maggie. Gaming was far more addictive than any opiate could ever be, and he was no different from a drug addict.

Damn it.

His father had disowned him because of his gambling. He was deeply in debt—Andrew refused to pay his creditors. Because of his dissolute nature, because of his weak, flawed character, he was living in this goddamned hotel, about to marry a woman he no longer liked and, in fact, could barely stand. Now he would never have a chance to become acquainted with Maggie Kennedy, and discover if his feelings were reciprocated at all.

The key turned in his lock. Evan was too much of a gentleman to curse aloud, but in his mind, a few unsavory words echoed. Bartolla stepped inside, clearly quite outraged.

Evan sat up. He slept in the buff, so he stayed under the bedcovers. Now he recalled why she was so livid. He had failed to meet her for their engagement last night.

"Well, at least you aren't with another woman," she said, stepping into his suite.

And something inside of him snapped. He stared at her, in her striped burgundy suit, garishly low-cut and far too fitted across the hips. In the past, such a style had inflamed him; now it repulsed him. Suddenly her body, which he had once considered magnificent, seemed overly ripe. It occurred to him that her hair was as distasteful, too, the shade more ruby than red and clearly unnatural. Maggie's soft blue eyes filled his mind, her regard tender, worried, searching.

She always put everyone before herself; never would she put her own needs first.

He held his simmering temper in check, slowly threw off the covers and got up. He ignored Bartolla, aware of her gaze upon him as he went to the love seat at the foot of the bed, where he had left his trousers. He quickly stepped into them, keeping his back to her.

"What happened last night? We had supper plans," she snapped.

He needed a glass of water, he thought, although he knew

that would not alleviate his throbbing head or his disgust with her—and himself.

"Evan! What is wrong with you? I thought you were going to pick me up, and when you didn't, I went to the Farleys' alone, thinking you were meeting me there. But you never showed up!"

He poured himself a glass of water, his hands shaking. Bartolla marched around him to face him. She grabbed the glass from his hand. "I was humiliated."

He met her heated eyes. "I am sorry—"

"I should hope so!" she said, cutting him off.

"I am sorry, but I cannot marry you, Bartolla," he continued.

She turned white. "I know you do not mean what you just said!"

"As for last night, I was gambling." He turned away from her, ill once again. What was wrong with him? Like a drunkard suffering from the effects of a binge on the next day, he regretted every bet he'd placed.

She seized his arm. "I thought those days were over!"

He gently dislodged her. "I had thought so, too."

Her face softened. "Evan, I see you have had a bad night. I am sorry. We both know that gambling is a disease for you. I see I have overreacted. How can I help? Oh, I think I know the cure for what ails you," she said, her tone turning husky. And she grasped the waistband of his trousers, her fingertips pressing against his skin.

He did stir, but only slightly. "I have had a very bad night," he said, pulling away from her. There was only one woman whose comfort he wanted—whose touch he wanted—and while she might comfort him, he felt rather certain she would never touch him. "I want you to know that I will take care of you and the child. I will be very generous."

Bartolla cried out. She lost all of her coloring now.

He hoped that would be the end of it. He could not manage a scene right now. "I am going to get dressed."

But she followed him into the boudoir. "Of course we are marrying—we are eloping, as soon as possible. I am carrying your child!"

"And I said I would take care of you."

She trembled in anger. "How?" she spat. "You have been disowned and you work for a lawyer. You can't even afford a decent ring! And clearly, you have not recovered from your urge to game. That will certainly tighten your purse strings!"

He was suddenly alert. "Bartolla, I was a penniless clerk when we first agreed to elope. You did not seem to mind then."

She shook her head. "I have always minded! And I have always assumed it was a temporary aberration on your part." Suddenly she reached for him. He stepped back, but she managed to place her hands on his chest. "Darling, I am a countess. I would never agree to marriage to a clerk. I intended to encourage you to make amends with your father after we wed. I know you had a rotten night, Evan, but we have to think of the child."

"I *am* thinking of the child. I am thinking that I will grovel before my father and beg his forgiveness so that I can support you and the child in the manner you deserve. But I am not marrying you."

She had become still. Her hands slipped from his chest. "You are going to go to your father and patch things up? So you can support me?"

He could not breathe. There did not seem to be enough air in the small chamber for them both and he walked out. Maggie's eyes followed him, sad and somewhat reproachful. She was going to be very disappointed in him, he thought, as she had made it clear that she thought he should marry Bartolla. He hated letting her down. And she would be horrified when he told her how he had slipped back into gambling last night. "I do not lie." He did not look at her now. "My one redeeming quality, I suppose. You need not fear for the future, Bartolla. Until my son or daughter comes of age, you will be taken care of."

Bartolla had followed him back into the bedroom and she sat down, appearing thoughtful. After a moment, she said, "My heart is broken, Evan."

He wasn't foolish enough to believe her. "And I am also sorry for that."

"I think I should send my lawyer to meet yours so we can finalize all of the arrangements."

He shrugged. "Just give me a day or two to speak with Andrew."

She stood. "Of course." She hesitated. "I will be here if you change your mind. We are a good match."

He tried to smile and failed. He wasn't going to change his mind, but he did not tell her that. "I am late for work. That is, if I haven't lost my position."

"Well, after you speak with Andrew, you won't need your employment, now will you?" She started across the room, reticule in hand.

He suddenly thought of what Maggie had told him. "Bartolla?"

At the door, she paused. "Yes?"

He walked over to her. "My support is conditional upon one thing."

"What is that?" she asked, unperturbed.

"I want you to stay away from Mrs. Kennedy and her children."

Her expression changed. "Is that what this is about? Are you breaking it off with me because of *her?*" Disbelief heightened her tone.

"I care for her, but no, that is not the reason I have broken things off."

Bartolla was shaking. "You fool! You jilt me—a *countess*—for a seamstress with four children and callused hands?"

He felt an answering rage sweep through him. "She is a true lady, Bartolla," he warned. "And she would never have me. So no, I did not jilt you for her."

"She would not have you?" Bartolla gasped. "Are you mad? Are you in love with that trollop? Are you so in love that you cannot see clearly?"

Evan just stared, her words striking him with the force of a gale wind. He was dumbfounded. Bartolla was precisely right. "It doesn't matter."

"Oh, it matters," Bartolla cried. And her cheeks flushed, she stormed out.

"I WAS HOPING YOU would be in," Francesca said, from just outside of Bragg's office.

He stood up in surprise, glancing at the clock on his desk. "It's only half past ten."

Francesca slipped inside and closed his office door. She hurried to him. "I wanted to call you last night. I have learned something very interesting, but out of respect for Leigh Anne and the children, I waited until this morning. And of course, I did not want an operator to overhear us."

He walked around his desk. "What has you so excited?"

"Joel has been tailing Farr. It appears that he is having an affair with Rose."

Bragg registered her words. "Are you certain?"

"No. But yesterday, he was leaving Daisy's house when I arrived to speak with Rose. Homer said that they met briefly behind closed doors. Rose claims he was on official police business, but Joel saw them in an embrace last night."

"You think that she was with Farr the night of the murder, and she is afraid to name him as her alibi?"

"Well, that is my first thought. If Rose was with Farr that night, then she is not our killer. But I have another notion." Francesca had done nothing but think about Brendan Farr's involvement in the case and crime last night. When Hart had left her, she had made copious notes, and in the end, she had drawn the same two conclusions. "Either Farr was with Rose and she had a solid alibi, meaning she is no longer a suspect, or he and Rose are involved in the murder together."

"Francesca!" Bragg exclaimed. "That is a huge accusation to make."

"I knew you would react that way. But Farr hates me. He has hated me from the moment we met. I have never discovered why. I have no doubt he would love to hurt us both by seeing Calder take the fall for Daisy's murder. And why didn't he come forward to tell us he was with Rose that night?"

"His silence is suspicious, but he might want to avoid a besmirched reputation—just like Gillespie."

"He isn't married. Who would care if he frequents a prostitute?"

"You know the press would make a cause célèbre out of it. I probably would have to dismiss him," Bragg said pointedly.

"Are you going to call him in? We need to ask him about this, Rick."

Bragg studied her and she stared back. "Of course. Do you want to look over that report on the knife while I get him?"

Francesca smiled then. "I would love to."

He handed her the folder, his gaze suspicious. "You are in very good spirits today, all things considering."

"Calder was framed, and if Rose is not our killer, then we will merely have to keep looking."

"That is not what I meant, exactly." He regarded closely.

"I am feeling much better," she admitted. She had weathered this latest new development with Hart and intended to embrace the future in any way it chose to come at them.

He stared. "You have reconciled with Hart."

She met his gaze. "Not exactly. But I realized that he has to do this—he feels compelled to protect me. I can understand that now. And I also realized that we do not need an official relationship to remain committed to one another."

Bragg flushed. "I hope you know what you're doing," he said tersely.

"I think that I do. But I am certainly not abandoning Hart."

"So what happens now? You will be his lover, with no commitment on his part? How fortunate he must feel!"

"If I am his lover, that is not your concern, Rick. I must tell you, you are misjudging Calder once again. And given that he has just gone out of his way to lend you a significant sum to pay off O'Donnell, I think you owe him the benefit of the doubt."

Bragg looked apoplectic. "I'd rather see you engaged than carrying on with him. I don't like this."

"I am sorry you feel that way," Francesca said. She meant it, but she was disturbed that he was so judgmental. "I think you have crossed the line, Rick. My private life is just that—private."

"Then do not speak so openly of it!" he snapped. Abruptly, he strode out to get the chief.

Francesca sat down with the file, sighing. How complicated the most important relationships in her life were. Then she opened the file and read exactly what Bragg had already told her.

Bragg entered the office with Farr. His eyes slid over Francesca and he greeted her in a civil tone. "Good morning, Miss Cahill."

"Chief," she said coolly, standing and closing the file. She looked at Bragg.

"Chief, take a seat."

Without any emotion flickering in his blue eyes, Farr bent his long frame into the chair beside Francesca. Bragg went to stand behind his desk but he did not sit. "I have a source that tells me you have been involved with Rose Cooper. Is it true?"

Farr looked at Francesca with real distaste. "Let me guess. Miz Cahill's been snooping?"

Francesca smiled but her temper soared. "You were seen with her in an intimate embrace. Will you deny it?"

Farr's cheeks turned red. "If I want to see a whore, I think that's my own business."

Before Francesca could rebut, Bragg said, "I disagree. We both know the press would take a liaison like this and blow it all over the news pages, until I dismiss you or you are forced to resign. You're no staff sergeant—you run this entire force."

Farr bared his teeth. "Then maybe we should keep a lid on this, don't you think?"

Francesca could not contain herself. She leapt to her feet. "Were you with Rose the night of Daisy's murder? Are you the man she was entertaining? Because if she has an alibi for the time of the murder, we have been wasting our time considering her as a suspect. If that is the case, *Chief,* you have withheld information crucial to an official police investigation!"

He was on his feet, towering over her. "Don't you dare tell me about police rules and investigations! For some damned reason, the boss lets you in here like you own the station. But you're no copper—you're a little woman who fancies herself an investigator. I've known Rose and Daisy for years. I've been in both their beds! Yes, yesterday I took myself a little piece of action. But I was not with her the night of Daisy's murder. Why don't you check the logs? I worked late that night, right here at headquarters."

Francesca was cowed, and she knew she had turned white, but her mind sped. Rose remained a suspect, but could Farr be put on that list now, as well? He had known Daisy for years. He had been one of her clients. "When was the last time you availed yourself of Daisy's services?"

"You mean, when was the last time I was in her bed? Not since the New Year. She was always hard to book and then she went exclusive with your fiancé—oh, excuse me, your ex-fiancé. I forgot, Hart dumped you."

"Chief, you need to change your tone," Bragg warned.

Farr looked at him, his eyes sparking. "She shouldn't be here and she shouldn't stick her nose in our business! We got our own inspectors and they're good *men*."

"Francesca has been privately hired to investigate, and I for one am pleased that she works with us. The more minds, the better."

"If you say so," Farr said, clearly struggling for his composure. He faced Francesca with a cold smile. "Sorry if I got rude or crude. In the old days, little girls did not dress up and act like the boys." He glanced at Bragg. "You want me to sign an official statement?"

"I don't think we need one. And I'll try to keep a lid on this," Bragg said. "Thank you, Chief."

Farr grunted and strode out.

Francesca collapsed in her chair. "What an odious man!"

FRANCESCA SAT ALONE IN the conference room with a cup of bitter coffee, a notepad in front of her. Two officers had been sent over to the Fifth Avenue Hotel to bring Gillespie in, but she hardly needed to make notes to know what she wished to ask him. Her mind kept veering back to the interview with Farr, and a shudder of revulsion swept her. With no information on Rose's supposed alibi, she finally asked herself if she seriously thought Rose guilty of murder.

Rose had loved Daisy so much. No matter how angry she had been about being rejected, Francesca could not imagine the other woman killing her best friend and lover. Such a heinous act would have had to have been committed in such a fit of rage as to temporarily make Rose insane.

She had no real reason to suspect Farr, but she had little doubt he could take a human life. Maybe that wasn't fair, but if he wasn't involved, then why hadn't he come forward to admit to his prior relationship with Daisy? Unfortunately, there was a simple answer—he wished to avoid being associated with her, just like the judge.

"Francesca?" her father asked softly from the door.

Francesca leapt to her feet, stunned to see Andrew standing there. He looked uncertain and very weary. "Papa! What are you doing here?" she cried, filling with hope.

"I had hoped to find you at your sister's, Francesca, but by the time I got there, you had already left. An officer downstairs told me you were here. May I come in?"

"Of course." Francesca wrung her hands. She had missed Andrew terribly, and seeing him now made her realize that.

He smiled gently at her and stepped into the room. Automatically, Francesca went to him and they embraced as if nothing were wrong. She then straightened his dark blue tie. "You seem tired, Papa."

"I am very tired," he said. "How can I sleep when you have left the house? Francesca, I was at an important supper last night for the Citizens Union—we are planning our next electoral campaign. I got home after midnight, but your mother was still up and she told me what happened. Are you all right?"

"I am fine," she assured him, smiling. "It was just a tap on the head. Someone does not want me following a certain lead. Have you heard? Hart was falsely arrested because he was framed."

"I hadn't heard, but I am happy for you. Did you see the morning's papers?"

Francesca tensed with dread. "No."

"The fact that Miss Jones was Judge Gillespie's daughter is all over the news."

For one moment, Francesca had been afraid that the fact that Daisy had been with child at the time of her murder had made headlines. She sighed with relief. "Papa, Hart is innocent."

"I never said I thought him capable of murder!" Andrew exclaimed. "But the scandal has begun in earnest. He was actually a topic of discussion last night. Everyone wanted my opinion on the affair, due to your involvement with him."

"And what did you say?"

"I said that he is innocent and I changed the subject. Did he end the engagement, Francesca?" Andrew asked, gently. "I read that press release, too."

"Yes, he did. You see, he *is* noble, Papa. He insists on sparing me from scandal."

Andrew pulled her into his arms. "And you will still defend him, won't you? No matter what?"

"Of course. Nothing has really changed, except for a formality. I still love him, and he still loves me."

Andrew stepped back. "The act was a truly selfless one," he admitted.

Francesca bit her lip. "I am glad you can finally say something positive about Hart."

"You still want to marry him, don't you?"

Francesca didn't hesitate. The truth was so obvious. She could claim she was eccentric and liberal, and that she had no use for traditional arrangements, but deep in her heart, she wanted to be his wife. She wanted that commitment the way she had never wanted anything else. But she was prepared to go forward with him without any formal agreement if she had to. "Yes."

"Will he be proved innocent?" Andrew asked.

Francesca nodded.

He touched her cheek. "When this is over, I will sit down with Hart and have a long talk with him."

"What does that mean?" Francesca asked.

"It means I will try to lay my prejudices aside and genuinely comprehend the man. I will give him a chance, Francesca, to prove to me that he is worthy of being your husband."

Francesca flung her arms around him. "Papa! I love you so much! I have hated being at odds with you this way."

"Francesca, will you please move back home?"

In that moment Francesca realized just how much the living arrangement with her sister suited her. She had much more independence and the freedom to do as she pleased. "Papa, I am enjoying my visit with Connie. You know that we have not been spending very much time together, due mostly to my sleuthing, but now we get to see each other several times a day."

"But you will come home?"

"In a few days," she said, wondering how she could make her stay at her sister's permanent.

Andrew smiled. "I am so glad we have worked things out."

"So am I, Papa," Francesca said, smiling happily in return. And then she saw Bragg appear in the doorway. He said, "Gillespie's coming up."

Francesca seized her father's hand. "I have to go. We are interviewing a suspect." She quickly kissed his cheek and ran after Bragg. In the hall, she saw Gillespie step out of the elevator with a uniformed officer. He seemed annoyed and angry.

"What is this about, Commissioner?" he demanded. "I was ordered by your men to come here."

"We have some questions to ask you," Bragg said, gesturing to his office. He nodded at the young officer, dismissing him.

"I don't know what you could possibly wish to ask me," Gillespie said, marching into the center of Bragg's office. He did not sit down. "You arrested Calder Hart yesterday."

"Hart was released on bail. More importantly, we have discovered he was framed. He was falsely arrested, Your Honor," Francesca said.

"The charges have been dropped," Bragg added.

Francesca hadn't known that. She thought about Daisy's letter. She was not going to show it to Bragg, no matter how guilty she felt for withholding it. Hart had been through enough. "Your Honor, sir, did you know that your daughter received a significant sum of money last month?"

He started. "No, I did not. How would I know that? I told you,

I had no idea what had become of Honora until you showed me that sketch."

Francesca exchanged a glance with Bragg. Softly, she said, "Sir, we have a witness who will testify that you were at Daisy's home last month."

He paled.

"And we also have proof that the money she deposited, all twenty thousand dollars, came from the First Federal Bank of Albany," Bragg said.

"What in God's name does this have to do with her murder?" Gillespie exclaimed.

"Your Honor!" Francesca was stern. "You have lied to me and you have lied to the police. You knew that your daughter was here in the city, using the name Daisy Jones. Yet you have insisted you knew nothing. Why, sir?"

Gillespie sank into a chair. "Why do you think?" He covered his face with his hands, apparently about to weep. "I am an elected official. My daughter turned herself into a whore. Why do you think I denied ever knowing of her and her new life?"

Francesca went to him, clasping his shoulder. "I am sorry," she said. "And I understand. When did you first learn that she was in the city?"

"I ran into her by accident, outside of a restaurant. There had been no word, for eight endless years. We hired private investigators, Miss Cahill. They worked for me for two years, but they turned up nothing. We had given up!" he cried. "But on May 3, I saw her on the street as she was getting out of a handsome coach, looking as elegant as any lady. I knew it was my beautiful daughter the moment I first saw her."

"And she invited you home?" Francesca asked.

He nodded, wiping at his tears.

"Did you tell your wife and daughter?" Bragg asked.

"No! They know nothing! They knew nothing—not until after she was murdered."

Francesca knew that was a lie, for he could not look at them now. Had he returned to Albany and announced his discovery of Honora's whereabouts? Or had he privately confided in Martha? Perhaps Lydia had somehow overheard what had transpired. However it had happened Francesca was quite certain that had all three of them had known about Honora's life as Daisy by the night of her murder. "And the money?"

"I am her father," he said. "It was a gift. I was hoping she would change her life. We wanted her to come home."

"We?" Bragg demanded.

"A figure of speech. Martha and Lydia grieved for her for years, Commissioner."

"I have one more question. When did she tell you what she had become?"

"She didn't." He paused. "But she was living alone, unwed, and she would not come home. It was obvious that someone was keeping her." He covered his face with his hands again.

Francesca took the opportunity to look at Bragg. He shook his head. Clearly, he also smelled a rat.

"Sir?" An officer knocked on the open door. "Rose Cooper is here, and she has asked to speak with you."

"Bring her up to the conference room." He turned to Gillespie. "Excuse us."

"How long will I have to be here?" the judge asked, clearly intent on leaving.

"Just a few more minutes," Bragg assured him.

Francesca followed him out. The moment his office door was closed, she tugged on his sleeve. "Rose must have some information she wishes to share," she said in excitement. Perhaps this would be the break they needed.

"I doubt it is a confession of murder," Bragg said mildly.

Rose appeared at the far end of the corridor. Although immaculately dressed, she was haggard with strain. Francesca wasn't certain if she remained stricken with grief or if some other event had occurred to distress her. "Rose? Are you all right?"

Rose paused before them, shaking her head. "I doubt I will ever be all right again."

"Let's go inside," Francesca suggested. She guided Rose into the conference room, Bragg following. She hesitated and then decided not to waste time. "We know about your relationship with Chief Farr."

Rose turned white. "You must tell him I never said a word!"

"It's all right. He knows that. Joel was following him and he saw you together."

Alarm immediately showed on Rose's face. "Are you sure he doesn't think I told you the truth?"

"Has he threatened you?"

"Of course not! But he is chief of police. He can make my life miserable!" She glanced at Bragg with more worry.

"Did Farr promise you protection in exchange for your services?" he asked.

Rose shook her head. "No. I...I like him. We're...lovers. That's all—and that's no crime."

Francesca had never despised Farr more. She had not a doubt he had availed himself of Rose's services simply by threatening to arrest her if she refused him. "Were you with Farr the night Daisy was murdered?"

"No," she whispered. "I lied. I never had a customer. I'm not stupid—I know how it looked. I knew you'd think about all the fights I'd had with Daisy after she took up with Hart. And I really thought he did it...but now I am not so sure."

Francesca was eager. "What has changed your mind?"

"Her father," Rose said, her tone stricken. "I have been thinking about him all night, ever since you told me that you found Daisy's family. Then I read in the newspaper this morning that he is here to bury her. And I can't let that happen!" She began to cry.

Francesca put her arm around her. "What is it that you are not telling us? Why don't you want Daisy's father to bury her? Rose, what do you know?"

"I promised," Rose wept. "I swore to Daisy, and I promised I would keep her secret forever. But how can I do that? She's dead and I think her father did it."

Francesca trembled. "Rose, whatever you promised Daisy, if keeping this secret is preventing us from finding her killer and bringing him to justice, she would want you to come forward now."

"I'm not sure she would ever want me to come forward, Francesca. We only spoke of it once, long ago, when we first became friends."

"Rose, you can be subpoenaed to testify in court. Refusal to do so would merit charges and a jail term," Bragg said quietly.

She looked at him through glazed eyes, and then at Francesca. "Daisy hated him. She hated him with a passion. She wished him dead, Francesca! He was the reason she ran away from home."

Francesca nodded. "Why? Why would she hate her own father so much? Did he betray her mother—did she catch him with another woman? Was he cruel, or punish her with force?"

"Did she catch him with another woman?" Rose laughed bitterly, hysterically. "She *was* the other woman, Francesca."

For a long moment, Francesca did not understand.

Bragg said, "Are you saying what I think you are?"

She nodded. "She was only a child. She was twelve years old when it started—that is what she said. Gillespie was sharing her bed."

CHAPTER NINETEEN

Friday, June 6, 1902—Noon

FRANCESCA WAS IN SHOCK. She looked at Bragg, whose expression was filled with revulsion. She finally began to understand. Daisy had been molested by her father, perhaps even raped. No wonder she had left home.

"You may have to testify to this in court, Rose," Bragg said.

She nodded, wiping her eyes.

Francesca faced her. "Did you know Gillespie was in town last month?"

"She never mentioned it, Francesca, just like she never mentioned the money," Rose whispered hoarsely. "Just like she never told me she was with child."

Francesca ran to the door, tearing it open. Bragg raced after her. "Wait! You had better let me handle this."

Francesca did not pause. "How much do you want to wager that Daisy was blackmailing her father? No wonder he claimed he did not know who she was!"

Bragg seized her arm outside of his office door. "You are too upset to interrogate him!"

"Upset? That hardly describes how I feel—I am ready to commit murder myself! That man deserves the death penalty, Rick."

"There is no death penalty for molestation or rape."

"There is for murder." She turned and pushed open the door.

Gillespie was standing by the window, staring out of it. Abruptly, he turned. "Am I free to go?"

"I don't think so," Francesca said.

Bragg took her arm. "Your daughter was blackmailing you, wasn't she?"

Gillespie stepped back. "I have no idea what you are talking about."

Francesca shook Bragg off. "We know why she ran away. And we have a witness—Daisy's best friend—who will testify in court that you were molesting your own daughter when she was twelve years old."

Gillespie stared, and then his face began to collapse.

"You horrid, despicable, inhuman man!" Francesca exclaimed, shaking. And tears finally filled her eyes.

"Francesca, stop," Bragg said softly.

Gillespie sank into a chair and began to quietly cry.

"Don't you have anything to say for yourself?" Francesca demanded.

"I didn't know she hated me so much until I saw her last month," he whispered, not looking up. "I loved her. I loved her so much. And she hated me. She said such ugly things. She told me she was a whore, she told me about all of the men. She was so cruel, so hateful! And then she wanted money. I didn't even have it, but she threatened me. My beautiful, beautiful daughter! I only loved her and I never meant to hurt her…I dreamed she would come home one day. I never meant for any of this to happen." He looked pleadingly at Francesca. "I love her."

Francesca was ill, but she could not look away from the quivering, depraved man sobbing in the chair. "Bragg, he has motive, he has means."

"Judge, I am afraid you are not leaving, not yet," Bragg said. "I'm sure you know the law. I can hold you for twenty-four hours and that is what I intend to do."

Gillespie leapt up, realization dawning. "I didn't do it! I didn't murder my own daughter!"

VERY SLOWLY, FEELING FAR more ancient than her twenty-one years, Francesca walked up the corridor of the sixth floor where the Gillespies had their suite of rooms. She was sick to her stomach and she had the urge to flee to Hart and bury herself in his arms, where she could cry for Daisy's life, but that would not solve the case. She had no doubt now that Daisy had hated her father enough to threaten him with exposure—her own exposure. The problem was that Gillespie's denial had rung true. As mentally ill as he was, as sexually depraved, she could not be certain that he had murdered his own daughter.

Poor Daisy. The words were a litany in her mind. She could not imagine how the twelve-year-old girl had felt or what she had gone through. But now, somewhat, she could understand the woman she had become. No wonder Daisy had wanted Hart back. He had given her a life of freedom and independence and he had been kind.

Francesca paused before the Gillespies' door, struggling for some composure. Had Martha known what was going on under her very roof? Had Lydia? She needed to learn exactly what mother and daughter really knew. If Gillespie was innocent and if Rose was also innocent, then she was at a loss for suspects and she was running out of clues—and time. Family members usually filled out the roster of suspects, but for the life of her, she could not imagine why either Martha or Lydia might want Daisy dead. If anything, she thought grimly as she knocked, they would want to murder Gillespie instead.

But Francesca knew Lydia was hiding something, and it was time she came clean.

Lydia opened the door, looking surprised to see her. Francesca tried to smile. "May I come in? I have some questions for you and your mother."

"Of course." Lydia opened the door and stepped aside so Francesca could enter.

Francesca glanced around the elegant sitting room, but

apparently Martha remained in one of the bedrooms. She waited until Lydia had closed the door. "I just saw your father."

Lydia's expression was strained. "What is it that you wish to say, Miss Cahill?"

"I have learned why Daisy ran away."

Something flickered in Lydia's eyes. She walked away. "Then maybe you should share that information. I would like to know why my sister abandoned me."

Francesca went to her, mulling over Lydia's choice of words. She decided to take a terrible risk. "Did he go to your bed, too?"

Lydia jerked. "I don't know what you are talking about!"

"I know that Daisy was molested by your father, Lydia. I am horrified, and I am very sorry."

Lydia stared, her expression frozen into unreadable lines. "You need to leave."

"I know this is a painful subject—"

"I think you know nothing, Miss Cahill, nothing!" Lydia was trembling but her face remained as tight as a drum.

"Did you know what was happening? Did you share a room with your sister? Or was she in her own room down the hall?"

Lydia's eyes became moist. "I have no idea what you are talking about! What difference does it make if we shared a room or not?" Her voice caught.

"They had their own rooms—with an adjoining door between."

Francesca whirled to face Martha Gillespie. She stood in the doorway of the bedroom, clad in a black mourning dress, her alabaster skin starkly pale, her eyes red from weeping.

"Miss Cahill was just leaving," Lydia said tersely.

Francesca looked at Lydia, wondering if she was protecting her mother. She turned her shocked gaze on Martha. Surely Martha was not the killer here. Daisy—Honora—had been her daughter. But why was Lydia being such a watchdog? What were they hiding?

"I'd like to ask your mother a few questions," Francesca said, her gaze riveted on the older blond woman.

"My mother is in mourning! Can't you see that? She needs to be left alone!" Lydia almost shouted, and she appeared desperate.

This family had already suffered terribly, Francesca thought. She didn't want to be the cause of any more suffering. And while she wanted to ask them both if they thought the judge capable of murdering Daisy, in order to gauge their reactions, her compassion won the day. "I am very sorry for your loss," Francesca said to Mrs. Gillespie.

She nodded, a white-knuckled grip on her handkerchief.

"Please, Miss Cahill. This is not a good time," Lydia said hoarsely.

Francesca hesitated, looking from daughter to mother. "I know you both want justice for Honora," she said. "But I need your help. So please, consider another interview—at your convenience, of course."

Martha Gillespie just stared. No one could be more despondent.

"Please go," Lydia cried.

Francesca nodded. She let herself out, but the moment she had closed the door, she pressed her ear against the smooth, polished wood. Her reward was instantaneous.

"She is going to find out," Martha said, her tone choked.

Lydia said, "No, she won't. Not if you do not say *anything.*"

BRAGG KNOCKED ON THE door of O'Donnell's flat. The thug was not expecting him and Bragg hoped that he was home. As he waited for a response, the wrapped leather handle of the case burned his hand. The money inside felt terribly heavy, like an anchor, dragging him down.

Images of Leigh Anne came to mind, tearful and afraid, begging him to fix this crisis, begging him to pay O'Donnell off so he would leave them alone. Another image followed, and Dot grinned at him, waving one chubby fist, while Katie regarded him out of her huge, questioning and somber eyes.

This was the right thing to do, Bragg reminded himself. Never mind that he was commissioner of police and his mandate was to uphold and enforce the law, not break it. *He had to protect his family.* The choice was clear. Leigh Anne was so fragile now. Every time he looked at her he saw the anguish and fear in her eyes. How much longer could she go on this way? Even Francesca agreed that the best course was to pay O'Donnell off and get rid of him instantly.

Bragg waited at the door, closing his eyes. The images in his mind were gruesome—O'Donnell gasping for his life as Bragg choked it right out of him, slowly, cruelly, purposefully. Everyone had a dark side and his had chosen this moment to assert itself. He had never hated anyone more—he had never feared anyone more.

But he would not succumb to such primitive rage. He was a rational man and he could control himself.

Bragg heard footsteps on the other side of the door. He stiffened. This was it, then.

He thought about how he knew O'Donnell as intimately as if they were lifelong acquaintances, because he had known men like him time and again. He was the scum of the earth, he would never be reformed, and he would come back to cause trouble, time and again.

He would come back, one day, for more money.

Sweat trickled down Bragg's temples. If he wasn't a man of the law, murder would be the only way to really ensure that the man never came back to harm them.

"Yeah?" O'Donnell opened the door.

Bragg stared.

FRANCESCA STOOD OUTSIDE THE closed front door of Daisy's house, waiting for Homer to answer her knock. The sadness she felt for Daisy remained, and its weight was crushing. She simply could not take it.

Homer opened the door. "Miss Cahill!"

She was surprised—he was not in his dark suit, but far more casual dress. "May I come in? Are you going out?"

"We have no duties now. The house is as clean as a whistle, considering we are not allowed to touch the study or Miss Jones's private rooms. Mr. Hart has left no instructions. I had hoped to visit my daughter on Staten Island."

"I'm sure he wouldn't mind." Francesca managed a smile that felt wan. "You need not stay here on my account. I came here to think."

"Is everything all right?" Homer asked, his dark eyes on hers.

"Not really," Francesca said.

"But...Mr. Hart has been released. He is innocent, is he not?"

Francesca tried out another feeble smile. "Yes, he is innocent. This isn't about Hart. I have just learned some very sad facts about Daisy. I wish she were alive. I wish we had never, ever exchanged a single harsh word."

Homer was startled, and Francesca recovered her composure, which was shaky indeed. "Please, I prefer to be alone, actually. I don't need anything."

Homer was hesitant, but Francesca encouraged him again, and finally he went to get his things so he could leave.

She was alone in the front hall, the door closed behind her. Francesca glanced around at the pale, cream-colored walls, the smooth polished floors, and into the first salon, the doors of which were open. Suddenly Daisy appeared, rising from a sofa, her grace as fluid and elegant as ever. She was smiling.

Francesca sighed. It was so easy to imagine Daisy alive, the way she had so recently been. She wiped some tears from her cheeks.

"I wish I had known you better," she whispered, walking to the threshold of the salon where Daisy had entertained her several times. "I wish I hadn't been so frightened of you, but you were so beautiful, and I admit that I am insecure." The empty beautifully furnished room was absolutely still. She realized she had been hoping to feel Daisy's presence, not that that would solve or change anything. But this room was entirely impersonal now.

Francesca walked out. There were more tears. How terribly had Daisy suffered as a child? How could any man behave so foully to his own daughter? Why hadn't someone realized what was going on and prevented it? She paused on the threshold of the study.

"I am sorry that we fought," she whispered. "But I understand now. I really do."

The study—small, dark and unlit, should have been cozy, but it was not. Even in the shadows, there were bloodstains all over the multicolored Persian rug on the floor. "Who did it? Daisy, I will find your killer, but I am currently at a loss. Did your father murder you?"

Of course, there was no answer. But this room did not feel empty and vacant, like the salon.

Francesca tensed. She was not alone in the small study. The hairs on her nape prickled and, filled with unease, she turned.

Martha Gillespie stood there. "Why won't you leave the dead alone?"

Before Francesca could answer, Martha raised a small gun.

"Why won't you leave *us* alone?"

IN THAT MOMENT, as he stared at O'Donnell, he wished he were more like his half brother. If the roles were somehow reversed, if it were Hart who was defending Francesca, he would not think twice about really getting rid of O'Donnell. Bragg had no doubt.

Surprise and even fear flashed in O'Donnell's eyes. Then he saw the case Bragg carried and his relief was evident. Bragg walked past O'Donnell, thinking about the gun he wore, thinking about the East River, where so many bodies were tossed. An odd desperation had filled him. How had he gone from the pursuit of justice to a desire to commit murder?

Beth O'Brien stood by the kitchen table, her blue eyes on the attaché case he held. O'Donnell closed the door. Bragg saw that he, too, stared at the briefcase. Their greed filled him with revulsion and disgust.

"I guess your pretty wife has been telling you how hard it's been for us these past few months," O'Donnell asked, walking over to him.

Red rage filled him. O'Donnell had terrorized Leigh Anne. But when he spoke, he was surprised at how unemotional and calm he sounded. "She has told me that you wish for a fresh start. There are better employment opportunities in the south, I believe." He went to the kitchen table, not looking directly at either the man or the woman, but very aware of them from the corner of his eye. Both O'Brien and O'Donnell came to stand there, as well. He laid the case down and unbuckled the two straps. Then he opened it completely, revealing the stacks of bills inside. "I imagine such a gift will be very helpful," he said, his heart thumping with a peculiar and sickening force. He added very softly, still not making eye contact, "You can count it if you wish."

O'Donnell chuckled and reached into the case. He removed one bound stack. "That won't be needed, Commissioner. Hey, you know what? With relations like you, we might never have to worry about anything again."

Bragg stepped away from the table. He could no longer control the forceful pounding of his heart. It would be so easy to seize his revolver and get rid of these two. If he didn't, they were coming back, he knew it the way he knew the sun would rise tomorrow.

"Guess I got the little lady to thank for that." Grinning, O'Donnell put the stack back inside the attaché case. "A wife like that would make a man do anything."

Bragg was never aware of moving, but suddenly his hands were around O'Donnell's throat, squeezing as hard as he could. O'Donnell was against the kitchen wall, his eyes bulging and his face turning red. "You fucking bastard! Never speak of my wife again."

O'Donnell's face changed from red to purple. *It would be so easy now.*

"You're killing him!" Beth screamed, seizing him from behind.

He was killing this lowlife, and no one would ever know. They would be free.

O'Donnell began to wheeze, panic in his bulging eyes.

He would know.

Bragg released him, stepping back. "Never mention my wife again," he snarled. "Do you understand me?"

O'Donnell fell to his knees, clutching his throat, now blotched red.

O'Brien cried, "Get out. Just get out. We have the cash—get out!"

He turned to look at her. Her eyes were filled with hatred and her face was no longer benign or grandmotherly at all. He couldn't kill O'Donnell—and he could not do this, either.

"You are both under arrest," he said, and he reached into his jacket. Then he snapped one manacle on O'Brien's wrist, the other on the leg of the table, his actions forcing her to sit down. She gaped in shock.

He hauled O'Donnell to his feet. The thug was coughing now. Bragg cuffed him, as well.

"You will regret this!" O'Donnell managed hoarsely.

"I almost did," Bragg said.

MARTHA GILLESPIE AIMED A double-barreled derringer directly at Francesca's head. Francesca's heart plummeted. She was almost certain that she had found Daisy's killer.

"What are you doing, Mrs. Gillespie?" she asked very carefully. She still clutched her purse, where she had her own pistol, but she did not dare move.

"My family was destroyed a long time ago," Martha said harshly. A tear tracked down her face. "Now you will destroy what is left of us."

"I don't want to destroy anyone," Francesca said softly. "I was Daisy's friend. I only want justice."

"If only you had left us alone!" Martha cried, her hand shaking, the gun wavering.

"You knew, didn't you? You knew that your husband was taking advantage of Daisy."

"Not at first," Martha whispered. "Of course I didn't know, not at first! But then Daisy began to act strangely. She stopped smiling. She never laughed. She would not speak to Richard. She had adored him, but then she flinched when he touched her. I was glad when she ran away!"

Francesca was stunned. "Maybe *Richard* was the one who should have left."

"It was not his fault! She was always too beautiful, even as a little child. Then, when she became a young woman, the way she walked, the way she carried herself…everyone noticed. She was temptation, Miss Cahill, evil, carnal temptation. I have no doubt that she lured Richard into her bed."

Francesca felt ill. "She was twelve years old."

"Was that when it began? I didn't realize what was happening until just before she left. Richard had said he was coming up to bed, but he never did. I wasn't well. I needed a doctor, so I went looking for him. You can imagine where I found him." She trembled even more and more tears fell.

Richard had been sexually abusing Daisy for three years and her mother had never known it. "Surely, surely, you made certain that it never happened after that night."

"I left them alone—I had to leave them. Richard doesn't know that I ever discovered his secret."

"You had a duty and a responsibility to protect your child, Mrs. Gillespie. You never confronted your husband?" Francesca was aghast.

"I never confronted him," Martha cried. "How could I? Could you? I am sorry, I did not have the courage!"

Francesca's grief for Daisy grew. "When did you decide to kill her?"

"I am not an evil woman—like she was. There is a reason she became a prostitute. She was blackmailing us! Richard told me that he had found her and that she refused to come home. I was glad—I would have never let her back in the house. One night I found him crying. He told me he was sending her money, that he wanted to help her, but I knew instantly that she was blackmailing him with her dirty secret."

"So you hated your own daughter?"

Martha lifted her chin. "I loved my daughter. Until she became a harlot—until she lured Richard into sin. And then I had every right to hate her."

Francesca could only stare, sickened.

"Mother, don't say another word!" Lydia rushed into the room, her wide eyes going from her mother to Francesca and back again.

"She is trying to destroy our family, Lydia," Martha said firmly.

"That isn't what she intends. She only wants to find Daisy's killer, Mother. She did not know that would destroy what was left of us."

So Lydia knew her mother had murdered Daisy. "You knew, too, didn't you? You knew what your father was doing to your sister?"

Lydia faced her, beside Martha. "Yes." Her expression was ravaged. "I knew. In the beginning, when he left her room, I would go to her and she would cry in my arms. But it didn't take long, Miss Cahill, for the tears to dry up."

"Why didn't you say something?" Francesca demanded.

"I was ten years old!" Lydia cried, her eyes shining with unshed tears. "I hardly understood. I was *thirteen* when Daisy ran away, Miss Cahill, and we both pretended that nothing was wrong after it all began. It hurt too much otherwise." She was a ghastly shade of white. "The truth is," she managed, shaking, "it wasn't until I learned that Father had found Honora here in the city and that she was a prostitute that I really understood what had happened when we were children."

Lydia had managed to block the ugly reality out. "I'm sorry. Why did you frame Calder Hart?"

"To protect my mother. Hart's involvement with my sister, and the fact that he was here the night she died, made it so easy to frame him. All I had to do was come back to the city and put a bloody knife in his coach. I did it Wednesday. Now please go away!" Lydia cried. "Go away and leave us alone."

Francesca was shocked. "Lydia, this is a tragedy. But your father needs to pay for what he did to Daisy and your mother *murdered* her."

Lydia stared at Francesca, her expression tight and strained. Then, never removing her gaze, she said, "Mother, give me that gun."

Instantly, Martha handed it to her daughter. As instantly, Lydia pointed it at Francesca. "I know you won't understand. But please, try. I hate my father. I have hated him since he first went to Honora. I loved my sister—I missed her every day that she was gone—but I was glad she had left. I prayed she would find happiness, but she didn't. Because of my father, she is dead. Mother is all I have left. Please try to understand. Please, don't take her away from me, too." And tears began to slowly fall down Lydia's cheeks.

Francesca ached deeply for her. "Your mother killed Honora, Lydia. You do know that?"

"I know. I discovered her in the act—and I helped her flee."

Francesca stared. Lydia was an accessory to murder. "Where is the murder weapon?"

"I threw it in the bushes of the neighbor's. What are you going to do, Miss Cahill?" Lydia asked.

"How can you ask me to walk away and pretend that I know nothing?" Francesca replied, aware that Lydia was no longer aiming the gun, but held it loosely at her side.

"I am not asking you, I am begging you," Lydia whispered. Then she raised the pistol. "And if my pleas do not move you, then maybe this will."

Lydia trained the gun at Francesca's head. Did she know how to fire the weapon? How good was her aim? "You are not a killer."

"I will protect Mother at all costs. We should have never come to the city!" she cried, and her hand wavered.

Francesca rushed her, tackling her at her waist. As Lydia fell backward, the gun went off, but the shot was wildly off any mark. If the gun was fully loaded, Lydia had another shot left, but Francesca wasn't sure that was the case or that Lydia even knew it. Francesca seized Lydia's hand, which held the gun and their eyes met.

"Please," Lydia cried, and she released the gun.

Francesca took it, shifting off of Lydia and onto her knees. She pointed it at the younger woman. "There is another shot." Or so she hoped.

Lydia looked helplessly at her.

Francesca backed up and rose, quickly pointing the gun at Martha. "Don't move, Mrs. Gillespie. I do not want to shoot you, but if I have to, I will." That was a bald lie, because she had no intention of shooting either of these women.

Martha sank down in the chair in front of Daisy's desk. "Don't hurt my daughter," she whispered.

FRANCESCA MET BRAGG IN the front hall when he arrived with two officers and Inspector Newman. She had left both women in the study with their hands tied behind their backs. Lydia's pistol had not been fully loaded, and there had not been a second shot in it. "Thank God you are here!" she cried, seizing his arm as he rushed into the house.

"Who is it, Francesca?" he demanded. A patrolman had delivered her message that she had Daisy's killer in custody.

"Martha Gillespie murdered Daisy," Francesca said, restraining him. "Bragg, this is a terrible tragedy. Apparently Martha hated Daisy for what transpired. She blamed Daisy for seducing the judge. She knew that Gillespie had found Daisy here in the city, and she realized quickly enough that Daisy was blackmailing him."

"She confessed to all of this?"

Francesca nodded, filled with worry. "There is more."

"I thought so," he said, his concerned gaze on her face.

She shuddered. "Lydia witnessed the murder and helped her mother flee."

Bragg was grim. "That makes her an accessory, Francesca."

"She did not conspire to the crime! She loved her sister and she has been every bit as much a victim as Daisy was, Rick! She has hated her father since he first started molesting Daisy. Rick, she was trying to protect her mother."

"What would you have me do? Are you asking me to withhold

the details of Lydia's involvement, are you asking me to tell the D.A. not to press charges against her, too?"

Francesca hadn't realized she still gripped his sleeve and now she released him. She wrung her hands. "I guess it is unfair of me to ask you for such a favor."

He was clearly unhappy. "I almost murdered O'Donnell today, Francesca. I was this close to killing him with my bare hands and tossing the body in the river. But I didn't. And I didn't pay him off, either—I arrested him and his aunt. I have spent my entire life being the most honest man that I can be. I am sorry about Lydia. We can recommend a suspension of her sentence. It is very likely a judge would respond favorably to such a plea." He gave her a dark look. "Or you can ask Hart to help you. I am sure he could manage the suspended sentence easily enough."

She stiffened. "What does that mean?"

"I think you know." He signaled to his men and they started through the front hall.

She chased him. "Is this about his bail?"

He gave her a look over his shoulder. "As I said, ask Hart to make certain Lydia doesn't suffer any further."

Francesca stopped in her tracks as Bragg and his men went into the study. Her head was aching from the blow she had sustained yesterday. She rubbed the back of her head but it was tender and she winced. Once, a lifetime ago, knowing right from wrong had been so easy—it had been black or white. Now the world had suddenly become every possible shade of gray. She did not know what to do. Her every moral fiber refused to succumb to the temptation of further bribery, yet she could not stand the thought of Lydia suffering any more than she already had. She was also aware that there would be more charges against Lydia if she told Bragg that she had attempted to frame Hart for the murder.

The two women came out of the study with the police. They

were both in handcuffs. Instantly, Lydia's gaze met Francesca's, and no plea for help could have been clearer.

The officers and the two women left the house. Bragg came to stand beside her and he put his arm around her. "I will hear what Lydia has to say and I will think about it," he said softly.

Francesca threw her arms around him. "Thank you."

He disengaged himself somewhat awkwardly. "I happen to agree with you," he said.

Francesca smiled. Then a new thought occurred to her and her smile vanished. Consternation filled her now. "Rick! What will happen to Gillespie?"

"His sexual crimes were committed more than eight years ago."

Francesca cried out. "Are you saying that he is going to walk away from his heinous deeds a free man?"

"Francesca, there is a statute of limitations. Besides, there is no evidence at all—it is all hearsay."

Francesca knew he spoke the truth. "So there is no justice for Daisy after all."

CHAPTER TWENTY

Friday, June 6, 1902—6:00 p.m.

HE HAD NOT A CLUE as to what he was doing. Evan stood outside Maggie's door, and he could hear the boys' voices from within. Because he could not show up at her door empty-handed, he had ordered an entire family supper from his hotel, which was in the woven wicker hamper at his feet. But the supper was an excuse for his visit. He was acutely aware of being overcome by nervousness and anxiety. He reminded himself that there was no need. He was just a family friend. He was only bringing supper. He could not court her, not even if he wanted to, not when another woman carried his child. That would be dishonorable in the extreme. And he certainly could not court her when he remained obsessed by the gaming tables. No woman needed a suitor like that; no woman needed such a delinquent husband, and especially not Maggie, who had more than enough hardship for an entire lifetime.

His heart lurched with hollow fear. Surely he wasn't thinking about marriage in the same instant as he was thinking about Maggie?

Earlier today, he had told Andrew he was sorry and his apology had been accepted instantly, much to Evan's surprise. Andrew had offered him a brandy and before Evan knew it, he had been telling him about some recent investments that he expected Evan to oversee at the family company. If Andrew learned about last night's gambling, he would be furious—and disgusted. Evan tried to imagine his reaction, should he inform him that he was seriously interested in a widowed seamstress with four children. Evan knew his father would not approve.

Suddenly Evan leaned against the wall beside Maggie's door. He did not want to be a lowly lawyer's clerk, but he'd tasted freedom in these past few weeks, real freedom, and he did not wish to work for Andrew, either. While returning to the familial fold and the company gave him great status, it felt as lowly as being a clerk. Every decision would be his father's, while he did all of the hack work. And should he ever reveal his feelings for Maggie, Evan could not even begin to imagine the uproar that would cause.

But did it matter? Maggie was not for him. She could do so much better, and he had to support Bartolla and the child in a very generous manner. But he needed Maggie in his life, if only as a friend.

"I will be right back," Maggie was saying, opening the door quite suddenly. She had a light blue shawl in her hands. She saw him and stopped, her pale brows arching in surprise.

His breath escaped, as if he had been socked hard in the chest. "I was just about to knock," he managed. "Hello, Maggie."

"Evan!" she gasped. Then she smiled, as if she was thrilled to see him, but her gaze was searching. "Are you all right?" Her eyes veered to the large hamper by his feet, widening with surprise.

He wanted her approval, desperately. "Care for a picnic? An indoor picnic? Or we could take the children to Central Park—I have a coach and driver downstairs."

"I was just running to the grocery—I am out of salt, of all things!" She blushed.

He reached for her hand and he felt the tension instantly ripple through her. Suddenly he was afraid.

"What is it?" Instead of pulling away she squeezed his hand

reassuringly. "Why have you come? It isn't safe! What if the countess learns you have been here?"

"She won't." He had to tell her everything, he thought. She had every right to know. "It's a beautiful night. Can we sit outside? I should really like to speak with you."

"On the stoop?" she asked in surprise.

"Maggie...I am not marrying the countess."

She dropped his hand, staring at him in shock. Then she took a breath. She closed the door to her flat and, leaving the hamper there, proceeded down the narrow corridor to the stairs. Evan followed.

It was a beautiful June evening, despite the elevated train distantly roaring two avenues behind them, the men shouting at one another in the traffic of drays in the cobbled street or the raucous noise from the corner saloon. A couple in one of the flats above them was arguing, as well. But two boys were playing jacks not far from the stoop, a grinning mongrel with them, laughing with every turn, and just above their heads, a pair of pigeons was cooing. Evan quickly removed his jacket and placed it on the top step, so Maggie had a clean place to sit. She sent him a small smile of thanks and carefully sat down. He sat beside her, badly wanting to put his arm around her and hold her close. He did not.

She glanced at him. Not for the first time, he thought her profile adorable. She had such a small face with a tiny, upturned nose, a hint of freckles scattered there. She was so terribly pretty.

"Evan? What has happened? You seem upset."

"Do I?" He glanced at his knees. Then he met her sky-blue gaze. "I can't marry her. I simply cannot. Maggie, I don't even like her."

There was distress in her eyes. "But she is carrying your child!"

He grimaced. "I have some doubts about whether she is carrying my child or someone else's."

Maggie's cheek turned pink.

"She may be a countess, but she is not a lady—and certainly not half the lady you are."

Maggie suddenly shifted away from him. "I don't know what to say."

That wasn't the response he had hoped for. "I am going to take care of her and the child, no matter whose it really is. I have sworn it, and in order to do so, I have reconciled with my father."

"Oh, Evan, I am so happy you have made amends with your family," Maggie cried, reaching impulsively for his hand. Then, realizing what she had done, she started to withdraw.

But he held on tightly. "It was more like groveling," he said.

"Evan, no. Family is everything." Their regards held.

"There is more," he whispered after a moment. "I am ashamed."

She studied him with worry. "Evan, you must never be ashamed with me. I would never be so bold as to judge you, not after all you have done for me and the children."

He felt rather certain she would judge—and condemn—him shortly. He hesitated. "Maggie, I am weak, dissolute. Last night I succumbed to the devil. I went to a club."

He saw her eyes fill with dismay.

"I didn't mean to play—it was only going to be one bet," he said desperately. "I have been feeling so trapped! And when I placed that bet, that terrible sense of being ensnared, of sinking into quicksand, went away! I forgot about Bartolla, the child, eloping. Instead of despair, there was excitement. I stayed most of the night. Maggie, one bet became a hundred bets."

Her eyes were shining with tears. "It doesn't matter," she finally said. "Today is a new day. You were upset about being forced into marriage with a woman you do not care for. But today, today you can start over. You will start over, won't you?"

"That is precisely what I intend to do. I woke up this morning hating myself…and now I am afraid you will hate me, too."

She shook her head. "I could *never* hate you! Evan, you have helped me through some terrible times. Maybe this time I can help you."

He had not a clue as to what she meant. "I don't want to drag you into anything sordid. And I certainly don't want to add to your worries."

She hesitated. "I will always worry about you." Then she smiled briefly. "Please, let me help. The next time you are thinking of gambling, come here instead. We can talk about it—we can take a walk—we can read together."

His heart accelerated. "Are you serious?" he asked, filled with hope.

She bit her lip, nodding. "Maybe it's my turn now to be the strong one, to offer hope."

He realized he wanted to lean on her now, just a little, if he really could. "I thought you would berate me for refusing to marry Bartolla, for spending the night at a club. But you didn't, not even once. How can you be so kind and so understanding?"

She did not look away, her color high. "How can you even ask me that? I have always wanted you to be happy. Evan, you deserve a good life. I know you are battling the devil when it comes to gaming, but I also know you will win, because you are a good man, a strong man. I have seen that, time and again. As for the countess, I simply don't want you to make a terrible mistake. You are wonderful with children. If this is your child, you will love it as you have never loved anyone or anything before." She refused to look at him now. "I thought you were in love with her."

"I was never in love with her!" He recovered his composure somewhat. "When I told her I will provide handsomely for her and the child until the child is of age, she was very pleased. Do not feel sorry for Bartolla," he said. "I think she may have been after my inheritance from the start."

Maggie gasped. "Surely she fell in love with you! Oh, I am certain of that!"

He grew still. He touched her cheek. "Why are you so certain, Maggie?" he whispered, his heart thundering in his chest.

She shook her head. "I just am."

He hesitated, his eyes on her beautiful face. "She is jealous of you, Maggie."

"Jealous of me?" She was incredulous, daring to meet his gaze. "There is nothing to be jealous of!"

He swallowed hard. "Isn't there?"

She turned red, glancing away. "We are only friends," she murmured, so low he could barely hear.

That was not what he had hoped to hear. "We will always be friends," he agreed firmly, meaning it. He could not imagine life without Maggie in it. But as he thought about the future, he saw Maggie in his arms, the embrace hardly platonic. He did not know what to do. "I don't ever want to disappoint you," he muttered, more to himself than her.

"You couldn't! You could never disappoint me," she cried fiercely.

"You can't possibly have that kind of faith in me—"

She cut him off. "I do! If you have decided to break it off with the countess, then that is the right decision, especially as you intend to provide for both her and the child."

He reached for and found her hand and he refused to let it go. "I came here with supper, but that was only an excuse to call. I needed to see you and tell you everything, and I needed to know that you do not think badly of me for what I have done. You have no idea how relieved I am. Your opinion means everything to me, Maggie."

She wet her lips. "I am glad you are not marrying her." Then, "I can help with the child, if you ever need my help that way."

He was overwhelmed. She would help him, never mind that his child belonged to another woman. "Come here," he said. It was reflexive on his part—he put his arm around her and leaned down to claim her lips.

She froze.

He hesitated, teetering there on the brink of a second kiss. But this would not be casual or impulsive; this kiss meant everything. He looked into her eyes. "May I?"

She hesitated and then nodded.

He put both arms around her, found her lips and gently opened them. His heart felt as if it had expanded impossibly, with more profound emotion than he had ever felt before. He felt her hands on his shoulders, her response to his lips, and urgency exploded in him. Because he had never felt such frantic need before, he quickly pulled away.

Maggie stared, dazed.

He felt as stunned as she appeared. "The countess was right to be jealous of you," he finally whispered. "Because it has always been you that I want, not her."

LEIGH ANNE WAS IN the girls' bedroom with both girls and Mrs. Flowers. Katie had put her own linen nightdress on and Mrs. Flowers was preparing Dot for bed. Leigh Anne sat in her chair, close to the bed, a book in her hand. As always, she would read to them for a few minutes.

But she strained to hear the front door opening downstairs.

It was almost eight. Rick often worked late, but Leigh Anne could not help herself now. She had been listening for the front door for hours, waiting for his footstep, for his news. At first the act had been subconscious, but now she was very aware of what she was doing. When he had left that morning, he had told her he would meet O'Donnell and give him the money. He had also said he would telephone the house the moment it was over. There had been no call. Leigh Anne had called headquarters herself a few hours ago, and she had been told that Bragg was in the field. She hadn't left a message, but Sergeant Shea had called the house recently to tell her that Bragg was on his way and she was to know that all was well.

What did that mean? She tried to reassure herself. She could not help but think that if all had truly gone well, Bragg would have called to tell her himself. Still, she knew the life he lived. Anything might have happened to prevent him from either meeting O'Donnell or calling her to tell her what had happened. Likely some police affair had prevented him from picking up the telephone.

"Mama?" Katie shyly approached, her eyes dark and huge and searching. "Why are you so sad?"

"Darling, I am not sad," she cried, smiling brightly. She reached out for her and Katie slipped awkwardly into her arms. Once, Leigh Anne had despaired to try to embrace her daughter from the special chair. Now the embrace was firm. She understood the slightly awkward manner in which they had to cling, but dismay and despair did not fill her heart in response. An image flashed in her mind, as it had all day, of her husband smiling down at her, his eyes dark with desire as he moved over her, in her, straining with her to reach that miraculous place of completion, of wonder, of love.

Warmth tingled through Leigh Anne's body, causing her skin to turn hot. She released Katie, smiling a little, still dazed whenever she dared to recall what had happened in their bed last night. But her body was a traitor to her mind. She knew she was crippled and ugly, yet her body begged her for his.

The front door slammed.

Leigh Anne started. "Katie, darling, help me into the hall!"

"It's only Papa," Katie said.

"Hurry!" Leigh Anne cried. Her heart raced even more quickly now, fear so swiftly replacing the treacherous desire.

Katie wheeled her from the bedroom and down the short

corridor to the top of the stairs. Leigh Anne saw Bragg in the front hall. He looked up at her—and he smiled.

Relief caused her to collapse in her chair. It was all right, she thought. *It was over.*

Bragg came swiftly up the steps.

"Is it done?" she managed to ask, and as she spoke, the butterflies that had nothing to do with fear and everything to do with last night returned.

"Yes." His gaze slipped over her face, lingering very briefly on her mouth, and then he turned to Katie. "Hello! Am I in time to tuck you and your sister into bed?" he asked, lifting her into his arms. He smiled at Leigh Anne over Katie's shoulder. "I'll put the girls to bed. Then let's have a drink," he said.

She knew he was prepared to discuss whatever had transpired with O'Donnell, but the look in his eyes also told her that he was thinking about last night, too. She knew he was thinking about making love to her again, and she felt her cheeks heat. How could this be happening? This was not the plan! She was not a seductress anymore—she was not about to delude herself—but the ache in her had grown, and so had a thick and familiar excitement.

Leigh Anne watched him take Katie into the bedroom and she heard him quietly speaking with the girls, his voice soft, strong, caring. She wheeled herself into the bedroom, the task no longer as difficult as it had once been. The bandages she had wrapped on her hands made it much easier, as well. She rolled her chair directly to the bureau, and as she did, there was no way she could avoid the reflection of the woman in the mirror there. The woman was breathtakingly beautiful, her pale skin flawless. Two spots of pink brightened her cheeks, and her eyes were bright with the same heat, too. No one looking at that dark-haired beauty would ever know she was confined to a wheelchair for the rest of her life.

Leigh Anne looked away. She knew she was a fool, but she

reached for the bottle of eau de parfum, anyway, adding a drop to her wrist and cleavage. Her hand was trembling.

Leigh Anne glanced up at the mirror again. Rick stood in the doorway, watching her intensely. His eyes smoked and he launched himself forward, closing the door, his strides unhurried. He paused behind her, their regards locked in the mirror, and clasped her shoulders gently. She shivered, the caress sweeping through her like a hot wave.

"It is going to be long time before he ever bothers us again."

"What?" She wanted him to tell her that O'Donnell was *never* coming back.

"I arrested him," he said, staring at her in the mirror. "I had to follow the law, Leigh Anne. I actually thought about killing him. I couldn't do it—I couldn't commit murder—and I couldn't be a party to extortion, either. I'm an officer of the law."

"You arrested him?" she cried in dismay. "What if he isn't convicted? What if he is released on parole. What if next time he abducts or hurts the girls?"

"That is a lot of 'what-ifs,'" he said. He wheeled the chair around and then knelt so they were face-to-face. "And what if I had paid him, and in a month or two he decided to come back and extort us yet again? He is in jail. He can't interfere in the adoption now, not from a prison cell with these charges hanging over his head. He will be convicted, because he is guilty. He is going to get ten to fifteen years. And if he gets out on parole, if he dares to ever approach us again, I will deal with him then as I dealt with him now. Please trust me," he said soberly.

"I do trust you," she whispered, and it was the truth. "I am still afraid, Rick."

He suddenly cradled her face in his hands. "I know you are. So you have to make me a promise, a pledge. If this man ever approaches you again, you will come directly to me. I don't care what he says, you come to me. I can manage a thug like O'Donnell."

She nodded, aware of a tear falling. "I wanted to tell you, I really did."

He softened. "Leigh Anne, I know how hard these past months have been. But isn't it time to let go of doubt and fear and actually live? We have so much to live for."

She met his amber eyes, her heart and body begging her to agree. For she knew exactly what he meant. If she dared to have the courage, she wanted a genuine marriage, too.

A real life, a real family and a real marriage with this noble man.

She wet her lips. "I am not brave. If I were brave, I would have never left you all those years ago."

"The past doesn't matter—we need to live in the present and plan the future. And you are very brave," he murmured, his tone turning thick. "If you don't know it, I do."

She knew he was going to kiss her. She shook her head in a hopeless warning she knew he would not heed. "How can you still want me that way? *How?*"

"Because you are so incredibly beautiful. Because you are my wife," he returned, "and because I love you. I need you, Leigh Anne, but you already know that."

She did. She saw the passion in his eyes, on his face, and she heard it in his tone. "I'm not ready," she tried.

"I don't believe you," he whispered, and he brushed her lips with his.

The aching threatened to explode and she gripped the arms of her chair, her eyes closing. She felt his tongue testing her lips, tasting them, probing, and she could not stop a moan. His mouth firmed, insisting that she open, and when she did, their tongues met in frantic urgency.

Abruptly he lifted her from the chair and carried her to the bed. She looked at him as he laid her down and could no more dampen the desire than she could stop her harsh and heavy breathing. He sat by her hip, his eyes glowing, and kissed her again.

She could not wait. It had been so long, and yesterday had only been a teasing. Leigh Anne started to weep as he quickly unbuttoned and removed her dress, his hands caressing her shoulders, her breasts, her thighs, as if he could not wait, either. Clad only in her chemise, stockings and drawers, she looked at him. He smiled just a little and he bent over her to taste her where she desperately wanted him to be.

Leigh Anne gasped as his tongue delved deeply against and between her flesh. She heard herself plead and could not stop because in another moment, she was going to explode. She begged and he listened, his tongue clever, skilled.

"I love you," he gasped, moving over her, against her, his thighs spreading her legs wide as he released himself.

Leigh Anne met his gaze. *I love you, too,* she thought. And she could not understand what had happened to tear them apart and then to keep them apart for so long.

His jaw flexed, and he surged hot, hard and so thickly into her. Leigh Anne gripped his back, hanging on as he rode her. And then there was no more thought at all—there was only his hard, aroused body, the power and the heat, so deep, the friction and frenzy, and finally, the explosion of sheer ecstasy. This time, she held him and refused to let go.

FRANCESCA PAUSED JUST OUTSIDE of the library. The two massive engraved doors were open and she could see Hart at his desk, engrossed in some papers, his shirtsleeves rolled up, his tie hanging with his suit jacket on the back of his chair. He appeared immersed in what he was doing, but she also saw the signs of strain on his face. Still, his seductive appeal remained as strong as ever. She could not wait to tell him the news, but she was also afraid that he would not react as she wanted him to.

Hart suddenly sensed her presence and he looked up. As their eyes met, he smiled at her and Francesca warmed. There was no doubt that he was glad to see her. Did that mean he had conquered his own personal demons? Did that mean he would change his mind about their engagement when she told him that she had found Daisy's killer?

"May I come in?" she asked softly.

He swiftly rose to his feet and came around his desk. "You never have to ask."

She approached, and halfway across the room, he reached her. His gaze was searching as he found her hands, and surprise instantly filled his eyes. "You have found Daisy's killer?"

"Yes, I have," she said, pleased that he knew her so well now that he could almost read her mind.

"What happened?"

"Daisy was being sexually abused by her own father, Calder, and that is why she ran away from home."

It was a very rare moment, for she saw that Hart was truly stunned.

"Her mother blamed her, Calder. Can you believe it? Martha felt that Daisy had somehow seduced her own father. In any case, the judge happened upon Daisy purely by accident in May. He approached her and she began to blackmail him. She hated him with a vengeance! Martha had no intention of letting her do that and she murdered her. Worse, Lydia witnessed the murder, helped her mother escape and then framed you when she realized she could do so and deflect suspicion from Martha."

"Poor Daisy," Hart said roughly. He seemed shaken. "I had no idea, Francesca, none."

"It is such a tragedy!" Francesca exclaimed. "Lydia adored her sister, and despised their father, too. She was only protecting Martha, because she feels her mother is all she has left. Hart, I do not want to see Lydia suffer anymore. I feel so badly for her. She is as much a victim as Daisy."

He pulled her close. "Francesca, I won't press charges against her, but the police and the D.A. can obviously charge her with quite a few crimes."

"I am aware of that. I have begged Bragg to withhold information on her behalf."

His gaze flickered. "And did he agree?"

"He said he would think about it."

Hart regarded her steadily for a moment, his expression impossible to read, and then he walked slowly away from her. He paused before a window, but seemed to stare out at the fading day with unseeing eyes. Francesca walked up behind him. "What is it?"

He shrugged, glancing at her. "I suppose that if anyone can get Bragg to circumvent his own morals, it is you."

She tensed slightly. "What does that mean? I had to ask him to treat Lydia differently than he would someone else."

He softened, clasping her cheek with one large hand. "Of course you did. She is a victim and you remain the kindest person I have ever had the good fortune to meet."

She searched his gaze now for some inkling of what their future might be. She saw that the shadow of grief lingered in his eyes. "Hart, it is over. I know this has been a terrible time for you. But Daisy's killer is in custody. You have been proved innocent, and that is how tomorrow's headlines will read."

He shook his head. "It has been a terrible time for you, Francesca, and I cannot stop blaming myself for what I have put you through."

"Don't! I wouldn't have wanted to be anywhere but here with you during this crisis, Calder. That is what friends are for—and we are quite a bit more than friends, even now." She trembled as she spoke.

"You never wavered, not even once, this entire time."

She was surprised. "I could never stop believing in you."

And his composure crumbled. "Your sister said you would have raised my child with me."

She nodded. "I would have loved your little boy or girl as if it were my own," she whispered roughly.

Anguish appeared in his eyes, but only briefly, because he pulled her suddenly into his embrace, reaching for her mouth with his. Francesca threw her arms around his neck and kissed him back with all of the love pounding in her breast. His grip tightened, and his lips firmed, demanding even more of a response from her. Francesca gladly gave it.

He finally held her face in his two hands. "This morning, I woke up feeling as if I had lost everything. I never dwell on the past, but that is all I have been doing, Francesca. I have been regretting the way I behaved when Daisy told me about my child. And I have been thinking about the moment we first met, and every time I have seen you or been with you since. Remember the first time you wore that red evening dress? I will never forget it—I wanted to ravish you on the spot. But you only had eyes for Rick."

"That feels like a lifetime ago," she whispered. "Calder, almost any man would have reacted to Daisy's news the way that you did. Please, don't be so hard on yourself. Had she lived, I know you would have adored that child."

"There you go again," he said roughly. "I don't want to ever see the day where you lose faith in me."

"You won't!" she exclaimed. "Calder, I love you just as much now as I did an hour ago."

He pulled her face close instantly and kissed her again, hot, hard and deeply. Then he pulled back. "Francesca? I love you now even *more* than I did an hour ago, as impossible as that seems."

She looked up, stunned by such an intimate confession, meeting his dark and very weary eyes.

He smiled slightly and released her. "I think I should be the one to make the arrangements for Daisy's burial," he said. "There needs to be a service, small and private. I will make certain Lydia can attend. Is Gillespie going to be arrested, as well?"

She reached for his hand. "What happened ended eight years ago—and there is only hearsay. It is unbelievable, but he is going to walk away from all of this a free man."

"Then he will undoubtedly appear at his daughter's funeral. How unfortunate."

Francesca hesitated. "May I help with the funeral arrangements?"

He looked at her. "Francesca, I need some time to myself now."

Hart needed time to grieve, but would he also use that time to distance himself from her? "Of course. Calder? I do need to attend the funeral."

He squeezed her hand. "I know you do." He paused. "Thank you, Francesca. Thank you for everything."

HE WAS SO TERRIBLY TIRED, a kind of fatigue that he didn't recall ever having experienced before. It was raining. The few mourners, all of whom had been either his family or Francesca's, had left the cemetery some time ago. He stared down at the small marble stone that commemorated the child he had not wanted and now would never know. Francesca had chosen the inscription. "Here Lies Innocence; the Perfect Soul." Remarkably, tears filled his gaze, blurring it. He had thought his tears long since dried up.

"Calder? It's pouring."

He started, unaware that Francesca had come to stand beside him. He hadn't seen her in the past four days. He slowly turned to her, and his heart began to expand with life as he looked into her worried eyes and at her beautiful face. Something inside of him that had felt frozen began to melt.

She did not carry an umbrella and she was soaking wet. He

jerked off his jacket, draping it about her shoulders. "I thought you had left!" he exclaimed. "Francesca, you could catch pneumonia!"

She pressed against him. "I was not going to leave you standing here in the rain by yourself. It was a beautiful funeral, Calder."

The lump of anguish that had been choking him for days surprised him by not rising up. Instead, it began to recede. He found himself putting his arm around her. She was warm, alive, and he had missed her terribly. "Thank you for the inscription."

She smiled just a little at him. "Raoul is waiting. Send your driver on—I will give you a lift home."

He realized he would like nothing more than to share a carriage with her. "I have missed you, Francesca."

She reached out, laying her fingertips across his cheek. "The feeling is a very mutual one."

He had spent the past four days in his own personal hell, mourning his child through four sleepless nights, all the while haunted by the little boy he had once been. He pulled her close and they started toward the coach. "How are you?"

"I have been worried about you."

She had halted and so did he. And before he knew it, he was holding her small face in his hands and his feelings were pouring forth, fervent and uncontrollable. "Francesca, since we first met, I have wanted to show you every possible pleasure here on this earth, from Paris in the moonlight to Tahiti at sunset. I only want you to experience the wonders life has to offer—the finest Rothschild wine; the rarest, flawless diamonds; French couture; van Gogh. Since we first met, I have thought of hundreds of ways to show you the finest things in the world. I have wanted to take you by the hand, travel the globe, enthrall you—especially in my bed. I *never* wanted to be the cause of your hurt and pain. I am so sorry!"

She was crying. "I am undone, Calder. Has any woman ever told you that you are the most romantic of men?"

"If I have become romantic, Francesca, it is because of you. Thank you for allowing me my privacy these past few days. I cannot begin to tell you how much your consideration means to me."

She sniffed, the tip of her nose red. "I will always respect your needs, Calder. By now, surely you know that?"

He wiped two teardrops with his thumb. "I think I am beginning to understand that."

She laughed a little, the sound shaky. "But I did speak with Alfred every day, to make sure you weren't locked in the library with a case of Scotch—to make sure you didn't need me, in spite of what you said."

"You are a miracle," he said, a powerful image of Francesca in his hallway, sneaking a conversation with Alfred while he wept in the master suite, overcoming him then.

"Hardly," she said, rolling her eyes.

He would have laughed, because she was so adorable and so modest, but he had yet to say what he had to say. "By trying to protect you from the scandal of Daisy's murder, I have hurt you—no, do not interrupt! You have been so brave and so strong. This has been so hard for you, hasn't it?"

She did not hesitate. "It has been very hard, Calder, but I understood that you only thought to protect me from scandal. Your motives were very noble. You see? You are a true gentleman after all!"

He almost laughed; the sound was choked instead. "Only you could be so forgiving when I put you through such hell. You are an extraordinary woman," he said unevenly. "I don't know you half as well as I intend to. I can think of nothing more exciting than spending the rest of my life uncovering every facet of who you are."

She became still. "I should gladly allow you to spend a lifetime searching for such hidden facets, although you are giving me far too much credit, Calder. I am really rather ordinary."

He actually laughed. "There is nothing ordinary about you!" he exclaimed, and then sobered. He had never missed anyone the way he had just missed Francesca.

"Calder?" she asked, her eyes shining with love and hope.

And in that instant he had an epiphany. His feelings were a miracle, he realized. *She* was a miracle—his miracle. What had he been thinking? "Fracesca, darling, I want that lifetime with you," he said thickly. "But can you ever trust me again? And are you certain that is what you still want? Society is gleefully lined up, waiting to throw their newly sharpened knives at me, I have not a doubt. I don't want a single barb aimed at you—I will not allow it, if you give me another chance."

Francesca cried out, flinging her arms around him. "Foolish man! I would give you a hundred chances—no, a thousand!"

He held her tightly. "God, I hope I do not need a hundred new chances."

"You probably will," she whispered teasingly, "as you are so arrogant, high-handed and resolute."

He did smile, even as his body came fiercely to life. "I do not know what I was thinking, to offer you a platonic friendship in exchange for what we had." He cradled her face in his large hands. "I cannot live without you, Francesca. These past few days have shown me that. My life is black without you. Without you, it hurts."

She became still as their gazes locked, his darkening with the smoke of desire. Need rose up in her so swiftly her knees buckled. Instantly he reached out to steady her. "I am very glad to hear you say that," she whispered shakily, "because I cannot live without you, either. I will always be at your side, whether you want me there or not, to ease your pain. But—" she smiled "—will you at least admit that perhaps you overreacted to the crisis at hand...darling?"

"I have a feeling that I will always overreact where you are concerned," he said roughly.

She had to smile at him, and their hands slid together. "I like the sound of that, Calder."

His dark gaze softened and was searching. "I committed myself to you long ago, before you ever accepted my proposal, and at the time I did not even know I was making such a commitment. It was a commitment that came from my heart—perhaps from my soul. It was a commitment I never dreamed I would ever make—and it will never change."

She was overcome. Somehow, in spite of their engagement having been briefly broken, their love had grown. Somehow their commitment had become even greater, as impossible as that seemed.

"Nothing has changed for me, either," Francesca whispered. "I love you and I will remain with you through thick and thin. If from time to time you think that you must protect me from your dark side, I do understand and I will accept it—protestingly, of course."

"Of course." He smiled, his hands splayed now upon her hips. "And you will always be here, to ease my pain?"

Her heart skipped in excitement. "Hart, I was referring to your battered heart."

He smiled just a little at her. "Oh! I misunderstood." His grin was suggestive. Then it vanished. "As badly as I wish to kiss you, there is something I must do first."

She began to tremble.

He was deadly ernest. "Francesca, I know I am a difficult man. I know I have a sordid past. This past week proved that. I know you could do far better than me. You deserve better. But I am in love with you. Deeply, darkly, hopelessly in love with you. And I wish to marry you—if you will really give me another chance—as soon as possible."

Francesca laughed and cried and kissed him, at first quickly, and then deeply and slowly, her tongue thrusting deep.

He returned her kiss for a long, long time. Then, when they were both out of breath, he whispered, "Is that a yes?"

She kissed his fingers. "It is a thousand yeses, rolled into one." She waved her hand at him.

He laughed. "I thought you might refuse me, or at least pretend to be coy. But you are still wearing my ring."

"Of course I am! Even if you married someone else, I wouldn't take it off!"

He laughed, the sound happy, his pleasure lighting up his face, his eyes. Then he became serious. "There will never be anyone else, not in my bed, my heart or my life."

"I can manage that," she said as happily, seeking his hand with hers. Their palms clasped. "So what do you think we should do? Papa has said he wants to sit down with you and get to know you somewhat. He is coming around, Calder. That means we can have a small ceremony, just family and friends."

"We can invite all of society, if you wish, and have a scandalous, impossibly expensive society wedding, so our detractors can be green with jealousy."

"Ooh, I do like that idea."

He laughed. "I thought you might," he murmured. He kissed the top of her head.

Francesca met his gaze and smiled. Did they dare have the wedding of the decade and taunt society in such a manner? She wasn't sure it mattered, but the idea was so tempting.

Her wildest dreams, her dearest hopes were going to come true after all. Only that morning she hadn't been sure if their relationship would survive as she wished it to, but it was hardly over. This was a new begining—better and more promising than ever before. The joy inside her was threatening to make her burst. "Maybe we should get out of the rain and go somewhere private—to discuss our wedding," she said in a silken tone. It had been far too long, she thought.

He grinned briefly. "Yes, somewhere private, a good idea, darling." The last word dripped from his tone like cream and there was no mistaking his intentions.

She went still. "You wish to discuss the wedding?"

His gaze was dark. "Of course. However, I recently—very recently—heard you claim that you could never refuse me." He gave her a sidelong look.

Every heated moment they had ever shared raced through her mind. Francesca tried to breathe, but her chest had never felt so tight. "I will never refuse you," she said softly. "Just tell me what you want." And she simply looked at him.

"You know what I want," he said thickly, pulling her completely into his arms. "I want to take you to my bed—right now—and I want to show you how terribly I have missed you and how much I have regretted our separation."

"Then we should call your driver," she whispered. "Because I am no longer shy and innocent and I want to show *you* a thing or two." She could not smile, not now.

"A thing or two?" He blinked, amused.

He had been poised to kiss her for several seconds now and she somehow smiled, quite incapable of drawing a normal breath. "I want to show you how much I love you, Calder. And I am going to show you—in your bed—I am going to remind you, again and again, that I am here to stay, no matter what demons you think to fight, and I will never leave you, or doubt you. But I must warn you. My passion does not feel controllable tonight."

He stared, his gaze smoldering. "Warning taken," he murmured, and he wrapped his arms around her, kissing her very, very thoroughly, tongue to tongue, for a very long time.

When he was done, she was breathless and dizzy, the grass beneath her feet tilting quite precariously. Worse, he had set a fire and it needed to be extinguished, as soon as possible—the carriage would do. And then, of course, there was the wedding they must plan. She could barely wait. "Take me home, Hart," she said.

He gave her a lazy, heavily lidded look. "I think that can be arranged, darling."

* * * * *